WRATH

LOVE IS CURE, VOL. 1 - VICES & VIRTUES SERIES

BOOK SIX

BROOKELYN MOSLEY

85 MEDIA LLC

ALSO BY BROOKELYN MOSLEY

Novels/Novellas/Novelettes/Series

No Fraternizing, Pt. 1

No Fraternizing, Pt 2

No Fraternizing, Pt. 3

First Came Love: The Love, Hate & Revenge Prequel

Love, Hate & Revenge, Pt. 1

Love, Hate & Revenge, Pt. 2

Love, Hate, & Revenge, Pt. 3

Girl Code

Mr. & Mrs. Jones

Forbidden: An Anthology

They Call Me Mello

A Love Deferred

Indecent Arrangement

Last Comes Love

Ebb & Flow

PRIDE

Meant To Be

LUST

Loveless

GREED

Rekindled

My First, My Last

ENVY

Ready or Not

So This is Love

Home Before Midnight

GLUTTONY

When Luke Met Juliette

When Life Gives You Sunsets

In Love, I Trust

Short Stories

Just Friends

Chateau Luxure

Lena's Ex-File

Dream Boss

Unsilent Knight

Twice In Love

Home For Christmas

ByBK Exclusives

Bed Bully
Stuck
LHR Rewind Series
Home Before Midnight
Maybe This Time Will Be Different
Lovekilla
Incoming Call
Rough
WYD
Drinks on Me
Cali & Lee
Ray & Jay
Living Out a Love Song
Glimpses
One Mic

(All books listed are available on ByBrookelynMosley.com. Type this link into your browse to find the books listed above: https:// bybrookelynmosley.com/collections/ebooks)

MESSAGE FROM THE AUTHOR

Thank you for purchasing your copy of *Wrath*. *Wrath* is book six in the *Love is Cure, Vol. 1 – Vices & Virtues* series. Although *Wrath* is a part of a series, similar to the previous five books in the series, you can read *Wrath* as a standalone. *Wrath* follows the journey to love for Lauryn James and Asher Truesdale. Lauryn is a kidnapping and sexual assault survivor. With that said, there are content warnings I need to make you aware of. Throughout *Wrath*, Lauryn recalls her kidnapping and sexual assault. Although there is no on-page scenario of the kidnapping or assault, Lauryn mentions in detail her kidnapping and assault throughout the story, most notably in a therapy session that appears in a later chapter in *Wrath*. There are also discussions of suicide and abortion. With that said, I handle all mentioned gently and with attention to sensitivity. However, if you are uncomfortable reading stories that include what I've mentioned above, *Wrath* may not fit the reading experience you're seeking. If you are ready to travel on a journey that captures how transformative and healing love is, turn the page and enjoy.

BK.

Acknowledgments

A loving thank you to my husband, who I have always thanked in my acknowledgements because he deserves all the thanks and then some. You continue to inspire me and push me even when you see the vision clearer than I do, and I'm so grateful for you. To my son and my daughter, who are so patient and understanding whenever mommy must write, I give my best because of your sacrifice for my time and dedication. You two and daddy are the real rock stars in all of this.

To my reading family. Thank you for your support and your continuous trusting of my pen. To the people who mention me in rooms I have yet to enter, those of you who constantly tell other readers they should read my work, your love and support is true blue. When I wrote my first story, I wondered if anyone would enjoy reading what I created and it sincerely feels enriching knowing that I've found you. Thank you for your continuous support. It means more than words can ever express.

And finally, thank you to the Lauryn James' of the world. I praise your strength and your bravery to find triumph over trauma. I pray you find as many tiny spaces in this world that are big enough and lit enough so your joy can thrive. I see you. And I hope this story proved that and inspires you to keep on seeking joy and love. You deserve.

Dedicated to the saints and the sinners...

PROLOGUE

A NEWS CLIP FROM A BREAKING NEWS
REPORT THAT AIRED ON NEWS 16 BROOKLYN,
IN OCTOBER 2004...

"Our on the field reporter, Angelina Areli, is in Flatbush this afternoon. She is outside of the property where a 25-year-old male held a young teen captive for four days," the news anchorman reports. "Here's Angelina with more."

The image on screen switches to a black woman with short curly black hair and eyes that appear fixed on those viewing.

"Thanks Kirk," she starts, pressing a finger to her ear, as she lifts her microphone with the microphone flag displaying News 16 Brooklyn around its tiny box surface. "I am live outside the abandoned property in the Flatbush section of Brooklyn where a thirteen-year-old, Lauryn James, was rescued yesterday evening in an event that has left this tight-knit Brooklyn community shaken."

The camera pans to a two-story property that is noticeably empty. Grass grows through the cracks of concrete that is the walkway, and weeds and shrubs intrude around the unkept lawn. Viewers' eyes go to broken windows with jagged edges on either side of the property's splintered door. On either side of the abandoned property are neighboring homes that are also visibly abandoned and are in similar dilapidated condition.

"As you can see, this abandoned property isn't the only abandoned property on this block," Angelina continues. "Residents in this neighbor-

hood confirm they have filed several complaints with the city regarding concerns about the easy access the abandon properties provide. According to residents, for over two years they have complained about the abandoned properties and the lack of window boardings to prevent entry by squatters, making the properties a breeding ground for illegal activity. Unfortunately, this property was the place a convicted felon not only held a young girl captive as a city searched for her, but this property was also where he brutally assaulted her for days."

The footage changes to scenes from the day before.

Video frames that transition from the blue and red siren lights on parked police vehicles and other emergency vehicles, lights that glowed brighter against the late night background behind them. The camera captures a growing crowd of people standing on the other side of yellow caution tape, all their attentions pointed at the abandoned property.

"Police received a tip yesterday afternoon that Lauryn James, a teenager living only two blocks from this abandoned property, was inside. Her name has become well known these past few days thanks to an article written by Holidae Press's Desmond Ellis II. An article that caught the attention of a city of residents demanding more media attention so her family could bring the girl home."

A photo of a young man appears on the screen. He's brown skin, with light hazel-brown eyes. Hair shaped up into a curly high-top. He looks to be in his mid-20s, unsmiling in the mug shot.

"A 25-year-old Corey Reynolds was wanted at large after Lauryn's mother detailed to officers on her hospital bed how Mr. Reynolds shot her when she walked in on Reynolds assaulting her daughter. Soon after wounding Lauryn James's mother, Reynolds abducted Ms. James at gunpoint. The family members of the abducted girl contacted authorities soon after the family discovered Lauryn's mother and learned of Lauryn's abduction, and authorities conducted a search around the neighborhood for two days. With no leads, the search efforts went cold. However, an article published in the Holidae Press by an off-beat reporter, Desmond Ellis II, raised awareness and subsequently a reignited citywide search for the teen, garnering nationwide attention centered on her abduction."

The camera returns to the reporter as she turns to face the camera again.

"Neighbors across the street from the abandoned property recognized Mr. Reynolds from a news report as he was entering and leaving the property several times, and they contacted authorities. When authorities arrived on the scene and attempted to enter the property, Reynolds claimed to have Ms. James at gunpoint and threatened to pull the trigger. As the officers attempted to negotiate entry, Lauryn's father, Jayshawn James, fought past uniformed officers and entered the property forcefully through the porch window, fatally shooting Mr. Reynolds once inside of the abandoned property. Scenes of Mr. James, emerging through the abandoned property's door with his daughter unconscious in his arms, have appeared on the cover of several of today's major newspapers, the community referring to him as a hero."

The image on screen shifts to an elderly woman. "Any father would have done what he did. I don't fault him at all."

"That monster needed to be taken off the streets," another resident, a middle-aged gentleman wearing a Yankee's ball cap, added in another scene. "That man deserved what he got. Hopefully, they don't lock that girl's father up for doing what is right."

"We have been complaining about these properties for years," another elderly lady is recorded explaining. "It's not the only property in this neighborhood not boarded and easily accessible. What happened to that girl was avoidable. The city is as much to blame for this situation as her attacker."

The camera returns to the news reporter.

"Family members confirmed that Lauryn's mother, who Lauryn's attacker wounded, succumbed to her injuries shortly after Lauryn's rescue. Lauryn James is under the care of those family members this afternoon. Lauryn's father, Mr. James, is in custody, with no further information given by the precinct commander or precinct executives. Spokespersons from Brooklyn's elected officials' offices, including the New York City Mayor's office, have all declined to comment. The community is calling for swift action so that what has happened to Lauryn James doesn't happen to another young girl in the community. Reporting live from Flatbush in Brooklyn, I'm Angelina Areli with News 16 Brooklyn."

ONE

AUGUST 2020 - 16 YEARS LATER...

LAURYN

Smiling is one of those things I don't do often. For one, it doesn't come naturally and, in my experience, it gives off the wrong impression that I'm approachable. And I'm not.

I've lost count how many times I've been told to smile. Lost count how many times I've had to tell a nigga to eat a dick because of it. But tonight, I couldn't help it.

There was no sound coming from the news report playing on the flatscreen my eyes focused on. But the images that appeared and then replaced with a new set of images were enough to stop me in my tracks.

Rap music reverberated around me, bouncing off the floors and ceilings of the club. I drowned it out like I did most nights, but tonight was different.

She seemed so happy, my former co-worker Ayanna. Cheesing from ear to ear as she stood wrapped in the arms of her boyfriend, Dallas Roque. Well, her fiancé, according to the banner of text printed beneath their photo as their engagement, made the ten o'clock news here in New York City.

Between the candid photos and paparazzi video capturing Ayanna and her NBA boyfriend, I could tell she was doing all right out there in Cali.

We used to work with each other when she lived in New York. I always knew she wouldn't be here for long. She was in college and just had a good head on her shoulders. She was cool. I was happy for her.

"Is that Ayanna?" I heard one dancer ask as she stopped beside me.

I peeked that way to see the dancer, Shyla, approaching. She had her fingers wrapped around a wad of wrinkled cash, her mouth moving as she chewed on gum. She'd just left the stage, likely done for the night, definitely nosy about what had my attention.

We were in the Black Bamboo, a strip club in Dumbo, Brooklyn. I hated it here. With a passion.

There was nothing to love about it. Then again, there was nothing to love about the city itself. But it was my home. A home I've been trying to escape for years.

"It is," I answered, refocusing on the screen.

"Got that nigga to lock it down, huh?" Shyla popped her gum as she giggled. "She 'bout to be crazy paid for life. She lucked out."

I rolled my eyes to myself. That's all they talked about was money in here. Granted, it's a strip club, but damn. Ayanna blushing and showing all her teeth beside that man was not because he had money. You could just tell it was something else. I just couldn't put my finger on that something else.

Couldn't stay in the moment long enough to figure out what lent that sparkle in Ayanna's eyes that was likely brighter than the diamond she now sported on her left ring finger. A hand landing against my ass in a swift slap pulled me from my thoughts.

I gasped, turned my head, then my body to face the fool. Because he had to be stupid.

"Yo, Mo, chill," Shyla cautioned, stretching out her slender arm to move Mo away from me. "She doesn't get down like that."

"Like what?" He questioned, eyes focused on my black halter top and matching short shorts.

His grills gleamed beneath the club lights as he flashed a menacing grin. Winked, then attempted to close the distance between us.

"She doesn't dance," Shyla tried this time.

"And even if I danced," I added, "what made you think you could put your dirty fucking hands on me?"

Shyla grabbed my hand, closing her fingers around my wrist because she knew.

Shyla, like everyone else in here with sense, understood I was off limits. I didn't have protection or anything like that. I wasn't the daughter of the club owner. Shit, he didn't even like my ass. But everyone knew I had no patience and a short fuse. And if Mo didn't create some distance between us, he was about to find out, too.

His grin grew into a toothy smile. The changed expression on his face made me take a step into his space with narrowed eyes.

Shyla tried to pull me back, but she wasn't quick enough. And even if she were, she'd still be too late.

"Lauryn," she tried.

"*Mmm,*" he groaned.

My heart dropped, and I stuttered a breath. It almost felt hard to swallow. The sound, though innocent, made my stomach do tricks, churning and somehow sending bile up my throat at the same time.

"I like my bitches feisty like you." Mo moved a step closer.

Too close.

Making me snap.

Some would say I blacked out. But it was more like everything slowing down and blinders being slipped on, like always, whenever I went from cool to hot.

But even though things slowed down, my hands moved quick. As was the case tonight, when my hands balled into fists. And one of those fists landed flat against Mo's bottom lip.

His head flung back, exposing his neck and Adam's apple. So I hit him there in the throat with a second jab. Neither one of those punches was easy to land. Mo had about two feet on my 5'2" height.

But fuck it. Whenever I got into the headspace of being cornered, I felt ten feet tall.

That second punch created the space I needed between us again. And it did some damage. A light pink thin line appeared down the crease of Mo's bottom lip before ripping by the seam, gradually pooling with blood.

The satisfaction that rushed through me almost brought a grand smile to my lips.

His hand quickly covered it all as he stepped back.

Strong hands wrapped around my biceps, damn near lifted me off the ground, as four big-bodied men emerged out of nowhere to step in front of Mo. One of them ushered him away from that area of the club.

The brawny arms behind me kept pulling me away from the area, too. They did it so quickly, I only had time to see who it was when they got me behind the bar counter, turning me roughly to face them.

"What the fuck did I tell you?" My boss, Larry, yelled, pointing his finger in my face.

I sucked my teeth. "Larry, I'm standing over there minding my damn business and he comes over—"

"I don't give a fuck what he does," he interjected. "That's fucking Mo' Money."

"And *I'm* fucking Lauryn James."

"Man, listen." He ran a big hand down his face. "You're either threatening them, cursing them out, or just last week, slashing their tires when you leave here from work all because these men take a liking to you."

My brows went up.

"Yeah." He nodded. "One of the chauffeurs told me he saw your ass slash a customer's tires after you argued with the nigga the hour prior to you getting off work."

I kissed my teeth. I should've slashed the customer's face. He also was too hands on for me.

"Now you're hitting them?!" Larry shook his head. "You can't punch my customers, Lauryn. You can't fucking do that."

"He violated me." My bottom lip trembled, but I quickly gained control because there was no way I'd let Larry, of all people, watch me break. "Grabbing my ass—"

"You work in a strip club."

"As a waitress," I yelled. "Not a fucking hoe!"

"Nobody in here is a hoe."

"Then nobody in here should get grabbed up like that, right?"

He shook his head. The club lights shined in his deep waves.

"You tryna fuck up my money, Lauryn," he growled. "And like I told your ass two years ago when I hired you, I don't like trouble."

"But he—"

"These niggas in here are paying good money and when I opened this joint, a lawsuit is not something I had in my plans."

I folded my arms over my chest.

"Mo may be a little aggressive." Larry shrugged nonchalantly. "But he's a paying customer, a high paying customer. He's also an upcoming rapper with a big enough following to have it be dry as fuck in here if he made one bad comment about this place. Now, I said nothing about the other dudes you've gotten into it with around here. But Mo? I gotta draw the line with him."

"So, what does that mean?"

"You gotta go home, ma." He formed prayer hands and used his fingers to point my way. "You're suspended for a week without pay."

"Suspended without pay?!" I shrieked. "We do that now?"

"We do that now."

"Since when?"

"Since you, shorty."

I scoffed. "But suspended for what?"

He used his thumb to gesture over his shoulder. "You just punched my fucking customer in his mouth and you asking me *for what*?"

"He wouldn't have gotten hit if he kept his hands off me."

"This is the environment you are in, baby." He smirked. "You're a pretty girl. You got a fat ass on you. Every so often, a nigga's gonna like what he sees and express that with a touch or two. You should be used to it by now. What's up with you?"

My hands were balling into fists.

"Get your stuff out of your locker and head home," he added, backing away. "Don't come back here until next Saturday."

"Wow."

"And the next time you do this shit," he added. "The next time you cause any kind of trouble in my business, Lauryn, you're fired. I promise you. Pretty or not."

I shook my head as I followed Larry with my eyes as he swaggered out of sight. His exit helped me quickly realize all the eyes in the area focused on me.

Music still blasted around the club, but to me, it was white noise quiet.

I clenched my jaw, gritting my teeth, watching as everyone's attention shifted off me to focus on the latest act on stage. I witnessed how everyone went back to what they were doing, doing nothing.

They did nothing when shit was happening to me.

Like always.

———

"Thank you," I said to my chauffeur as I pushed open the back seat's car door to step out.

After changing out of my club uniform and into a matching gray loose tee and bikers shorts, I collected my things from my locker at the Black Bamboo and got into one of the black cars Larry made available for the dancers and waitresses during late nights. The drivers parked in the reserved parking spaces in Black Bamboo's parking lot were specifically there to take us ladies who worked at the club home. That was the only good thing Larry did for us over there. And I think the only reason he supplied us girls, who didn't own cars, with a black car service, was more to benefit his ass than anyone else. Can't make money off a woman who doesn't make it home from work. So Larry made sure we got home safely so we could get up and do it all again the next day. My apartment on Flatbush Avenue was the only place I enjoyed being, anyway.

I fumed inside the black car silently the entire ride home. While the dancers always had my back, reminding me if I ever needed anything to let them know, security, the bartenders, shit, even Larry never did what was right. The women in the club were only pawns in Larry's game of trying to win wealth. The fact he thought he'd be able to do it with his sleazy ass club was laughable. Especially when it attracted people like that fucked up Mo' Money.

I asked the chauffeur to let me out of the car a block away from my building. I always did that whenever I had drivers bring me home.

I don't trust men. Not anymore. Most of them, if not all, were barbaric by nature. Unchained animals that refused to be trained. They didn't understand the word no, and they often took a woman's disinterest as rejection or worst an insult. So my knee jerk reaction was learning how to defend myself. Sometimes hurting them before they hurt me. A lot of times, gaining some kind of satisfaction from the latter. Life is a bitch of a teacher and class is always in session. It will teach your ass if you don't stand up for yourself, no one will.

The neighborhood looked alive, as usual. Even at 10pm. I rarely knew what Saturday nights at ten looked like. I spent most of my Saturday nights at the Black Bamboo.

This Saturday felt different. And not because I was home for a change.

I noticed the moving truck in front of my building as I waited at the crosswalk for the light to change to cross. Men moved in and out of the truck, hauling boxes toward my building's front door.

There was a guy who stood at the center of it all and in the middle of the block with an older woman by his side.

His skin was dark like midnight, eyes bright like two moons. As he spoke with the older woman, his eyes bounced between her and the men moving the boxes from the truck, walking them into the building.

He was average height, no taller than 5'11" with a medium build. Though he dressed himself simply in jeans and a white tee with white canvas sneakers, he had a certain air to him. His mannerisms gave me the impression he wasn't from around here. Yet, he seemed comfortable.

Self-aware and secure.

This part of Flatbush had straightened up a little. People criticized gentrification a lot, but since the white people moved in around here, things were looking better.

The neighborhood still had its flaws threaded in its growth, though. Like me.

I guess that's one reason I remain here, even when I don't want to be here. Finding my pinch of comfort in the uncomfortable.

I'd gotten within a few feet of the guy when I got a better view of him. He had a strong jawline I noticed even through his well-trimmed beard. His shape was that of an action figure, but he wasn't bulky at all. The guy's attention was razor sharp, too, never not scanning his surroundings. His eyes returned to the truck where the men were unloading again. As his attention moved with one mover, walking a box to the building's front door, those eyes slammed into mine.

Squarely on me, I realized his attention had a warmth to it.

Which is weird right?

How can attention have a temperature?

But he had it.

It made me feel warm. He didn't appraise me like the other men I was used to dealing with on a day-to-day basis. He didn't visually grope me like Mo and other men did. Or itemize and object me like Larry. This guy's attention was one I'd never experienced before. Gave off a sense of curiosity and intrigue... in me. A simple take notice gesture that offered room for me to introduce myself instead of having something or someone introduce what and who they thought I was.

Still, it was a male gaze. And I hated that shit to my core. So, I made a show of not wanting his attention by blinking hard and shooting a glare his way before rolling my eyes hard and focusing forward to enter the building.

That didn't stop me from tossing a glance over my shoulder the second I was inside, though.

And realizing he was still looking my way, surprisingly, made me feel... good?

Two

ASHER

"Dreadful," my mother spat beside me. "Why are there so many active bodies out at this hour, anyway?"

I tuned her out. A few minutes ago, I could do so by focusing on the movers transporting my belongings off the moving truck and into the building I would call home for the next few months.

"Out of all the places you could have chosen, you chose *here*."

What had my attention now aiding in my escape of my mother's chastising was a presence I couldn't blink out of staring at.

She assumed the appearance of someone so sad but so damn beautiful, too.

Long gorgeous black hair, clear taupe brown skin, full bow lips enhanced with bright red lipstick. Her eyes, though. They were stunning and appeared on the verge of tearing up. And while her eyes were the most fascinating thing to me, her several sizes too big baggy shirt, gray shorts, and sneakers made her standout.

I'd never seen such a mix of femininity and masculinity played up so well.

"Look at this sidewalk," my mother continued beside me. "Cracks everywhere. An uneven pavement. Look at this! Asher, this is the ghetto."

I tilted my head to my right to afford myself an opportunity to continue to admire the woman as she stopped in front of the bank of elevators inside of the building.

Her clothing was baggy, and yet I could still spot her curves through them. A complete contrast to the women I'd been around all my life, including the woman standing beside me. Appearance was everything to my mother. Your clothing spoke before you uttered a word, according to my mom and the women like her. If that were the case, the woman who'd just entered the building wore clothing that whispered she didn't take herself too seriously. They promised she chose comfort over judgement. And I liked what her laid-back style was telling me. Even though the glare she gave me could freeze fire.

"Oh, don't even think about it," my mother shrieked next, interrupting my thoughts. "Absolutely not!"

I furrowed my brows and forced my attention off the woman I'd been watching to focus to my left.

My mother's perfectly waxed brows furrowed as well. Lips tight as she stared at me. She'd only broken eye contact to gesture in the direction where I'd been staring, and to add, "No."

"No, what?"

"No, to *that*." She jabbed the air, gesturing at the woman inside of the building.

My mother, pointing that way, gave me a reason to glance in that direction again. In time to see the woman disappear into the elevator. Not before sharing another glance with me, though.

Couldn't help biting back my grin because of her last-chance glance, either.

"No girl who lives here should be interesting to you."

I sighed, moving my attention to the truck again to focus on anything but my mother and her bullshit.

My eyes did a quick scan of the surrounding neighborhood instead. The area was lively around us. The ten-story building I was moving into appeared out of place compared to the other modest properties around. It was the only spot in Brooklyn my mother would approve of. Even though her approval meant little to me, I agreed to appease to her comfort, so she'd shut the fuck up about it.

"I still don't understand what has gotten into you, Asher."

I took a breath and let it out slowly through my nose. My keep-calm routine whenever we shared the same space.

"You drop out of your doctoral program at Brookville to live like a pauper in Bali."

"Mom—"

"Return to the states after I had to practically beg you to come back in tears," she continued. "Only to decide not to return to the Hamptons, but to move *here*?"

"I'm restarting my doctoral program," I reasoned.

"After you completed five years of Brookville's acclaimed doctoral program."

And hated every moment of counseling psychology. But it wasn't the psychology I hated. I loved it. I've dreamed of owning my practice in the city and it's a dream I decided I'd see come to life. It was my life at Brookville. I couldn't take it anymore. My life as a Truesdale had become an even harder thing to tolerate.

Life got too monotonous with each passing birthday. Insignificant things dressed up and made to seem like the only things that mattered. I'd yet to leave home, doing exactly what my parents wanted. Even though I lived on campus at Brookville, my parents still had access to me. My father's father had a building named after him. Everyone expected me to attend Brookville before I even had the option to choose what university I wanted to make a home. My family tightly weaved their legacies into the foundation of BU and that meant mine was too. It was exhausting. I felt like I was dying, or at the least, had become the walking dead. A shell of a person. A puppet. My peers were in school, expecting to find themselves, and I was there to continue in the footsteps of the men before me. I had no sense of individuality, no encouragement to find myself. I never had a why. My parents robbed that of me, deciding my life for me and how I would spend it, leaving no room for discovery or for me to grow into the man I would like to be. Someone who I would admire. I had no vision. So... I quit school. Backpacked through Europe and made a home in Indonesia living off the grid.

"Now you have to start from the beginning, since transferring credits in a doctoral program is impossible." She shook her head. "And out of *all* the places you could continue your doctoral studies, you chose Langston University," she added with so much disgust you'd think I was earning my Ph.D. in a crack house.

I shrugged. "Summer went to Langston."

"And now your cousin works at some no name non-for-profit, making barely pennies and living off her trust fund. All because she went to Langston." She kissed her teeth. "It was a terrible decision. And Priscilla hates to admit it."

"Well, at least Summer is happy." I turned to face my mother. "And happy is what I'm aiming to be. I get it." I extended my arm and gestured around me. "This isn't what you'd choose for you. But I chose it for me and for a good reason."

"What could be a good reason to live in the slums?"

"First, it isn't the slums," I started. "I lived in the slums and the slums are not as bad as you think they are."

Her eyes bulged. "Asher!"

"And two." I held up my two fingers. "I wanted something different. I *needed* something fresh in my life."

"So much for fresh," she sniped. "It smells like pure shit out here, if you ask me."

"It's my new home," I declared. "Brooklyn has a rich culture filled with unique personalities and not the carbon copies, walking around, doing the same things, talking the same way, and boastfully calling the Hamptons home. There's a lot to learn and experience here. Brooklyn has tons of potential. And I already like it here."

"Son," she started, laying a hand against my chest. "I only want the best for you. You deserve the best. You are Asher Truesdale. My one and only son. Your father and I have worked and built a beautiful life, so you wouldn't have to know the likes of this place. Just because you haven't experienced the woes of life doesn't mean you haven't lived. I promise you aren't missing anything."

"This place isn't bad."

"It's terrible, Asher!"

I took another breath. This one deeper than the last.

"Absolutely awful." She exhaled loudly, then adjusted the strap on her designer handbag. "Your father wouldn't even accompany us here to assist with your move."

Because he's with his young mistress, of the moment, like always, popping Viagra and making a sport of keeping it up like he's been doing every Saturday night since I was a child.

I don't say that, even though I really want to.

Instead, I give, "His absence has little to do with the neighborhood, Mom, and you know it. So please digress."

"*Hmph.*" She balled her lips together and turned away.

Because she knows she subscribes to the belief, that everything has its cost. And turning a blind eye to my father's infidelities is a minor exchange for living the life of the rich, financially secured, and pampered. Most importantly, turning a blind eye afforded her a life that everyone thought was perfect.

Their envy was her validation.

My mother. Patricia Truesdale. Imposing on my life since 1991 while having so much shit to clean up in hers. It would be her greatest project righting her own life. But it is simply too much work, so she'd much rather tell me how to live mine.

I shifted my attention inside the building again, searching for any trace of the woman I'd just seen. I knew she wouldn't still be there but, I don't know, I still wanted to try.

"I saw the way you gawked at her," my mother spoke again. "That *girl* that walked in there recently."

"You mean that woman?"

"Listen to me." She turned to me again, this time with a finger pointed my way. "Your ancestors have tailored and refined your blood-line to be mixed with the upper echelon of our society."

"Here we go," I mumbled, canvassing the truck again.

I wish the movers would hurry and finish so she could just leave.

My mother turned my face so I would focus her way again.

"That *girl*," she stressed, "is *not* in our society and never will be. Dressed like a boy with her baggy clothing and street sneakers. *Please.*"

Her sneakers caught my eyes, to be honest. I kind of liked that about her. She was different at first glance. And her different left me curious.

"I may accept your poor choice of school and your poorer choice of where you plan to lay your head, but your choice of woman? *That* I am not willing to compromise on."

"Relax." I folded my arms over my chest. "All I did was take notice."

And liked what I saw.

THREE

LAURYN

I anchored my head back to read the floor numbers lighting up, showing what floor the elevator was currently on.

On a Sunday afternoon, I was on my way to the park. It was something to do. Anything to get out of my apartment. Most Sundays, I spent the earlier part of the day at home after waking up after noon because I returned from work that same morning.

But suspended with nothing to do had me choosing to leave my unit for fresh air.

Although my apartment was my haven, I didn't like being inside of it alone the whole day with only my thoughts keeping me company.

I sucked my teeth, noticing the elevator car stalled on the seventh floor. The elevator barely worked in this building, and it was one of the new ones they just installed a month prior. Mostly college students or the elderly rented out of here. I moved here because it was on the busiest part of Flatbush. My windows faced the street, which allowed there to constantly be street noise booming through my window blinds, and I liked that. Noise let me know I wasn't as alone as I often felt.

When the elevator car finally arrived on the fifth floor, my floor, I was already front and center, ready to enter.

The doors peeled opened and my eyes found his almost immediately.

The guy from the night before.

Skin like midnight and eyes like the night sky, with the whites around them like two moons.

Beneath the elevator lights, I could see his features clearer than the night before. Though he wasn't very tall, his presence was domineering, but not in an intimidating way.

In a providing way. Built just right for something, anything, life might throw at him.

I recovered from my falter in step and entered the elevator. I quickly diverted my eyes and clutched the spine of the book I carried while making my way to the corner of the elevator.

There was another resident in the elevator with him. She stood close, as if they knew each other.

I'd heard the other residents refer to her as Delilah.

We never spoke. I didn't speak to many people in the building. Hardly spoke to people, period. But I knew Delilah didn't like me because I didn't care to speak, and honestly, that was probably more my fault than anything else.

"Good afternoon," he greeted once the elevator doors closed.

I turned my head slowly in his direction.

There was that warming feeling again.

A cascading comfort that spilled from the gaze we held and washed over me in a familiar calm.

It was weird, in a good way. It was in a good way because I didn't feel my skin prick when he tracked me with his eyes. And because I didn't experience the urge to tighten the muscles in my body to be on guard for any sudden moves he made while we shared the same space.

Everything in me was lax.

Despite that, I didn't return the greeting. I rolled my eyes forward. Did my best to relax my shoulders and focused on the floor location indicator that lit up the floor numbers above the lobby.

Delilah snickered to herself and uttered low, "She says nothing to no one, so don't take it personally."

"*She*," I spat, "can hear you, bitch."

Her jaw dropped, and she scoffed, forcing her attention forward, which was probably for the best. I hadn't added slapping anyone on my list of plans for the day.

While she broke eye contact, he didn't. He stared for a bit, then guided his eyes to the spine of the book I clutched in my grip. He tilted his head a little as he skimmed the title; I guess.

He asked, "Is it a good read?"

The elevator chimed, and the doors opened.

I wanted to share the book was my favorite read lately.

How to Be Soft in A World That's Hard by Halo Behari. My latest self-help book I'd been rereading for the past month, which I usually did with books I found and liked. I wanted to share how I was on my fourth read of it and had learned things I missed the first three times.

Oddly, I felt comfortable enough to do it.

But I didn't, leaving his question unanswered.

Though I was the last to enter the elevator, I made it a point to be the first to leave.

FOUR

ASHER

My cousin Summer's giggles traveled around the outside space. Seated outside of a Manhattan eatery, she, myself, and her fiancé, Jayce, enjoyed brunch under the sun.

"Jayce, quit." She playfully shoved him while blushing. "I do not."

Jayce glanced at me and nodded. "She does."

I snickered.

"She's not even into the cute little salads or cutesy shaped finger sandwiches she swore she always loved eating."

Summer rolled her eyes.

"She wants the sloppiest, messiest, most greasy chop cheese from my hood bodega whenever we visit my family."

"Oh, whatever!"

"I'm thinking she looks forward to getting the sandwiches at the bodega more than she does seeing my extended family the way she gets excited about going to Brooklyn." He gestured at Summer. "Even after my mother got her house out in Queens. Summer still loves going back to Brooklyn for the chop cheese."

She laughed to herself.

"Because we can't find any of that where we live now," Jayce added.

"Not surprising." I emphasized my point by gesturing around us.

He laughed and pointed. "Exactly."

It was my cousin's idea to meet up for brunch. On a Sunday, the last day of summer, which meant summer was unofficially ending.

The three of us met up at a restaurant that wasn't far from their Upper West Side condo. I only agreed because I wanted to do a little exploring around the city. Get acquainted with my area by venturing out of it, intending to find my way back home.

"I can't believe you're actually here," Summer gushed, her excitement brightening her expression. "I can't believe Aunt Patricia actually allowed you to be this far away from her since you've returned."

I cringed at the thought, but quickly recovered. I was a 29-year-old man and the idea that my mother would need to *allow me* to do something at my age just rubbed me so wrong.

"And I can't believe how bubbly you've become," I said, my attempt at changing the subject.

I shifted my attention to Jayce. "What the hell did you do to my cousin, man?"

Jayce barked a laugh, which made Summer and I laugh as well.

"I like it." I nodded, reaching for my mimosa. "She's more laid-back, funny, she's smiling. With her teeth. Incredible."

"Oh, shut up!" She shouted. "You act like I was some kind of monster."

I stared at her from the side of my eyes.

Jayce snorted, and Summer shook her head in response.

"So, how long are you here for?" Jayce asked. "Living in the city?"

"A while." I leaned back in my seat. "School starts in a few days. I'm back at square one."

"Summer told me you were at Brookville, studying for your Ph.D. until a year ago."

"Yup," I confirmed. "Dropped out at the end of my fifth year."

"Something Aunt Patricia won't let us hear the end of." Summer perked up in her seat. "Do you know she literally busted into tears when recalling you coming to her and Uncle Jon to inform them you'd dropped out of Brookville and was leaving the country with no plans on returning?"

I scratched the back of my head.

"It was bold as hell and inspiring, honestly," she added.

"It was stupid," I admitted. "Short-sighted. Not well thought out, but extremely necessary. Kind of like pulling out a decaying tooth with pliers because it was causing excruciating pain."

Silence fell on our table for a few breaths.

"But." I shrugged. "I needed to make that move. As crazy as a decision I knew it was, I had to do it. For me. And I'm glad I did."

Summer smiled sweetly. "Is studying psychology still the plan?"

"Absolutely." I ran my hand down my trimmed beard. "My time living off the grid helped with silencing all the chatter. In my head, in my heart. I feel at peace. Going from having everything to having nothing and finding so much joy in the nothingness." I pressed my hand to my chest. "Showed me how important being mentally healthy truly is. How it's the real wealth. I want to be that solace for others. That awakening was truly nourishing. That was the only reason I came back." I shook my head. "I don't know. I needed my fix of something different, if that makes sense. I needed a dose of real life and out of the bubble my parents created while convincing me they did it for my own good. They were doing more harm than good, curating every damn moment of my life. I just... desired to be on my own. I was dying to hear my voice." I pressed a hand to my chest. "Make my own decisions whether they be bad or good, but at least I'd know they were mine and came from me, you know?"

"I get it." Summer shook her head. "It gets so exhausting having to meet the standards of others. Especially when your mother's names are Pricilla or Patricia."

I blew air out of my mouth.

My cousin Summer and I had little in common. But the one thing we could and probably will always connect on is the overbearing natures of our mothers.

"She isn't happy I've chosen to attend Langston," I revealed.

"I know," Summer acknowledged. "But it's a wonderful school."

"It's an excellent school," Jayce added. "I owe everything to LU."

I smiled and nodded.

"Before I started there, all I had were dreams but no plans," Jayce revealed. "When I graduated, my dreams had bloomed into a brotherhood, a plan, and a lucrative internship that led to an amazing career."

"An internship I let him have when I quit it," Summer stated.

Jayce poked her at her side and she snickered. "Oh, you *let* me have it, huh?"

"*Mm-hmm*. Yup"

He leaned in close and whispered something in her ear that had her giggling like a schoolgirl again.

The most annoying thing to witness, but also the most adorable thing as well. My cousin was in love, and it looked great on her.

The waitress returned with our platters of waffles, French toast, cheese grits, and spinach quiche.

When we were all settled into our meals, Jayce asked. "What part of Brooklyn are you staying?"

"Flatbush."

He pressed his hand to his chest. "I'm from Flatbush. What part?"

"I think east?" I answered, lifting my napkin to clean my mouth. "I'm still getting acquainted with the area. But I'm not too far from Prospect Park."

"Aight, dope." He beamed. "I used to live around that area."

"It's nice."

"Yeah," he agreed with me. "Things are changing, but the culture is still rich."

"Aunty Patricia has already called mother complaining about the building," Summer informed. "And of course mother called me. She wanted me to ask around about units in Jayce and my building so we can save you from yours."

"Not surprising." I scoffed. "She started complaining the moment we pulled up with the moving truck."

"Met any of the neighbors yet?" Summer asked next.

"Only a few," I replied. The mention of neighbors brought my mind to a particular one. The one who gave me the heated glare on my move-in night and then the cold shoulder hours prior to me attending brunch with my cousin and her fiancé.

"She's the bitch," insisted the lady, who'd introduced herself to me as Delilah when she entered the elevator a floor after me.

She was referring to the young woman who I'd tried to strike up a conversation with. The one who rode on the elevator with us but quickly left the elevator moments ago. A part of me wanted to take off behind her. I was never the type to believe what others said about someone when the person could speak for themself. But Delilah gently grabbing me on the forearm when I tried to leave behind the woman, stopped me.

"She's always so nasty to everyone," she reported, following me off the car. "The only person in this building who doesn't speak to anyone. She's so weird."

I glanced in the direction the young woman took off in.

I wish I got her name.

I wish she gave it to me.

I would have loved to learn more about her. But at least I knew something.

She held a book.

How to Be Soft in a World That's Hard.

I didn't catch the author's name, but the title was intriguing.

She liked to read.

That was very good to know because I did too.

I guess my recollection showed more on my face than I thought.

This was clear when Jayce said, "The few neighbors you've met must have been great the way you're grinning over there."

I didn't even realize I was.

"Am I grinning?"

Summer's smile grew wider. "You were smiling."

I chuckled.

"What's that about?" She asked next.

I fanned my hand in the air, nonchalantly implying it was nothing.

"No," she insisted. "What?"

I exhaled in defeat and said, "The night I moved in, there was a woman—"

"I knew it!" Summer shouted.

I laughed.

"Asher, man." He chuckled. "It was in the eyes."

She nodded incessantly. "Right?!"

I held a hand up. "It's nothing. I mean." I shrugged next. "She's beautiful and intriguing. But I'm pretty sure she hates me... for some odd reason."

"What makes you say that?"

I waved a hand in the air. "It's nothing. She's just closed off. Distant by choice."

"Oh, I know all about that life," Jayce revealed. "Summer hated me for years."

Her jaw dropped.

"Oh, don't even try to act shocked!" He hollered a laugh. "The audacity."

"I didn't hate you, per se."

"You just really liked me and hated the fact that you did."

Summer seesawed her head from left to right. "I'm a little pissed you're able to explain that so well."

We all laughed at that.

"Aye, Asher," Jayce spoke again. "If you ever need advice or need someone to vent to about it, call me."

I tilted my head to one side. "Are you sure?"

"Definitely." He nodded. "It'll also give us an opportunity to meet up independent of Summer and you can tell me all the things she wouldn't dare tell me about herself."

"Asher would never," Summer mumbled before sipping her mimosa.

I laughed.

"As for your new neighbor," Jayce added. "Give it some time." He winked. "They always come around."

FIVE

LAURYN

Another day of nothing to do.

I sat on a wooden bench beneath one of the giant trees that populated the surrounding space. People either jogged along the paved path in front of me or on the blacktop road a few feet up. Beside them, bikers pedaled past along the bike lane framed in a thick white line that seemed to extend forever.

I was at the park, Brooklyn's Prospect Park, on a Monday afternoon trying to kill time.

Though Black Bamboo's owner, Larry, put me on suspension a couple of days ago, I wasn't sure how long I would last having nothing to do.

The Black Bamboo was nothing like a haven. On any night, wall-to-wall men packed the club. As one of the few strip clubs in Brooklyn, all kinds of men from rappers to Wall Street types filed in once the doors opened at 9pm. Regardless of class, the men were all there to see the ladies dance with nothing on, paying these guys the attention they found hard to get outside those club doors. Money was the exchange, the romance, and while I saw a fraction of the cash as a waitress, the money wasn't what kept me at the Black Bamboo.

It was the last place I should be in, but oddly, it was where I felt the most comfortable outside of my apartment.

Standing under Black Bamboo's roof, I knew what to expect. I knew the men came tuned into WPFP - will pay for play.

There was an unwritten agreement at Black Bamboo between the men who patronized and the women who worked there. If the guys offered the dancers money and the ladies are interested, it's a successful transaction. But if a woman is not interested, she has the safe option of declining and there will be no hard feelings about the rejection because there are plenty of other beautiful women in the room to proposition. Mostly, everyone respected the unspoken rule. But sometimes there was the outlier, the rebel with no cause like Mo Money the other night, who had no respect for order.

Overall, though, the men who frequented Black Bamboo were predictable. If they walked through the doors, they weren't there for the drinks or the wings. They were hungry for the things not on the menu. They wanted to see titties and ass. And nothing about that surprised me. As long as they kept their hands off me, I was fine.

Most of all, working at the Black Bamboo was something to do at night. I barely slept when the sun went down because of my night terrors. So working, making money, while forcing myself to stay awake at night worked out perfectly for me.

Plus, the owner kept the lights dimmed low and all the waitresses practically looked the same under dark lighting. So, I could get by unseen and unbothered most nights. Though I wore way less under Black Bamboo's roof than I did when I was out of the club, it was so dark in there; I knew no one would notice me.

But here, out in a park, fully lit by the late August summer sun, I felt my most naked.

I inhaled a deep breath and dropped my attention onto my notebook. A black classic grid notebook with tiny blue boxes I used as a guide since I always wrote off the lines in traditionally wide lined notebooks. My notebook was simply a place for my thoughts. I'd been purchasing the same notebook since I was nineteen. Every time I leafed through to the last page in my last one, I'd buy a new identical one.

It wasn't a journal. It was a book of letters.

Addressed to my father.

He was the only man in this world I trusted. Even with him behind bars, miles away, he still was my superhero.

I'd peeked up every so often while seated on the park's bench. And every time, after writing a line or two, I looked up to find I had someone's attention. He sat on the bench opposite me on the other side of the park. The blacktop road and paved sidewalks divided us.

I tried not to make eye contact with him the few times I looked up from what I was doing to find him watching me. I wanted nothing to make him think I was the least bit interested.

Finally able to block him out, I wrote a page of words and was turning it over when I heard, "Good afternoon, queen."

I'd purposely chosen to sit away from view. On the bench far off from the others with iron legs nailed to the concrete along the park's walking path. This was about to happen.

"I've been working up the courage to walk over to comment on how beautiful your aura is," he said.

I shut my eyes and exhaled into my throat, forcing myself to think of something to write to reclaim my attention.

"Your aura," he continued, "it's as sunny as this beautiful day we're having."

So much for being able to read an aura. Because I was sure *sunny* was the last word someone would use to describe my aura.

I didn't bother looking his way. Didn't want to give him a reason to think he could approach.

But as always, my avoiding him wasn't enough.

"You know..." He took a seat beside me. "You're way too pretty to be wearing this frown. Smile."

He invaded my space not only with his presence but also with the aroma of Frankincense and Murr. It automatically brought me to the block I grew up on. I had a neighbor who would burn it outside her door on her stoop. And the memory brought back more memories I didn't care to entertain.

I shot him a glare from the side of my eyes, hoping it would help. But it made him lean in closer.

"While I sat over there." He pointed at the bench he previously occupied, continuing to speak to me despite me not saying anything since he walked over. "I noticed you have the most beautiful eyes. What's your name?"

From the side of my eyes, I noticed he asked his question to my breasts. Commented on my eyes but had yet to meet my gaze because he was too busy scanning everywhere else on me.

I shook my head, closed my notebook, and finally gave him my full attention.

He dressed himself casually. Graphic tee and stonewashed jeans. His locs were short and unkempt. Nothing truly stood out about him. He resembled most of the guys I'd seen around Flatbush. But I would prefer to see him and not hear him.

"Can you get away from me?"

His brows went up.

"You saw me over here minding my business," I started. "I didn't call you over, so I don't know why you thought you should approach."

He licked his lips, lowered his eyes down my neck to return to gawking at my breasts through my baggy tee. Men like him would gawk at a woman in a potato sack and still make an X-rated movie based on what they couldn't see.

"I just wanted to know your name, love."

"You don't give a shit about my name."

My comment got him to pull his attention off my body and to finally focus on my eyes.

I narrowed them at him and he smiled in response.

This was what I was talking about when I said I felt safer in the Black Bamboo even though it wasn't a haven.

The Black Bamboo is probably not the best place for a woman who experienced trauma when she was thirteen, but at least I knew what to expect.

Which meant I knew never to let my guard down under Black Bamboo's roof. I understood I could never relax. I had a purpose for my anxiety and oddly, that worked for me.

I expected for the men to want to be touchy in there. I expected for the men to focus more on my ass and less on my eyes. And because I expected it, I knew never to get the kind of comfortable where a man could do what a man did to me years ago.

Out in this park, though? A place where I *expected* to visit, sit alone, be unbothered, and not get hit on by the likes of this guy? I didn't expect that.

Anything could happen. It's on the news every day.

I was once in the news for a week.

"Now why would you say that?" He asked. "Of course I care about your name."

With his words, he scooted closer, and I curled my fingers into a tight fist.

He noticed and snickered. "Why are you making a fist?"

"Because I'm about to knock you the fuck out."

He slacked his jaw and created space between us.

"That's not enough." I blinked twice. "You need to get up because I will start swinging and I promise you I will not miss."

"All right, okay." He stood to his feet and threw his hands up in front of him while backing away, saying. "I'll leave you alone."

"Bye," I countered.

On my face I probably gave off a level of calm, but inside my heart was racing. Having a man sit so close to me made inside my throat feel like it was closing. Breathing got harder; my head got lighter. All the feelings I wasn't used to feeling in spaces like a park rolled through me like thunder I had to force myself to contain.

As I watched the guy walk away, staring until he became a dot in the distance, I wondered if I would ever feel comfortable with it.

Having a man be so close.

That wasn't something I always wondered, though.

Honestly, I'd only started wondering that yesterday when I entered the elevator and saw the guy from two nights ago.

His eyes.

They seemed so sincere.

Which is weird, right?

First, his attention felt warm and now his eyes were sincere.

I scoffed a laugh and shook my head at the thought.

But still I wondered, could the same comfort I had at an inanimate place like Black Bamboo extend to a person... like him?

I shook my head, attempting to shake the thought too.

It was random and unrealistic and... why was I thinking about him?

I opened my notebook and pressed my pen's ejector to get back to writing the one and only man who had my trust in life.

Because I shouldn't have been thinking about the other guy.

Because...

To me, regardless of how warm that man made me feel or how sincere his eyes appeared, he was still a *man*, and life and the pain I'd experienced in it proved that men must stay at a distance.

From me, at least.

Six

ASHER

"Very impressive, young man," the elderly lady, Elsie, complimented beside me. "Very impressive. You know, we need more black psychologists in this world."

I smiled and nodded as we both entered the elevator.

"If we saw ourselves more in those roles," she continued inside the car, "we'd feel more comfortable unpacking all the baggage we carry. Getting a lot more off our chests simply because we're speaking to someone who shares our ancestral features and who we believe will understand us best. What a blessing."

We'd met for the first time on my floor. I found Elsie waiting in front of the elevators when I left my apartment to take the elevator to head out for a walk around the area. That day was one of my final available days before the semester started at LU. I'd already received my syllabus from my professor, and the course work looked more than I'd had to complete when I attended Brookville.

Or perhaps it was so long ago, I didn't realize how much work a first-year doctorate student had to take on.

It was fine. I anticipated it all. This time around, I had a purpose. I knew my why, and listening to Elsie speak about the necessity of black psychologists was inspiring me to stick with something I knew would be hard.

A simple greeting and introduction between the two of us had me revealing I'd moved into the building to attend Langston University in Manhattan. As soon as I told her that, her face lit up with a bright expression.

"Head doctors," Elsie started. "Uh... that's what we used to call psychologists way back when... probably still do."

I chuckled.

"They weren't popular with us the way they are with you all now." She shook her head, the overhead elevator lights shining down on her cropped gray hair. "Telling strangers our business, often family business, was not something people close to us encouraged us to do, you know? They forced us to hide it. But talking about it even just a little would've helped so many people."

"Oh, I'm sure."

"Instead, we kept it all inside and between family. Passing down our traumas like how people pass down land for their children to inherit. And their children passed it down to their children. A sad reality, honestly."

The elevator chimed again, but this time it stopped on the fifth floor.

When the doors peeled apart, the young woman I had been seeing since the night I moved in was on the other side of those doors again.

Her brown eyes found mine almost immediately before she shifted her attention to Elsie, then back to me again.

"Well..." Elsie gestured at the young woman with a wrinkled hand. "Come on in here, pretty girl. I got an appointment to get to."

The young woman rolled her eyes and stepped into the elevator. Like the last time we rode in an elevator car together, she walked to the opposite end of the elevator, practically pressing her shoulder to the elevator's wall.

Today she wore an oversized graphic tee that was several sizes too big. The tee hung inches above her knees. Beneath, she wore black leggings and on her feet she sported another pair of cool sneakers. Lips still a shade of red, hair a beautiful straight silken black. Skin a clean and clear light brown.

I liked her style a lot. To the point, I was staring and only realized I was when she shot me a mean glare.

"Uh... hey," I tried with a smile the moment the elevator doors closed.

The young woman glanced my way again, looked me up and down this time, and returned her eyes forward, anchoring her head a bit to watch the floor location indicator lights.

The car traveled down the next floor and another until a sudden jolt rattled the car and it stopped at a floor, but the doors did not open.

Elsie sighed. "It does that sometimes," she assured, while leaning forward a bit to push the floor selection button for the lobby. "You gotta press your floor button again."

I furrowed my brows.

"For a new building, you would think everything would act brand new." She chuckled, pressing the floor button again. "Not this one." She jabbed the button some more. "They should have renovated everything besides the units on each floor. Should've knocked down the entire building and started over from scratch, if you ask me."

The elevator jolted once more and continued descending, as Elsie promised.

We were only a few floors above the lobby.

I scratched the back of my head and cleared my throat, turning toward the young woman again.

"Hey... *uh*..." I cleared my throat a second time. "How's the... *umm*... the book?"

The young woman turned her head slowly to refocus on me. Dark brown eyes, soft round lips that seemed to be in a permanent pout now in my line of sight.

"The book you were reading?" I clarified. "How is it?"

She stared at me for a beat before her top lip hiked slightly. She kissed her teeth next, shook her head, and focused forward again.

I let the exhale I'd been holding in go slowly through my nose as I mentally kicked myself.

How's the book you're reading?

God. I'm a fucking loser.

I dropped my forehead into my hand and shook my head at myself.

Could I be any more pathetic?

The elevator arrived on the ground floor and the doors peeled opened. Like the last time we shared an elevator, the young woman was the first one to leave the car, taking large steps towards the building's front door, exiting without glancing back.

I stepped out of the elevator, pinching the inside corners of my eyes. I was a second away from cursing myself for being so corny when I felt a hand rub over my shoulder gently.

I turned to glance behind me to find Elsie smiling up at me.

"You did fine."

I pointed behind us toward the elevator we all just left. "*That* was not fine."

She snickered to herself. "It was. Lauryn has been through a lot."

"Lauryn," I repeated. "Her name is Lauryn."

"*Mm-hmm.*" Ms. Elsie nodded while grinning. "Lauryn James."

A name as beautiful as the woman herself. I didn't allow myself enough time to bask in the revelation of finally having a name to go with a face, because Elsie's words echoed in the corners of my mind.

"Been through a lot," I parroted. "What do you mean by that?"

She held both hands up in front of her. "I'm not one to gossip."

"Right, no." I shook my head. "I'm not asking you to gossip—"

"It's a discovery you should make on your own." She nodded, her eyes going from bright to cloudy with tears.

I tilted my head to one side. "It's something terrible."

Elsie smiled again. "All I can say is, hang in there. Few people talk to Lauryn because they fear her. But they don't realize she's more scared of them than they are of her. She doesn't have many friends..." Elsie pointed up at me and smiled wider. "But something tells me that's about to change."

With that, she ambled off with the help of the cane she walked with.

I stood in front of the elevator, the doors now closed. I was more intrigued and interested.

"Lauryn," I said low, a smile slowly pulling at my lips.

Seven

ASHER

“Oh my God,” I whispered. “Fuck me.”

And not in a good way.

I stepped away from my door, hoping they wouldn’t notice I was in front of it.

“Asher, love,” my mother called on the other side of my apartment’s door. “Open up.”

Unfortunately, she was not alone.

“What on earth is that smell?” My aunt Priscilla queried. “Smells rancid.”

“Natural scent of ghetto.” My mother turned to my door to hammer her fists against it. “Asher, what is taking so long for you to open this door?”

I hung my head in front of me. Clenching my teeth before forcing myself to face my door to unlock it.

I could have thought of a million other things I would've preferred to do on a Saturday morning. Opening my door to let my mother and aunt in was not one of those million things.

They both held fake smiles that looked painful to maintain on their faces when I allowed them past the threshold.

"Well," my aunt started, "at least it's nice in here, Patricia." She turned to face me next. "You've done good Asher."

"Good?" my mother spat, moving around my apartment, her designer heels clicking against my hardwood, dragging in the debris of Brooklyn's sidewalks onto floors I mopped an hour prior.

I didn't allow shoes in my space these days. After living in Indonesia and assimilating to their culture, bringing in the dirt from outside into my living space was a thing of the past.

Wish I could have left my mother and her sister in the past as well.

"It's so small, no?" my mother quizzed my aunt.

"Well, yes," my aunt agreed. "It is small, but at least it doesn't call to mind the neighborhood it's in."

"*Hmph*," my mother huffed, her disappointment clear. "How about this punching dummy, though, Priscilla?" She gestured at the BOB body bag in one corner of my living room. "I tried like hell for him to get rid of the thing, but he insisted he bring this barbaric tool with him."

Going for a few rounds hitting that barbaric tool was the only reason my patience was at the level it was with her and all others.

I signed up for boxing lessons at a gym on the less picturesque side of Long Island when I was eighteen. Kept my training a secret for two years and kept going despite my parents' disapproval when they discovered I'd been spending my weekends learning how to fight. But after I discovered how calming boxing was to me, I refused to give training up. Though I hadn't been to the gym after dropping out of Brookville U, I maintained my practices.

"Well, *that* I can't defend," Aunt Priscilla conceded with a giggle. "Sorry Asher, but it seems violent."

"I wasn't expecting you two," I chimed in. Tried my best to say it with as much patience as I could muster up. "I had plans."

"Oh, love," my mother replied. "They can wait. Your aunt and I wanted to see how you were getting along here. You know, your cousin is looking into condominiums in her building in Manhattan."

I took a deep breath.

"It's closer to Langston," she offered next.

"Oh, your cousin's home is simply stunning, Asher," Aunt Priscilla added. "Beautiful. One of the few things that fiancé of hers got right."

My mother giggled. "I still don't understand how you're dealing with that."

"With what?"

I shook my head as they continued to carry on a conversation in my space. A space I didn't formally invite them to enter before they showed up unannounced.

It was the weekend and my first day to myself. Or what should have been to me.

I'd started school earlier in the week and the workload was making my head spin. Though I'd completed five years of doctorate studies, the course material seemed to have gotten harder and a lot more in quantity to complete, with even less time to complete them.

The day these two popped up was supposed to be my day to decompress. Instead, I was feeling more stressed than before.

"Summer getting ready to marry someone with such..." My mother cleared her throat. "*Humble* beginnings."

"His career helps," Aunt Priscilla insisted. "Because Lord knows, when Summer mentioned she was involved with him, I almost hemorrhaged in my brain."

I dropped my head into my hands.

"Thankfully, his mother and siblings no longer live in the ghetto, but my goodness, Summer loves returning to the slums. I'm just dreading having to share a space with his family members at their wedding—"

"You know," I interjected, unable to take another minute of their visit. "I met Jayce, and he's a great guy. Summer did good."

They both turned to look at me and only blinked.

"He loves her," I added, voice and tone balanced. "And let's be honest, Summer can be a lot."

Aunt Priscilla shrugged. "A lot how? Summer's like me."

Exactly.

"I'm just saying," I added, "they're perfect for each other."

"Well, don't you go getting any ideas," my mother jumped in. "Your cousin may have lucked out, dating down, but *you* won't because you will not even try to."

I arched a brow.

She turned to face her sister. "Did I tell you who your nephew was surveying the night he moved in?"

Aunt Priscilla glanced my way. "Someone's caught your eye already, Asher?"

"More like some*thing*," my mother answered. "The girl, who, by the way, I could barely assign that label to, dressed herself like a boy. Baggy this and baggy that. Sneakers on her feet."

"Oh no." My aunt shook her head.

"Just dreadful," my mother added. "And he was staring at her, Priscilla." She shared a glance with me and commented, "I'd much rather you be gay if that's the case."

"Oh-kay, um." I walked toward my door and placed my hand on the knob. "I had a very rough week, starting school and all—"

"I swear he's trying to kill me, Priscella." My mother pressed her hand to her chest. "First, he drops out of his doctoral program at Brookville to gallivant around the world doing God knows what..."

Living peacefully is what.

"Then he returns to not only attend Brookville's lower rated rivals but also to move into *this* place. This place of *all* places in New York City. My God. Manhattan was right there!"

My mother looked at me, eyes beginning to water. "What have I done to deserve such wicked treatment from you?"

I shouldn't have opened the door.

Because of all of this.

All this drama within the first ten minutes of me letting them in.

In my mother's eyes, the world revolved around her. The world did not exist as she slept, only when she opened her eyes and began her day. So everything happening or about to happen was contingent on her taking her next breath.

I truly believe my mother and her undiagnosed bout with narcissism was one of my earlier inspirations to pursue psychology. So, I could professionally diagnose her as a fucking nutcase and recommend we immediately begin treatment.

"It's been a challenging week restarting my studies again."

My mother opened her mouth to say something, and I quickly followed up with, "And while I'm grateful that you both stopped by, I really should get my rest today."

My aunt smiled and laid a hand on my mother's shoulder. "He's right Patricia. Let's catch a cab and do brunch in the city, then a mani and pedi at the spa."

My mother immediately lit up, and I took another calming, deep breath.

"Yes," I agreed. "That's a great idea Aunt Priscilla." I shifted my attention to my mother. "You ought to go, Mom. You deserve it."

No, she didn't, but honestly, the two of them could walk off a cliff at that moment and I would have encouraged it.

"Very well," my mother said, approaching me and giving me her cheek. "I will check in with you tomorrow."

I bit my tongue to resist telling her she didn't have to and instead gave her the kiss on her cheek she was gesturing to receive. She was leaving, and that would have to be enough.

"Be good, Asher," Aunt Priscilla said as she stepped out into the building's hallway.

"Yes, Asher," my mother added as she exited behind my aunt. "Be good and be sure to stay away from you know who."

"Was she that bad?" my aunt asked my mother as they made their way to the elevator that was only a few steps away from my front door.

"Terrible," my mother answered as she pressed the call button for the elevator. "Stereotypical hood roach."

My aunt snickered. "Patricia, I think it's called hood rat."

The both of them cackled, their voices traveling down the eighth-floor hallway as I closed my door, needing to keep my cool.

Because hearing them discuss Lauryn in that fashion bothered me somehow.

She was a stranger to me, but my mother's comments about her bothered me.

"Lauryn," I said, fighting the urge to bite back my smile.

I wondered how she was choosing to spend her Saturday morning.

EIGHT

LAURYN

I sat up in bed with my back pressed against the headboard. My bedding on my mattress was still a tangled mess. The bed had yet to be made up and would remain that way.

Because I never made it up.

It was my way of controlling my environment. My way of having a choice of what my space looked like around me which was important to me.

A new artist, Cleo Sol's voice, played low on my phone. Her "Young Love" was on a loop and had been for the past two hours.

I got a little sleep the night before.

Bad dreams led to insomnia and me turning on my TV and watching my favorite cooking show on a cable cooking channel. When that got old, I just laid in bed with the TV off. Eyes fixed on the ceiling, witnessing as daylight poured in through my windows and listening to the natural sounds of Brooklyn waking up.

My bad dreams were more like bad recollections. Night terrors. Many of which woke me from sleep around four that morning and I hadn't been back to sleep.

I didn't trip over it. In a few hours, I could return to my usual routine of getting out of bed, preparing myself to leave my apartment to head to work.

It had been a week since my boss and Black Bamboo's owner Larry put me on a weeklong suspension for punching a customer. Today was the last day of that suspension. I called Larry the night prior before going to sleep to ask if I could come back to the club. He agreed to me returning to the club to work my scheduled night shift.

I still had a few hours to burn, and the rest was nowhere to be found, so I did what I usually did when I had free time.

Write to my father in my notebook.

I flipped opened the notebook and leafed through the pages. Eyes scanning the words quickly as I turned the pages in search of a blank one.

My letters to him felt like diary pages. I'd tell him what I was feeling at the time of my writing. Tell him about my day and, of course, how much I missed him.

I'd update him on everything that was changing with me or changing on the outside of his prison walls.

It almost felt like a duty to do it. An obligation I didn't mind meeting. Even though he probably will read none of the letters, I write to him.

A child laughing outside made my ears perk up. I glanced toward the window only to see the tops of neighboring buildings and the clear blue sky.

On my eighteenth birthday, I rode the bus to the correctional facility where my father was serving a life sentence to visit him. It was the only thing I wanted to do on my birthday and I had been excited to see him for months after I got the idea to go. I didn't tell anyone I was going. Had I told my aunt, Aunt Evelyn, she would have talked me out of it. So, I kept it a secret.

I got all pretty and dressed up in a new sweatsuit and sneakers I'd purchased weeks prior with the visit in mind. I wanted my dad to see that I'd been taking care of myself since he's been away and that he didn't have to worry about me.

I needed to prove to him that his sacrifice was worth it. I wanted to show him I was okay... though I really wasn't.

The bad dreams were worst back then because I didn't know how to manage them so I wasn't sleeping, which didn't help with being angry all the time. I could manage the anger better after graduating high school that year. But when I was a student, I would get into fights with boys at school. A lot of the fights I started. In high school, all the girls my age were praying the guys at school liked them. I was fist fighting those same guys if they showed any type of romantic interest in me. And I'd always fight them publicly so that other guys could see and know not to step to me on the same shit those guys were getting their asses handed to them for doing.

Besides graduating that year, going to see my father was another thing I was excited to do.

But when I arrived at the facility, he took forever to come out, even when the guards promised they'd let him know I was there.

He never came out of his cell to see me. Instead of coming out to see me, my dad sent the correctional officer to speak to me. The officer told me my dad didn't want to see me and didn't want to see me in *there* again.

Right after the correctional officer uttered those words, they asked me to leave. And I wanted to do more. Fight my way through, because I couldn't believe that my father would say such a thing. It confused me.

I couldn't wrap my mind around what he said to me.

Was he upset?

Did he have a bad day?

Did things get better after I left?

I figured my father was angry with me. And he would have every right to be.

I pushed down on my pen's ejector and started writing.

Today's letter would be all about the sleep I didn't get the night before. I made a mental note to keep out what the dream was about.

I was the reason they locked him up to begin with.

Because I was his third strike. The reason he was behind bars for the rest of his life.

I was writing so hard in my notebook. My thoughts drifted to feeling more and more alone the more words I jotted down on the page. I had plans to visit my aunt on Sunday but besides her; I had only me these days.

The sound of the pen's tip slicing into the grid lined page made me quickly relax the tension in my hand. I was physically putting all my weight and burden on the page.

Sometimes it was too heavy to keep to myself. Too difficult to focus on.

Outside, it was clear the residents in Brooklyn were now awake. Voices scattered outside my window, coming in and out. I could make out what they were saying. Other voices got drowned out by the chorus of horns honking at once, likely because someone was holding up a line of cars at the red light.

I focused my attention on it all, needing to preoccupy my mind with anything besides what was on my mind. In my heart.

Because the memory of being pinned down, unable to move, unable to breathe. Unable to do anything besides take *it*, waiting and hoping now would be when it ended wasn't what I wanted to focus on. But I couldn't help it.

I shut my book and shut my lids tight.

And when that didn't work, I threw my notebook across the room. And when that didn't do enough, I turned to pick up the glass of water sitting on one of my night tables, throwing the glass against the nearest wall.

And that still wasn't enough.

Books I had stacked together on my night table hit the floor with one swoop of my arm along the table's surface.

And when none of that worked, I snatched up my pillow and pressed it to my face and screamed into the cushion long and hard. The strain of my vocal cords giving me the release I was in search of.

I screamed again into the cushion until my eyes watered. Until things felt under my control again.

"You're okay," I whispered to myself, closing my eyes. Feeling the scratching ache in my throat, knowing my voice would be hoarse in a few hours. "Just stop fucking thinking."

I dropped the pillow from my face and quickly realized I had tears in my eyes when the tension of squeezing my lids closed caused two pearls of tears to slide through.

I squeezed my lids tighter and clenched my teeth together. I held my breath and did my best to gain control, any control I could muster, to stop my chest from heaving.

I could hear my heart hammering in my ears and clenched my teeth tighter. I refused to take a breath until my heart slowed down. Figured if I died, at least I wouldn't have to feel *this* ever again.

Sixteen years had passed, but some days it felt like *it* happened only yesterday.

I quickly wiped my face and stood off the bed. It was too early to get ready for work, but I needed to shake the feeling.

Because it was the first day of work, at a job I didn't like, but at least it would help me not think or dream about a time in my life that ruined me.

NINE

ASHER

The sun was setting behind the neighboring buildings. I pulled opened my building door and stepped in. In one hand, I carried a plastic bag that had a stapled brown paper bag inside of it. That bag held three takeout Chinese containers.

It was Sunday evening, and I was returning from a day out, ready to wind down and prepare for another ruthless week of school.

I didn't regret many things, but I was regretting dropping out of my doctoral program the year prior.

I would've been done.

Now I was starting all over.

The whole thing made me grunt and drop my head into my hand as I approached the bank of elevators.

I pushed the call button and dropped my head back, shutting my eyelids to lull the faint headache looming.

"I really hope this was a good idea," I said lowly to myself.

I felt the air move a little beside me. A gentle force of energy that pulled me out of my woe-is-me mood.

I leveled my head to see the young woman, Lauryn, approaching the elevators where I stood.

I did a double-take and held onto my breath a second longer than usual when she stopped inches away.

Our last few interactions left me unsure of myself. Feeling a little defeated.

While I struggled a little to get a handle over my course load at LU, women, to me, were much easier to understand.

Women liked their men to be triple A's – attentive, assertive, and adventurous. They had to be attracted to them, of course, but attraction is so subjective that one could find themselves attracted to someone they never thought they'd like. But those triple A's along with a man who listens were always a formula to depend on for me.

Because I wasn't the tallest guy or the bulkiest, but I knew what women liked. Or at least I thought I did.

I'd studied them long enough, at least the ones I grew up with. They were simple to me. Their likes easy to identify. I didn't consider their wants complicated for me to meet.

Lauryn, though...

She was a mystery I wanted to solve.

The two neighbors I'd spoken with gave conflicting opinions about this illusive woman.

I was dying to find out who she was for me.

I parted my lips to give a greeting when she moved her eyes off me, faced toward the elevator doors, and tilted her head back to check the floor location indicator lighting up above.

I released my exhale and turned forward to do the same. Her body language was saying what she was thinking loud and clear.

No.

And I had no choice but to respect it.

The doors peeled opened, and I waited for a moment for her to enter the car, but she didn't move.

I gestured inside. "After you."

"You go first," she replied.

Her voice.

Not what I was expecting after witnessing her interaction a week ago. When she called our neighbor Delilah a bitch, she sounded angry, aggressive.

With me, though, in that moment, was different.

Her voice this evening.

It was soft.

Light.

Like a Disney princess.

Which was not what I was expecting at all.

I nodded, stepping into the car. She followed, moving to the far end of the elevator as always.

I pressed my floor, eight, and pressed hers, five.

I turned to glimpse her way as the doors closed. "Fifth, right?"

I knew her floor. I just had to hear her voice again to make sure I wasn't mistaken. The trickle in of information on this woman was like the serving of a full-course meal. Each plate delivered, elevating my palette, and satisfying my curiosity about her.

First her presence, then her name, now her voice.

I wonder what she thinks about?

She didn't reply with words. only a simple nod.

The elevator ascended. Second floor, then third.

By the fourth, the elevator jolted, then stopped.

Remembering what Elsie, the elderly lady who lived on my floor, told me, I simply leaned forward and pressed button five.

Nothing.

I arched a brow.

I also heard when Lauryn cleared her throat at the other end of the elevator.

I moved in closer to the elevator's cab controls and pressed five again.

Unlike the day Elsie did it, the elevator didn't move. It did nothing.

"Fuck," I whispered to myself, tilting my head back to check the floor location indicator. Pushed the eighth-floor button this time once, then twice.

Only stopped when I heard the heavy breaths she was taking beside me.

I turned my attention her way and noticed her chest was heaving. She focused her attention forward as her breaths got even heavier.

"Are you okay?" I asked, approaching.

"Don't." She turned to press her back to the elevator's wall. "Stay over there or I will swing."

She clenched her fists, and her eyes bugged a little.

I held up both hands, the bag of Chinese food dangling in one as I backed away. "Absolutely. I just wanted to make sure you were—"

"I'm cool," she interjected, pointing now. "Just stay over there."

Her reaction was interesting. She almost appeared scared of me, but I couldn't be too sure because she came across as if she was ready to fight me, too.

Which was odd a little, but also made sense.

At least in terms of what I'd been reading in the book she carried when we first met after I moved in.

I returned to the cab of buttons. Instead of pressing any of the floor numbers, I pressed the emergency alarm button. Pushed it three times before a voice boomed through the cab control speakers.

"Hello," the voice echoed around the car.

"Yeah, the elevator is stuck," I informed. "It should have stopped on the fifth floor."

"Yes, sir," the voice replied. "We are working on it right now. I apologize for the inconvenience."

I peeked over at Lauryn to see her chest still heaving, fists as clenched as the first time I noticed, and her attention entirely on me as she stared at me from the side of her eyes.

"How long?" I asked the guy.

"Please give us at least ten minutes," he answered.

Lauryn released a shaky breath out of her mouth.

"Our maintenance guy is only a block away and will be here soon," he added. "The moment it's repaired, the elevator will make its way to the fifth floor and any other floors selected on its own. Please do not press anymore buttons as you wait."

"Please be quick," I urged. "We have someone in here who is claustrophobic."

"I'm not claustrophobic," she explained to me once the guy ended the conversation.

I turned to face her. "I'm sorry. I thought... you were breathing heavily and—"

"I'm not weak."

"No." I shook my head, pressing my hand to my chest. "Of course not. Claustrophobia doesn't mean you're weak. It only means you're nervous in confined spaces." I gestured around me. "Like elevators."

She stared at me for a moment, eyes scanning mine, in search of what I wasn't sure.

But I softened my gaze on her, so taken by the complete picture that stood before me.

"I read your book," I revealed.

Her brows furrowed.

"How to Be Soft in a World That's Hard."

A brow piqued.

"It was..."

"Not for you," she cut in.

I dropped my head and chuckled to myself briefly before lifting my gaze again. In time to catch the ghost of a smirk on her lips.

Lauryn was beautiful, like a doll. Big brown eyes, full lips, painted red again today, and long black hair she wore loose. But with the hint of a smile on her red lips, goodness... she was gorgeous.

"I'm not the target audience, no," I acknowledged. "But I'm a reader. I read a lot."

She tilted her head to one side.

"And I saw you with the book and the title sounded interesting and..." I scratched the back of my head, suddenly realizing how weird I was sounding. "I was curious why a woman like yourself would read a book like that."

"A woman like myself?" She questioned. "And what's a woman like me?"

She had a thick Brooklyn accent; one I've grown to really like since living in the city. Growing up in the Hamptons, the closest to the city I'd ever gotten was Manhattan, when my family and I would travel out of Long Island for a show on Broadway or for dinner at a fine restaurant. Brooklyn was only a bridge to me. Never a place I'd ever been to, or even thought to visit. But now I lived here, and I realized how rich in culture it was. It was like its own part of the world. A melting pot of cuisines, languages, and unique accents.

Her Brooklyn accent sounded pronounced. It complemented what I saw on the outside.

She was so intriguing.

"A woman who appears soft already," I answered.

The gentle whirring of the elevator's filter filled the silence for a beat before she scoffed a laugh and shook her head, dropping her attention to her sneakers.

Another fresh pair, women's size fives, maybe. This one was a successful collaboration of pink and red, with laces that resembled a strawberry shortcake mosaic.

"I'm Asher," I said next. "Asher Truesdale."

She looked up at me again.

"We've seen each other a few times and I've wanted to introduce myself to you, but it never seemed like the right moment to."

"Lauryn James," she said back.

I smiled, pleased that she shared her name with me. Even though someone had already beaten her to it, something about her feeling opened enough to share it with me herself made me feel good.

"Nice to meet you, Lauryn."

The sound of metal squeaking followed by the car swaying, then jolting, had us both pressing our back to the elevator wall.

Soon the elevator was moving upward, ascending once again, and quickly stopping once more.

This time the doors peeled opened and there were people standing on the other side.

"There we go," announced the gentleman dressed in a cobalt blue maintenance jumpsuit with his name, Paul, stitched over the top of his left chest. "Sorry about the wait, and I apologize for the inconvenience."

He shook his head. "These elevators. It should be good now for you to make it to your floors."

"This is mine," Lauryn announced, moving toward the elevator opening to step out and exit.

"Thank you," I said to the maintenance man, watching as she left.

Right when I was feeling a way that she was leaving saying nothing, she turned before the doors were closing to say, "Later, Asher."

And before I could say anything in return, the doors shut in front of me, reflecting my big smile on the elevator's chrome surface.

Ten

LAURYN

Asher.

Every time I thought of his name, I had to fight tooth and nail to keep myself from smiling.

I didn't expect his name to be Asher. He reminded me of a Rahim or a Jamal. But Asher suited him. The name gave off the impression of strength and protection like the guy himself.

The whole elevator situation could have gone all the way left. Especially with me being there. Because as soon as the car stopped on the fourth floor and the doors refused to open, my throat felt like it was closing on me.

He called it claustrophobia, but I knew that wasn't it at all.

I was in a small space with a man I didn't know.

Though he wasn't a towering man with big muscles, or an intimidating presence, he was still a man.

And it wasn't looking good... for either of us.

I glanced up from my notebook to stare out at the lake view in front of me. Ducks and white swans paddled their legs in the water, appearing to float along the surface.

On a bench in Prospect Park, I sat penning another letter in my notebook. I was back at work and scheduled to start my shift at the Black Bamboo later that night. That week I had off, because of my suspension, helped me discover how relaxing the park could be, so I'd added it to my outdoor routine. Figured sitting in the park would be good for me for the next few months before it got colder outside. Eventually leaving me with nothing else to do. Might as well enjoy it as much as I can before then.

Asher was on my mind that day in the park. So, he was the subject of my letter to my father in my notebook. Well, the elevator getting stuck was the subject.

Asher was simply a mention.

A mention that had me fighting not to smile.

A giggle to my left fluttered in the air, attracting my attention.

I turned my head to glance that way and saw the couple I found sitting here when I arrived. They were kissing now.

It wasn't tacky or anything.

It was kind of... cute.

I found myself caught in their world, watching them. He eased strands of hair out of her eyes. Caressing her shoulder as they talked, then focused forward to watch the ducks in the lake.

Relationships have always been an interesting thing to me. The closest thing I had to a representation of one around me was my aunt, who had been with her boyfriend for two years now. Before that, it was only her and me. And she made being alone and without a romantic relationship appear doable. Which is why I believed it was doable for me to move out on my own two years ago when she started dating again.

The woman's giggles traveled around me once more. I glanced again, then quickly blinked away when her boyfriend caught me staring.

I returned my attention to my notebook and immediately read Asher's name again.

He had a calming energy to him, Asher. The way he analyzed me was unlike any other man. It was as if I were a glass figurine to him. But not crystal clear. More like frosted. While others accepted I was difficult to see-through, Asher studied me like he was trying to peer through the blur to discover what was inside.

A smile pulled at the corners of my lips as I pushed my pen ejector down to write again.

The scent of vanilla and musk invaded my space before I could look up to see where it was coming from.

"Hey," he greeted, taking a seat beside me.

My muscles tensed immediately.

It was the guy who was sitting on the bench a few feet across from me with his girlfriend.

I leaned forward a bit to peek that way to see that the bench he sat on with his girlfriend was empty.

"She's gone," he informed, reading my expression. "What's your name?"

I furrowed my brows and stared at him. "Why?"

He smiled, revealing a mouth full of plaque teeth. "Because I saw you looking."

I closed my notebook and laid my pen on top. "Excuse me?"

"I saw you looking," he repeated. "When I was sitting over there with my girl. I saw you checking me out."

"Checking you out?" I scoffed. "No."

"Listen, it's cool." He scooted closer to me, draping one arm over the back of the bench where my back rested.

I held onto my inhale.

"I sent her off so I could talk to you." He licked his lips and my stomach knotted. "So, what's up?"

It was only us two on this side of the lake. Though people were present around the perimeter of the water, including people sitting on building balconies in neighboring buildings with units that overlooked the lake, having him this close was making my heart race so fast my head was feeling light.

"I was not checking you out," I told him. "And you need to get out of my face."

"Chill." He leaned in more. "My girl doesn't mind. We have an open relationship."

"And you are about to have an *open* lip after I bust it opened if you don't get the fuck out of my face."

He jerked his head back.

"Get the fuck up!" I shouted. "Or I will get you the fuck up."

He jumped to his feet.

"You're crazy," he spat, lip hiked on the right. "And not the crazy I can fuck with. It ain't even that serious."

Damn.

Just when I was allowing myself to lean into the warmth.

I watched him leave. Did so to confirm he actually left so I could take my breaths easy again.

Once upon a time I would swing and talk after, taking great pleasure in inflicting pain on men who didn't keep their distance. So, he was lucky.

But this was exactly why I didn't trust men. They were not to be trusted. If they weren't breaking you physically, they were breaking your heart.

I wonder if she knew they were in an open relationship.

I opened my notebook and pressed down on my pen's ejector again. Dragged the tip of the pen along the paragraph with Asher's name, crossing everything out. Every nice thing I wrote, all the feelings I mentioned, he made me feel. I blackened it. I got rid of it so I wouldn't have to see it ever again.

Because he probably wasn't a protector. Possibly pretending to be one to get close to me and hurt me like they all do.

The warmth I was experiencing was most likely misguided energy. And if I wasn't careful, I could find myself in a situation like the one I found myself in years ago.

And I already told myself never again.

Crossing out his name wasn't enough in that instance.

I ripped out the page next and made a paper ball of it. Stood to my feet and tossed it in a nearby trashcan on my way out of the park's lake view area.

Because no man would ever catch me slippin' again.

Definitely not Asher.

ELEVEN

ASHER

I grunted the moment we stepped through the doors.

They dimmed the overhead lighting so low. The lights might as well not have been on. Bright green strobe lights were the only thing lighting the way. People packed the space all around us but stood cluttered near the stage.

Women sauntered around us with practically nothing on. Some had nothing on at all. It smelled of musk, money, and malt.

"This is not my scene," I commented, following behind a friend.

Printed on the black awning outside in green lettering was Black Bamboo. On a Saturday night, the Black Bamboo was not where I wanted to be.

But a friend of mine from Brookville U, who had made a home for himself in this part of Brooklyn, begged me to meet up with him that weekend so he could show me a good time.

"When you said the club," I shouted over the music, turning sideways to make my way through the crowded area without bumping into anyone, "I thought you meant a lounge kind of club."

And for good reason.

Tyler worked as a financial advisor on Wall Street. His clients were trading stocks that totaled more than millions. He lived in a co-op that overlooked the East River. Tyler wore pressed dress shirts and crisp dress pants, always designer. It was practically his uniform. He was what many called respectable. My mother loved him.

But somehow, we were here.

"There's this rapper, Keith Aaron," he shouted over his shoulder at me. "He comes here all the time. Swears, it's one of the hottest up-and-coming spots in Brooklyn and I agree."

That was Tyler's flaw. Growing up in a sheltered life of wealth and status in Long Island, hip-hop, more so rappers, were his heroes. While kids our ages found wonderment in Marvel comic book characters, Tyler idolized rappers, wishing he could live the lives they lived.

For an intelligent man, he was stupid.

We stopped at a section, divided off from the rest of the club by a thick velvet rope that encircled the space. There were three other sections like it within walking distance.

"Only VIP for my VIP," Tyler grinned. "This is us."

The section was a few feet away from the main stage where a woman danced seductively around the thick silver pole.

I sighed as Tyler unhooked the rope, releasing it so we could step inside.

Already I was regretting agreeing to step inside the club.

The dancer on stage dropped into a squat, balancing herself on the arches of her feet to bounce her ass to the beat of the rap song reverberating around us.

"Man," Tyler shouted, reaching for the bottle of champagne that sat in a silver bucket of ice next to him. "All the girls in here are fine. The waitresses too."

"Tyler." I leaned in so I wouldn't have to shout. "This is not my scene."

"Oh, come on!" He handed me a champagne flute and filled it with champagne. "I haven't seen you in a fucking year."

Hordes of dollars fluttered in the air in front of us.

"You up and drop out of Brookville, leave the country, and don't so much as call me." He laughed. "You're back. This is cause for celebration."

Tyler and I met at Brookville University our freshman years when we lived in a dorm together. We lived together our four years in undergrad and remained friends after we finished our bachelor's programs. He joined a firm, and I started my doctoral program at Brookville. Though life was taking us in different directions, we always stayed in touch and hung out occasionally, maintaining a friendship.

"No one knew I'd left school and the country except my parents," I explained.

"And still I'm crushed, but…" He held a finger up. "You can make it up to me by having a good time. Just sit back and enjoy the show. And what a show it is, my man." He winked next.

It was so hard to make out faces. There was so much going on around me, it was impossible to form a cohesive thought. The music was loud, the space congested. I didn't feel good about the environment at all. Who could?

Time seemed to crawl. Half an hour felt more like two. While I nursed my glass of champagne and had yet to finish it, Tyler was on his third and the bottle was now empty.

His hand went up before he was gesturing at the empty bottle.

I shook my head. "Don't you think you've had enough?"

"Don't be a dad, Ash," he chastised. "It's the damn weekend. I don't get many opportunities to get out and have some fun. This is my fun. Some people get high, others fuck bitches. I like to get high, fuck bitches, and watch them shake ass. It's a vice that does me right and it doesn't hurt anybody for me to enjoy."

I closed my eyes and shook my head again.

Another hour, I thought to myself. *I'll stay for another hour and that's it.*

When I opened my eyes, I saw a pair of round hips, a small waist, and full breasts heading our way. Though she dressed herself in all black, no color could mask the natural bounce of her curves.

Her face was the last thing to come into view because of how dark it was in the club. The only thing helping to make out her facial features were the sparklers, sparkling from the neck of the bottle she carried. But once I recognized her face, I nearly choked.

My eyes bugged when they locked with hers. "Lauryn?"

In her hand, she carried an identical bottle, like the one Tyler had just finished draining.

Lauryn faltered in step, her jaw dropping the closer she approached.

"You know her?" Tyler quizzed.

I couldn't respond. Couldn't help my eyes from moving off hers to review the outfit she had on.

The woman who covered herself completely in baggy clothing, hiding everything, was now exposed in a way that made me stand to my feet.

"What are you doing here?" Lauryn asked, shouting over the music while setting the bottle down on our table.

"That's what I want to know, but about you," I said back.

"I'm Tyler." Tyler stood to his feet, immediately reaching for her hand.

She pulled her hand back.

I pushed Tyler back into his seat.

He was drunk, and I was too much in shock and a daze to check on him.

Lauryn shook her head while backing away.

"Wait." I walked out of my area to follow behind her. "Where are you going?"

"Back to work."

"Work?" I grabbed her arm gently, and she immediately pulled her arm free. She stopped walking, though, and turned to face me.

"Why do you work *here*?"

"Why do you care?"

My eyes scanned her face, my attention kept falling to her body.

I didn't know what I was feeling or why I was feeling it. I wanted to rip my tee off and to give it to her. Pull her out of the club and take her home. My mind couldn't compute why I wanted to do that.

I couldn't answer her question either.

She pouted her red painted lips and spun on her heels, strutting off, and leaving me standing there stuck for a few breaths.

An hour came and went, and I was still there.

Not standing where Lauryn left me. Back in my seat in Tyler and my VIP section. I worked hard to see through the dark to find her every time I lost her in the scuffle of activity in the club.

I watched Lauryn from a distance in VIP as she serviced neighboring tables. Bringing food to one, clearing the bottles and glasses off another.

Every so often she would glance my way and I made it a priority for her to always see me watching her.

The glass Tyler poured for me sat on the table in front of us, still practically filled to the rim. He'd empty his second bottle and was dancing offbeat to the song blasting in the club.

I tuned him out. Tuned everything out. I had tunnel vision, all focused on Lauryn.

As the hour progressed to hour two, the club didn't get emptier. It only got more crowded.

People were bumping into each other as they moved about the space. It was a mess.

Tyler had stopped trying to get me to have fun and was now having fun for the both of us.

My eyes followed Lauryn as she approached the section beside Tyler and my section. She carried a bottle, not like the one she brought to Tyler, to the section. As she was placing the bottle down on the table, one guy who was standing outside of the section slapped her on the ass as she was leaning forward.

I sat up straight in my seat.

She popped up instantly and turned to face him. I noticed she clenched her hands into fists for only a second before she released the tension in her fingers and was turning to walk away.

But the same guy who'd slapped her ass stopped her by grabbing her arm.

And that got me up on my feet.

"Hey," Tyler slurred. "Where are you going?"

I left his question unanswered and rounded our section's table to step out of it and to walk my way over to the section Lauryn was in.

As I walked closer, I heard her shouting for him to let her go. I fixed my eyes on his grip on her arm. My pulse pounding now in my neck the closer I approached.

"Let her go," came out as a growl from me.

The guy had me by about a foot and was likely ten pounds heavier than I was, too. He had a mouth full of glittering gold and a bruise that extended down the center of his lip.

"Nigga, who the fuck are you?" he asked, still holding tight to her arm.

"I said, let her go," I repeated, stepping closer into his space.

He did. He shoved Lauryn away next, but only to turn to give me his full attention. The other guys in his section, who lounged in seats, stood to their feet and moved closer to me, too.

I glanced in Lauryn's direction to see her eyes fixed on mine. She looked visibly worried.

"Are you crazy or are you dumb?" the guy asked. "Do you know who the fuck I am?"

He grabbed me by my shirt collar, intending to lift me off my feet.

And... I snapped.

My fist was cutting through the air before I could stop it. Connecting with his jawline before someone lifted me off my feet from behind and threw me to the hard ground. I didn't stay there long. Never did when I got into this state. Between the lack of lighting and the competing smells in the air, the environment sent me into a mental whirlwind that had me hitting anything and anywhere my fist could land.

If it had eyes and a face, it was getting hit. They weren't people anymore around me. They were all just punching dummies.

Things were crashing to the surrounding floors, and I felt hands grabbing me, but again, I was so wrapped up in the moment that all I saw were eyes and faces and if I saw them; they were getting hit.

Everything moved fast, including when someone tackled me to the ground. More than one pair of hands lifted me into the air shortly after and forced me to my feet.

"You gotta get the fuck out," I heard spat behind me. "Get him the fuck out of here!"

Strong arms shoved me toward the front exit. The people in front of me cleared the way. My nostrils stung from the influx of air I was inhaling in my attempt to calm myself down while being pushed forward. The crowd that was impossible to walkthrough when Tyler and I arrived, now seemed to part like the Red Sea for me.

One big shove out the door had me catching my balance on the concrete outside. With the fresh air to greet me and the sounds of Brooklyn instead of rap music polluting my listening space, I came to.

The guards, who came close to triple my size, stepped back, hands up in front of them in surrender.

"You can't come back in here, boss," one decided, shaking his head. "I'm sorry."

"Yo, you a wild guy, though, my dude. Gahdamn," the other commented while chuckling. "I could barely get you out of there on my own."

"Man, what the fuck?!" Tyler shouted, staggering out of the door before the guards closed it again. "What the hell, Asher?"

I could finally get control over my breathing. Didn't even realize I was breathing so hard until all I heard was the sound of night behind me.

Tyler's eyes were glassy, but moving wildly as he stared at me in shock. "What was that?"

"They…" I started, swallowing to catch my breath. "They grabbed me—"

"You took on all of those guys in there like some kind of maniac." He stepped closer, eyes scanning my face. "And you left with not even a scratch. You went berserk, Ash! How did you do that? And most importantly, can you teach me?"

None of that mattered to me at that moment. All I wanted was to know if Lauryn was okay.

Why did I even care?

I still didn't have that answer for her or myself.

And although I would've liked to have handled things at Black Bamboo differently, knowing she wouldn't have to worry about being grabbed like that was comfort enough.

Twelve

LAURYN

Onions and garlic sizzled in the skillet, releasing an aromatic scent throughout my aunt's apartment. Her boyfriend moved around the kitchen like a seasoned chef, reaching for this and sprinkling that.

My aunt sat beside me, pressing the buttons on her TV's remote control. She was sifting through movie titles on her movie streaming app. Legs kicked up, a fresh cocktail prepared for her icing in a glass.

It wasn't her birthday or any special occasion. It was only Sunday.

"They got a few seasons of the cooking show you like watching on here," she informed, her eyes fixed on the TV screen. "We can watch that."

I didn't respond.

I was too busy staring at the bouquet of bright red roses; the green stems sitting in a vase of water. My aunt positioned the vase at the center of the coffee table in front of us.

Usually, when I visited my aunt's apartment, I spent the bulk of the time staring at my mother's picture. Aunt Evelyn kept a framed photo of my mother wearing her signature red lip-stained lips in a portrait she had taken at JCPenney before I was born. I hated the attention I attracted from men whenever I wore red lipstick. But I still wore my lips red as an homage to my mother, since red was her favorite color and she loved wearing red lipstick all the time when she was alive. My aunt's homage to my mother was keeping my mother's photo next to the silver urn that held my mother's ashes on the shelf beside my aunt's TV.

My mother's urn always had my attention. Not that evening, though.

"You good?" my aunt asked beside me.

I turned my head to find her eyes fixed on mine. Those eyes scanned my face, searching for my answer before I could give it.

"I'm fine," I told her. Not to calm her concern, but because I really was.

Her dark brown eyes continued to scan, though. She had the longest lashes, something she and my mother shared.

The sound of a pot being set on the stove drew my attention to the kitchen again.

We were in her apartment in Brooklyn, about three miles from my apartment building. Dinner at my Aunt Evelyn's was something I'd been doing since I moved out two years ago.

Coincidentally, that was when she started dating her boyfriend William, whom she called Will.

She took me in when I was thirteen. Thirteen was the year everything changed.

"You look like you've seen a ghost." She giggled to herself.

"Might as well." I pointed towards the kitchen with my thumb. "What's he doing in there?"

Aunt Evelyn smirked. "Cooking."

I leaned in. "You got that man cooking for you?"

She hollered a laugh, and her amusement almost made me smile.

She shrugged nonchalantly and returned to surfing through movie titles. "He insisted, so I obliged."

"Does he know how to cook, though?"

Aunt Evelyn inhaled the air and replied with, "Smells like it."

For many years, my aunt was single. Or appeared single.

Because she never brought guys around after I moved in to live with her.

I realize now that was a conscious decision on her part, to not date. A sacrifice of sorts, because of me.

"I didn't know men did that." I admitted.

She turned her attention to me again. "Did what? Cook?"

"Yeah." I gestured at the flowers. "Or *that*."

Her eyes went where I pointed, and she smiled. "They do nice things sometimes. A good amount of them do nice things *all* the time."

"*Hmph*," I replied, leaning back in my chair. "I ain't never seen it."

"You see it now," Aunt Evelyn countered.

I glanced toward the kitchen and nodded.

I saw it last night too.

"I got fired."

"From Black Bamboo?"

I nodded again. "Yup. Last night."

"Why?" she asked, turning completely in her seat on the couch to face me. "What happened?"

"You do nothing but bring me trouble up in here," Larry shouted at me, while pointing behind me.

I allowed my eyes to wander that way, spotting the shattered glass sparkling beneath the green strobe lighting. Where there wasn't glass, were pools of spilled liquor. And turned over tables and chairs. That one area of the club mirrored the aftermath of a tornado. I couldn't believe it.

"Why am I being blamed?" I shouted. "I didn't even do anything."

"You didn't do nothing?!" Larry got louder. "That nigga lost his fucking mind because of you. Throwing punches and shit. Wildin' out on my loyal customers. All that was because of your ass."

"Your stupid ass loyal customer put his hands on me, again," I argued. "Why isn't he banned from coming in here?"

"This is a fucking strip club, Lauryn!" he yelled. "A strip club."

I took a breath and shook my head. "That doesn't justify him grab-bing me when I don't want to be grabbed, Larry."

"You're fired."

My jaw dropped. "What?"

"You're fucking fired," he said this time. "Get out. Get your shit and get the fuck out of my business, Lauryn."

I jerked my head back, my jaw dropping the more his demand set in.

His attention returned behind him when he turned and pressed his hands to the top of his head. "Do you see what this crazy nigga did to my place, man? Fuck!"

"Damn," my aunt whispered. "Well, I can't say I'm mad about it. You know how much I hated you working there."

"It paid good money."

"You got money, Lauryn," she reminded. "You don't need to be working. I still have your money—"

"It's not my money, Auntie."

"It *is* your money," she swore. "The money from that company—"

"I don't fucking want it!" I interjected, a little too loud.

William stopped moving around the kitchen and glanced back at us. "Y'all all right out there?"

My aunt held up a hand, her attention still on me. "We're fine."

A smile and nod from her were enough confirmation for him to return to moving around the kitchen.

"I will say this last thing and I'll drop it."

I rolled my eyes closed.

"The awarded money from the real estate company for the aban-doned house belongs to you, Lauryn. You deserve it." She pressed her hands to either side of my face and turned my head to face her. When I opened my eyes to hers, she titled my head down to kiss my forehead.

I released all the air I held in, wanting to lose myself in her comfort. Although my aunt wasn't identical to my mother. They shared similar features. They had different mothers, but the same father. But my aunt's love for me was much like my mother's. Aunt Evelyn didn't have chil-dren of her own. Never wanted them. So I was her baby, something she always told me and showed me even more.

"If you want the money," she said. "Just say the word. I've been waiting to sign everything over to you."

I shook my head.

"All the money is sitting in accounts, untouched." She pointed toward her bedroom. "I have the information and account numbers for them all in my—"

"I'm good, Auntie," I told her. "I saved a lot of my money whenever I got paid. Only paid rent and bought sneakers and notebooks with it. I'll be fine."

She sighed in defeat. "Okay."

We were quiet for a little. My aunt returned to sorting through movie titles on screen.

"I know him."

She arched a brow.

"The guy who tore up the club over me?"

"How do you know him?"

"He lives in my building," I revealed. "His name is Asher Truesdale."

She stared at me for a moment, her lips working into a sly grin.

"What?"

"Nothing," she said, "Only that I see you fighting a smile wanting to shine through."

I shook my head. "I'm not smiling."

"You want to though, huh?"

I dropped my eyes to her hardwood floors.

She nudged me on my shoulder. "It's okay to like a guy."

I looked up at her and she winked.

"It's even more okay to admit it, too," she added.

William poked his head out of the kitchen long enough to announce, "Food's ready, y'all."

"Perfect," my aunt said back. "We'll be right there. Thank you, baby."

She leaned in close and said low, "Because when you like them and they like you, they might cook for you and buy you flowers... just because it's Sunday." She stuck her tongue out and I couldn't help but to laugh.

Couldn't help but to consider her words, too.

Because I think I do like Asher.

———

A few days later, on a Friday evening around 7pm, I stood in front of Asher's door.

I'd been hoping to run into him by the elevators or outside of the building like we always did, but he was nowhere to be found.

The day before, I'd rode up in the elevator with one neighbor, Ms. Elsie. I didn't talk to the residents in the building because I didn't like them very much. They loved discussing other people's business, and they knew very little about mine. Which was a problem for them, I guess. It's like the more you kept to yourself and minded your business, the more people wanted to be in your business. But Ms. Elsie was cool and made it easy to like her more than others.

When I hadn't seen Asher for a few days, I worked up the nerve to ask her if she'd seen him around the building lately. The three of us had shared an elevator not too long ago, and they were already talking when I stepped on the elevator on my floor, so I figured she'd have to know something. I asked her what floor Asher lived on without saying his name because I didn't want her mind to wonder.

Ms. Elsie was nosy. So I used her nosiness for my benefit.

She told me he lived on her floor. The eighth. His apartment's door was the first unit door seen when the elevator doors opened.

"He's usually home around 7pm," she shared when I asked. *"He's in school. Did you know he's studying to get his Ph.D.?"* She flashed a grand smile next. *"He's a good one."*

I didn't bother asking her how she knew all of that. That would have meant us talking for longer. Plus, like I said, I already knew she knew all about him because she was nosy like the other older residents living in our building.

I took her intel though and used it, deciding since I wasn't running into Asher by accident these past few days, I'd run into him on purpose.

The thing was... when I arrived in front of his door, I froze.

It was going on five minutes and I was still standing there and still hadn't knocked or rang the doorbell. The way I imagined approaching him was not as easy in real life.

After another minute of standing there, staring at his bell, I couldn't bring myself to ring it. So, I turned on my Nikes and approached the elevator.

I pushed the call button when I arrived in front of the steely doors and was waiting for the elevator to reach the floor when I heard the click of a lock and glanced toward his door.

Another click echoed around the hallway and soon his door opened.

Asher appeared in the doorway.

As always, he dressed himself casually. A gray Henley tee and black jeans, designer slides on his socked feet.

In his hand, he held a white trash bag.

He was so out of place here, but still he made himself comfortable.

His brows shot up the moment he recognized me. "Hey."

The elevator arrived on the eighth floor as he was closing his door behind him.

"Got off on the wrong floor?" He asked as he approached the incinerator, that was only a few steps away, to discard the trash bag he carried.

I glanced at the elevator, then back at him as he was making his way to his door again.

I thought about getting on it and riding the car to my floor, then pretending I didn't have the stupid idea to stand at his door to begin with.

"I came up here to see you," came out of my mouth instead, with a lot of effort.

My throat in the short time had dried up, my head was feeling a little light too. The only thing that calmed me was the surprised expression on his face.

The intrigued yet stunned expression he wore on his face made this clear.

He pointed at himself and asked, "Me?"

I couldn't believe the guy standing in front of me was the same guy who ripped through the VIP section at Black Bamboo like the Tasmanian Devil taking down everything in sight.

Asher on the surface was so nonthreatening. Average height, medium build. Handsome and easy on the eyes, but... still average. His voice was deep, but not too deep. He was tall compared to my 5'2" making me look up at him a little, but he wasn't very tall either. His demeanor was calm, relaxed. Cool, confident. He would probably fit right in on one of those billboard ads for Ralph Lauren I could see from my bedroom window.

But that night, at Black Bamboo, he was throwing punches and dodging them like someone seven feet tall and who grew up in the grittiest part of New York.

The contrast was insane to what I thought I knew about him.

That intrigued me.

"I..." I started. "I wanted to thank you for the other night."

He cringed, shutting his eyes and holding them tight for a beat.

"I really appreciate what you did."

"Well, I apologize for not keeping my cool. It wasn't my best moment." He scratched the back of his head. "It was actually..."

"Really dope," I added, low. I felt my lips wanting to slide into a smile, but I dropped my eyes to the hallway's floor and kept them there long enough for the feeling to go away.

He scoffed a laugh. "There are other things that are more *dope* in this world to admire, I am sure."

We were quiet until I said, "Would you like to have lunch with me tomorrow?"

Asher's brows went up so high I thought they'd touch his pristine hairline.

His brows, I was learning, were the best way to predict what he was thinking. He communicated with them. It was something I realized in the last few interactions we had with each other.

It was... cute.

"Uh, yeah. Yes." He nodded. "Absolutely. I would... *love* that."

He said yes.

His response made the nerves shooting through my body from the moment I stepped off the elevator subside.

I guess me standing there and saying nothing seemed like an invitation for him to point at his door. "Did you... want to come inside and sit for a little?"

I shook my head incessantly and stepped back. "No."

"Okay, yeah. Cool." He threw his hands up in front of him. "I thought I'd ask."

I exhaled the breath I purposely held.

"So, tomorrow," he confirmed. "Noon sound good?"

I nodded.

"Cool." He smiled and my heart skipped a beat. "We'll meet in the building's lobby at noon."

"Cool," I echoed, turning to approach the elevator.

A thought occurred to me the moment I pressed the call button. And thankfully it was before he closed his apartment door after stepping inside.

"Asher,"

He pulled opened his door immediately. "Yeah?"

"Don't look me up online."

The serene smile he wore on his lips seconds ago slid off his face as easy as it originally appeared. Soon his brows were nonverbally communicating his curiosity.

"I don't want you to look me up online," I clarified.

His smile returned when he asked, "You're not a killer, are you?"

He thought I was joking, but I was serious.

I wanted to introduce myself and not have what reporters or journalists had to say about me introduce me. My aunt had been figuring out ways to scrub my name off the internet to no success. Though my name was common, news articles about what happened to me as a teenager were still present. Thankfully, not on the first page of search engines, but still very much there.

I didn't want him to see any of them.

"Just..." I shook my head. "Don't do it, okay?"

His smile was gone again. Asher formed his lips into the shape to question me, but stopped himself.

"Okay," he agreed.

I turned to press the elevator, and the car was right there, so the doors slid opened a few seconds later.

I stepped into the car and turned to the wall of buttons, pressing the one labeled five.

Asher watched me with the same curious brows until the doors closed between us.

THIRTEEN

ASHER

I didn't listen.

I should've listened.

Why the hell didn't I listen?

"Fuck," I said low to myself, my voice echoing around me. I shook out my arms next and rolled my head around my neck, trying to get it together as I rode down in the elevator on my way to the building's lobby. As agreed, I was heading down to the lobby to meet Lauryn for our lunch date at noon.

Shocked couldn't describe what I was when she asked if I'd have lunch with her today. Seeing her on my floor the day before when I opened my apartment door to throw out my trash surprised me. But then for her to reveal her reason for being on my floor was specifically to see me?

Yeah, she shocked me. I thought I'd somehow slipped into a waking dream.

She had one request, though.

One damn request.

And I didn't honor it.

"Fuck," I said again, a little louder this time.

I exhaled loudly in the elevator, my heart picking up in rhythm as the elevator's floor indicator light lit up on the L for lobby.

I inhaled a deep breath and released it quickly through my lips.

Lauryn wasn't waiting in front of the elevators when I stepped out of the car I rode.

Thank God.

Because that gave me time to get my face and my feelings in order before I saw her.

"Hey," I heard uttered softly behind me.

I turned quick toward the voice in reaction.

Lauryn wasn't standing in front of the elevators, but she stood near one corner of the lobby. She was standing in an unusual spot. Most people rarely stand in that corner when waiting for the elevators.

Because her presence came as a surprise, in that instance, I didn't have time to prepare my expression.

My eyes locked on hers and my heart felt like it melted into a puddle of tears. I fought hard to fix the frown, trying to weigh my lips down and the sympathetic tilt of my head, but I wasn't fast enough.

She'd already read it all on my face.

Lauryn wasn't a smiler, but I saw a hint of one when I first turned around after stepping off the elevator. The moment she read my expression, though, her lips gradually morphed back into the pout I'd grown accustomed to seeing her wear.

"You looked me up," she surmised, shutting her eyes and releasing an audible exhale.

I pulled my laptop onto my lap and got comfortable against my bed's headboard. I'd just finished showering... and jerking off if I'm being transparent.

Seeing Lauryn again after seeing her at the club was my reason.

She arrived on my floor in her usual outfit of a baggy shirt, leggings and sneakers, but all I could see was her dressed in her club uniform.

Couldn't get the vision of her out of my head from that night at Black Bamboo. And seeing her again, dressed down, looking the complete opposite of what she looked like at the club, was such a fucking turn on to me. Knowing what she hid underneath when she stood on my floor had me rock hard while taking my hot shower. I had to relieve the tension somehow. I kept the vision of how her ass sat in her shorts at the club and the way her breasts relaxed high and full in her matching crop top, practically spilling out. I swore I could see her nipples poking through the fabric. Imagining holding the tight ball between my teeth as I buried myself inside her sent me off the edge and spurting everywhere.

Fresh and drained, I sat in bed with my laptop.

Lauryn's been an extremely hard read, to put it lightly. And although she instructed me not to look her up, I had to know why.

"What are you hiding, hmmm?" I asked out loud as I typed in my password. "Because who the hell says don't look them up?"

I scoffed.

My curiosity led me to searching for her social presence first.

Nothing came up on any of the social media sites I browsed using her name.

So I turned to Google, positive I would have to find something. Often Google can pick up old social accounts that sometimes we forget exist.

I typed in her name, Lauryn James and Brooklyn, NY, in the search engine's browser box. The first page gave me a bunch of results that had the name Lauryn James in the hyperlinks, which was to be expected. Her name was common, so I already knew I would have to do some deep diving past the first page of results. I was ready to see anything with her digital footprint. Instead, by the time I got to the third page, my eyes landed on a full page of hyperlinked articles with headlines that made my curiosity immediately turn into regret.

Each headline wrinkled my brows more and made my heart plummet into the depths of my stomach, making me queasy.

Brooklyn Teen, Lauryn James, Found In Abandoned Property.

Missing Teen, Lauryn James, Rescued After Kidnapped and Assaulted In Captivity By Family Friend

"What?" I whispered to myself.

I really should have stopped there. But the thing about curiosity is, once you give into feeding it, that one thing you feed curiosity is never enough.

I clicked into the article published on the Holidae Press website. A repurposed article, previously published in their daily newspaper, but this one formatted for online reading.

"NYPD officers found Lauryn James, the thirteen-year-old girl who went missing last Friday, on an abandoned property in the Flatbush section of Brooklyn," I read out loud. "Authorities confirm Lauryn, who was abducted from her family's home only a few steps from the abandoned property, was held hostage and sexually assaulted by Corey Reynolds, a twenty-five-year-old male who was a family friend."

I slammed the lid of my laptop closed and pushed my laptop away as if shit covered it. Pressed my hands together and pressed the side of my fingers to my lips.

"Oh my God," I whispered to myself. "Why the fuck did I do that?"

My eyes softened as they locked on hers.

She stared at me for a moment, eyes darting between mine.

I tried to find the words to say, but I was at a loss.

She was so beautiful, so fucking delicate.

Who would do that to her?

What monster would do such a thing?

Lauryn kissed her teeth and turned to walk away.

"Lauryn, wait." I reached for her arm.

"Don't!" She jerked her arm free and jumped back. "Don't touch me."

Her voice echoed around us. It was only her and me in the lobby at that hour. But if there were people there, I wouldn't have cared for the stares.

Nothing else mattered at that moment.

I held my hands up in surrender and created as much space as I could between us so she'd be comfortable.

"God!" she shouted, eyes watering. "I literally told you not to look me up online, and you fucking did it, anyway."

"I did," I admitted, forming prayer hands and pressing my fingers to my lips. "I did. And I'm sorry. I didn't listen to you. I apologize."

She sighed, looking away while shaking her head.

"But Lauryn, I'm also glad I did."

Her chest heaved up and down in her baggy tee. Her eyes were turning red because of the tears forming in them.

"Because now I understand," I added. "I get it."

"You get *what*, Asher?"

"You."

We stood there for a moment, quiet. Her eyes scanned mine, searching again. Likely for the bullshit. And I stood there, not thinking about hiding a thing. Because I wanted her to see me. I wanted her to see I meant every word in the purest of ways. I needed her to feel safe with me. I needed her to know I understood and was grateful to.

I had the strongest urge to hug her. An even stronger urge to fight for her, to hit something, in her honor. I was both sympathetic and angry all at the same time. This weird feeling of accountability I couldn't shake had only gotten stronger seeing her that afternoon.

"You're clenching your jaw," she acknowledged.

"What?"

"Your jaw is tight," she added.

I didn't realize it was. Likely because of my thoughts. I took a breath and immediately released the tension. "I'm sorry."

"For clenching your jaw?"

"And for all you've been through." I said, gaze softening. "My God, Lauryn."

"I don't need you to be sorry." She pointed up at me. "I don't want you to feel bad for me."

"I don't."

Lauryn narrowed her eyes.

"I mean, I feel for you," I explained. "But... I feel for you in a way of wanting to take some of what you've been through... mainly what you're feeling, because of what you've been through, off you. I want to bear that weight."

She scoffed.

"And I know that sounds crazy as fuck. I know it might sound like

I'm talking shit." I chuckled nervously. "It honestly sounded like shit to me too, but..." I shook my head. "I don't know any other way to say I wish I could lift what you have been through off you so I can carry it."

"You don't even know me."

"The crazy thing is..." I sighed. "I feel I do."

She tore her eyes off me to look away.

"Just let me."

She shook her head, eyes still diverted.

"It's okay for people to empathize with you."

She grunted, pushing past me to approach the elevators.

"Lauryn."

"No," she turned to point at me. "I told you *not* to look me up, and you did, anyway. Now you're in my face with some bullshit about..." She shook her head. "Whatever the fuck you're telling me right now. I don't want to hear it. I'm out." Lauryn stabbed at the call button. "I don't even want to go out anymore."

I walked in front of her and pressed my back to the elevator button.

She stepped back.

"Move."

"Lauryn—"

"Move!" She balled her hands into fists.

"I'm sorry," I whispered. "I was wrong. You told me not to do something, and I did it, anyway. I didn't respect your privacy and I'm sorry. But please don't go upstairs right now."

She turned away from me to peer out of the building's front door.

"I promise I'll never do something like that again," I said, walking into her view. She refused to make eye contact with me, though. "I promise we'll have a great time and I swear on everything holy I won't bring up any of the stuff I found in my search."

She focused on me again.

"I will get to know you through your own narrative. Nothing more, nothing less." I pressed my hand to my chest. "Because I genuinely would like to get to know Lauryn James through Lauryn James. Because..." I smiled. "From the very first day I saw you, all I ever wanted was to get to know you through you and no one else."

That part was true.

I hated myself a little, though. Because after what I'd learned about her, I couldn't shake my physical attraction to her. Couldn't shake my attraction to her beauty and the light I knew was there, but dimmed.

After reading what I read in the article about her kidnapping, I felt like shit about jerking off thinking about her. I felt dirty.

The physical attraction was still there as I admired her, but now I wanted to show her a good time. A genuinely good time.

"I want you to be soft with me, so please allow me the opportunity to provide a day where you can be soft."

Her eyes locked on mine when I said that.

"If you want that," I told her. "I can be that. No problem. Give me another chance to show you I can be."

"And you won't ask me questions about what you read?" she quizzed.

"Not a single one." I pressed my hands together again. "I promise."

Fourteen

LAURYN

"I like this," Asher commented, eyes scanning the diner. "Your favorite eatery is nice."

It was a tiny diner on Flatbush right by the train station. There was nothing fancy about it. It had your typical service counter, cooks sporting grease-covered aprons cooking breakfast, lunch, and dinner foods over a grill nearby at eye view. They kept weathered wooden tables pushed up against the opposite wall, with matching chairs beneath them.

Asher had done well to make me feel comfortable in his presence despite him revealing he did the one thing I told him not to do.

"You don't have to say that," I mumbled, folding my arms and leaning my back against my chair.

A small smile appeared on his lips. "I know." Asher leaned forward in his seat, his attention fully on me. "But I mean it. I like it in here. Your favorite spot isn't pretentious, busy, or trying to do more than it actually is. It's honest and modest. I like honest and modest."

We stared at each other for a moment before Asher lifted the laminated menu off the table.

"What do you usually get when you come here?" He asked.

"So you don't have questions?"

He lifted his gaze off the menu and focused on me.

"After reading all that stuff about me?" I shifted in my seat uncomfortably. "You don't have questions about what you read?"

He inhaled deeply, placing the menu down on the table in front of him.

The sounds of the diner filled in the space the silence left between us.

"I do." Asher folded his hands over the menu. "But I also want to respect your privacy."

I scoffed.

"And I know it's ironic for me to say something like that, but I do. I want you to be comfortable, Lauryn. With me."

"Why?"

He fought, but lost to the smile that pulled at his lips. It was telling. Not innocent, but still not concerning either. Asher's smile in reaction to my question was genuine. So I knew his answer would be too.

"Because I like you. A lot."

I blinked, then blinked a few times again in response. All so I wouldn't give into the smile trying to force my lips up.

"You're obviously *very* beautiful, but I just..." He sighed. "I don't know. There's something about you I'm drawn to besides your beauty."

"Hi there," the aging waitress greeted the second she approached our table. "What can I get you two today?"

Asher and I placed our orders. We both ordered burgers and fries, and two strawberry milkshakes.

"Do you have questions for me?" he asked once the waitress walked away, and we were alone again.

I had plenty.

"Where are you from?"

"Long Island."

"Where in Long Island."

"The Hamptons."

I nodded, glancing away. "I could tell."

"How so?"

"How not?" I focused on him. "You don't give off the impression of someone who's from around here or anywhere near here."

His brow arched, and I tucked my lips into my mouth to keep from laughing. Those brows seemed to have a mind of their own.

"What about me gives off the impression I'm not from around here?"

"To start," I said, "the way you dress. Then there's how you talk. How you carry yourself."

"*Hmph.*"

"What's throwing me off, though, is how you cleared Black Bamboo's VIP section the other day all on your own."

He cringed, then shook his head.

"You gave that same reaction yesterday," I noted. "What does it mean?"

"I was..." He ran his hand down his mouth. "I am *still* embarrassed by what happened."

I jerked my head back. "But why?"

He scratched the back of his head.

"You know how many guys wish they could take down a group of niggas trying to jump him?"

"I..." He started. "I've spent many years working on my short fuse. My temper. It was terrible as a child. Got worse as a teenager. A lot of therapy, boxing lessons, and conscious work finding the tools to build my patience helped teach me how to manage my temper. And what happened that night at the club, for a moment, undid all the work I've put in."

The waitress returned with our food, sliding our plates in front of us and setting our drinks down soon after.

We'd begun eating when Asher asked, "Have you tried it?"

"Tried what?" I asked, lifting a fry to my lips.

"Therapy," he answered. "After everything that happened, have you spoken to anyone?"

I shook my head.

"Would you... be interested?"

"Are you saying I need it?" I ground out, communicating my annoyance with the snap of my neck.

Asher stared at me for a breath before breaking eye contact to briefly focus on his plate of food. "I think it could help."

"Help what?" I folded my arms over my chest. "What good will it be for me to talk about what happened to me? Relive it?"

My pulse raced. I could feel my blood running hot. I was growing pissed at just the thought of doing any of that, talking and reliving, with a stranger who would analyze the shit out of everything I said.

"You're getting upset," he acknowledged calmly. "Let's change the subject."

"No, let's talk about it," I challenged. "You already read about everything, right?"

"Lauryn—"

"I can still hear *him* some nights," I blurted, swallowing hard once the words left my lips.

Asher froze in his seat.

"In my memory. I can still hear what he sounded like hurting me," I added, then shook my head. "The sounds from him were so angry, like he was mad at me, but also something else. He sounded like he didn't like what he was doing. Which was confusing. It's still confusing why he sounded guilty doing what he did, but he kept doing it. But... I don't remember what happened much. Only bits and pieces that show up in my dreams. But the bits and pieces lack details or isn't clear enough for me to make sense of what I remember. And I don't want to feel like putting in the work to make any of it clear to me."

Asher nodded next.

"Some nights, when I hear him in my sleep? I force myself awake. Just like you've found the tools to build your patience. I've trained myself to wake up whenever what he sounds like creeps up in my dreams. I do it because I'm worried that if I make the memory of what he sounded like go on for too long, it'll trigger the other memories and make them more vivid, and I'll remember everything that happened to me and I don't want to."

Asher's lips balled as he clenched his jaw.

"You're clenching your jaw again," I noted. "Really tight."

He released the tension immediately and sat up, seesawing his head from side to side.

"Are *you* upset?" I asked, sure of the answer but unsure why.

"I am," he answered curtly.

I wrinkled my brows at that. "About what?"

"About what happened to you. I'm upset about what you carry because of it—"

"I carry nothing, Asher. And you don't have to feel sorry for what happened to me," I said. "I don't need you feeling bad for me."

"I don't feel bad—"

"You weren't even there."

"I wish I could've been."

I scoffed, biting at my bottom lip. "You barely know me."

"God, I wish I did," he remarked low and sighed a stream of air right after. "At the very least, I wish I met you sooner."

I stared at him and he stared back. We were quiet for a bit, neither one of us touching our food.

Talking about that time in my life was never something I wanted to do. Not even with Aunt Evelyn. We never discussed it and probably never would. She rarely, if ever, pushed me to do anything uncomfortable after everything that happened. I was grateful for that because to me there was never a good time to discuss it.

But despite the little talking I'd done with Asher, my heart felt lighter. I could literally feel the heaviness those thoughts often made me feel, lift a little. And my fears about discussing my assault subsided slightly, realizing the world had not ended. The world still spun, and the day continued to go on after I revealed what I revealed and I almost felt compelled to reveal more. But I simply wasn't ready.

"Well, you know me now," I said to him.

He nodded. "And anytime you ever want to talk about anything, you can talk to me." He lowered his chin to meet my eyes. "Okay?"

I nodded too.

I was reaching for the ketchup when Asher said, "We should come back here again. Next Saturday?"

"You wanna come back?" I questioned. "With me?"

"Oh, absolutely." He smiled big while nodding his answer. Asher had a beautiful smile. One that reached his eyes and made it slant a little. And the movement of the slant allowed the lights in the room to sparkle in his pupils. Like carbonado. Black diamonds. My father's favorite. Asher's eyes were fascinating to stare into because of this.

"They have so many things on their menu that I must try," he added. "Might make it a thing to get through this entire menu."

A little chuckle left my mouth before I could stop it, and Asher caught it.

He took a breath and held it for a bit. I could tell he did from the barely noticeable indent in his neck.

"What?"

"I never seen you laugh or smile and I saw a hint of both, and... it was..."

I waited for him to finish his thought, but he shook his head and smiled.

"Anyway." He lifted a fry out of his plate, tossing it into his mouth. "I think I'll try the wrap next time. What else is good here? What do you like to order besides the burger?"

FIFTEEN

ASHER

"Man," I sighed, shaking my head. "I've been in Brooklyn for less than a month and I've already gotten myself into some shit I do not know what to do with."

Jayce, who sat across from me, chuckled to himself. "I can see why falling for a woman so soon can be some uncomfortable shit, but I don't see the problem."

I scratched my head. "I wouldn't call it a problem, but it's not all that great either."

We were outside of a Caribbean restaurant, The Green Palm. The weather in Brooklyn was still on summer's time, so the sun was shining, the breeze was minimal, and the heat blazing hot.

Jayce and I kept cool under The Green Palm's giant umbrella. We sat at their outside table, waiting for our meals.

I'd called Jayce, as he advised, and invited him out to lunch in Brooklyn. He told me he would be in Brooklyn visiting his aunt and cousins, and would be happy to link up.

So, we did.

"I mean, it's only a problem if she's crazy." Jayce leaned in. "Is she crazy, Asher?"

I snorted. "No, not crazy. She's just been through a lot."

"A lot," he repeated. "Care to share what *a lot* is in context?"

"No." I shook my head. "I can't."

"You can't." He sat up in his seat. "This is serious."

"Extremely."

Though I could get through Lauryn and my lunch date the day before, her words weighed heavy on me long after we returned to our building and she agreed for me to walk her to her door. I was unsure of how to behave after learning what I'd learned. Hearing her reveal her innermost feelings. The night before I was jerking off to the memory of what this woman's body looked like when she wore barely nothing, only for her to tell me she'd been trying to forget the terrible memories of the worst time of her life.

The amount of guilt I was feeling was debilitating me mentally.

"The problem is, I'm extremely attracted to her physically, and..." I pressed my hands together and gestured with them. "Without saying too much, I'm going to have to calm my physical attraction because of what she's been through physically."

"Oh." Jayce nodded his understanding. "Shit. Okay." Jayce dropped his head to blink a few times. "Damn."

"Yeah." I exhaled. I shut my eyes and exhaled the air out of my mouth. "After learning her story, I just... I want to be her reason she smiles. I no longer want anything from her. I simply want to give and give endlessly. You know?"

Jayce grinned.

"And not on anything selfish or..." I pointed my eyes above my head, in search of the words. "Like I'm doing it with ill intentions. I don't want to do all this nice shit to get something from her. But the truth is, I *wanted* something from her. I kind of still do which is what is fucking with me so bad. I can't come with that kind of energy, at all. I'm going to have to get to know her by moving differently, and I'm honestly not used to it."

Jayce nodded once more.

"At first, when we first met? My thoughts weren't all that pure."

"Understood," Jayce said.

"But now." I shrugged. "I want the opportunity to show her the good side of life, you know? The beauty in the cracks. Where people scream from excitement and cry tears of joy. And where men do kind acts, expecting nothing in return."

I dropped my head, a little embarrassed. "I sound like a simp."

"You sound decided," Jayce countered. "You want to give her fresh memories to soothe the bad ones... but with a selfless heart."

"Yes," I agreed.

"You want a place to exercise your superhero complex," Jayce stated matter-of-factly. "Ain't nothing *simp* about that."

I hollered a laugh, and he laughed too.

"Yo, I get it. I do it all the time with Summer." He chuckled some more. "I save the day just to see her face light up. It's one of the greatest feelings. And there are worst things you can do besides wanting to carry the weight of the world for a woman you like or love. At least that's what I think."

"That's what I believe, too. But I'm at a deficit. She doesn't trust me. She doesn't trust men, from what I've noticed. And for a damn good reason," I acknowledged, staring beyond Jayce and down the city street. "Women already feel like men sexualize them; you know? Everything we do for them is with an expectation of something in return. Transactional most times. They're already naturally on guard when dealing with us because they believe that what we do, *all* we do, is with a primary goal of getting between their legs, which essentially..." I seesawed my head from side to side. "Is true."

"It's facts, my man." Jayce barked a laugh. "It's true."

"But now, I'm attracted to a woman..."

"*Mm-hmm.*"

"A woman, who I must move differently with. I must move differently with her because it's the right thing to do. For the both of us," I noted. "It's the right thing to do for her comfort, and the right thing to do in my effort to build her trust. I only need for her to recognize my intention and to know I don't want to hurt her."

"You want her to feel comfortable." Jayce acknowledged, following along.

"Yes." I nodded. "So, I can be her burden bearer, even though it's not clear to me why I would volunteer myself for such an endeavor. I don't know." I shook my head this time. "Maybe because I want to show her a side of life, her past trauma is making her fear. But to do that, my motivation has to shift."

"Lean more on being empathetic, which I know you won't have an issue doing."

"No issue at all, but she hates that, a lot, interestingly." I laughed. "And I don't want her to take a good thing and make it toxic. Which, by the way, I'm still not sure why I'm willingly wanting to take on such work." I pinched the space between my eyes. "Jayce, I barely know her but then again I feel I know exactly what will turn her off and I don't mean in the sexual way."

"Well." Jayce folded his hands on the table. "I think you trying to figure out a way to navigate the aftermath of her circumstances proves you have her best interest in mind. Your honorable intentions are motivating your thinking."

"Yeah."

"And you know the most challenging women are usually the women well worth it."

I nodded.

"Because everyone sees challenges differently," He continued. "What might be a challenge to me wouldn't be a challenge to you, and vice versa. But the fact that she is a challenge for you, and you still want to pursue her? It's giving... she's more than just your pretty neighbor that you only like."

"*Hmph*," I huffed, my mind drifting into thoughts.

Our waitress finally arrived with our food and placed it on our table in front of us.

"I think I'm going to ask her out on another date," I stated once we were alone again. "Like, a proper date."

"Oh, so the one you two went on wasn't real?"

I nodded. "It was. We went to her favorite place, so it definitely stood for something."

"Okay...?"

"I'd like to take her somewhere that gives off the unmistakable vibe of a date and not just us going somewhere to eat."

"Got you." Jayce beamed a winning smile. "Yeah, I think you should do it. What kind of date did you have in mind, though?"

I smiled back, not caring to hide it. "One that will seem ripped from the pages of a superhero romance."

Sixteen

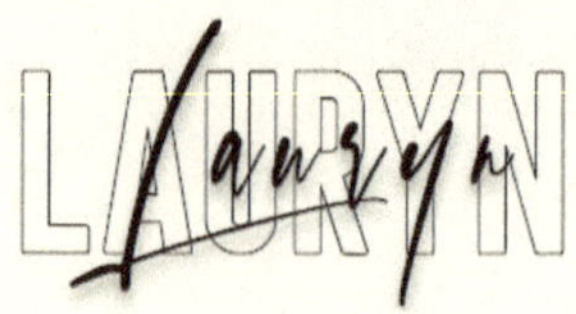

LAURYN

Asher pulled opened the door and gestured for me to walk inside.

"It's okay," I told him. "You can go first."

As always, he didn't protest. He only did as I suggested.

I hadn't seen him since our lunch date that past week. He was busy with school most of the days during the week, as he told me when we met up for lunch earlier in the day.

After we finished our meals at the local diner, I expected for us to return to our building and to our separate apartments, but Asher suggested we stop somewhere else first.

The moment we walked through the door, I inhaled the air deeply.

It was a crazy thing to say, but I loved the smell of bookstores.

"This is huge," I commented, my eyes wandering around me, falling on tall shelves lined with various colors of book spines. "I can't believe I've never heard of this place."

"It isn't much of a secret," he said while reaching for a nearby book. "It just isn't in a very busy area in the neighborhood."

At all.

The bookstore was on a dead-end block. I'd walked past this block several times on my way around the neighborhood. It's one of those places you don't bother glancing down. Because you don't expect to see anything. Across from the bookstore was a green market that sold fresh vegetables and fruits. Trucks that carried those vegetables and fruits transported from local farms parked along the curb of the dead-end block, shrouding passerby's views of anything.

What a hidden treasure this place was.

"What do you like to read?"

Asher turned to me and smiled. "Everything."

He almost got a smile back.

The two-story shop was practically empty. A few people were on the ground floor, with a few more here and there that I could spot from my vantage point.

"It's hard to imagine a guy like you sitting and reading."

Asher turned to face me. "A guy like me?"

I slid my hands into my black joggers' pockets and shrugged. "I said what I said."

He chuckled, flashing his beautiful smile.

His smile always made me stare a little longer than I should have, but it told me things his words would never reveal.

I couldn't trust that, though.

"I read a lot in my Ph.D. program," he revealed, turning to the table behind us that had a stack of books displayed across it. "A lot of reading and writing. I like to read books to give my brain a break from all the studying."

"I would think the more reading and writing would be stressful since you're already doing a lot."

"Depends on the type of reading." Asher turned to face me while holding up a book. The cover had a black woman who stood beside a wolf. In the background was a dark blue sky and a bright white moon.

"This kind of reading is like an escape. Like TV in my head. My kind of thing."

I arched a brow. "You like to read stuff like this?" I pointed. "Shifter romances?"

"Oh, hell yeah." Asher flipped the book over to the back matter. "About to get this for sure."

That got a laugh out of me.

His head popped up, and I quickly fixed my face.

A small smile appeared on his lips and I turned my attention elsewhere.

He made me feel different. Whenever I was around Asher, I didn't think about all the wrong that were happening around me or that happened *to* me. I was in every bit of the present moment with no care of time or how much longer I could do this.

This simple thing of standing in a bookstore discussing his like for shifter romances. He made me think of things other than myself and I liked that.

"So..." He gestured with his head for me to follow him when he walked away. "Judging by your interest in How to Be Soft In A World That's Hard, I'm thinking self-help books are your thing."

"I prefer them," I confirmed. "I like romances when I need a break from self-help."

"Romance?" he asked, intrigue clear in his brows.

I shrugged.

He smiled again. "We have that in common."

Asher led the way, guiding us to the stairs to climb to the next level in the bookstore. Based on the aged wood of the shelves and the basic appearance of the cash register I could see from my angle on the stairs, I could tell the bookstore had been in this neighborhood for a few years. Likely decades. I'd never been inside a locally owned bookstore. Only Barnes and Noble or I ordered my books online. Something about this tiny little bookstore in the hood gave me a vibe of belonging.

Comfort.

That, and no one was paying me any mind with their noses buried in the books they were shopping for.

"This is the section you want to be in," Asher pointed out, turning down one aisle.

I followed, my head on a swivel, eyes scanning the shelves.

Not that I preferred self-help books. They helped make sense of the world around me, though. Made life seem doable by having names for things and situations. Solutions where they seemed to be none. It all was great as I was reading. But actually functioning in the world self-help books try to make sense of has always been a struggle.

So I keep reading them until it all becomes clear.

"Oh," Asher said, walking up to me and reaching over my head.

My breath hitched in my throat as he drew near.

His scent of something woodsy and citrus hijacked the air as he moved it towards me with his reach.

Asher was in the middle of pulling down the book when he glanced down at me while I lifted my gaze to him.

Time honestly froze.

So fucking cliche, I know it.

But it did.

We were staring at each other. Definitely for different reasons.

Or were they for the same?

Because those eyes of his, that were so calming, so assuring. I couldn't understand the comfort of his gaze and what it did to me.

Made me feel safe.

He blinked out of his stare at me, sliding the book out of its place behind me on the shelf.

"This is a good read," he said low, holding the book up in front of himself. Hesitated at first to hand it to me, but eventually did and waited for me to take it out of his hand.

I dropped my eyes to it. Not at all interested in the book. I'm sure it was an excellent selection. But my heart was racing like it was competing with my pulse and I needed a distraction, a way to cool it all.

"I didn't bring my wallet," I said to the book before glancing up to meet his eyes again.

God, those eyes.

"I only brought enough for lunch, which you refused for me to pay for again this week."

For another Saturday in a row.

"And I'm going to refuse for you to pay for this." Asher slid the book out of my hand. "It's on me." He turned to face the opposite shelf and approached it. "Let's see what else they got. Mess around," he added, glancing over his shoulder while wearing a smirk. "I might fill at least one of your bookshelves at home."

"I don't have a bookshelf," I admitted. "Or a bookcase, for that matter."

That made him turn around to face me again.

"I keep my books on a side table by my bed pushed together with metal bookends." I shrugged. "I do most of my reading in bed, so..."

A full beam smile pulled at his lips. "Oh, then we've got to get you a bookcase right now."

"Right *now*?"

He nodded. "Immediately."

Asher gestured with his head toward the area we entered through. "Come on."

———

Asher sure moved fast.

Fast in deciding we'd swing by a local Target to purchase a simple wooden bookcase.

Fast in ordering a black car to get us and the wooden bookcase, that was only wood pieces in a box in that instance, back to my apartment.

"Would you mind if I put it together for you?" He asked on our ride back to the apartment.

I couldn't believe a simple second lunch date was turning into *this*.

I said nothing in response, simply rummaging through my thoughts for the answer.

"You can say no," he insisted, lifting his hand with emphasis. "I can put it together at my place and bring it down—"

"You can put it together in my place."

It was such a ballsy decision for me. Different. Because no one had been in my apartment besides Aunt Evelyn and sometimes the maintenance guy, but Aunt Evelyn would be present with me whenever he made an apartment call for repairs.

But here I was. Sitting on my green velvet armchair, watching Asher put together a bookcase, not once glancing at the instructions.

I watched as every muscle in his upper body flexed whenever he twisted a screw onto one end of the shelf, then lifted that shelf to slide into the solid standing case.

He worked quietly, only making slightly curious sounds as he searched around him for a tool or for an accompanying piece of wood to add to the bookcase's structure.

"Are you going to read the instructions?"

I'd been trying to think of something to say to him and that was the best I could come up with. Although I was nervous having him in my place, only us two, he made me feel so comfortable. He gave me no reason to be nervous and that helped a lot with my anxiety.

"No need," he insisted, eyes preoccupied with his work. "I can just study the picture and can tell where everything needs to go. Plus, all the pieces have sticker letters on them. See?" He held up one of those pieces and looked at me.

I couldn't care less about the pieces, the bookcase, or the numbers separating them all.

He was in my apartment, building me a bookcase. A man who embodied the hallmarks of a man who never had to use his hands in his life to build anything. And he was building something for me. A practical stranger. I couldn't believe it.

I nodded, though, acknowledging his remark about the numbers on the pieces so I wouldn't make things weird.

Asher glanced around himself as he picked up another piece to continue working. "Your place is beautiful."

I turned my attention to my apartment and the surrounding things.

My apartment was my little piece of heaven, away from the hell outside of it. I knew when I left Aunt Evelyn's apartment that I would have to create a place that would provide the comfort she wouldn't be able to give me while I was away.

My Aunt's love of magazines fostered my love for it too. So I created artwork out of the ones she used to throw away. I placed vintage black magazine covers in picture frames. Other art from local artists hung beside them.

In the sitting area where I relaxed on my crushed velvet green armchair was a magazine holder beside it. Depending on how much I loved the cover, after reading the magazines they graced, I'd rip them off and would place them in photo albums.

It was an odd collector's hobby, but it was mine.

Most of my furniture were items that were discarded by the new fancy neighbors who overestimated the space they were moving into. Thanks to gentrification, I had a beautiful vanity table and side tables in my bedroom, the velvet couch I sat on, and antique end tables in my living room. All of them like new.

"Thank you," I said. "And thank you for this. You didn't have to."

"I wanted to," he replied, busy at work. "Thank you for allowing me to."

We were quiet again for a bit as Asher continued to work. He was almost done. I could tell this by how finished the shelf looked. It resembled the box's photo.

"Have you ever built a bookcase before?"

He chuckled. "I have."

I twisted my lips to one side to bite the inside of my lip. "Have you ever built a bookcase for a woman?"

He stopped twisting the screw into the final shelf end when he peeked over his shoulder and held his gaze with me for a breath.

He smirked. "You're my first and only."

Thankfully, he returned his attention to the bookcase. Because I couldn't help the smile that pulled at the corners of my lips. Every time I tried to ball my lips together, my smile tugged at my lips harder.

"Okay," he announced, dusting off his hands and gesturing at the bookcase. "It's done."

I nodded as he walked over to the bookstore's branded tote he purchased. Asher pulled out the book he bought for me and sat it on the bookcase's first bookshelf.

He held his hands in front of the bookcase as if he were presenting the new model of a car. "What do you think?"

It was beautiful. The bookcase was your normal five shelves tall wooden bookcase with nothing too fancy about it, but it was beautiful to me.

The man standing in front of it, too.

"It's cool." I bobbed my head up and down. "I like it."

He smiled big. "Cool."

A moment later, Asher was cleaning up the tiny plastic bags that held the parts needed for assembling the bookcase, walking them to my trash bin in my kitchen and returning shortly after.

He had the cardboard box the bookcase arrived in and his book he purchased from the bookstore in hand when he told me, "I'll get out of your hair."

He was leaving and I couldn't help but to feel sad about it.

Asher was taking steps to the door when I said, "Asher."

I didn't want him to leave, but I wasn't sure if wanting him to stay was a good idea, either. I was both surprised and proud of myself for finding the comfort of having him in my apartment. Us all alone. A part of me enjoyed having him around, alone. But the other half of me didn't want to push it either. A few minutes may have been all I could stand without letting my nerves get the best of me.

He stood near my door, waiting for me to continue.

But I couldn't say anything.

And he just smiled. Knowingly. Nodded to himself, then met his eyes with mine.

"Some other time." He gestured with his chin in my direction. "Okay?"

Without another word from me, he opened my door and left.

And I finally let my smile rip through.

No fighting this time.

Seventeen

ASHER

As an idea, asking Lauryn out on a proper date seemed easy. For a month, I planned it and even considered how I would approach her with my invitation. I played out the scenario in my mind a dozen times. And as an idea, it seemed simple.

But actually getting Lauryn to agree to go out with me, away from her home, her neighborhood, and in another borough...

Not as simple.

"Why?" she asked, over her plate of a chicken Caesar wrap and fries.

We'd been grabbing lunch at her favorite spot for a month. This was the fourth weekend we were spending our Saturday afternoon at the diner. I'd just asked her if we could do something a little different the following week.

"We come here every week," she noted. "Why switch up now?"

"Because we've been going to your favorite spot for a month and I would like to take you to a couple of my favorite places in the city."

"A couple?" She questioned. "More than one?"

"Yes, Lauryn." I smiled. "More than one."

"What favorite places you got?" She scrunched up her nose, and I found it to be so damn cute. "You're not even from here. How do you know they're your favorite and not just some place you like right now?"

"Oh, they are definitely my favorites." I pushed a fry into my mouth and chewed while smiling. "And you're going to love them."

Lauryn eventually agreed. And we were now stepping into the ride share vehicle I ordered to take us to our first location.

A place I hoped she'd love.

"When was the last time you visited Manhattan?"

"It's been a while," she answered, eyes focused out of her window.

We were crossing the Brooklyn-Queens Expressway en route to the FDR Drive. My plan was to instruct the driver to drop us off as soon as we exited the parkway in Manhattan and for Lauryn and me to explore a little.

It was a beautiful autumn Saturday. The leaves were changing on the trees; the sun beginning to take on a golden hue because of the late afternoon hour.

I noticed Lauryn kept things local to her. She barely left Brooklyn, which I found to be interesting. Though the borough has everything one could need without having to cross a bridge, going to alternative places was exciting.

I wanted her to get excited.

I wanted her to know excitement more than she knew caution.

"I want to eat here," she argued one of the Saturday afternoons we'd designated for our lunch outing.

"I know, but..." I glanced away from the diner. "Wouldn't you be interested in trying somewhere new today?"

"Nope," she answered, stalking toward the diner's entrance. "I'd like to stick to what I know. Come on."

She hated trying new things, something I assumed before actually attempting to change up our plans.

Because she knew caution more than excitement. She's known

caution for so long. Known it so well, it was likely encoded in her DNA now.

"Where are we going, anyway?" She turned in her seat to face me.

"To parts of the city that will seem like a getaway."

She pursed her lips and made a face that made me laugh.

"That's cryptic as hell." She shook her head. "But, I'm curious."

"Curiosity is the zest of life."

"*Mm-hmm.*" She nodded, fighting back the faint hint of a grin.

The more we've hung out, the more I've caught her doing that. Resist smiling. I'd never seen her actually smile with me. Or laugh.

It almost happened in our building when we'd returned from one of our lunches. One resident, a mother of a toddler, had organized a mommy-and-me meet up of sorts, so our lobby was a little busier than usual.

Lauryn pushed her back against the elevator wall and I did my best to stand at a distance from her.

The elevator wouldn't fit all five of the moms, their toddlers, or the strollers they rolled on. So a few stepped on the elevator with Lauryn and me while the rest of them waited in the lobby for another elevator to arrive.

Even with just two mothers on the elevator with us, it was still very crowded because of their toddlers and the strollers they sat in.

I moved, turning to speak with Lauryn before the doors closed to take her to her floor, when a third mom insisted, "I think I can fit."

She couldn't, but she tried anyway, shoving her high-end stroller into the car and right against my ankle.

The impact made my leg buckle and I lost my balance. Lauryn reached out to catch me, but was unsuccessful. Luckily, I could regain my footing. But that meant me falling into her a little, stopping myself from colliding right into her by pressing my hand to the elevator wall behind her.

"Oh, gosh!" The mother shouted. "Shoot, I'm so sorry. I'll just wait for the next one."

Lauryn and I were the closest we'd ever been. Up close, I could see how brown her eyes really were, and how perfectly shaped her lips appeared. Her natural scent wafted up my nose and stayed there. At least, that's how it felt.

That moment locked her scent in my memory for sure.

"Sorry about that," I told her, quickly creating distance between us.

And right then, it almost happened. The corners of her mouth lifted just a little for a hint of a smile to appear.

She quickly corrected it, though, but it was too late. Getting her to smile was my new favorite challenge.

Aside from that, getting to know Lauryn on a personal level in the past month was interesting. We hadn't spoken about her past since that one Saturday. She didn't bring it up, and I had found other ways to get to know a woman that was even more intriguing the more layers of her personality I peeled back.

We only had the weekends to do that though. My first year of my Ph.D. program at Langston inundated a lot of my time, and when I wasn't there at school, I was studying the rest of my hours away. To say my classes were stressful would put it lightly. But as the saying goes, tough times don't last, tough people do. Plus, I always had Saturdays to look forward to.

This Saturday would differ from the previous ones, and I hoped it did in a good way.

When we arrived in Manhattan, about a half-a-mile walk from the park, we got out of the car and walked the rest of the way.

Lauryn's eyes were everywhere. Scanning her surroundings and taking in the sights.

Autumn in Manhattan was one of my favorite times of year to visit. The leaves were switching in shade and the weather was not too hot or too cold. It was perfect for a walk with something hot. The vibe was just warm in presence.

"Are you going to tell me where we're going, Asher?" She asked, focusing elsewhere.

"There," I answered, pointing across the street.

She scoped out the direction I pointed, squinting her eyes a little. "Greenacre Park?"

"That's it."

She took a breath and released the tension on her lips. The corners of her mouth did that thing again.

"I figured you'd like it," I said. "You love going to Prospect Park. At least you mentioned that once when we went out to eat."

"You made us drive all this way to go to a park?"

I smiled big. "This one is different. I promise." I gestured with my head next. "Come on."

We crossed the street and made our way to the stairs at the park's entrance.

"Where's that water sound coming from?" She asked when we were close.

"What you'll see will be way better than what I can describe."

Up the smooth paved stairs, we stepped into a green oasis filled with trees and potted plants.

To our right, water from the constructed fountain trickled down the cemented stones, creating a rich soundscape.

People sat here and there in front of tables, relaxing in green chairs, all facing the major attraction.

I heard her gasp beside me, and my head whipped that way.

It was the softest sound. An expression of wonderment I didn't realize Lauryn could make.

To the eyes from a distance, she was soft. She had dainty features and appeared to be a beautiful woman.

But when you studied her eyes, the fear mixed with a wall of defense was clear. Lauryn seemed forever on guard on any other given day.

Today, though, in the park, staring straight ahead at the waterfall of water cascading over two pillars of rock, she took on the appearance of an angel.

She hadn't blinked once, nor did she move. We were on the level of the park that was still inside of it, but still far from the waterfall's entrance, located down another level of stairs.

I almost didn't want to disrupt her gaze or her daze, but I had to get her closer.

"Do you want to get a better view of it?" I glanced at the beauty that had her attention. "It looks even better up close."

She said nothing in response to me. Only nodded.

We approached the entrance and took the steps down. The closer we got to the waterfall, the louder the cascade of water grew.

Right there between two high-rises, and sandwiched between two walls of orange and gold leaves, was the Greenacre Park waterfall.

The park was one of my favorite places to visit in the city. While my mother drove into Manhattan to satisfy a shopping, hair, or manicure appointment, I always tagged along. Not because I enjoyed her company.

All so I could come here.

The water appeared white and frothy as it fell from what seemed like nowhere. It coated the two beds of large rocks. And the impact of the water against the rocks offered a sound like an undulating ocean kissing the shoreline.

When we arrived at a spot that gave a direct view of the waterfall, I took a seat in the nearby chair while Lauryn remained standing in front of the table.

She looked mesmerized, and I knew that feeling well. I'd experienced it too.

The shock. The wonderment.

An actual tropical waterfall in a concrete jungle like New York City.

It was a fascinating thing to witness.

"Wow," she exhaled, turning to glance at me over her shoulder.

And my breath caught in my chest.

Because she had the most beautiful smile pushing her cheeks back and slanting her eyes.

She had the whitest teeth, the softest features wearing that expression.

"Yeah," I nodded, spellbound by *her*. "Wow."

A soft gasp escaped Lauryn's mouth the moment we stepped through the terrace's glass door.

We were in Loft 88 - a rooftop restaurant in the midtown section of Manhattan.

The rooftop restaurant was popular because of their celebrity patrons. But when people weren't gushing over celebrity sightings, the view left them in genuine awe.

The terrace was unique in that it offered an option for outdoor dining in cushioned lounge chairs, with the New York City skyline in direct view.

Loft 88 was a place to be seen. To have your photo taken and shared with those you knew would get jealous because they weren't there, and you were.

I'd arranged for a private area of the terrace to be blocked off for Lauryn and me.

It was a little later in the day. We spent a few hours at Greenacre Park. She didn't want to leave, and I would not insist or rush her, either.

Watching her get lost in the sights and sounds of the waterfall was fulfilling. As I planned our date, I worried it would be too much out of her scope of things. But I wanted to show her beauty outside of what she knows. I wanted to wow her. And based on her reactions to both places, I'd nailed it.

"This entire area is ours?" She asked, in front of one of the wooden tables. White frosted candles glowed orange on the surface of those tables, adding to the setup's ambiance.

"Yup," I answered.

Surrounding the lounge chairs and tables were a forest of green potted plants with specs of colors from roses and other colorful flowers.

The sun was setting behind the Freedom Tower, making the sky a sorbet color of peach, gold, and blue.

"This is really beautiful," she commented, eyes fixed on the skyline. Lauryn turned her attention to me. "I can see why it's another favorite."

"The burgers and fries are great here, too," I informed. "I know that's your thing."

Her eyes dropped to the menu book on the table. "I'm gonna see what else they have."

My brows went up. Trying something new in a new place, though not a big deal to others, was an interesting thing to me about Lauryn. She barely stepped out of her comfort zone and for good reason. On any weekend, the place we ate was always the same. What she ordered never changed. She was comfortable in the habit.

It seems a change of scenery gave her the confidence to step out of comfort a bit more.

An hour had elapsed since we'd been on the terrace. Night had fallen, our plates of brick oven pizza held only crumbs, and the glow of lights from the surrounding skyscrapers that made up the New York City skyline had our attentions.

Lauryn and I sat across from each other on cushion lounge chairs. The temperature had dipped a few degrees, turning the warm autumn day into a cool winter night preview.

Lauryn had rubbed her hands together at least twice in her seat, but had made no mention of the cold.

A breeze passed between us, causing her to shiver.

"You're cold," I commented.

"I'm fine." She glanced at me before returning her attention to the view.

"Do you want to head out—"

"No," she answered to the skyline.

From my seat, I could see her eyes scanning the surrounding area in wonderment. It was fun to watch, but not so much fun seeing the dip in the temperature making her uncomfortable.

"Here." I stood to my feet and removed my jacket. With it off, I walked it over to her and when I was close, I draped my jacket over her shoulders.

"Asher—"

"Please don't refuse it," I protested over her. "You want to stay? We can do that. But I can't watch you shivering yourself crazy."

I turned away with plans of returning to my seat when she told me, "You can sit here."

"Sit... here?" I pointed at the space beside her.

She nodded.

I stared at her for a second. "Are you sure?"

"Yeah, come on." She gestured with her head.

Her eyes remained on mine as I took my seat beside her.

The lounge chair wasn't a large one. It only provided seats for two, so she and I were close.

"Lauryn," I voiced. "Are you sure you're okay with me sitting here?"

Her eyes remained on the skyline when she answered with, "Can you just relax?"

At that, I released the breath I'd been slowly inhaling.

"Anyone else?" she started. "No. But you're cool, Asher."

Lauryn finally looked over at me.

"You're different."

I held her gaze.

"This." She glanced at the skyline again. "This is different. And you brought me here."

"You came with me," I corrected. "You accompanied me."

"My point is," she said, turning her head my way again. "I would have never known of this place, or the park, if you hadn't introduced it to me. It was thoughtful, and that makes you different from any other guys I've ever known or encountered." Lauryn blinked a few times and added, "And I like that."

Her gazing at me with softer eyes I've never seen her have with me was influencing my breathing.

In a good way.

She wasn't on guard or visibly uncomfortable. She understood and acknowledged my intention for the outing with no need for me to say a word.

I dropped my head for a little to smile with myself and when I lifted my head again to look at Lauryn; I noticed she was closer. Her lips specifically were closer, as she leaned into me for a kiss.

Our lips brushing against each other made me jump back in my seat.

Why the hell did you just jump back, Asher?!

Because I thought that I may have moved too close at some point. In my mind, I thought it had to be me who tried to kiss her because it couldn't have possibly been Lauryn coming in for a kiss from me.

Right?

"Sorry." Her voice sounded so small with her hand pressed against her mouth. "I don't know why... I figured..."

I was at a loss for words.

Did Lauryn just try to kiss me?

"You don't like me like that," she surmised low.

"No," I voiced in haste. "That's... that's not it—"

"You have a girlfriend," she tried next, tucking her lips into her mouth. "Of course you have one. You're handsome and that's what people have, right? Relationships? Well, normal people do."

My brows knitted over my eyes.

"I'm sorry." She closed her eyes for a moment. "I shouldn't have—"

She stopped speaking as soon as I took her face into my hands.

In that moment, I thought of how I used to wreck my brain trying to figure out how to get this beautiful woman to talk to me. Then how I spent the time, after getting her to talk to me, figuring out ways to make her comfortable around me.

To now this.

"Is this okay?" I asked, staring deeply into her eyes.

She nodded.

I caressed her cheeks with my thumbs and asked. "I can kiss you?"

She nodded again, but this time told me, "Yes."

I wasn't sure how it happened, how we got to here and the details mattered little either.

Because when I leaned in and pressed my lips to her lips and kissed them softly, nothing else mattered.

My mind wanted to take over, clutter my thoughts with trying to figure out how to kiss a woman who had experienced such pain in her past. I forced them out.

Well, normal people do.

Her words echoed in my mind. That indirect expression of feeling like an alien compared to so-called *normal people* when she was everything but that.

Lauryn was real. She was raw. And her kiss was as sweet as I knew she was underneath all the fear and armor she wore because of her circumstances.

I moved in closer when I parted her lips. Carefully slid my tongue into her mouth in search of hers.

And she let me.

The moment our tongues made contact, she moaned into my mouth, releasing the tension in her body. That made me release any tension left in mine.

I caressed her cheeks with my thumb as I guided her deeper into our kiss.

I'd gotten a little too relaxed because I realized I was growing hard in my jeans.

I broke our kiss immediately.

She panted beside me, chest moving up and down. It was only after I'd broken our kiss that I realized I needed the air too.

Lauryn's eyes met mine, and a smile pulled her lips up, revealing a perfect sparkling smile before she covered it with her fingers. She caressed her lips before dragging her fingernails down the center of them.

"Wow," she expressed with more air than tone.

And I couldn't tell what was better, the kiss or her brilliant smile.

"Yeah." I caressed the side of her face with the side of my hand. "Wow for sure."

EIGHTEEN

LAURYN

Aunt Evelyn stood over her stove, turning over a golden brown chicken wing using silver tongs.

The smells and sounds of Sunday filled her apartment.

William, her boyfriend, was in the living room watching a football game, mumbling comments to himself whenever the team he rooted for messed up a play.

Hot oil and the seasoning from the chicken traveled around the unit and were the strongest in the kitchen where my aunt and I were.

Aunt Evelyn sipped her white wine and made a gratifying sound each time. Her attention volleyed from the frying pan to the collard greens cooking in the large pot on the burner to the right of her.

My mind was still on Saturday. I couldn't get Asher off my mind.

After we returned from Manhattan and he escorted me to my apartment door, once inside, I reminisced myself to sleep, remembering the day.

I had such a good time. A better time than I was expecting. I didn't know what this preppy guy from Long Island had planned and if it would be anything worth crossing an expressway and a parkway to enjoy.

But it was so worth it. And the outing really had me thinking.

"Hey, Auntie?"

"Hmm?" She'd reached for her glass of white wine and took a sip, her back still facing me.

"What does sex feel like when it's good?"

That sent her into a coughing fit.

She gasped for air while trying to clear her airway with hard, persistent coughing.

I straightened my back in my seat. "Auntie, you good?"

She held a hand up.

"You all right in there, Ev," William asked from the couch in the living room.

"I'm fine," she pushed out in a hoarse voice.

He stared at her for a moment, and she reassured him with another hand up in the air.

"I'm fine," she repeated, glancing at me, then at him.

William returned to watching the game when my aunt turned to focus on me again.

"What did you ask me?" She asked in a whisper.

I scoffed. "I know you heard me."

"Shit." She pressed a hand to her chest. "I can't be too sure I did."

Aunt Evelyn placed her wineglass on her counter and removed the chicken out of the oil, placing the fried wing on a paper toweled plate with the other fried wings.

After turning off the stove, she dropped herself into a seat near to me at the kitchen table and leaned in. "Lauryn, why did you ask me that?"

His kisses seemed to get better the more we kissed.

Asher and I stood outside of my door after returning from our date in the city. His kiss the first time out on the terrace of that restaurant made my heart do things it's never done. I mean, my heart has hammered before, but it's never done so in a way that made me feel like I was being energized by every beat.

His fingers were in my hair as he twirled his tongue with mine, encapsulating my lips with his. Asher's kiss was so gentle and so was his touch. The three times we've kissed, he's cradled my face in his hands and although his kiss was amazing, his touch was the best part.

I'd moved in closer to him, not at all caring to unlock my door to go inside and end the night. When I moved closer, I noticed a hardness in his jeans against me.

He immediately broke our kiss and stepped back a little.

My eyes fell to the bulge in his jeans, and he stepped back a little more.

"Sorry," was the first thing out of his mouth.

I'd say before meeting Asher and hanging with him, my mind had rarely gone to thoughts of men and what women did with men... in a good way.

I always saw the bad. The problems, the catches of being in any close contact with men.

But with Asher, I didn't feel repelled by the effect that our kissing was having on him.

I was curious.

"And he left after?" Aunt Evelyn asked.

I nodded. "We only kissed and then he went home."

A smile spread across her lips as she nodded, too.

"I didn't know what I was doing half the time, but I must've known something because he had *that* reaction."

"And how did that make you feel?" She quizzed this time. "Knowing he had that reaction?"

"Curious."

She arched a brow. "Hence the question?"

"Yeah?"

"So... you want to..." She took a breath and scooted a little closer. "Do you want to have sex with him?"

"Well, not tomorrow, Auntie."

She dropped her head and released a long sigh of relief, and that made me laugh.

Her head popped up so quick I thought she'd lose it off her neck.

She stared at me for a moment before pressing her hand to her chest. "You're smiling."

I scratched my head, then ran my fingers through my strands. "Am I?"

She bobbed her head up, then down. Her eyes were watering, but she inhaled a deep breath to keep the tears from falling.

"Well, you're grown." She said, inhaling a deep breath. "You're 29 and more than old enough, Lauryn. Seeing a guy is an on-brand behavior for 29."

I blinked in response.

"But I want to meet him first," she asserted. "Before you do other things, that's on-brand behavior for 29."

I laughed, and she smiled in reaction.

"This guy," she continued. "What's his name?"

"Asher," I answered. "He's the guy I told you about. The one who fought those guys at Black Bamboo because of me."

"Asher," she repeated low. "Right. Okay." She nodded next. "I remember you mentioning him. Invite Asher over for Sunday dinner and also ask *Asher* what he likes to eat, and I'll hook it up. Next Sunday."

I smiled to myself. "Okay."

"And let him know that turning down my invitation is not an option."

I twisted my lips to one side. "Okay."

My aunt's eyes darted between my eyes as she drew in another one of those deep breaths through her nose. She nodded to herself and stood up again, returning to her post over the stove.

"When it feels good," she started, turning on the stove's burner under the oil again. "It makes time seem like an illusion and extremely unreal. Because the feeling fools you into thinking it will be there forever. And technically, it is because it is powerful enough to find a home in your thoughts. And every time you think about it, it transports your mind and body back to that time and place, and your brain will not know the difference."

"Sounds heavenly."

"Oh, honey." She tossed a glance over her shoulder. "It's like a little piece of heaven on earth... when done the right way. "

"And what's the right way?"

"Selflessly," she answered. "When you're thinking of him and he's thinking of you."

My aunt turned to face me and said lowly, "The way a man is in bed reflects how he is in life. If he's selfish in it, he's selfish when he's off the mattress too. That's why I want to meet this, Asher."

"I think you'll like him," I said with confidence.

"We'll see." She winked.

NINETEEN

ASHER

"Okay!" the petite woman with short, cropped hair said the moment she opened her door. "So far, so good."

I chuckled to myself, then looked at Lauryn, who smiled up at me.

I was still getting used to that. Seeing a smile on her face. And I'll admit, no number of times she's flashed a smile my way has made it lose its sparkle.

"Well, come in," the woman invited, gesturing into her apartment.

"Aunt Evelyn," Lauryn announced the moment she and I stepped over the threshold. "This is Asher." Lauryn glanced at me and added, "Asher, Aunt Evelyn."

"Pleasure to meet you," I said with a nod.

"The pleasure is all mine." Evelyn smiled big. "Happy to have you."

A quick glance around me showed me a home that was feminine from the custom blown glass lighting hanging from the ceiling to the furry pink rug in the living room. There wasn't anything minimalist about anything in Evelyn's apartment. This gave me insight into the woman I would meet today.

"Your home is beautiful," I commented.

She giggled. "Could it get any girlier, right?"

I snickered. "I like it."

"And so far." She winked at Lauryn, then focused on me again. "I like you."

I smiled shyly.

"I'm still finishing up a few things in the kitchen, but dinner will be ready soon."

"You need help Auntie?"

"Normally, you know I would say yes, but we have a guest." Evelyn smiled at me.

"It's no bother to me," I insisted. "I can help too."

Evelyn's brows arched.

I motioned at the table. "I'm sure I can set the table or something."

Evelyn turned her attention to Lauryn next and grinned. "Okay."

Lauryn and I joined Evelyn to get everything ready for dinner. While I focused on walking the plates and utensils from the kitchen to the dining room, Lauryn assisted her aunt in the kitchen.

"So how old are you, Asher?" Evelyn asked.

"29."

"Okay." She nodded approvingly. "Same age as Lauryn. Where are you from?"

"Long Island."

"Where in Long Island?"

"The Hamptons."

Evelyn's head shot up from the pot she stood over. "The Hamptons. Really?"

I chuckled. "Yeah. Most of my family lives in The Hamptons."

Evelyn left her post at the stove to stand in front of the island that divided the kitchen from the dining room.

"I don't hear too much about people *living* in the Hamptons," she explained. "The Hamptons around here are a magical place you escape to, to vacation in the summer, or to attend a party. What does your family do?"

"Auntie," Lauryn spat. "You giving him an interview before we can sit?"

"Well, I didn't intend to." She laughed. "I was trying to have small talk, but Asher is more interesting than I was expecting."

"I'm flattered." I snorted. "My family is in real estate. My father owns a few real estate businesses around New York City."

"So, you're a rich boy."

Lauryn's eyes bulged. "Auntie."

"It's okay." I smiled at Lauryn, then switched my eyes over to her aunt. "My family is well-to-do, yes. Some would call them rich, but I always believe the true rich has more to do with character than the number of commas in a bank account."

"Yeah... until you need them commas," Evelyn insisted. "Then you wish you were richer than a motherfucker and want as many commas as the bank can hold."

I laughed.

"But yes, I agree, wholeheartedly." She nodded. "Rich character should definitely be the priority."

I lowered my attention to the table.

"What is a man from The Hamptons doing living in an apartment building in the renovated hood?"

"Renovated hood?" I questioned.

"Gentrification."

"Ah, got you." I laughed. "Well, I moved there because it's close to the trains and the trains are close to Langston U, where I go to school."

"You're in school?" Evelyn made a shrugging expression with her lips, impressed. "Studying what?"

"I'm studying for my Ph.D. in psychology."

"You're P..." Evelyn's eyes went wide. "Lauryn! You didn't tell me any of this."

Lauryn shook her head.

"He's amazing," Evelyn commented low, returning to her position over the stove to stir the pot of food. "I can't believe you didn't tell me how amazing he is. Talking about some guy. This ain't just some guy, girl! Have I taught you nothing?"

Lauryn rolled her eyes while fighting back a smile.

"He's perfect." Evelyn returned to the island where I stood on the other side of. "You're perfect. A little too perfect." She leaned in. "So, what's wrong with you?"

"Oh, my God," Lauryn mumbled.

I bit back my smile. "Justified question. If I can be as upfront about the good, I can be as open to sharing the not-so good, I guess."

Evelyn nodded.

"I'm impulsive and extremely hardheaded."

Evelyn arched both brows. "And honest too. I'm listening."

I turned to face her. "I'm studying for my Ph.D. *after* dropping out the first time I was studying for it, five years into the program."

Her jaw dropped. "Why would you do that?"

My eyes moved to Lauryn to find her as engaged as her aunt.

"Boredom, a little stupidity. Perhaps slightly because I wanted to be defiant." I sighed, leaning my backside against the edge of the table. "I dropped out of school to live in Bali for a year. Arrived with a temporary visa, then used the money my parents put aside for me as a lump sum allowance while in school to invest in Bali's economy so they would allow me to live in their country for that year."

Evelyn leaned forward on the island that separated the kitchen from the dining room, completely tuned in.

"It's not like I didn't love studying psychology." I shrugged. "It was the only thing I wanted to study when I was told what school to study it in. But that was the thing. My parents always dictated my life. Which was to be expected since I understand every parent wants what's best for their child. But my set of expectations was different. The expectations as an only child to a family that makes wealth their religion was far beyond what I wanted to meet."

Evelyn giggled. "Sounds like first world problems to me."

"Which is why I dropped out and left the country." I nodded. "Lived modestly in a small village in Bali for my first few months in Indonesia. I moved to another part of Bali to live out the rest of my time there after those few months. The part of Bali I lived for the first few months was nothing like the Bali you think about when you hear the name. The village I lived had no running water or electricity. I cooked my food over a kerosene stove which was terrible to inhale. Extremely unhealthy. I felt every weather condition. Deeply. From sweltering heat to torrential rain. I might as well had been homeless because of the impoverished housing conditions I lived in by choice. But I wasn't alone. Everyone in the village lived like that and had been living like that for most of their lives. So, I never complained."

Her brows went up.

"No phones, no TV." I inhaled a bountiful amount of air and smiled. "Only meditation, journaling, and yoga. And worrying about nothing that wasn't related to simply surviving the day because, for those few months, I forced myself to have nothing. I spent a lot of time getting in touch with myself and it gave me the privilege to uncover and acknowledge the things that once served me but that I needed to release to be a whole and better person."

"Damn." Evelyn glanced over at Lauryn, then focused on me again. "You've lived many lives for 29, Asher."

I chuckled, returning to setting the table.

Dinner followed the theme of the conversation we'd fallen into. A lot of questions about my background, my upbringing, and eventually Lauryn.

"So," Evelyn said as she cleaned her mouth with the napkin I'd placed beside her plate earlier while setting up. "I have to have the real talk with you."

I chewed the last of my food and nodded.

"I understand that I'm a woman and may not have the same threatening effect as a man who would say this..."

My attention turned to Lauryn, who sat next to me.

"But... that's my favorite girl sitting beside you," she said with a serious expression. "And to say she's been through a lot would be an understatement."

The sadness in Evelyn's eyes was palpable. In the short time we'd been in each other's presence, I realized she was a fun loving, effervescent, cool aunt who didn't let age determine how she related to others. But in that moment, all of that subsided. And I could understand why.

"I'm aware," I told her low.

Evelyn blinked a few times, pressing her hand to her chest, visibly trying her hardest to hold the tears in.

"Auntie," Lauryn whispered and shook her head. "Please don't do that right now because you know if you cry I will too and I will be so mad if you make me do that right now."

The mood in the room shifted. Lauryn was balling her lips to my right. Evelyn was patting her eyes dry across from me.

I knew the gravity of what my involvement with Lauryn would be. I knew it when our neighbor Elsie hinted at it. Knew it when I searched Lauryn up online and read only the few lines in the article. Even knew it when I spoke with Jayce about her.

And none of that made me want to run.

There was something pulling me to Lauryn. Tethering me to her. Something that just felt right. Something that made me refuse to see her or what she'd been through as too much to handle too.

I wanted this. Despite what *this* was. I wanted it with her.

I moved my plate of food out of the way to place my hands on the table and thought for a moment about my next few words.

"I don't know everything about what happened," I started. "I know some things, but I want Lauryn to tell me everything in her own words at her time."

I turned to Lauryn. "Okay, Lauryn?"

Lauryn nodded.

"Whenever you're ready. Whenever it feels like too much to keep inside. I'll always be ready to hear it from you."

Lauryn broke eye contact and took a breath.

"And before then and after she does," I continued, refocusing on Evelyn. "I will handle her with care. Beyond that being necessary, it's the right thing to do. Now, I know it won't be easy. But like I've told you, I'm extremely hardheaded, so easy isn't what I've ever gone after."

Evelyn scoffed a laugh.

"I like your niece a lot," I admitted, looking fixedly into Evelyn's eyes. "I care about her. And my heart is big, so I know I could love her too. Because I want to."

Evelyn smiled.

"I know I can't make her forget all she's been through, but I want to give her new things to think about, you know? Because... yeah, life is hard, but there are tiny spaces in it that's big enough and have enough light for joy to thrive."

I looked over at Lauryn.

"And I would love to be one of those tiny spaces in this world for you."

Lauryn held her gaze with me, her eyes darting between mine. The vulnerability in her gaze communicated fears she would never admit in that instance. And I didn't want her to. I didn't need to hear them.

Because I was way ahead of them.

"Okay, so..." Evelyn chimed in. "Should I leave?"

Lauryn focused on her aunt before I turned to look in Evelyn's direction.

"That longing gaze made me feel like I was intruding on you two... in my own damn apartment."

I chuckled, then focused down on my food. Snuck a glance at Lauryn from the side of my eyes to see a smile pulling at her lips as she resumed eating, too.

***

We spent another hour at Lauryn's Aunt Evelyn's apartment before Lauryn and I returned to our apartment building.

The dinner after the brief discussion was lighter and more relaxed, just as it was when Lauryn and I first arrived at Evelyn's.

Evelyn shared a few things about Lauryn in her childhood that were great to learn and very insightful about the woman I was getting to know.

The ride back to the apartment building was quiet. Lauryn didn't sit as far away from me in the black car that I ordered to take us home. But she also said little.

I didn't feel the need to fill the silence. So, we just chilled.

Back at our building and in front of her apartment's door, I stood facing her and smiled.

Since the ride back to the building, she seemed deep in thought about something. Like I said, the ride back was quiet. With no interest in filling the silence, I believed her having nothing to say was because she had a lot on her mind. Which was to be expected.

"Well," I started, "thank you for inviting me to Sunday dinner with your aunt. I had a lot of fun—"

"Do you want to come in?"

I hadn't been back inside Lauryn's apartment since the day I built her bookcase.

It was a surprise she allowed me in there, much less to build the bookcase, which took some time.

I never asked to return and hadn't expected her to invite me back soon, either. I'd been moving at her pace, and I wanted to continue to do that.

"I would like to but," I answered, "only if you want me to."

Lauryn bit at her bottom lip.

The day she agreed to have me in her apartment to build the bookcase, it was broad daylight. The sun was out, the hour late afternoon. It was very clear I was in her apartment with a purpose.

Tonight though, after 8pm, autumn's habit of making the days short and the nights long again after summer had it looking later.

"I want you to come inside," she said.

I searched her eyes for any hint of hesitance or uncertainty and found none. So, I nodded and said, "Okay, yeah, sure. I'll come in."

She arranged the living room differently. At least from my recollection and what I could see the moment Lauryn opened her apartment's door. The furniture was in a different spot. Not drastically far from where they were before, but it was clear she'd moved some things around.

Everything except for the bookcase.

"It looks different in here," I noted, eyes scanning. "You moved around your furniture."

She scratched the back of her head, then began stepping out of her sneakers. "Only a little."

I used the toe of my right sneaker to pull down on the back of my sneaker on my left, removing it, then repeating the move on my opposite foot.

Lauryn switched on the lights around her apartment, first the living room, then her kitchen.

Her place was lovely and did the job of revealing parts of Lauryn she had yet to share with me.

She was nostalgic. In love with things from a time that was nowhere close to now. This was clear in the type of furniture she had; the vintage magazine covers she kept in picture frames on her living room wall. Everything was nice and well taken care of. There was the occasional imperfection in the wood paneling on her walls or the gash in paint that was slight, but still noticeable to me. But her place was so lovely. Soft in appearance. The soft I believed she was hoping to be.

I pulled myself out of analyzing my environment long enough to look for her and to find her standing a few feet away, watching me.

I turned to face her and asked, "You okay?"

She nodded. "Yeah."

Lauryn took steps towards me, then stopped when she was within arm's reach. She toyed with her fingers as she approached. Pinching and tugging at her fingertips. A sign of nervousness. Anxiety.

"I can go," I reminded. "It's fine. You can ask me to leave at any time. You know that, right?"

She continued taking steps towards me and stood close. Lids blinking, eyes darting between mine.

Finally, she asked, "Can you kiss me?"

I would never let her ask twice.

Not when the first time sounded so sweet and had me calling on my patience not to rush her to grant her request.

I took my time closing the space between us in a few steps. Tilting my head at the perfect angle once I arrived in front of her, to press my lips against hers.

And when I did, they felt soft. Like always.

Kissing Lauryn had become my new favorite thing to do. More than reading. More than eating at my favorite eatery in Brooklyn. She was my new thrill. There was an innocence about it I loved so much reconnecting with.

I parted her lips with mine to slide my tongue into her mouth. She pulled back.

My eyes flew open.

She inhaled a deep breath and let her exhale slide through her lips slowly.

I took a step back, and she followed me, taking a step forward.

"No," she expressed softly. Then balanced herself on the arches of her feet to press her lips against my lips again. Exhaled against me and parted my lips with hers this time. She melted against me, pressing her chest to my chest. Her body heat leaned up against mine, made me sigh in her mouth. We'd gotten into a rhythm; one I didn't want a break from. Tongues caressing. The exchange of inhales and exhales in a cyclical pattern. It made me want to draw her closer to me to lock her in place. So, I attempted to do just that, wrapping my arm around her waist, but then she broke our kiss again.

This time more abruptly than the first.

She dropped her head, frustrated, and exhaled in defeat.

I was a little frustrated too. Right when it was getting good.

But I caught myself.

I want this.

So, I tucked my lips into my mouth and bent my legs at the knees to meet her eyes again. "Lauryn, it's okay."

"I can do this," she whispered, lifting her head again.

"You don't have to."

"I *want* to."

"I can leave—"

"I don't want you to leave," she countered, her voice raised higher than mine.

I shook my head, confused. "Why are you so adamant about this..." My voice trailed off when a thought occurred to me.

She wanted not only a kiss.

She wanted what could come *after* the kiss?

"Oh," I said low to myself. "Do you...? Are you...?" I cleared my throat to gather my next few words. "Do you want more than a kiss tonight, Lauryn?"

She rubbed her lips together and just stared at me.

"Damn, *ummm.*" I blew air through my lips. "Lauryn, I don't know if you're ready for that." I shook my head again. "I don't know if *I'm* ready for that—"

"I want us to be," she affirmed. "I want to be."

She stared up at me and didn't break eye contact until she started speaking again.

"It's just that..." She ran her fingers through her long hair. "I've never done it in a way that normal people do it."

"Normal people?" I questioned.

"You *know* what I mean." She licked her lips. "I was a virgin before my assault and I have never had sex after it happened, okay?"

"Okay," I answered quickly.

She exhaled a shaky breath. "I've never *wanted* to do that after everything happened. I'd have desires like normal people, I guess, but the thought of doing *it* was never one I wanted to act on... until you."

Breathing became a struggle suddenly.

I suspected as much, but hearing her say it was a different revelation.

"And you've given me no reason not to want to with you, so... I want to. With you. Tonight."

I puffed my cheeks with air and exhaled through pursed lips.

"I bought condoms," she revealed. "They're in the room."

"Wow." I chuckled nervously. "You've prepared for this. I... don't know what to say."

She blinked in response.

"I'm honored, Lauryn."

She said nothing in response. Just waited. And I refused to make her do that for long.

I inhaled an encouraging breath. "If this is what you want to do... we'll have to talk through this, okay?" I nodded. "Because this is a first for us both, in a way, and I need for us to be always on the same page. Do you understand what I mean by that?"

She nodded.

"No." I shook my head. "You can't do that. Because I can't hear a nod and we must literally talk. I need to hear from you. I need to hear your voice. Hearing your voice will let me know you're with me the entire time." I licked my lips. "A 'yes' or a 'yeah' will do. Or any other way you choose to give me your approval. I need to hear you *every time*, Lauryn."

Lauryn held my gaze.

"And if it's not yes, if you don't like or want something, I need to hear 'no' instead." I looked her deeply in her eyes and told her, "I'm going to always need your consent. Always. Okay?"

She nodded once again, but this time gave me a "Yes."

I nodded and grinned. "Good."

I looked away for a moment to scan her apartment before locking eyes with her again. "Should we go to your room?"

She smirked, and I had to take a breath to calm the growing stiffness in my groin. "Yeah."

"Where is it?"

She pointed over my shoulder. "Through there."

"Do you want to lead the way, or should I?"

"You can go."

As I expected.

So that is what I did.

Before we arrived in her bedroom, I insisted we stop in her bathroom to wash our hands. I needed the moment to catch my breath, allowing the water from her silver faucet to ground me and to keep me calm as I cleaned my hands.

And when we arrived inside of her room, my nerves had settled.

Even more nostalgic beauty that was first highlighted in her living room met my eyes.

Her mattress was large enough for the both of us. Queen-sized. The white bedding wrinkled. The bed, unmade.

I turned to see Lauryn a few feet away.

Without saying another word, Lauryn pulled opened the side table's drawer closest to her and pulled out the box of condoms she mentioned. The sound of her ripping the box open and pulling out a single condom echoed around the spacious room. Her eyes stayed on mine as she stretched her arm with the condom in my direction, handing the wrapped condom to me which I took.

Her hands grabbed the hem of her shirt next, lifting it, pulling her hooded sweatshirt up with the shirt high enough to remove over her head.

I heard my exhale leave me heavily and the condom wrapper crinkle as I squeezed it in my hand, when all I could see were her full breasts in her solid black bra.

I followed her lead and pulled at my shirt to remove it. After a moment of my view being blocked while removing my shirt, when I could see again, it was just in time to watch her pull the waistband of her joggers down and over her hips, letting the pants fall to her ankles.

She stood there only for a moment, allowing my eyes to pore over her body. Full hips and thighs, a cinched waist and soft stomach. Tawny brown skin with long bra strap length jet black hair that flowed over her shoulders with the ends covering her breasts.

Lauryn took the few steps to her bed as I stepped out of my jeans. I watched her peel back her white blanket, then climbed onto the mattress, retreating beneath the bedding.

I joined her shortly after, climbing onto the mattress and getting beneath the covers too. I turned to face her the moment I was comfortable in bed.

We held our stares for a beat before I told her, "I'll ask again."

Her eyes darted between mine.

"Are you sure you want to do this?"

TWENTY

LAURYN

"Yes," came out of my mouth with ease. Because doing this had been on my mind for the past few weeks.

I bought condoms. And honestly, I knew I was sure I wanted this the moment I had the thought to buy them.

Before Asher, sex was something I had no interest in. I still kind of had no interest in it, but I had this desire to take what Asher and I had to another level. And it was so strong it was all I could think about lately.

It just felt right to do it.

Even with my heart pounding so damn hard, I was nervous he could hear it, too.

"Can I touch you here?" He asked, caressing the side of my face.

I was prepared to nod my answer, but remembered what he told me.

That he would need my consent.

Every time.

And when he said that, when he told me he would only do what I allowed, I knew then not only did I want to do this, *but I also* needed to do this with him.

"Yeah," I uttered.

Asher took his time, gliding first his fingers, then his hand farther along my face, stopping at my hairline. He buried his fingertips into my hair soon after, and I closed my eyes to his touch.

He caressed my cheek with his thumb, and I instinctively pulled on my walls. That reaction made my heart beat harder than it was already beating.

"You're so beautiful and so brave," he expressed with more breath than voice.

I opened my eyes to him. He gazed at me with soft eyes that were fixed on mine before I could focus completely.

"The most beautiful woman I have ever seen in my life."

I parted my lips and inhaled deeply through my mouth.

Asher glided his thumb from my cheek to my lips. "Can I touch you here, sweetheart?"

"Yes," I whispered against his thumb. And with my approval, another layer of nerves subsided. My heart calmed a little more, the rhythm thumping a little less in my chest.

He strummed the pad of his thumb along my bottom lip.

And I moaned in an exhale. What should have been the release of air brought with it a sound I'd never heard come from me.

"Does this feel good?" He asked me.

"*Mmm-hmm*," I replied, accompanied by a nod.

"Feels good to me too."

Asher bit his bottom lip then released it to wet it with his tongue and I just wanted his mouth on mine.

So I closed the space between us, pressed my lips and then my body against his. I parted my lips, and he did too. Sliding his tongue into my mouth in search of mine.

And I met him halfway. Moaning again against his lips. Completely unsure of what I was doing, but somehow able to keep up. Like always.

All of this was new.

The desire.

The want.

The pure satisfaction from having his heat against me.

His fingers moved deeper into my hair, and he pulled me closer to him with his grip on my head and I swear I melted.

I felt the stiffness gradually pressing more and more against me. And right when I was about to panic, he told me, "You're doing amazing, sweetheart."

And I instantly relaxed.

"So amazing," he added, pulling me closer, and I allowed it.

Allowed myself to get carried away with the rush of energy pulsing through me that made my heart hammer and my pulse quicken.

We were nothing but heavy breaths when Asher turned over with me so that he was now on top.

The weight of him on top of me made me gasp softly.

"Are you still with me?" He asked in a whisper. "Can I lie right here with you?"

A chill ran down my back and I shivered beneath him, and he held me tighter.

"Should we stop?"

I shook my head.

"Lauryn," he panted.

"Please don't stop."

I lifted my head off my pillow high enough to crash my lips into his and he obliged, kissing me back while gently guiding me down to my pillow. Our tongues danced in our mouths in no rush as he hardened more against me. Between my thighs felt like my heart had fallen there in this new position. Thumping with so much life, just the feeling of it, made me want more.

Fingers soon slid there. Asher's fingers.

He asked, "Can I touch you here?"

Asher rested those fingers against the seat of my panties and moaned when I trembled beneath him.

"Ye-yes," I exhaled.

He lifted them high enough along my abdomen and paused at the waistband of my panties. "Can I touch here?"

"Yes."

And with no further hesitation, Asher smoothed his hand, fingers first, into the seat of my panties. Gliding down trimmed coarse hair and into the valley of it all.

I whimpered beneath him when he slid a fingertip between the folds of my pussy. And we moaned together when my wetness slicked his finger.

I held my breath when he guided one finger slowly inside of me.

I dropped my jaw as he glided his finger farther in.

"Focus on me, sweetheart," he whispered over me. And when I did, he asked, "Can I keep touching you here?"

"Yes."

"Can I keep going?"

"Keep going."

Asher stroked another finger into me, and I angled myself to receive what he was giving.

I moaned each time he guided his fingers deeper into me and curved his fingertips up just enough, repeating the action all over again. I couldn't believe my innate reaction to gyrating my hips and pushing myself onto his hand each time he tried to pull back.

Asher extended his arm for the condom he placed on my side table, still curving his finger as he slid his digits in and out.

Our eyes locked as he ripped the condom opened with his teeth, then he slid his fingers out of my warmth.

Filled with a sudden feeling of emptiness, I wanted him back there, touching me between my thighs again immediately.

He only needed a moment to slide the condom on beneath the covers, but our eyes never wavered.

Soon I felt the slick feel of his sheathed erection as he slid the tip up my slick folds.

"May I?" He breathed.

I'd never seen the desperation in his eyes that was present at that moment. Pleading eyes, quick pace breathing.

It was all so damn beautiful.

"Lauryn, may I?" He asked again, panting.

I nodded, and he sighed, frustrated.

But still patient.

"Lauryn," he exhaled, pausing all his actions, literally freezing over me. "May. I?"

I didn't want to speak because I didn't want to change my mind. I had never thought this far when thoughts, only the prospect, of Asher and me like this crossed my mind and I was too curious to turn back, even when my anxiety was threatening to creep up.

I reached down between us and took his dick into my hand, coiling my fingers around his heavy, thick muscle that was so hard I could feel the veins through the condom. The realization made me skip more than one breath.

I inhaled at the same time as I lifted the length of him high enough to be at level with my warm opening. Then I slowly guided him inside of me.

And he let me, eyes never leaving mine. In fact, he was scanning my face the whole time. His lids fluttered the deeper I guided him inside me, past the initial resistance. I winced and sighed as his girth forced my walls to give way to him, and the only thing that kept me calm was knowing it was happening at my pace. Asher hadn't moved a muscle. He remained still over me, balancing himself on his forearms, watching me.

He blinked a few times before he couldn't help but to shut his eyes and drop his head to take a breath before he lifted his head again, but only long enough to press his lips against mine.

I kept my hand around the base of his dick as we laid there motionless and kissing for a moment.

His first thrust forward was a shock to my system. The sensation it produced, him thrusting into me only once, made my ears ring. His second thrust made me gasp. The third made me want the fourth. And by the fifth stroke, nothing else mattered. I could feel nothing else other than Asher moving in and out of me now. Slowly. And with so much patience, my toes were curling from the ease of his moves.

My heavy breaths became slow building moans.

I held on to his dick at the base as he stroked, feeling his hardness slide back and forth between my grip around him. Feeling everything happening inside and out of me.

"You're doing so good, sweetheart," he whispered against my lips. "You feel so good, too. Do I feel good to you?"

So good. Too good to respond at that moment.

Half the time, I couldn't kiss him back. My breath mimicking his pace and the glide of his erection between the curve of my fingers.

The feeling kept morphing the longer I stayed in it. His weight against me, his exhales brushing against my face. It just all kept getting better.

Until finally, I let my hand fall away, releasing my grip around his shaft.

He kept going, now deeper, and I wanted him to.

I moved my lips off his and let my head fall to one side as I drifted more into the now.

Hyperaware of what was happening between my thighs. Wanting each stroke, each glide of his erection between my walls to continue forever.

I was happy to give up control.

Feeling the hairs all over my body stand higher. My nerve endings tingling in places I didn't know nerves existed.

And soon I couldn't feel anything besides pressure, weight, and tingling heat. I could see nothing but colors with my eyes closed.

Asher's lips were to my ear when he asked me, "Do you feel that, sweetheart?"

I wasn't sure what *that* was, but yeah, I could feel something. Though I didn't know it, I trusted it.

Oddly enough, although I had felt nothing like it, I was okay with it building to a physical peak I no longer could control in any form. I couldn't control what it was or for how long I would allow it to take over me.

And take over me, it did. Causing me to push myself more onto Asher, meeting his thrusts, feeling him tap something soft and sensitive inside of me.

It was so sensitive. Each time he made contact, my body shook, but the feeling was so raw, so sweet, so I pushed myself more than before onto him so I could experience the true strength of it all.

I opened my eyes to Asher's and kept them on him as whatever was happening to me happened.

My legs shook, my body trembled each time he thrusted forward. My walls were fluttering like crazy, and it seemed to make him grow harder between them.

I didn't know what was happening. All I knew was that it felt like nothing I'd ever felt before.

Not so I could ever think hard enough to describe, nor would I want to bother with trying. Not in that moment.

It rushed me. Making me arch my back while rocking my quivering core out of sync with Asher's thrusts. The sensation felt like a possession, pulsing through me in a repetitive sonic pattern that started from the top of my head and bottomed out at the soles of my feet.

I couldn't say anything even with my mouth slacked wide.

Asher was grunting when the feeling reached a level that made me feel like I would burst.

But instead of bursting, a warm sensation swept through me in waves and caused my eyes to roll and the walls inside me to flutter uncontrollably like a heartbeat. It heightened the kiss Asher pressed into my lips and made me feel high and like I was not in this world anymore.

Made me feel something I'd never felt in my life.

Bliss.

———

I let all my weight go in Asher's arms. Relaxed the flex in my muscles and my tongue against the roof of my mouth. I let it all go and allowed myself to get caught up and lost in the scalp massage he'd started as I rested against him.

When I got up earlier that morning, I didn't know we'd be in this position by night. I was naked beneath my covers and pressed up against a naked Asher.

I'd read about this in a book or two. Fictionalized scenarios of women after rapture clinging to the afterglow they were in after making love.

I made love.

I smiled to myself at that realization.

"What's on your mind?" He asked.

What wasn't?

The hour had to be after midnight. After we finished making love and catching our breath from the high of it all, Asher pulled me to him, and I nuzzled myself into the nook of his arm. And there I remained.

"My dad," I answered.

Asher's finger massaging ceased for only a moment before they started up again.

My dad. Not someone most would think about after doing what we'd just done, but my reasoning was valid.

I'd just experienced something I believed I would never want in my life. After everything that had happened to me, I wanted nothing to do with sex or anything next to it.

But as I laid in Asher's arms, I couldn't wait for us to do it all again. And soon.

"Your dad," he repeated. "*Hmph.*"

I tilted my head back to look up at him.

"Not the answer I was expecting."

I bit at my bottom lip.

"But, okay." Asher pulled me close to press a kiss onto my forehead. "Do you speak to him often?"

"No," I answered curtly. "He's in prison."

Asher froze against me this time.

"He's in prison because of me."

Asher created enough space between us to turn over to face me. He lowered his chin to his chest and looked at me from the top of his eyes.

"He killed the guy who hurt me."

Asher's brows relaxed and all he did was nod twice.

"I was my dad's third strike." I blinked away to keep the tears in. "I haven't spoken to him in years. Went to see him once for my eighteenth birthday, but he never came out to see me. Sent an officer to tell me never to come back to the prison. That broke me a little."

Asher wrapped an arm around me and brought me close to him again.

"With my mother gone... all I have now is my father and my aunt. So..." I exhaled. "Me not being able to see him hurts."

Asher ran his fingers through my hair, moving the strands off my shoulder.

"I write him like every day but in a notebook." I scoffed a laugh. "Several notebooks, actually."

"Did he say why he didn't want to see you?"

I shook my head.

"I'm sure he had his reason."

"Does that make you like me less?"

Asher pulled back long enough to meet my eyes.

"Because my dad is a murderer?"

"He isn't a murderer," he avowed and with his eyes fixed on mine. "He's a hero. Meeting him would be an honor. So, no, that does not make me like you any less."

I closed the space between us and lifted my lips to his, pecking him once before sliding my tongue into his mouth.

I was thinking of my dad because I wished he could see the kind of man who liked me. Someone with heart and who wanted to protect mine. And I knew that from the many times Asher and I have spent time together getting to know each other. But after making love, I knew it for a fact, and I wanted to tell the whole world about him.

Starting with my dad.

Asher broke our kiss long enough to ask, "Do you want me as much as I want you right now?"

I nodded, and he grunted, which made me giggle.

"I don't like the nod, but I think you giggling is my new favorite sound from you," he commented with a smirk.

I bit my bottom lip and lowered my hand between us, without pause, taking him into my hand. "And I think I want you more than you want me right now."

"Impossible." A full beam smile pulled at the corners of his lips. "And I'll show you why... if you say it's okay."

I tightened my grip around him beneath the covers and he groaned while briefly closing his eyes.

When he opened them again, he asked, "So, may I, sweetheart?"

I smiled and nodded slowly. "Yes, you may."

Twenty-One
One Month Later...

LAURYN

The moment I stepped off the elevator, I walked straight to Asher's door.

I'd just returned from the shopping mall a few miles from my apartment. My trip to the mall was to pick up something I knew Asher would like. It was a Friday night, which meant Asher was home. Out of all the days in the week, his course load was the lightest on Fridays, which meant he spent less time on campus. So he always made it home at a decent hour, just in time for the weekend.

I moved the bag I carried onto my opposite hand to knock on his door once and waited.

Like always.

It had been a month since we'd taken our relationship to the next level. A month of getting to know this new side of him. This new side of myself.

"Asher," I heard on the other end of his door.

I jerked my head back when I noticed it was the voice of a woman.

I heard the slide of the peephole cover being moved out of the way, then the click of the locks, and finally the door opened.

The first thing I realized were her eyes. They were like him. The only difference was hers had faint wrinkles at the side of each one.

She blinked hard when our eyes met.

"Hello," the woman greeted.

"Hi," I returned.

"Lauryn," Asher called behind her, gesturing for me to come in. "Mom, can you please step to the side so my girlfriend can come in?"

She whipped her head so fast in his direction. "Girlfriend?"

I was still getting used to the title myself.

His lips were on my neck as he drew in the soft skin into his mouth. I never knew I could feel such pleasure having lips on my neck the way I did when Asher pressed his lips there. It had honestly become my favorite feeling he helped me experience.

"Let's make this official," he said against me.

My eyes were closed, and I really wasn't paying much attention to what he was saying. Too excited about what would come the moment we moved past kissing.

"Official, how?" I asked.

He pulled away to meet my eyes and smiled. "I want you to be my girlfriend."

My smile was pulling my lips up before I could stop them. "You want that?"

"I need that," he confirmed, pulling me close to him by my waist. He slid his hand from my waist to the top of my ass. "Can I touch you here?"

"Yes," I whispered through my smile.

He bit his bottom lip as he slid his hand over the fullest part of my ass through my gray joggers. Asher used his grip on my backside to bring me closer to him so he could kiss me.

"Will you be my girlfriend?" He sucked my bottom lip into his mouth and bit it gently, making me skip a breath.

I nodded and told him, "Yes, I'll be your girlfriend."

"Since when?!" His mother questioned. More like shrieked. She kept the apartment door opened after she made just enough room for me to step inside.

The sound of her voice made me tighten my grip around the handle of the bag I carried. Something about it didn't seem as warm as I imagined his mother's voice sounding.

Asher was so sweet. Literally the sweetest man I'd ever met. After a few weeks of getting to know him on a physical level, I gave up searching for one thing about him that had to be wrong with him. There just had to be a thing that would make him switch from being this amazing guy and into the man he truly was, showing the nasty side of his personality most guys show after getting what they wanted.

Like most guys.

Asher wasn't most guys, though. At all. I imagined his mother, the woman who raised him, would be the same, if not better.

I doubted that.

"Does it matter?" He asked, closing the space between us. When he was near, he wrapped an arm around my waist and pulled me to his side. "Lauryn, this is my mother Patricia, who was just leaving."

She scoffed.

"Mom, this is Lauryn, my girlfriend."

Her eyes bounced between us before she focused on Asher.

"I thought," she started, lifting a brow, "we *discussed* this."

He made a shrugging expression at the corners of his mouth. "I don't recall."

"Of course you do," she replied, wide-eyed.

I turned my attention up at him and couldn't help not relaxing the wrinkle in my brow.

"Mom, respectfully," he said, tightening his arm around me, "this is nor the time or the place to address whatever you're talking about. Because Lauryn is here, and we have plans. You popped up here, like always, which I'm always happy to see you, but my girlfriend and I have plans."

"Your girlfriend," she repeated, her voice losing power as she said girlfriend. "Well," she added, adjusting the lapel of her brown wool coat.

It was beautiful, along with the premium leather boots and the matching leather handbag she adjusted next over her shoulder. "We will have to do lunch or dinner. Something so I can get to know your *girlfriend*."

Again, she could barely get the last word out.

And she was pissing me off.

The only thing keeping me from expressing that was the understanding she was Asher's mother.

I had a soft spot for people's mamas after losing mine.

Asher left my side to press his hand to his mother's back to help guide her to the door.

"It was lovely meeting you, Lauryn," she said.

Her words were heavy in something I couldn't quite put my finger on and the fact she didn't bother to turn to look at me when she said it was setting off a bevy of red flags.

What the fuck was her problem?

"Sorry about that," Asher said, closing, then locking the door. "She popped up here half an hour ago, claiming she was in the area. Which, between you and me..." He approached, wrapping his arms around my waist when he was near. "Is bullshit."

I couldn't fix my face if I wanted to. Couldn't shake the feeling speaking to his mother brought over me.

Asher leaned back to look me in my eyes. "You okay?"

I twisted my lips to one side and shrugged. "I don't think she likes me."

"She doesn't like herself," he affirmed. Said it like there was no doubt about what he'd uttered. "I wouldn't give any value to her approval or disapproval." His eyes dropped to the bag in my hand. "What's that?"

That helped switch my mood.

"Something for you."

His brows shot up, and I snickered. My reaction to his reaction made him lick his lips really slowly.

"You're not supposed to get me gifts," he told me, gently taking the bag out of my hand. "I'm supposed to get you gifts."

"Oh, I'm sorry. I've never done this girlfriend thing before, so I don't know the rules."

He smiled that beautiful smile and shook his head. Asher peeled opened the top of the bag to peek inside. Saw what it was, then lifted his eyes to mine with an even bigger smile.

"It's a mug warmer," I said.

"I see that."

"You're always complaining about your coffee getting cold while you're studying, so... I figured this would help keep it warm for you."

Asher stared at me for a moment and nodded. He set the bag down on his couch behind him.

"This is incredibly thoughtful of you, sweetheart." Asher leaned against the neck of his couch and pulled me to him with my hand. "Now I have to find a better way to thank you."

I giggled. "No, you don't."

"Oh, I must." Asher licked his lips and lowered his eyes between us. "May I thank you in a way I've never thanked you before?"

I tilted my head to one side. "And what way is that?"

He smirked and tugged at my joggers' waistband. "Can I show you?"

Sex had become something of a routine between us. And by routine, I don't mean with any vibe associated with boring.

I mean our usual.

Frequent enough, I'd grown comfortable discussing it in conversation. "Okay."

Though his mother's energy left something of an aftertaste in her exit, this part of being Asher's girlfriend was exciting.

And it seemed to get better in the month we'd been together.

When we arrived in his bedroom, Asher closed his door. In front of it, he pulled up his shirt by the neck, removing it completely.

He looked great with his clothes on, always wearing something simple, but that something simple looked like it cost a lot. But nothing could compare to him naked.

Asher wasn't a big guy, by any sense of the word. His arms, chest, and abs defined, yes, and so were his legs, which I couldn't get my eyes to move off as I watched him step out of his lounge pants. Despite that, the most appealing thing about Asher, the thing that made it easy for me to agree to be in a relationship with him, were those eyes.

Like moons with an attention so warm I could feel the warmth running through me as he fixed his eyes on mine.

He placed a hand on the hem of my sweatshirt and asked, "Can I take this off of you?"

That hadn't let up. Even though I couldn't remember the number of times, this would be, we made love.

Every move he made in intimacy, from simply running his fingers through my hair, which he loved to do, to guiding himself inside of me, didn't happen unless I said it was okay.

His need for my consent was the sexiest thing about him and that's saying a lot, considering my boyfriend was fucking beautiful.

"Yeah." I nodded. "You can take it off."

"And the pants?" He asked as he lifted my shirt.

"That, too."

Asher guided me back against his mattress once all of that was off, instructing me to lie flat on my back. He hovered over me, holding himself up in a plank, and locked eyes with me.

"I want to make you come with my tongue."

My jaw dropped. "Wh-what?"

He smiled a cunning grin, then lowered himself on top of me. Kissed his way from my neck to my cheek, making me moan and needing to wrap my legs around his waist.

Sex was great, and so was coming. But this, simply having his weight on me, only like this, satisfied something in me that felt just as good as what he made my body do whenever he was inside me for long enough.

He kissed me past my lips, drawing in the lobe of my ear for only a moment. Asher released his lips and brought them to my ear to whisper, "I want to lick your pussy until you come for me, sweetheart. Can I?"

I exhaled a deep breath, feeling that area of me throb like it always did when he was this close. It always felt like my heart, and that part of me was in sync. Thumping in rhythm to a song only Asher could sing to me.

He'd never done this, though. This thing he was asking permission to do. And that alone made me curious.

"Okay."

Asher wasted no time. Kissing me from my ear to my neck again, sliding his way down the foot of the bed. He was on his knees on the floor when he pulled me to the edge.

His fingers were at the sides of my panties when he looked up at me.

Before he could ask, I told him, "You can."

He couldn't fight back the grin and I couldn't help pulling on my walls once he got those panties off and moved in close between my sprawled legs.

Asher placed a kiss against my lower lips, and I gasped. He nuzzled his nose between my trimmed hairs before opening his mouth and flicking his tongue between the folds once.

I jumped at the feeling. It both tickled me and aroused me all at once.

"Is this still okay, sweetheart?" he whispered between his kisses against my lower lips.

"Yes," I breathed.

"Good," he expressed. "Because I *really* want to keep going."

And that was the last thing he said before parting my lips with his and darting his tongue against my clit.

He'd brushed and rubbed my tiny ball with his fingers tons of times. Often, he'd massage it as he slid in and out of me during sex. But his tongue against my clit was a whole distinct sensation. A sweeping sensation that was wet and warm, and the overload of the combination had me pushing myself more into his mouth so I'd experience more of it.

Asher mimicked my hips' gyration with his tongue. My whimpers turned into moans and then pleas for him to continue.

He flicked, twirled, and sucked on me with a level of gentleness that nearly brought me to tears. Used his hands to hold me at his mouth's level while rubbing my ass, delivering the sweetest caresses.

You'd think he was getting the same pleasure he was delivering from how he moaned with me.

The sensation morphed into a pulsing that made me jolt each time the tip of his tongue glided against the roundest part of my clit. And when he sucked in the ball once again, a climatic high erupted in me and had me forgetting to breathe or be still. A moment of uncertainty because of the new feeling suddenly subsided. Replaced with my shaking, still gyrating, and sweating like crazy, while biting my bottom lip so hard I thought I'd draw blood.

Asher moved his mouth off me long enough to kiss his way up to my lips. I smelled my essence on his lips before he brought his mouth to me and I pulled him in for a kiss without thinking. I heard the crinkle of the condom. I reached down between us as he was sheathing his dick.

Could barely wait for him to get the condom on good enough before I was guiding him inside of me, which was easy to do because I was so slick.

"*Mmm*," he moaned in my mouth while sinking in deep. "Good, baby."

That was another new thing. Him calling me *baby* while we made love. The first time he whispered it in my ear, it was a second before he came and it has been a turn on ever since.

Tonight when he said it, he clasped one hand to the back of my head to hold my face in his hand as he started his first series of strokes.

I was so sensitive where we connected, the brush of his pubic hairs was causing raw friction that was competing with his deep strokes that filled me.

Asher balanced himself on his forearm while running his thumb along my cheek. Sliding in and out while gazing deep into my eyes. The bite of his teeth held his bottom lip in place and became all too much to see at once.

He only released his lip long enough to whisper, "I'm falling for you hard, baby."

"I'm falling hard too," left my mouth before I could even consider the gravity of the words I repeated. But something about saying it with Asher, acknowledging the mutual feeling, and like this, in whatever state of mind we were drifting off into together, felt so right my body agreed.

"I feel it, too," he panted, his torso quivering with mine. "I'm with you, baby. Come with me, baby."

And I did. Clinging to him, fingertips dug in deep into his back. My body humming a song only for Asher.

TWENTY-TWO

ASHER

I inhaled the air as I turned over to my other side in bed. Picked up her scent in my restful state and thought nothing of it to move closer and in her scent's direction.

Lauryn and I had never done this before, spend the night at each other's apartment. This was the first night. And to say it didn't feel good stroking her hair until she fell asleep in my arms would be a lie.

At some point in the night, my arm felt like it was falling asleep. So, I slipped her off it and turned over to fall asleep myself.

That was hours ago.

It must've been a little after three in the morning. The sky outside was pitch black. Though there was still activity outside of her window, it was light. Through her window, I could hear the sounds of cars driving over the blacktop road and the wind whistling through trees and the tiny gaps in power lines.

The temperature in her apartment was a little brisk because of that opened window. And me, lying there in just my tee and boxers, wanted to feel a little more warmth besides her blanket I covered with.

I guess in the night, Lauryn had turned over herself. There was a comfortable space between us. Her bed being queen-sized made us not have that much of a distance to travel to touch one another.

So that's what I did. I traveled the distance, even though my better judgement would've told me not to.

But I was half awake, slightly hard, and Lauryn and I had been going nonstop, making love whenever we were around each other.

I couldn't get enough of her. I'd literally move in for only a kiss and suddenly want so much more. What we had created between us was still very new. It had only been a month since we started having sex and she agreed to be my girl. There was a lot I was still learning about Lauryn in this way.

We'd just revealed to each other only a week ago that we were falling for each other when she visited my apartment, and my mother answered the door. There was still so much to learn about Lauryn. So much to learn about us.

And the learning would likely never stop, which I loved a lot. She wasn't an opened book. Lauryn only allowed herself to reveal new things every so often, so it was like finding a book with a beautiful cover with missing pages and discovering those pages scattered about during my journey, our relationship. While that would frustrate some people, it was exciting to me, honestly.

I rolled over and simply draped my arm over her waist. Though it was dark in her bedroom, there was enough light for me to make out where she laid, and to detect her body underneath the covers.

The moment I draped my arm over her waist and attempted to pull her close, Lauryn went from soundly sleeping to elbowing me hard in my chest.

"Don't touch me!" She shouted at the top of her lungs.

The blow she delivered knocked the breath out of me.

I tried to speak, but no words would come out of my mouth.

In my temporarily paralyzed state, I felt the bed move as Lauryn turned over quickly to face in my direction. And before I could make sense of what was happening, Lauryn punched me in my left eye.

I grunted. My hand flew to where she punched me. All I saw was darkness and an array of colors.

Between being half asleep and shocked out my mind by what was happening, I forgot to feel for the floor with my feet as I tried to move out of her reach and ended up falling off the bed and right onto my right knee, banging the joint against her hardwood floor.

"Ow!" I groaned. "Fuck."

If I wasn't awake before, I was now.

Feeling throbbing pain from my head to my feet. My body was hot, my mind in disarray.

The bed was moving above me and soon lights lit up the bedroom.

"Oh, my God!" Lauryn shouted, running to me. She dropped to her knees when close.

Lauryn rolled me over and through my one good eye, I saw the petrified expression on her face.

"Oh my God."

"It's okay," I pushed out. Barely.

My chest was on fire, my eye growing hot like hell, and my knee was concerning me because it was growing numb and I couldn't feel it.

"Shit." She jumped to her feet, then added, "I'll be right back."

I extended my leg and winced at the pain in my knee. Placed my hand against it and pulled back, then extended my leg once again, relieved the fall only bruised it.

Lauryn took quick steps back into the room and immediately pressed something hard and cold to my eye.

I winced again, and she sighed heavily. Or sniffled. I couldn't tell in that moment until I looked up at her to see her face wet with tears.

"No." I shook my head while pulling her by her arm to lie on me. "Come here, sweetheart. Come here."

She obliged, lying her head against my chest that still ached from her elbowing me. I cringed from the pain, ran my fingers through her hair, feeling as my eye continued to throb swollen. I knew I wouldn't be able to see through it in the morning.

"I'm sorry," she whispered against me, shaking her head. "I'm so sorry."

"It's okay," I told her, even though I wasn't.

"I felt your arms around me and I—"

"It's okay."

"It's not," she insisted, lifting her eyes to me. "Oh my God, your eye."

Lauryn raised her hand to my eye, and the gentle touch she gave it made me cringe in pain.

And more tears fell from her eyes instantly.

"Stop crying, sweetheart, please," I whispered. "I'm fine." I forced a smile next. "I was wrong."

"No, you weren't." She shook her head. "I'm just so fucking broken."

I placed my finger beneath her chin and lifted her head to look up at me.

"Don't say that."

"You didn't deserve this." She squeezed her eyes shut. "I don't deserve you."

"Aye." I tilted her head back a little more so she would refocus on me. The moment her eyes met mine. "I love you, okay?"

I'd been wanting to say that to her for a couple of weeks now. Realized it then and had been questioning why I felt love for a woman I barely knew. But it was true. I loved her.

"And I'm okay," I assured. "It's okay. We're just having a really bad first sleepover."

She scoffed a laugh. "You shouldn't be the one trying to make me feel better."

"I'll always be the one to do that. Come here." I lowered her head back against my chest and moved in close to her forehead to leave a kiss against it.

We were no doubt moving fast, but I wouldn't say that out loud. Deciding to sleep over only after a month of getting intimate was too fast. For *us*. But it felt natural. I should've known better. *We* should have known better.

I loved her, though, and saying it out loud made it even more real to me that I might have bitten off more than I could chew.

Twenty-Three

LAURYN

I woke up feeling terrible. Literally opened my eyes and couldn't fight the disappointment in myself.

My room was brightly lit by the sun shining in through my windows. Though my back was to it, I could easily see around my room with no effort.

Falling asleep after everything last night was so hard.

Although Asher assured me everything was okay, I was worried.

When he suggested he sleep over last night, I wanted to protest it. My night terrors had become the usual for me, but no one knew about them, not even my Aunt Evelyn. I promised myself I'd keep it all together, though.

Asher would only be there for one night. I told myself it would only be one night.

But then I felt his touch, which in my waking state would have been enough to make me melt against him. But, in that instance, his touch pulled me out of sleep and mentally transported me back to that abandoned house on the cold floor with my heart in my throat. Trying to scream but unable to.

I shook my head and turned over onto my back. I needed to see Asher so I could pull myself from thoughts of the worst night of my life. But when I turned over to glance in his direction, his side of the bed was empty.

I shot up from my pillow.

Heart pounding, eyes scanning all around my room.

He was gone.

His clothes he'd folded and placed on my dresser were nowhere to be found. There was no evidence he was still in my apartment.

Dread washed over me so fast my throat grew dry.

"Hey," I heard at my door.

I whipped my head so fast in that direction as my hand flew to my chest.

He paused in step.

My eyes fell on the tray in his hand that he carried. He filled it to the brim with things. Plates of eggs, bacon, pancakes, and toast. Two glasses of orange juice, and a bowl of fresh fruit.

"I thought you left," I said once I lifted my gaze to him again.

His eye.

Fuck. His eye!

The swelling had it swollen shut. Bruised like he'd just lost a bout in a boxing ring.

And the presence of it red and bruised immediately made my eyes well with tears.

Asher closed the distance between us, sitting the tray of food at the foot of my bed, then making his way over to me.

He sat in the small space between me and the edge of the bed and ran his thumb beneath my eyes, drying my tears.

"It looks worse than it feels." He smiled. "I promise."

"I'm so sorry," I whispered.

"It's okay."

She shook her head. "He raped me from behind."

Asher steeled in his seat in my bed.

"Every time." I closed my eyes and swallowed again. "And when he kidnapped me and kept me trapped in that abandoned house, he..." I exhaled. "He would attack me whenever I'd fall asleep, so sometimes, I would wake to him raping me."

"*Shh.*" Asher wrapped his arms around me and held me tight against him, and I let all my weight go in his embrace.

"I don't remember most of what happened those days of the assault, but I remembered that," I added to his chest. "I remember darkness and never seeing his face, so when you touched me and pulled me to you, I snapped without thinking."

"It's okay, Lauryn."

"It's like I couldn't control it," I continued, despite his intention to calm me down. "I just couldn't control it."

"Hey." Asher pulled back and cradled my face in his hands. "I'm okay. Did it hurt? Hell yeah. You've got a nasty right hook, sweetheart. Goddamn you hit very hard."

I scoffed a laugh.

"But I'm okay, okay?"

"It's not too late," I told him. "To end this. To get out."

He shook his head.

"I was wrong, still." I licked my lips. "And if you never wanted to talk to me again after everything that happened last night, I would completely understand."

"I'm not going anywhere." Asher brushed the pad of his thumb against my cheek. "So, you have nothing to worry about because I'm here. I'm all in. And I'm way too hooked on you to even want to leave, so let's not hear anymore about it."

I focused on his swollen eye and sighed in defeat. Leaned forward in my seat on the mattress to press my lips to the swelling and to leave a gentle kiss against his puffy eyelid before moving on to pressing my lips against his. He kissed me back, pecking at my lips twice.

"The food is getting cold." He stood to retrieve the tray from the foot of my bed.

"You made all of this?"

"Ordered it," he revealed with a smirk. "But the tray is mine."

I smiled.

"Got it from my apartment so we could have a little breakfast in bed."

"This should be the other way around," I said. "I should be the one making you breakfast in bed after what I did."

"Well." He shrugged, placing the tray to my left. Asher climbed on the bed to sit on the other side of the tray. "You got me a gift when I told you I wanted to be the one to give you gifts, so…"

I giggled.

"We're making our own rules in this relationship as we should."

I nodded, while standing to my feet to head into my bathroom to freshen up. "I'm gonna brush my teeth."

"Go for it."

After a quick brush of my teeth and wash of my face, I was back in bed, enjoying Asher's breakfast in bed. Conversation about the meal eventually shifted to talks about the upcoming holiday. We were twelve days away from Christmas, and nineteen days away from a New Year. I'd be spending Christmas with Aunt Evelyn, like always.

"I'll be on Long Island for Christmas and will travel there next Thursday," Asher announced between bites. "But New Year's Eve, I have nothing planned and would like to take you somewhere exciting."

"Somewhere like where?"

He shrugged. "I'm thinking Atlantic City."

My brows shot up.

"Ever been?"

I shook my head. "I haven't really been anywhere besides Brooklyn, to be honest. Manhattan sometimes."

"Perfect." He smiled big. "We'll drive out to AC on the 30th and spend three days and two nights out there." He winked next. "It'll be fun. I promise."

I smiled big, excited.

Little did I know, our little fun New Year's Eve trip would change my life forever.

Twenty-Four

ASHER

Only the sounds of our utensils scraping against our plates traveled around the table before my mother broke the silence with, "You won't believe what I learned when I visited your son a few weeks ago, Jonathan."

I cleaned my mouth and lifted my eyes off my plate, leaning back in my seat.

And so it begins.

Christmas at my parents. The only time my parents and I gathered around a table to eat together.

The days leading up to Christmas was the busiest in the house.

The night before Christmas Eve, we had extended family over where we exchanged gifts in front of the 17-foot Christmas tree in our sitting room. Christmas Eve, my mother hosted her high society friends and associates. There she boasted about all the wonderful things she's done that year not to be informative. To simply brag. *My house is bigger than yours, my son more handsome,* is what you'd hear her saying if you were in attendance. It used to be *my son is so smart,* but all that changed when I dropped out of my Ph.D. program at Brookville. She called them her friends and associates, but she hated them all. Still, they crowded our house until midnight, drinking and exchanging first world problems like hors d'oeuvres.

But Christmas was only for us.

Only the three of us.

Agony.

My father, Jonathan Truesdale, lifted his eyes from his phone to focus on my mother. I hadn't seen him in months. Talked to him often on the phone, our conversation always ending before the call duration timer in our phone call could reach one minute. We've never had a relationship for it to be good or bad. It was what it was.

"Oh, yeah?" He asked, eyes moving over to me, then back to her. "What did you learn?"

"He has a girlfriend."

My father's salt and pepper brow rose so high it wrinkled his forehead. "Does he now?"

He looked over at me with a smirk. "Good girl?"

My mother scoffed before I could utter a response.

"She's great," I insisted anyway.

"Ha!" My mother made her disagreement verbal this time. "Please. Jon, let's just put it this way. It wouldn't surprise me one bit if this *great girl* is the reason for his eye looking the way it does."

I shut my eyes for a moment, then quickly opened them. Although it had healed well since the week prior, the black and blue bruise had transitioned into a faint yellow and green that was still visible on my dark skin. I considered not traveling back to Long Island for the holidays because of it, but I knew that would only influence my mother popping up at my apartment yet again, so... I braced for impact.

My father tilted his head to one side. "Is that true?"

"He won't say," my mother spoke for me. "He won't tell me what happened." She kissed her teeth next. "And if it isn't her, it's that dreadful neighborhood he's taken up residence in."

"Let's change the subject please," I voiced, returning to eating my food.

Just a few more minutes to get through this meal and one more day to stay in my parents' estate and I would be back in Brooklyn. A place I'd only been living for four months, but Brooklyn felt more like home compared to the place I've lived in since birth.

Our maid returned to our table for the third time that night to refill our glasses before she returned to the kitchen with the rest of the help.

"We'll have to meet her," my father announced.

He meant my mother would have to meet her. It's like I said, this was the only time only the three of us sat for dinner together. During the Christmas holiday. Only the Christmas holiday. And it was likely my father would only remain in the house for another hour before he was gone again. To his mistress's house somewhere in the greater part of New York, perhaps. Or his duplex condo somewhere in the city that neither my mother nor I know where exactly.

Orderly dysfunction is how I identified my relationship with my parents and their relationship with each other. And neither of them has reasoned to repair any of it because to them nothing was broken. And if it isn't broken... you know the rest.

"I have been trying to get Asher to let me know the perfect time we can all meet up, but he's been mum about it all."

I forced myself not to roll my eyes.

"Lunch? Dinner?" She shrugged. "I'm not picky."

"Asher," my father spoke, eyes down on his phone. "Give your mother a time that works for you and your girlfriend so she can get to know her better. It's the right thing to do."

I clenched my teeth together and swallowed back the words I really wanted to say.

Which is *fuck no*.

I didn't want my mother anywhere near Lauryn. Only the few minutes the two of them met in front of my door earlier that month had Lauryn in her head. Lauryn's discomfort was obvious on her face after the brief meeting. It was one reason I axed our plans to go out that night, opting to stay in and make love. My mother has a way of scaring people I like out of my life and I didn't want her doing the same with Lauryn.

"I say in the New Year," my mother pushed, lifting her wineglass to sip her cherry wine. "No later. I need to get to know this girl because I swear to you, Jon, I knew your son would pursue her."

"That's interesting," my father chimed in, eyes still glued to his phone screen.

"Staring at her all smitten the night he moved in." She cleared her throat, hesitantly, as she looked at my father. "I'm sure if you were *there* though, Jon, you would've—"

"You handled it fine," my father interjected. "I don't doubt that."

"Yes, but perhaps if you were there," she continued, "you would have seen the girl for yourself and would have told him no way—"

"I said," he started, finally making eye contact with her but wearing a stern look, "you managed fine."

My father glared at me with the same stern expression on his face and told me, "In the New Year, you, your girlfriend, and your mother will sit for dinner to calm your mother's worries. Understood?"

My father had an unspoken rule. He stayed out of my way and I got to enjoy the freedom of not having my father breathing down my neck. And I was responsible for keeping my mother happy and not contributing to her worries, so he wouldn't have to calm her worries or needing to be around offering pseudo-assurance that his presence makes a difference. Which it could have. He simply did not want to be around her longer than he needed to and knew the only thing she worried about was me.

So, I conceded with a nod and told him, "Understood."

———

Lauryn stood at the wall window, staring at the view.

The bedroom in our suite faced the beach that was empty this time of year. The view didn't show the time of year we were in.

Ocean waves were calm this late afternoon, but still they created frothy white hems along the shoreline. Moving back and forth, kissing the sand, I was sure, was also cold.

I thought of walking up behind Lauryn and wrapping my arms around her, but stopped myself.

Didn't want a repeat of the first night I spent the night at her place. Especially when this trip was because of it.

Lauryn and I were in Atlantic City for New Year's Eve. We were one day away from the unofficial holiday, but the hotel we stayed in was still lively with activity.

People packed the property, and the New Year's Eve decorations sparkled everywhere, starting from the parking lot where Lauryn and I parked.

I'd rented a car in Brooklyn for our time in New Jersey. Lauryn and I drove out here. During the ride, she was quiet. Eyes and attention taking in everything around her. And I didn't interrupt her gazing. Didn't insist on having a ride that wasn't so quiet. This weekend was for her. A reason to get out of town and to offer a change of scene.

And hopefully everything worked out for the best.

She turned to look at me over her shoulder to find me staring at her from my seat at the foot of the bed.

Lauryn wore her hair down. Her sweatsuit was a bit more form fitting than the others she has in her collection. More feminine.

Definitely new.

And it was taking everything in me not to cancel our plans for the night.

"Ready to go out?"

Her brows hiked over her eyes.

"Out?" She glanced around herself. "We're going out?"

I chuckled while standing at my feet to approach. "We're definitely not about to spend our entire time in this room."

A smile pulled at her lips as I pulled her close to me. I wrapped my arms around her waist and held her a little tighter.

"I've missed you," I confessed.

Her grin blossomed into a beautiful, dazzling smile.

Those days away from her and at my parents' estate were not long, but I was getting used to seeing her often and felt her absence.

I lowered my hand to hers and threaded my fingers with hers.

"Come on." I winked. "Let's go."

The first place we visited when we left our room and then the resort was the boardwalk.

During the summers, the boardwalk was alive with energy. Long strips of wooden planks with most of Atlantic City's hotels lining the area.

Regardless of the brisk temperature outside, no doubt elevated because of the beach and ocean to our left, there were people everywhere we turned.

I held Lauryn close with my arm draped over her shoulder as we took our time walking the boardwalk and taking in the sights.

By the next day, this area would bustle with even more energy. Hosted parties would take place anywhere with a roof, and plenty where there aren't, along with fireworks shows that Lauryn and I could see from the boardwalk.

Lauryn and I would have the choice of viewing the fireworks with the crowd or in our suite. I'd purposely booked a suite that gave us a view of the beach from our bedroom and the boardwalk from our living room.

Tonight, we'd grab some drinks and play a few games at the casino.

But first we would go to dinner.

I'd reserved a table for the two of us at one of the Asian-fusion restaurants at the resort we were staying. We had to walk through the casino to get to it. Lauryn's eyes lit up as she saw all the lights and the bells and whistles of the slot machines.

Nicotine, alcohol, and the merriment of perfumes and colognes fragranced the air. There was something more potent in the air, though. One that made my girl all giddy beside me and I honestly loved to see it.

When we arrived at the Asian-fusion restaurant, the hostess seated us immediately. Patrons crowded the restaurant, which was to be expected. That was the reason I thought ahead to have a table reserved.

The smile Lauryn wore on her face the whole time was making me feel like nothing else mattered. My mind was racing with ideas about how I could make her smile grow even wider before the end of the night.

"Good evening," the server greeted before she arrived at our table. "I'm Stacia, your server for tonight."

She only addressed me, never breaking eye contact to address Lauryn as well. I thought little of it. So, I smiled politely and returned the greeting.

"Can I start you off with something to drink?"

"Yeah." I peeked down at the drink menu, running my finger down the laminated surface in search of something that would stir my interest. "I think I want to try your Mai Tai." I lifted my eyes to Stacia. "Are you all generous with the rum?"

She giggled so hard, and that made me jerk my head back a bit.

"I'll take care of you." She winked.

Now that was much.

I turned in Lauryn's direction, honestly to ask her what she wanted to drink since I noticed our server hadn't asked her yet. When I did, I saw Lauryn's jaw was tight. She narrowed her eyes up at the server and a quick glance down at Lauryn's hands showed me they were both in fists.

"Two Mai Tais will be great, thank you," I blurted in a hurry. "You can give us a few more minutes to decide what we want to order."

"A handsome man with a plan." Stacia finally moved her eyes off me to focus on Lauryn. "How lucky are *you*?"

Lauryn reared her head back, balling her lips next.

Stacia, oblivious or good at ignoring things, collected the drink menus and was on her way as I turned to face Lauryn in my seat.

We'd opted to sit beside each other in the restaurant. Really, I sat next to her because, like I said, I've missed her and wanted to spend every moment with her.

It was a wise decision.

"Hey," I said to her.

She didn't look my way. Her eyes tracked Stacia as our server visited the neighboring tables on her way to get our drinks.

"Hey," I repeated, this time taking Lauryn's chin in my hand and guiding her attention onto me.

She finally obliged and instantly the tension in her face and her body subsided.

I smiled and her shoulders relaxed a little next.

I ran my thumb along the seam of her lips, and she closed her eyes to my touch, and I swore I wanted to do a little more in that moment.

So, I did.

Leaning in for a kiss and she reciprocated, opening her mouth to let me slide my tongue into her mouth in search of hers.

But Stacia interrupted us.

Stacia returned to our table, clearing her throat and damn near slamming our Mai Tais onto the table.

Some of the drink spilled over the rims, which she needed to lean in close to us, more so me, to wipe up the liquid with a towel she kept at her waist.

"I'm sorry about that," she whispered to me.

I heard Lauryn shift in her seat.

The tension was becoming too thick.

"Have you decided what you want to order?"

She asked, again, only addressing me.

"Yes." I forced my eyes down on the menu. "*We'll* have the spring rolls, shrimp Lo Mein, fried chicken and vegetable fried rice to start. Thank you."

"And he has good taste, too." Stacia smiled.

"You know what...?" Lauryn spoke.

"Thank you," I expressed, handing the menus up to Stacia. "Here you are."

I grabbed Lauryn's hand as she was attempting to slide out of her seat as Stacia walked off.

Stacia checked over her shoulder at Lauryn when she was at a distance, still heading to the other end of the restaurant.

"Sweetheart—"

"I'll be right back," Lauryn interjected. She tried to slide out of our booth again, but I tightened my grip around her waist.

"Where are you going?"

As if I didn't already know.

"I'm just gonna *talk* to our server."

"Talk?"

"*Mmm-hmm,*" she answered through a tight jaw.

"Don't look like you want to just talk."

"She's a fucking bitch," she blurted, a little too loud. Loud enough to draw attention from two neighboring tables of patrons. "So you're right, I *don't* want to talk because you don't *talk* to bitches."

"*Shh,*" I shushed, moving in close enough to wrap my arm around her waist and to pull her near me. "I'll handle it."

"No, *I'll* handle it," she argued. Lauryn tried to pull her arm free, and I tightened my grip a little more.

"Do you trust me?"

Her chest was heaving, lips balled so tight it was leaving wrinkles on her lips. I could tell it was taking everything in her not to hit me just to get me out of the way so she could get to the server, but I wouldn't let that happen.

No good would come from it, and that went without saying.

Lauryn swallowed hard, but still gave me no answer.

"Sweetheart, do you trust me?"

"Yes," she said and exhaled a long, deep breath that relaxed her shoulders again.

"I promise I will handle it," I repeated. "Can you trust that, too, please?"

She was reluctant to respond at first, but eventually answered with a nod.

"No." I shook my head. "You know I can't hear that."

"I will trust that too," she said, fighting back her smile.

A few minutes later, another server delivered our food to our table. Once we started eating, Lauryn was back to her giddy self. Close to twenty minutes later, our plates were close to empty when Stacia returned to our table to check on us.

Well... to check on me.

"How's it going?" She asked, attention on me. "How's the food and your drink?"

"Both are great, thank you." I lifted my napkin to clean my mouth. "And I'm sure my girlfriend would agree. However, we may have a difference of opinion regarding the quality of our service being the same."

Stacia tilted her head to one side, feigning confusion.

"Your lack of communication with her has made her uncomfortable and her discomfort is mine, too."

"Oh." Stacia fanned her hand in the air and focused on Lauryn. "It's nothing personal, girl. I figured he was the one paying—"

"That has very little to do with anything," I interjected.

Stacia rolled her eyes and Lauryn kissed her teeth.

"Is there anything else I can get for you tonight?"

"Yes, there is," I replied with as much patience as I could muster up to keep a calm voice. "I would appreciate if I could get an apology for my lady. She doesn't feel like she received the same service as I did tonight and, as I said before, I agree with her."

"Well," Stacia started, glancing at Lauryn. "I apologize if you felt—"

"Not *if*," I interjected again. "Because she felt what you wanted her to feel."

Stacia tucked her lips into her mouth and shifted her weight onto her other foot.

"Look." I folded my hand on the table. "I would love for us to mediate this situation between the three of us because I would hate to get the manager involved. Not so close to the holiday, you know?"

Stacia blinked hard. "That's unnecessary."

"That's what I figured."

"I apologize," she stated to Lauryn. "I can appreciate a good man when I see one and you clearly have a good man." Stacia glanced over at me and licked her lips. "I just wanted to be polite."

"No, you wanted to be a flirt," Lauryn said, in an eerily calm voice. "And you're right, I have a good man. Because, thanks to him, you get the privilege of keeping all your teeth and taking them with you into the new year. Now, how lucky are *you*?"

"Excuse me?" Stacia exclaimed.

"Oooh, girl." Lauryn sighed. "Don't make me repeat myself. Because if I have to, I'll have to say it to your face and you don't want me that close."

"Lauryn." I squeezed her leg that was bouncing under the table.

Stacia's jaw dropped.

"We'll take the check," I said, forcing a smile at Stacia. "As soon as you can."

"Yeah," Stacia replied, "I'll have it over to you as soon as possible. You have a good night."

"Thanks, *we'll* have a great one," Lauryn shot back.

Stacia quickly turned on her feet and walked away.

I turned to Lauryn, and she shrugged, picking up the last of her spring roll off her plate and bringing it to her lips.

"What?" she asked, stuffing the roll into her mouth. "I didn't hit her."

I chuckled. "You didn't hit her."

I leaned in for a kiss, and Lauryn met me halfway.

"Progress," she said with a wink.

———

I awoke to a hand sliding down my abs and fingers disappearing into the waistband of my boxers.

Couldn't be too sure at first since I was still feeling the aftereffects of having way too much to drink.

After leaving the Asian restaurant, Lauryn and I stopped at a few of the casino tables and accepted a few rounds of the complimentary drinks as we played.

The casino was busy and the energy super live. Because it was the night before New Year's Eve, everyone was in great spirits, making the scene one that neither Lauryn nor I wanted to tear ourselves away from.

I lost a lot of money between the blackjack table and the slot machines. But it didn't matter. Seeing Lauryn laugh from her gut and smile so wide I could count all her teeth was a sight to behold. I didn't know what it was about this woman, but she made me want to give her everything I could just to see her face do the things it did when she was feeling good.

Regarding feeling good, the hand and fingers were inches away from my dick when I felt her lips by my ear, succeeding without a doubt with getting me up and out of sleep.

"Asher," she whispered.

And my name had never sounded sweeter.

I inhaled a deep breath and turned my head to look her way.

We'd forgotten to draw the curtains closed over the wall windows, so random lights around the resort and from neighboring hotels lit up our room. There were parties happening all over the boardwalk and surrounding strip. It had to be after midnight, but you wouldn't know it from the bevy of flashing lights all around.

I groaned when she tightened her grip around my dick. Folded in my bottom lip to bite as I turned to face her.

I took Lauryn's face into my hands and pressed my lips to hers, tasting the faint taste of liquor heavy on her tongue.

She moaned in my mouth, and I moved in closer, breaking our kiss long enough to ask, "Is this okay?"

Lauryn didn't reply. Instead, she moved in again and kissed me. She kissed me harder than the first time.

I slid my hand down her face and was journeying my touch down her neck, then her shoulders. By the time I got to her back, I realized she was completely naked already.

I pulled my lips from hers and she followed me.

"Sweetheart," I tried, taking her face into my hands. "Where are your clothes?"

She licked her lips as she leaned her weight into me to guide me down onto my pillow. Her simple move billowed the air between us beneath the covers. And her scent found its way to my nose.

I sucked in the air through my teeth. This was not how we'd discussed doing things. And while I would've loved to throw caution to the wind, to go with the flow, Lauryn's reaction to me trying to pull her to me in the middle of the night a few weeks prior wouldn't let me.

We had a process. We agreed to talk through this. And she didn't look or feel like she wanted to talk tonight.

"Lauryn," I said to her, pressing my hands gently into her shoulder. "Where are your clothes, sweetheart?"

"I want you," she whispered. More like slurred.

It's like I said, between the Mai Tais we ordered at the restaurant and the more than a few cocktails she and I sucked down through tiny red straws at the casino tables, Lauryn and I had enough drinks to have us stumbling a little through our hotel room door earlier when we returned to the suite.

"You're drunk, sweetheart."

"And horny," she claimed through a giggle.

I scoffed a laugh, feeling all the same but still feeling like doing it like this wasn't the best for us.

I had little time to think of a better way, though. Because a moment later, Lauryn kicked one leg over me to straddle me. She leaned forward in her seat over me to crush her lips against mine.

I groaned in defeat. Her mouth on mine, her hot pussy warming the area where my dick was firming up. The slit in my boxers was becoming more and more non-existent as my dick tried like hell to poke through it.

She moaned when she noticed it. Reached down between us to maneuver the hardness through the tiny opening.

"Baby, baby, baby," I uttered beneath my breath. "Wait."

My protesting wasn't assertive enough, though. I wasn't even convincing myself.

Because when Lauryn pulled me out by the shaft and lifted high enough on her knees so she could sit back on my erection, every muscle in my body relaxed.

She rolled her hips, albeit out of sync. Her body shuddered and her hip movements were inconsistent. But her inexperience did nothing to quell how fucking good she was making me feel as she slid me in and out of her pussy.

I dropped my head back and gave in. Placing my hands on each of her cheeks, helping to guide us both to a release.

Lauryn was a fast and determined learner, quickly catching on to the direction and the speed I needed her to move in. Soon she was feeling what I was feeling, and we were in sync.

I lifted my head to focus on her. Watching as her full breasts swelled from each breath she inhaled and how the movements she administered made them sway before my eyes.

I pushed myself up to suck on her nipple. My mouth was already on the tight skin before I remembered to ask her permission. She gave it, holding my head there. Pushing herself even more onto me, smothering me with her thick hips and rocking herself back and forth over me.

Slick sounds materialized between us.

I just knew my boxers were wet with her juices.

"You... feel... so good," she stuttered. Her torso vibrated each time she rode me in deep and I met her speed with well-timed upstrokes.

With nothing between us, I could feel everything. Her walls quivering and wet around me. The soft flesh inside her that was swelling each time I grazed it with my strokes.

I grabbed her by one of her thighs and leaned my body's weight against her, changing our position so I was now on top of her. I pulled out long enough to get rid of my boxers and slid in again, shuddering with my return.

Lauryn held onto her bottom lip with her top teeth while clamping her hands on each of my ass cheeks.

We both were loud now. Her wetness sounding so juicy between us as I sexed us both through a high I could no longer control.

I gazed down at her in my drunken, lucid state, and she looked up at me. I wanted to ask if this was okay. I wanted to pull on our usual thing of checking in with each other, so I knew she was with me.

But the twinkle in her eyes said it all.

She nodded and smiled a little, her teeth still holding the fullest part of her lip in a bite.

We both trembled and shuddered in my last attempt to keep stroking.

I was close, right there, and prepared to pull out, but her walls pulled me in, and her thighs squeezed so tight around me. I decided mindlessly in that moment, I wasn't going anywhere or doing anything but coming.

"*Ahh*," I roared into the silent room, and she gasped beneath me, gyrating her hips and shaking beneath me. Lauryn clung to me as I continued to stroke without control, riding the last of my release with no sense of restraint. I drove into her with literal reckless abandon. Our wet body parts clapping so aggressively, the sounds of our act echoed around us. Lauryn clung even tighter to me as I slammed in and out of her wet tightness. Even if I could stop myself, I couldn't. So I let it be.

At the end of it all, I collapsed on top of her and her arms fell to either side of her. Once I could, I pushed myself up high enough to check on her. Her chest rose and fell with each breath she took. Her eyes locking on mine.

For a second, I was worried.

Our act in those last few seconds was the roughest we'd ever done it.

I was trying to pull in air fast enough to talk when she lifted her hand to my face and caressed it gently.

"I'm okay." She nodded. "I'm good."

"Are you sure?" I panted.

"One hundred percent." Lauryn wrapped her arms around the back of my neck to guide me down to her lips. She told me, "I wanna do it like that again," right before she parted my lips with hers and slid her tongue in so softly. I moaned the moment our tongues touched.

The night was different on so many levels. And it was the start of something besides a new year.

Twenty-Five

2 MONTHS LATER...

LAURYN

"Shit," I whispered, then swallowed hard.

I shook my head as I stared down at the bathroom's vanity.

The words stared right back at me, and I still shook my head a second time, not convinced.

"No, no, no," I said in a chant, turning away quickly and dashing out of my bathroom and into my bedroom.

A bouquet of red roses and the card it arrived with laid on my bed. I bypassed it and headed straight to my night table to grab the box.

It was the morning of Valentine's Day. Half an hour to noon and already the day was starting off in a way I did not love or expect.

Asher had the flowers delivered to me and thankfully I was home to receive them. In his mind, I'm sure, he believed I would be home to accept the roses from the delivery guy. He probably would have never imagined I would be at a pharmacy the moment it opened to buy a double pregnancy test.

It was only a thought to take one.

I'd been late by a few weeks, too many weeks, and I just wanted to be sure.

The idea never crossed my mind that it would give me the result advertised on the box.

I took large steps towards the bathroom, pulling out the second test stick and raising the wrapper to my mouth to rip it opened with my teeth.

I glanced at the test stick I'd peed on a few moments prior and saw "pregnant" staring up at me again.

The shit might as well be in red and flashing brightly behind the test window.

I shook my head anyway. Pulled down my varsity shorts again and waited for a stream of pee to fall on the absorbent tip.

I couldn't stop my legs from bouncing on the arches of my feet. Couldn't keep my heart from pounding like it was trying to pound the fuck out of my chest.

To say I was freaking out would be a lie. I was slowly dying on the inside at the idea of what being pregnant would mean.

Because I couldn't be pregnant.

I placed the new test stick on the counter closest to me as I remained on the toilet. Dropped my head into my hands and dug my fingertips into my strands, pressing the pads of them into my scalp.

Atlantic City. It had to have happened in Atlantic City, and it was all my fault.

Asher would give me anything I wanted. It was something I knew after that night.

We didn't use condoms at all during our time in AC. Sex in the jacuzzi, sex on the suite's bathroom vanity. After the first night when I got up from sleep, still drunk and very horny. Deciding to rid myself of my clothes before trying to wake him up, I didn't plan for us to make love without a condom. We had them. Asher got them and they were in his bag. But I didn't want to bother with them and, as always, he gave me what I wanted.

There was no telling which time did it. Probably the first night. Likely the last.

A part of me was sad that we would have to return to reality. It was our last night in Atlantic City. The days were so much fun and the nights were everything.

We'd eaten at most of the restaurants at the resort we stayed at. Ventured out of the resort to check out the lighthouse not far away. But the most exciting part of the stay was returning to the suite every night and getting into bed with Asher.

Tonight was no different.

We hadn't opened the condom box once. Tonight, it sat on the night table closest to Asher's side.

Unopened.

Untouched.

I was in his face, like always since we've been here, pressing kisses along his face and him smiling from the attention.

I'd crawled my way close enough to straddle him. I still had on my bra and panties and he, his boxers. Still, he maneuvered himself out of the slit and simply slid my panties to the side.

And I took my seat. With no hesitation. No thought. Like how I'd been doing since we arrived.

I'd gotten better in this position. Rolling my hips to my favorite song, I imagined playing in my ear. Falling more and more in love with Asher's touch as he ran his hands up and down my body, massaging and grabbing at my ass as I slid him in and out with only my hips.

His eyes locked with mine and I smiled, leaning forward to kiss him as I rode him.

And he loved it.

Moaning and groaning in my mouth while wrapping an arm around my waist. Using his other hand to grip the back of my neck and to use his grasp to push himself more into me.

I'd found a new love in this position. Being able to feel him everywhere while being so close. I'd made peace with this feeling. Being full of him inside me. Curious how far in he could go and he could go far. It didn't jar me anymore. The pleasure had gotten better in the short time we'd been intimate. Because Asher shared control. He let me control the speed and the timing. Patient in every way, allowing me to explore and to find what I enjoyed sitting on top of him.

But like always, Asher changed positions on me. Instead of remaining connected though, tonight he slid out and replaced his dick with his tongue.

My jaw slacked, and I grabbed the back of his head as he flicked his tongue, then licked around the bulb of my clit. Sucked with his mouth and caressed my body with his hands, guiding his fingers up to my lips so that I could suck on them.

It was insane how in touch with my body I got whenever he pleased me.

I never thought I could find peace or comfort in pleasure like this, but with Asher, all things were possible.

I was close when he kissed his way up and guided himself inside of me, placing his fingers against my clit. My man sexed me and rubbed between my thighs until I couldn't figure out which source of pleasure to give agency to. So I gave into it all, feeling him give in too. Shuddering against me as he spurted warmth inside of me, rocketing us both into bliss.

And now I had to pay for it.

I was almost scared to lift my head out of my hands to glance to my right to check the test strip.

In my time of silence, I already knew what it would say.

It would match what the other one said.

And sure enough, after I lifted my head and did the thing I didn't want to do, I read "pregnant" on the new test stick too.

I shut my eyes and exhaled a long breath.

My phone rang a second later.

I stretched my neck beyond the positive test sticks and pointed my eyes on my phone's screen to see it was Asher calling.

My heart dropped.

This whole time I was thinking about myself and how I felt about this new situation that had become my situation only seconds ago. Not once did I consider how Asher would feel.

What would he say?

How would he feel?

The device continued to flash and vibrate on the vanity until I finally picked up the device to answer it.

"Hey."

"Hey, sweetheart," he said back. Even through the phone, I could tell he was smiling. "Got the flowers I sent you?"

Only the mention of them made me smile from my heart. "I did. They're beautiful. Thank you."

"You're beautiful, and you're more than welcome."

I was quiet for a moment, my eyes on their own, moving to the test sticks. I felt the wind leave my lungs with each breath.

"Are you okay?"

I sat up straight. "Yeah, yes. I'm fine. Why?"

"You sound like everything isn't."

I bit at my bottom lip.

I couldn't do it. I couldn't tell him. Not in that instance.

Because I wasn't sure how he would react. And Asher was a great guy who I didn't want to lose. A baby might make me lose him.

"I'm fine," I repeated. "I was... *ummm*..." I ran my fingers through my hair, desperate for a thought. "I was a little busy."

"Well, don't get too busy." He chuckled. "I'll be there to get you in an hour or two. I got some things planned. I can't wait to do them with you."

I bit my bottom lip as I smiled. "Some things, huh?"

He laughed sexily, and that got a little laugh out of me.

"I can't wait to see you," he whispered. I closed my eyes at the sound of his voice in my ear.

God, I loved him.

But I didn't love this... keeping something from him.

I was parting my lips to tell him I had something to tell him when he said, "Oh, before I forget... my mother has lost all patience about having to wait any longer to have dinner with the two of us, so I settled on next Saturday with her."

My eyes ballooned.

"Is that okay?"

"*Ummm...*"

"I know, sweetheart," he said in the most empathetic tone.

His pet names of sweetheart and baby did something to me and always let me know if he was being serious or sensual. I loved hearing them both, honestly.

"I'm not thrilled about it either," he continued, "but I'm also kind of happy too because now she'll get to see how amazing you are and why I'm so in love with you."

I squeezed my eyes closed and dropped my head. Lifted it shortly after to tell him, "Okay. Cool."

No, it wasn't. There wasn't anything cool about it. Not after I'd just found out I was pregnant with the woman's grandchild, and she probably wouldn't be happy about that.

But shit, it was better than putting it off for another week. Asher's mother has been pestering him about having dinner, just the three of us. Asher told me his father wouldn't be there. Explained his father was hardly around, so I shouldn't expect to see him much. But with his mother, as Asher explained to me, she needs constant reassurance that everything is fine with Asher or else she meddles.

"Once she meets you," Asher added, "We won't hear from her as often. It's how she is."

I nodded. "Then next Saturday is perfect."

I mean... what's the worst that could happen at dinner, anyway?

Twenty-Six

ASHER

I swear my mother chose the fanciest restaurant she could find in Manhattan.

I shook my head as I scanned the room. It was early evening, but patrons packed the space. Not a single vacant table available. The only reason *we* had a table was because my mother had one reserved.

By *we*, I mean my mother, Lauryn, and myself. As expected, my father was nowhere to be found.

My mother cleared her throat as she raised her menu to her eyes to peruse the selections.

She didn't tell me there would be a dress code at the restaurant. But the hostess and the restaurant's managers looked past it being that my mother was the wife of *the* Jonathan Truesdale, real estate magnate to the stars and, I, his son.

But here we all sat, my mother dressed in a forest green wrap dress with dainty, expensive jewelry sparkling in her ear, around her neck, and her wrists while Lauryn and I dressed ourselves like we were just swinging by the market to pick up milk.

Lauryn shifted in her seat as she forced her eyes to remain on the menu. In a gray joggers suit, her hair up in a messy bun and me in a black pullover hoodie, jeans, and white tennis sneakers, my girlfriend and I couldn't look anymore out of place.

And it occurred to me that's how my mother wanted it to be.

"See anything interesting, Lauryn?" my mother asked, not looking up from her menu.

Lauryn lifted her eyes out of the menu book to focus on my mother first and then me. "The chicken sounds good."

"Chicken?" my mother scoffed. "Everyone knows this place for their filet mignon and caviar, and you want *chicken*? Darling."

Lauryn tucked her lips into her mouth and refocused on the menu.

"The chicken sounds good to me too," I insisted, my eyes fixed on Lauryn.

She looked in my direction, and I winked at her. That brought a smile to her face, which I loved.

I glanced over at my mother to see her staring right at me now.

"I think we all should have the filet mignon," she decided, closing the menu book, then raising her arm in the air to get the attention of our server.

We'd only been in the restaurant for about ten minutes and already I was ready to go.

This dinner was definitely more for my mother and less for anyone else, and I wanted her to know that more than anything.

"If you wanted for us to have what *you* liked, Mom," I started. "*You* should have ordered ahead. Speed this up a bit more."

"Now, why would I want to speed this up?" My mother looked at Lauryn, her judgmental eyes scanning my girlfriend from her head to any place my mother could see above the table. "I want all the time I can get so I can learn everything there is to learn about Lauryn, and I would imagine she'd want to do the same with me."

I clenched my teeth.

At least patrons crowded the environment. Their presence forced me to keep it together and to stretch the strength of my patience, which was necessary for dealing with a woman like my mother.

The server arrived at our table and, in controlling fashion, my mother ordered our meals for us down to the dessert, which would be a crème brûlée.

"So," my mother started as the server walked off. "What do you do, Lauryn?"

I sat up in my seat. "Mom, please."

"What?"

I sighed.

"I can't ask what she does?"

"I do nothing right now," Lauryn answered. "I had a job at a club, but that didn't work out very well for me."

"A club?" My mother repeated. "Well... what do you do with your days now?"

Lauryn shrugged. "I read a lot."

"*Uh-huh*." My mother rolled her eyes and focused elsewhere for a moment. "Asher is in a Ph.D. program with plans to open his own practice as a psychologist. Do you have any long-term goals, or do you plan to just *read* for the rest of your life?"

"Can we get the food before you lambaste my girlfriend right in front of me?" I spat.

My mother held her hand up in front of her in mock surrender.

I peeked over at Lauryn and saw her press her hand to her chest and swallow back something. In response, I reached over to press my hand to her knee.

"You okay, sweetheart?"

She straightened her back in her seat and quickly nodded.

"No," my mother pushed, and I rolled my eyes. "What is it, Lauryn?"

"It's nothing," Lauryn said with the raise of her hand. "It's just... that... the smell of red peppers is very strong in here."

"Red peppers?" My mother sniffed the air. "You smell red peppers... specifically?"

Lauryn nodded, cringing and swallowing something back again. She gagged a little before reaching for her glass of water to drink.

My mother reared her head back.

I tilted my head to one side myself.

Our server returned to our table right on time, forcing us to focus on our meals.

Even with our plates in front of us, and our attention expectedly on eating, my mother still got in as many questions as she wanted.

Inquiries about Lauryn's city of birth. The schools she's attended. Why hasn't she traveled out of the country? Why didn't she choose to go to college?

"I didn't know what I wanted to study," Lauryn answered. "And I didn't want to waste money trying to figure it out while there."

"*Hmph*." My mother huffed before forking a piece of the well-done beef into her mouth. "You're not doing much of anything right now, so would it have been a terrible thing to figure it out in college?"

I briefly shut my eyes and sighed as I reached for my wine. My glass was almost done, so I raised my hand to motion at our server for a refill.

"This is going to be your second glass, Asher," my mother reminded. "And you have yet to touch your food."

I glanced at Lauryn, who was looking back at me. Her cheek was bulging with food as she stretched her arm in front of her to reach for the salt. At least she was enjoying the meal because my mother's company was getting worse by the minute. At least to me.

"I need more," I insisted, smiling at the server who knew to arrive at our table with another bottle of the wine we'd ordered.

Lauryn's wine still filled her glass. She hadn't touched it. But she was on her third glass of water.

"What do your parents do, Lauryn?"

I coughed, clearing my throat when the wine went down the wrong pipe.

Lauryn chewed the last of her meal and swallowed hard. "My... mother passed away when I was younger and my father's not around right now."

I exhaled a silent sigh of relief.

I knew little about Lauryn's past. She didn't speak of her mother much and her father, I already knew, was in prison. I didn't want her to hide that fact because why he was in prison should deserve a medal of honor. But I also didn't want my mother to form an even more skewed impression than she's already formed about Lauryn with that new knowledge.

"*Hmph*," my mother huffed again. "That's... interesting."

Lauryn took another bite of her food and was reaching for the salt again.

My mother's brows gathered over her eyes. "Is it not salty enough?"

Lauryn focused on my mother.

Mom giggled. She forked another piece of beef into her mouth. "Everyone raves over this restaurant's filet mignon and the decadent flavors they infuse into the meat, and yet you are salting it to the high heavens."

I shook my head and lifted my fork and knife to cut into the meat and to taste it.

And my mother was right. The chefs flavored the meal well, well-seasoned. Delicious and not needing to be salted.

My mother giggled as she cut into her meat, shaking her head for emphasis. "You're saying you smell red peppers, of all things, and you're salting your food with every bite. If I didn't know any better, I'd think you were pregnant."

I chuckled at that, dropping my head a little, lifting my head again to share in the humor with Lauryn.

But she wasn't laughing.

"That's ridiculous," I stated to my mother, my attention moving to Lauryn again to see her motionless in her seat.

My mother's eyes bounced between the two of us, her smile slowly shrinking. "Is it?"

Lauryn still had said nothing. Hadn't moved an inch either. Not even her eyes to glimpse my way, to give me any kind of assurance.

Sudden awkwardness fell on our table.

I jerked my head back.

"Oh, dear God," my mother exclaimed in nearly a whisper. "I was only joking."

I ignored my mother, choosing to fasten my eyes on Lauryn instead. "Lauryn?"

My heart was now picking up the pace in my chest. The room feeling like it was in the beginning stages of spinning.

I watched Lauryn swallow hard, then turn her head to face me. "*Ummm*," she started, before tucking her lips into her mouth.

My mother made a shrieking noise that traveled around the restaurant, garnering a lot of attention. She was out of her seat next, the chair she sat on falling to the floor behind her.

"Oh, God!" My mother clutched her chest. "I can't breathe."

I reached over to Lauryn so she'd say something. Tell me this was all a mistake. I was hoping she would crack a smile; tell me she was indeed not what my mother joked about, at least.

But all Lauryn did was dart her eyes away and told me, "I'm so sorry."

———

"Whisky," Summer decided the moment she opened the door. "We need whiskey."

Everything was all a blur. Me trying to calm my mother down well enough to escort her out of the restaurant, albeit still in shock. Me returning inside to handle the check, order a ride share vehicle for Lauryn so she could take it back home.

The only thing that was clear to me was hopping in a yellow cab to take crosstown to my cousin Summer and her fiancé Jayce's condo.

Summer left me at the door as she walked away to approach her home bar.

Jayce was feet away. All he could do was grab my shoulder and give it an empathetic squeeze while gesturing toward the island in their kitchen.

"This is a fucking nightmare," I uttered the moment I took a seat on the stool at the island.

I'd called them and asked if I could stop by at the last minute. I was in a complete daze. Playing back what happened at the restaurant. It all felt unreal.

Tonight was supposed to only be a dinner. We eat, get through the night, and I wouldn't have to deal with my mother until the next holiday or the next time she popped up unannounced.

Not this.

Pregnant.

What the fuck!

The slam of the high-end whiskey bottle as Summer placed it on the island's counter made a thud. She rounded the counter just as quick. Her long black hair feathering the air before she arrived in front of the kitchen cabinets. She pulled down two shot glasses, walking them over to me.

"Thank you," I said to her when she placed both shot glasses down in front of me. How she knew I'd need two shots of something hard I didn't know. But I was grateful.

Summer poured the first glass, and I was reaching for it before she lifted it off the counter and tossed it back.

"Whew," she sighed. "I *so* needed that."

I looked up at her, shocked. I glanced over at Jayce to find him snickering and shaking his head.

I couldn't help but to laugh as I grabbed the empty glass and poured myself a shot of whiskey.

"To the end of my life," I voiced, holding the glass up in a toast before tossing the whiskey to the back of my mouth.

"It isn't the end," Jayce assured, as I reached for the bottle to pour myself another glass.

"She's fucking pregnant," I said out loud. "The more I say it, the more I can't believe that she's fucking pregnant."

"How the *hell* did this happen, Asher?!" Summer hollered. "Mother said Aunt Patricia called her frantic. She could barely understand your mother through her hysterical crying."

I balanced my elbow on the island so I could drop my head into my hand. "New Year's Eve," I revealed. "We were away, got a little carried away with the nights. Didn't use protection once.

Summer sighed.

"I thought nothing of it." I shook my head. "It was just one or two times."

"It only takes one or two times," Summer replied.

"Baby," Jayce said gently. "Can you just... take a seat? You're shaking and this really isn't about you."

"To hell it isn't. I'm going to be an aunt," Summer avowed, pressing her manicured fingers to her chest. "And I must be a rich one. I'm broke and there's not enough time for me to change that. This is terrible! The worst."

Jayce squeezed his eyes closed.

I chuckled at the whole thing.

The news. Summer's reaction. My mother's near-death expression she wore the entire time after Lauryn revealed through her omission that she was pregnant.

Pregnant.

What the fuck!

"How does she feel about all of this?" Jayce asked.

"What?"

"Lauryn," Jayce continued. "How does she feel about all of this?"

I lowered my eyes from his and searched the counter for the answer. Went back to my memory to recall anything she said in reaction to us finding out she was pregnant.

"I... I don't know." I was up and out of my seat, pacing now. "Shit. I didn't ask."

Summer's jaw dropped. "Excuse me?"

I stopped pacing and shook my head to gather my thoughts. "Right after Mom made the comment, everything unfolded so quickly. I had to get Mom out of there and I did, then I put Lauryn in a ride share—"

"Well..." Summer fanned her hands in the air. "What did she say before you put her in the ride share, Asher?"

"Nothing."

Jayce cringed.

"Oh, my God." Summer pressed her hand to her chest. "Asher, she's probably freaking the fuck out, too. But alone and all by herself."

Shit.

"I have to go."

I was taking steps toward their door before they could say anything. Ordering a ride share before I could get out of the elevator.

The ride back to Brooklyn happened in slow motion.

Time seems to slow down when you have a lot of things weighing down the mind.

Out of the car, up the elevator, and on the fifth floor in front of Lauryn's apartment door, I didn't hesitate to ring the bell, then knock on the surface for good measure.

She appeared at the doorway shortly after. And when she opened the door, my heart broke in two.

Her eyes were red rimmed. Her nose was even redder.

She'd been crying.

I pulled her to me so fast, her head hitting my chest made a thud.

Lauryn's shoulders shook as she cried against me, and I held her so tight I could feel the pain she felt.

And I felt like shit.

I pushed my mouth into her hair, kissing her there several times while holding her against my chest.

And Lauryn clung to me. She held onto me like letting go was not an option.

"I'm sorry, sweetheart," I whispered against her. "I'm so sorry."

Twenty-Seven

LAURYN

For the second day in a row, I'd slept until noon. Since the dinner the Saturday before, getting up had been a struggle, and I wasn't sure if it was pregnancy symptoms kicking in or if it was something else. Depression?

Asher stayed with me from Saturday night and until Sunday evening. There wasn't a lot of talking. Only a lot of me laying in his arms and him placing kisses on my head or my forehead.

Saturday night, after his mother joked about me being pregnant and me not having the sense to deny it, everything seemed to fall apart.

It wasn't real to me, the pregnancy. I'd literally only found out the week before and had been trying to forget somehow... I think.

I don't know.

I wasn't sure if I wanted to tell Asher to begin with, so I don't know why I didn't laugh or calm either of their worries.

Why didn't I just lie?

My phone vibrating on my night table got my attention.

I peeked that way before turning over completely, to extend my hand behind me to scoop up my device.

Expecting it to be my aunt, who probably wanted to know why I missed Sunday dinner. Or even Asher, calling to check on me.

It was neither of them.

I didn't recognize the number, so that made it easy to ignore the call. Prepared to place the phone back on the night table's surface, the call came in again. From the same number.

This time I answered with plans to tell the caller to fuck off and to stop calling me because they had the wrong number.

"Lauryn," her voice poured in after I said hello.

And I instantly recognized it.

"It's me, Patricia Truesdale," she confirmed. "Asher's mother. Do you remember me?"

As if that could ever be a valid question after Saturday night.

She said nothing to me after I failed to deny what she was only joking about.

She looked like she died a little inside when my silence made loud and clear I was pregnant with her son's child.

Patricia had made it no secret, nor did she ever try to hide her feelings. She didn't like me. She probably wouldn't have an issue seeing me around whenever she visited her son in his building. But she certainly didn't like me being her son's girlfriend.

"Lauryn, are you there?"

"Yes," I confirmed. "I'm here."

"Good." She cleared her throat, then added, "How are you?"

"Okay, I guess."

There was silence on the line for a moment.

Why was she calling me?

"Look," she started. "I'm not going to beat around the bush with you. Asher did not give me your phone number. I had to get it on my own by searching you up, and when I searched you up, I learned some disturbing things about you."

My heart tanked.

"Darling, while I'm terribly sorry about what happened to you. Terribly…"

My heart was hammering now.

"We have to be honest in the situation and unfortunately, I will have to be blunt with you." She took a breath. "You *cannot* have this baby."

I couldn't.

I didn't even want to be pregnant.

I'd been trying to figure out how to say this to myself and to take the action to make it so I wasn't pregnant anymore. But every time I brought myself to look up a local clinic that could make me un-pregnant, I couldn't click any of the links that popped up to book an appointment, nor could I press the numbers to contact the facility.

"Asher…" she sighed. "Asher is in no position to be a father and *you*… well, you…"

I twisted my lips to one side.

"Darling, you wouldn't make a fit mother."

I said nothing.

"You aren't working, you aren't in school. It sounds as if you've just gotten up for the day judging by the froggy sound in your voice."

I swallowed hard.

"You have no plans for your future, and your past is just so—"

"I know!" I interjected, hollering it into the phone and feeling hot tears gather in my lower lids.

Patricia gasped on the line, then cleared her throat. I guess she was trying to get herself together.

She was throwing her perception at me so easily. It was both making me angry and breaking my heart. Asher assured me he loved me and that I was perfect for him, but I knew deep down I wasn't.

We were from two different worlds. His so wonderfully built and mine ripped out experiences with frayed ends for pain, glued together to create the most fucked up collage.

I had no business being anyone's mother.

"I can help, is what I'm trying to tell you, Lauryn."

I blinked the tears back, not wanting one to fall.

"I can make an appointment at a very good clinic, and we can handle it... privately."

My brows knitted over my eyes.

"Asher doesn't have to know."

Which would probably be best, right?

Though he had expressed no negative feelings about me being pregnant, not once. Not at the restaurant, not when he finally showed up at my door after sending me home from the restaurant in a ride share without a word. Even as he spent the rest of his weekend with me, making sure I was okay. He had expressed no emotions whatsoever. And I know that was to protect my feelings. He had to be freaking out. Asher had his entire future ahead of him. There was no telling we would last more than a few more months, if I'm lucky?

"I'll take care of it," Patricia continued. "I'll make the appointment and will stop by your apartment building with a car to take you to and from the clinic after the procedure. I'll pay for everything. All you need to do is show up. How does that sound?"

I nodded before saying, "Sure. Yeah, sounds good."

"Perfect," she replied. It was the happiest I'd ever heard her sound in the short time of knowing her. "I'll find out when their next appointment is and will book it. And Lauryn?"

I said nothing in response.

"Don't tell Asher, okay?"

I sighed into the phone.

"He doesn't need to know," she advised. "This is your choice. Your body. You understand more than he does, being a mother isn't a good thing for either of you. So, there is no need to tell him anything at all. We'll just... take care of it. Make it all go away and it will be like it never happened. Only you and me. Okay?"

Something about it didn't feel right. But I also didn't want to cause any problems for Asher. He'd been so good to me these past few months. Life has felt different with him. A great kind of different. And if it was just this one thing that would make everything go back to the way it was before it, then I'd do it. I'd honestly do anything.

"Okay," I agreed. "I won't tell him."

TWENTY-EIGHT

ASHER

I rode the elevator, holding the stems of the red roses in my grip and a bag of Chinese food in my other hand. I had classes tonight at Langston, but I'd taken the day off.

Because Lauryn had been avoiding my phone calls.

The elevator's chime pinged as it ascended to the third floor.

I hadn't spoken to Lauryn since the Sunday evening I left her apartment after spending the night the Saturday prior.

After rushing to her apartment that Saturday when I realized I hadn't checked to see how she was feeling about everything, she and I just spent time in each other's space. We talked a little. Didn't make love either. It was quiet and calm. And I thought we were all good.

But then when I showed up Monday night after I was done with classes, she didn't answer her door or answer her phone when I called her. I tried again Tuesday night, which was yesterday, going to her door and calling her, and she didn't answer her phone then either.

So today, a Wednesday, I took the day off and visited her in the afternoon. For sure, I would get her.

Everything was still sinking in for me. And I did not know what my course of action would be. Before Saturday night, I'd never considered being someone's father.

I shook my head as I waited in the elevator for the car to reach the fifth floor.

I was 29 years old, set to be 30 in August.

Obviously, children have been a topic of discussion in my family even if my parents hadn't mentioned it in years' past.

Despite that, I never thought of parenthood. Not when I dropped out of Brookville. Not after I moved to Bali for a year. Parenthood has never been a real thought or anywhere on my mental radar until Saturday night.

And now?

I still wasn't sure where I stood on all of this.

But I figured I could still be there for Lauryn, so she'd know she wasn't alone or dealing with any of this new stuff on her own.

The elevator arrived on the fifth floor and the doors opened. Lauryn's door was near the end of the hall on her floor.

I stepped out of the car and made a left, walking toward her apartment. The second I was out of the elevator, I saw who I thought was my mother standing outside of Lauryn's door, talking.

On closer inspection, I realized it *was* my mother.

I jerked my head back. "Mom?"

She whipped her head in my direction so fast. The first thing I noticed was how wide her eyes grew. My presence seemed to make them bug out.

Lauryn was standing feet away from her closed door's threshold, staring right at me.

It took me a second more to register what I was seeing.

My mother was in my apartment building, but not on my floor in front of *my* door.

She was at Lauryn's door.

Why?

"What the hell is going on?" I asked as I approached.

The closer I got, the more obvious the shock was on my mother's beautiful face.

When I focused my eyes on Lauryn, my brows relaxed.

She had guilt written all over her face.

It was the afternoon.

I wasn't supposed to be home, much less on Lauryn's floor.

When I arrived in front of my mother and Lauryn, I noticed Lauryn fully dressed with her coat zipped and her crossover bag securely sitting on her shoulder.

"What the fuck is going on?" I asked, this time with more bass.

Lauryn tried to form words with her mouth but couldn't get anything out. I focused on my mother.

"I scheduled an appointment for Lauryn to have a procedure," my mother confessed.

I reared my head back. "Excuse me?"

"Lauryn decided she would like to have an abortion—"

"Excuse me?!" I shouted this time.

My voice traveled down the hallway and echoed around us.

"She called me, and..." Lauryn started, her voice trembling.

"*We* decided," my mother jumped in again, throwing a hard stare in Lauryn's direction before returning her attention to me, "that it would be best for everyone—"

"Mom, what the fuck?!"

"Asher," my mother tried.

I shook my head and turned to look at Lauryn. "Open the door and go inside."

Lauryn's brows furrowed. "What?"

"Open the damn door and go inside."

I growled my words, trying hard to keep myself calm. Inside, I was feeling five alarms hot.

Lauryn's eyes grew wide. "What the fuck did you say to me?"

"Please, sweetheart," I tried this time, taking another breath to calm the rage that was bubbling in me and to keep my tone as even as I could. "Go inside. I need to speak to my mother."

"Asher," my mother chastised behind me. "Don't be ridiculous. The appointment is in one hour."

"Here," I said to Lauryn when she did as I asked, handing her the roses and the bag of Chinese food. "Put the roses in water, please. I'll be back."

My grip was on her doorknob, closing her apartment door and closing Lauryn inside before Lauryn could say anything in retort.

"Mom." I took my mother gently by her forearm with enough force to get her walking.

"Asher, what are you doing?"

"Getting you away from my girlfriend's door and out of the building."

She pulled her arm free, and I took her by her arm again.

"My God," she shrieked. "What is wrong with you?"

"That's what I would like to know about you."

With no help from her, really, I pulled her to the elevator and pressed the call button. And thank God we didn't have to wait long for the car to arrive on the fifth floor.

She gasped when I guided her into the elevator with resistance from her.

"That girl cannot have this baby, Asher."

I got on after her and quickly pressed the lobby button. Forced myself to take even breaths in and out to keep from going off on the woman who gave me life.

I couldn't believe what was happening, though.

This was absolutely insane... right?

Was Lauryn going to have an abortion and not tell me anything before she went through with it?

"Do you know her story?" My mother asked me wide-eyed. "She's a rape victim. The victim of a brutal rape, Asher."

"Mom," I said calmly.

"Her mother, who passed? She died during surgery, hours after Lauryn's rescue. Lauryn's rapist shot her mother before he abducted Lauryn."

"Please stop."

"And Lauryn's father is in prison for killing her rapist. He's a murderer, Asher—"

"Mom, I said stop!" I yelled. "Just stop it."

My mother pressed her trembling hands together in prayer hands and brought her fingers to her lips. She shook her head, her eyes welling with tears. "She cannot have this baby. Lauryn is not okay, not after *all* of that. Not after all that I've read about her."

"I love her," I declared. "And she's okay with me. She will continue to be okay."

She shook her head even quicker. "I don't want our family to have anything to do with that. The kind of life she has unfortunately lived. I don't want us to have anything to do with that. Now I'm sorry about what happened to her, happened, because what happened was horrible... but Asher, honey, you can't save her. Allowing Lauryn to bring a life into this world when she is *so* broken—"

"What the fuck is wrong with you?" I asked in a whisper.

The elevator doors opened to the lobby. No one was there to get on, so my mother and I remained in the car.

"How can you look at a woman like Lauryn and only see what she's been through? How can you be so indifferent? So heartless? So fucking negative? How, Mom? Really tell me."

My mother pressed her hand to her mouth, and that's when tears fell from her eyes.

"Because when I see her, I just—" I exhaled through my mouth. "I want to be everything that's right in this world for her since she's seen too much of what's wrong in it. I want to give her love unlimited and in abundance just to see her smile because when she smiles, Mom." I smiled, thinking about it. "God, when she smiles, I see peace. Despite it all, despite everything she's survived, I see her peace. The true peace I've always heard about that I've never known. The peace that isn't absent in the storm. And I want everything to do with that. Every damn thing."

My mother's bottom lip trembled as the tears continued to fall. "Aww, Asher."

I ran my hand down my mouth, then walked beside my mother to guide her off the elevator by the small of her back.

"Go," I told her. "And don't you ever show up at her door or call her again, because if you do… Mom, I don't even know what I'll do in reaction. So please. Let's both be responsible and never find out."

My mother stood outside of the car in the lobby, her jaw slacked, and eyes fixed on me.

I walked up to the wall of buttons inside of the elevator and pressed the number five. I kept my eyes on hers until the elevator doors closed between us.

———

I tried to take as many deep breaths as necessary before I returned in front of Lauryn's door, but with each inhale I performed followed by my exhales, I just got more and more upset.

By the time I was off the elevator and steps in front of Lauryn's door, I was more pissed than when I left the first time.

And the three bangs I did on Lauryn's door when I arrived in front of it demonstrated this.

She was at her door less than a minute later, pulling it opened.

"Asher, what the hell—"

"You were going to do this without talking to me?"

Lauryn kissed her teeth and walked away from her door. I stepped inside of her apartment and slammed it closed.

She turned to glare at me. "Asher, don't slam my door like that."

"How could you…" I ran my hand down my mouth and tried again. "Why would you…"

But the words weren't there.

I was so angry inside. Talking felt like a losing struggle.

"Was it wrong of me to agree to have your mother take me to a clinic to have an abortion behind your back? Yes." She nodded. "I'm not gonna lie. It was wrong."

"Fucked up is what it was," I said through my teeth.

"It's *my* choice."

"Since when?" I asked, gesturing with my hands. "Because when I was here with you the night you unintentionally revealed you were pregnant, you didn't tell me any of this shit."

"Asher, you practically pushed me into the black car outside of the restaurant after everything." She jabbed the air, pointing at me. "You didn't say a fucking word to me after you found out. You don't want this."

"I don't know what I want," I admitted. "But I would've hoped we'd have time to discuss this so we can both figure it out."

"There's nothing to figure out." She lifted and dropped her shoulders hard. "I can't have this baby."

"How are you deciding this without me?"

She sucked her teeth.

"How are you...?" I sighed. "Sweetheart, *why* are you leaving me out of this?"

"You will *never* understand, Asher."

I stood there quiet.

"I..." she started, inhaling a deep breath, then releasing it harshly through her mouth. "I'm so fucking damaged."

"You're not."

"Shut up!" She yelled.

"Lauryn—"

"I don't need you to convince me otherwise." She threw her hands in front of her. "I live a fucked up life. My head and all the shit that runs through it on the daily is even more fucked up. I can barely care for myself. There is no way I'm gonna be able to take care of no baby, Asher."

I stood there silent, chest heaving up and down.

She shook her head. "When I'm not crying, I'm pissed. I'm angry inside, always. Mentally killing every man I come across because I don't have it in me to do it in real life. My tears aren't the same as others. My shit? Is the calm before the storm okay?"

Lauryn pointed at the walls next. "You see those etchings on my walls?"

I glanced at where she gestured. Not needing to search too hard. The gashes in the paint were pronounced. They were one thing I noticed the first time I was in her apartment.

"That's from me throwing shit at it to get the rage that's always in me out, so I won't hurt someone. But throwing shit against walls never works. It never calms the rage in the way I need it to. But I gotta do it like I need to breathe. I have to see my rage in physical form, so I know that it's real. Because if I don't, I'll kill myself. I'll die from feeling defeated."

I took a breath and let it all go through my mouth.

"I move my furniture around at least once a fucking week because I need the comfort of doing something I can control because I feel it's the *only* thing I can control. Because I can't control my thoughts. Tried that, and I fail every time. I'm a mess, Asher. I'm not this person you want to believe I am. I'm ruined and I can't bring a baby into any of my shit. I can't do that."

"I'll be there," I tried. "I will *always* be there."

"What are you saying?"

I tucked my lips into my mouth and dropped my head into my hands, not sure *what* I was saying.

I wasn't sure what I was feeling.

But I knew torn was one of those feelings. A part of me understood where Lauryn was coming from. Though I'd experienced no hardship in my life, much less what Lauryn had been through, I understood her stance.

And with everything else, I wanted to help.

And fine. Maybe neither one of us was ready to be anyone's parent.

But I at least wanted to let her know I would be there if she kept the baby.

What the fuck?

"I'd be there." I nodded. "If you had this baby, I promise on everything. I'd be there every step of the way."

"Asher, no!" She shook her head incessantly. "We can't. This is a mistake."

"What if it's not?" I stared right into her eyes. "What if this is how it's supposed to go?"

She shook her head harder and stepped back. "I'm not having this baby, Asher." Lauryn shook her head harder. "Hell no."

And while I should've felt relief when she said that, all I could feel was pain.

Her decision not to keep the baby wasn't what hurt. It was her not believing me enough to at least consider the possibility.

I turned away from her and quickly left her apartment. Not saying another word, slamming her apartment door closed behind me.

TWENTY-NINE

LAURYN

My aunt sat on her couch with her jaw slacked and her eyes fixed ahead of her.

I was at her apartment on a Thursday evening. She'd just arrived home from work when she found me standing outside of her apartment building waiting for her to arrive.

My aunt knew me through and through, so the moment she saw me, she knew something was up. So, I told her I was pregnant before we could step into the building.

And the shocked expression she wore had been on her face and in her eyes ever since.

"Well," she finally said. "Pregnancy happens when you do the things that make babies without protection."

I scoffed a laugh.

The first laugh I'd expressed in a few days.

Laughing and smiling had been a thing for me for the past few months, so to go back to a state where it wasn't happening as often was an adjustment period.

I hadn't spoken to Asher since he stormed out of my apartment the day before.

Seeing him show up on my floor right before his mother and I left for the appointment at the clinic was jarring as fuck.

He wasn't supposed to be home, much less on my floor. That was the main reason his mother and I agreed that a weekday afternoon would be perfect. He would be at school and when he found out what happened, the procedure would have already been done.

But that plan fell through.

And as expected, I felt terrible.

"I made another appointment at the same clinic his mother setup the first time."

My aunt turned her attention to me. "His mother? She knew before me?"

"She'd somehow figured it out during dinner." I shook my head. "She made a joke, and I didn't laugh and her and Asher pretty much put two and two together."

"But how did y'all go from knowing about the pregnancy to setting up an appointment at a clinic, Lauryn?"

"Don't get mad, please."

My aunt clenched her jaw and turned her head away.

"I just." I sighed. "I wanted to fix it."

"Fix what?"

"*This.*" I gestured at myself. "Do something right. It's my fault I got pregnant any fucking way."

"It takes two people to make a baby, Lauryn. No one's blaming anyone."

"I influenced him to do it without protection."

"And he went along with it, now didn't he?" Aunt Evelyn quizzed. "Asher is a smart man. I'm sure he's aware of how people make babies. We will not acknowledge he's smart in many areas, but dumb in others."

"He's pissed at me," I recalled, eyes falling to my fingers. "He stormed out of my apartment yesterday afternoon and he hasn't called me since. He'd been calling me since he left my apartment Sunday, but I was ignoring his phone calls."

"So, you could end the pregnancy behind his back?"

I whipped my head in her direction, and she threw her hands up in surrender.

"I'm not saying it like that, but then again, Lauryn, I am saying it like *that*." She twisted in her seat to face me. "Baby, I can't *believe* you were gonna have an abortion and not tell me about it. *Me*?"

"I'm sorry," I expressed, my eyes welling with tears.

She wrapped her arms around my shoulders and pulled me into her chest. My aunt pressed a kiss against my forehead, then leaned her head against mine. And that's all it took for the tears to fall and for me to cry.

My aunt held me tighter in response.

"The worst thing I can do is have this baby," I confessed through my sobs. "No, the worst thing I could do is have this baby and she be a girl. Oh my God."

My aunt took my face in her hands and held it there as she cleaned the tears off my cheeks. "Don't say that."

"It's true." I sniffed. "This world is horrible and filled with terrible men. Straight up fucking monsters. There are some good ones, yeah, fine. But the monsters out number them and this world continues to raise them. When one dies, two more pop up. And girls must pay for it all because the world is worse on us in every way. Because if the monsters are not hurting girls, they're making them feel less than human. But the monsters don't see themselves as monsters. They call themselves children of God. That's why I hate them, and I hate God, too."

My aunt's brows knitted. "Lauryn—"

"He created them, right? God? So yeah, I hate him. With everything in me, I hate him. And God must hate my ass, too. Why else did what happened, all those years ago, happen to me?"

I had never spoken of that night with my aunt and she's never brought it up, likely because she wanted me to. She's tried to take me to therapy twice as a teenager, but I'd had an explosive reaction to only the thought of going.

As she sat beside me with her hands on either sides of my face, she gave me the attention of someone who was more than ready to hear me talk about it.

"I wanna die every day," I confessed. "*Every* day I wake up, I wanna end it and the only reason I don't end it is because I know it will make you sad."

My aunt squeezed her eyes together and when she did, tears fell from them.

"I don't even want to be here." I scoffed a laugh, gently leaning away from my aunt. I dragged my hands down my face once and sniffed back the tears that hadn't fallen. "So, why would I want to bring a baby into this hell?"

I nodded, even more sure about my next words than I'd ever been.

"I'm having that abortion next Monday." I turned to my aunt. "And nobody's gonna stop me."

THIRTY

LAURYN

I climbed the train station's steep stairs and took a deep breath the moment I reached the top.

The clinic was within walking distance, according to the receptionist who promised the facility was close to the subway.

It was the day of my appointment. The day matched my mood perfectly.

The clouds covered any light that tried to shine through. The air was dry and the cold bitter. For the first day of March, with the promise of spring in a few weeks, the weather was giving everything but new.

The night before, I sent Asher a text letting him know about the appointment. He answered with a simple "okay." We hadn't spoken since he left my apartment two days ago.

I was grateful the clinic could fit me in after I missed the appointment Patricia arranged for me a few days ago. Grateful to get all of this over with.

My aunt wanted to accompany me to the clinic, but I refused. I told her I would much rather do it by myself.

I wanted to make as little fuss about it as I could, and I prayed it would all work out.

I was only a few feet away from the clinic when I recognized Asher, leaned up against a parked car a few feet away from the clinic's door.

He was staring straight ahead, before he turned his head to survey his surroundings and did a double take when he saw me.

Asher pushed himself off the car and immediately approached.

"Why aren't you in school?" I asked as he walked in my direction.

"There are more important things to tend to today."

His getup was simple, but as always, stylish. Designer puffer coat that was opened despite the chill. A black tee and black joggers finished with white sneakers. It was his usual going-to-school outfit. Comfortable. Totally Asher.

"You've missed two days of classes."

He was standing in front of me now and he didn't hesitate to pull me by the hem of my winter coat, bringing me close enough for him to wrap his arms around me.

And the moment my head touched his chest, his warmth engulfed me. At that moment, everything was perfect.

Asher kissed the top of my head and I pressed myself snugged against him.

"Are you ready?" He asked, with his lips still against my hair.

I shrugged, not sure. "I just wanna get it over with."

I heard him inhale deeply and as he exhaled, he stepped back to take my hand to walk me to the door.

"I can wait out here for you or..." His eyes focused through the glass doors. "I can come with."

I said I wanted to do it alone, but I don't know. Asher was here, and it didn't seem like he was here to talk me out of anything.

"You can come with," I told him, tightening my grip around our interlocked fingers for emphasis.

Asher nodded, then pulled the door open. And the moment I got a whiff of the air inside, the breathing I was in the middle of doing ceased.

The smell in the air was familiar and not in a good way.

Medicinal.

Clinical

Sterile.

I pressed my hand to my chest.

Asher walked in front of me and placed his hands on each of my shoulders. He bent his legs at the knees to be in sight with me.

"What's up?"

I forced myself to shake my head and to take a step forward.

Without me even knowing, my breathing had quickened as my eyes scanned around me.

It was early morning, just after eight, and people packed the waiting area.

Were they all here for the same thing?

That didn't help my anxiety one bit.

"Good morning," the woman with brassy blonde hair greeted to the right of Asher and me.

The clinic was not what I imagined. Patricia promised she would find the best and the place, although in the ritzier part of Manhattan, did not sparkle like the best.

It was mysterious on the outside. Anyone passing by with no business inside of the clinic wouldn't know what it was because on the outside, it resembled any ordinary building. Building number and windows. That's it.

Inside, there were several posters and pamphlets advertising birth control, though.

Asher gently pulled me toward the desk, and I followed.

"Name?" she quizzed without addressing us with her eyes too.

And suddenly I didn't know how to talk.

The woman peeked up from her computer screen to focus on me. Her eyes darted to Asher.

He cleared his throat. "Lauryn James."

Without another word, she continued typing and said, "You're early. You beat the protestors by half an hour. Lucky you."

"Protestors?" I questioned.

"Anti-abortioners." She rolled her eyes. "We usually have an escort outside, but she called out from work today, so now that will be me in a few minutes. You missed them." She winked and smiled. "That's a good thing."

She was handing a clipboard with papers over to me before I could respond.

"Fill these out." She pointed to the waiting area with her pen before placing the same pen on the board for me to take. "You can do so over there."

As I mentioned, people packed the waiting area. Women of all shapes, sizes, and ethnicities crowded the space.

Asher and I said a lot of "excuse me" and "sorries" as we made our way to the far end of the room, where there were only a few empty seats.

The smell.

I couldn't get the smell out of my head.

The moment we sat on the seats, I let out all the air inside of me.

I only realized my hands were shaking as Asher took the clipboard out of my hand.

"I'll fill out what I know and when I'm done, I'll check with you to fill in the parts I missed." He smiled at me. "Okay?"

I nodded in response.

My eyes were roaming again, the wings of my nose flaring each time I inhaled the air.

I was trying my hardest not to be transported back to one of the worst moments in my life.

But the smell.

"The smell in here..." I started.

Asher stopped writing to look over at me.

I shook my head.

"No." He leaned in. "What is it?"

Asher placed the pen down on the clipboard and turned completely to face me. "You can tell me anything, Lauryn. I told you that."

I stared at him.

"Anything, sweetheart."

We were quiet for a few moments. The natural sounds of the clinic filling the silence.

"It smells like the hospital they took me to… after."

Asher's expression softened.

"The hospital room they put me in." I rubbed my lips together for comfort. "The assault was bad and honestly, I thought it would never end. And when it did, I believed the idea that the worst was behind me, but it wasn't because the exams after were terrible. The shots I needed to take. The pills to end any pregnancy. The combing of my pubic hairs. The black light they examined my body with."

I cringed, and Asher wrapped his arm around me tight in response.

"That room smelled a lot like in here and I'm just…"

"I know," he whispered against me.

"I really hate my life." I nodded.

"Lauryn James," someone called across the room.

Asher and I glanced toward where the voice came from. A woman, black, stood near an opened door dressed in a white coat and blue dress underneath.

"Lauryn James?" She called a second time.

Asher raised an arm in the air. "Over here." He peeked down at me next. "You ready?"

I wasn't.

Despite that, I stood to my feet and got out of my seat. The only thing making me do so was I wanted to get everything over with.

I still was holding Asher's hand, though.

"Sweetheart, I don't think I can go with you in there."

"Please," I pleaded, tightening my grip.

He sighed. "Let me see what I can do."

We were both approaching the woman when she smiled. She was parting her lips to speak when I asked, "Can he please come with me?"

The woman lowered her view to the folder in her hand. "According to this, you should only be eight weeks, which means you won't require a procedure, so sure. But." She held a finger up. "If the ultrasound shows you are farther along in your pregnancy and we need to do a procedure, he cannot be present for that. Understood?"

Asher and I both nodded.

"Sounds good to me," he answered for the both of us.

The woman escorted us through a frosted glass door and down a narrow corridor to an office at the end of the hall. The smell changed on the other side of the door. Likely because this side of the clinic seemed to be only offices with exam tables and machines.

"You can have a seat on the exam table," she directed, placing the clipboard on her desk. The doctor walked to a machine. It was a few feet away from the exam table she advised me to sit.

Asher picked up the armchair in front of the large wooden desk and moved it to the side of the table where I sat.

"I'm Dr. Faith Lewis," she started, glancing at me and Asher. "I understand you are eight weeks pregnant and would like to end the pregnancy. Is that correct?"

I cringed at the language. I mean, she wasn't wrong. I wanted that. But there was something about the way she said it that made me shift uncomfortably in my seat on the exam table.

Asher took my hand from his seat beside me. I glanced at him and he offered a small smile.

When I returned my eyes to Faith, she smiled. She leaned a little against the wall she stood beside. "How about I tell you what you can expect here today to ease your worries a bit?"

I nodded my agreement.

"Today," she began, "I'll give you a tiny pill called mifepristone. This pill will block your body's progesterone, which will jumpstart the termination. You'll wait twenty-four to forty-eight hours after taking the first pill I give you today to take misoprostol, which will be another set of four pills."

I inhaled deeply and exhaled with assurance. Pills I could take. Similar to the night the paramedics brought me to the hospital. If pills were all I had to take, I could do it.

"Now, while the first pill I'll give you today won't cause you any pain, the next set of four will. You'll experience some cramping and bleeding which can last for several hours, kind of like a heavy period. So, you'll have to take it easy for the next few days, okay?"

"That's it?" I asked.

She smiled and nodded for emphasis. "That's it. But." Faith turned away to approach the set of drawers at the nearby counter. "We'll have to confirm how far along you are to make sure taking those pills is still an option for you. According to your intake form, your last period was in December. Is that correct?"

I nodded.

Faith turned on the machine that stood beside Asher, then focused on the monitor and keyboard attached to it. As she typed, she told me, "I'm going to give you a quick ultrasound and then we can take it from there."

She'd finished typing and lifted her hand to turn on the overhead monitor that was a mounted flatscreen.

"We usually do a transvaginal ultrasound," Faith informed, "but judging from the information you provided, you should be far along enough for us to get an accurate read abdominally."

At the top of the screen, my name appeared in white letters, along with the date. The rest of the screen was black.

"Lie flat for me on the table and pull the waistband of your sweatpants down to the top of your pelvis."

I'd done as told, now lying flat on my back.

I was rolling my eyes up to stare at the ceiling when Asher asked, "You okay?"

"Yeah."

I said I was, but inside my heart was pounding.

Dr. Faith did a good job of calming my anxiety, but there was something about all this that wouldn't let me chill.

There was so much I didn't know about what was happening. I'd never considered I'd be here in any capacity. Pregnant and in an abortion clinic. I felt out of place, out of control. And I didn't like that.

Faith turned off the lights, then returned beside me.

"Lift your sweatshirt up to your bra, please."

And when I did as she instructed, she squirted my lower stomach with a cool gel and placed a transducer against the area.

The second she placed the wand against my stomach, quick rhythmic beats echoed around the room.

They were out of rhythm with mine but still in sync, and out of nowhere, a wave of emotions surfaced inside me.

"What is that?" Asher asked.

"*That* is *its* heartbeat," Faith answered nonchalantly, moving the transducer around while stretching her other arm to the ultrasound equipment cart to press a few buttons on the equipment's keyboard.

"It has a heartbeat?" I whispered.

"*Mm-hmm*," she confirmed as she typed and clicked at the keys. "Okay, you *are* eight weeks. You made your appointment just in time."

Her words went in one ear and out the other. All I could hear were the rhythmic thumps. They sounded like raindrops. In tempo and oddly soothing. They were so fast. Almost in sync with mine. It was beautiful. Calming. And soon the rhythmic thumps were gone when Faith pulled the wand away from my stomach.

And suddenly I felt empty again.

"Okay," she said as she made her way to the light switch to turn the lights on again. "We can get started." Faith pulled at the tissue sticking out of the tissue holder and walked two sheets of tissue to me. "Clean your stomach with this. I'll be right back with the pills."

She'd left the room, and I was still holding the tissues in my hand, eyes darting along the ceiling above me.

I turned my head to look at Asher, who was staring straight ahead, motionless. I noticed when his Adam's apple bobbed in his throat when he swallowed hard though.

I wasn't sure what he was feeling. What he was thinking. But I knew what was running through my head and my heart.

"Asher."

He turned his focus on me immediately. "Yeah?"

I closed my eyes and held my lids tight. "I wanna leave."

Asher sat up in his seat immediately. "What?"

I sat up from my recline and kicked my legs off the exam table. My mind was so cluttered with thoughts and responses. I pulled my sweatshirt down, feeling the cool gel soil my knuckles.

"I wanna leave," I repeated. "Can we leave, though?"

He blinked hard. "What... what are you saying?"

"I don't know." I ran my fingers through my hair. "I don't know. But... I... *ummm*... I don't wanna be here. I don't think I wanna do this."

Asher jumped to his feet immediately. He nodded incessantly and snatched my coat off the other chair that sat opposite Faith's desk.

"Then let's go."

———

Asher and I laid facing each other in my unmade bed. His hand was against my stomach, the side of his thumb caressing it back and forth.

Every so often, a smile pulled at the corners of his lips. Or he'd scoff a laugh as he kept his eyes fixed on my belly button.

I should freak out. The thoughts running through them should've had my mind all fucked up.

Because we'd left the clinic and I was still pregnant.

"Where are you two going?" Faith asked as Asher and I took large steps down the corridor. The same corridor she walked us down minutes earlier. "I have the pills."

"Thanks, but you can keep them," Asher answered for us as he pushed opened the frosted door for us to leave through the lobby.

He didn't order a ride share to take us back. The car I found Asher leaned up against when I saw him was a rental. He'd rented the car in preparation to take me home after the procedure, or what we thought would have been a procedure. Asher held my hand the entire ride back home. Kissing me on the forehead at what seemed like every red light and asking me if I was okay as he drove us home.

"This is crazy, right?" I asked in a whisper.

It was the first words I'd spoken since we left the clinic.

Since we climbed into my bed after arriving at my apartment.

Still pregnant.

That thought continued to keep my mind in a Vise-Grip. I was pregnant and didn't want to get rid of it anymore. Which meant... I would have it?

Could I have it?

"I wanna keep it," I confessed out loud. "That's crazy... right?"

He smiled at me and lifted himself up by his elbow to gaze down at me. "Not at all."

I sat up too. "But we can't, right?"

He grinned. "Sweetheart, we can do whatever the hell we want as shown by today."

I burst out laughing and he chuckled.

"No." I shook my head. "Asher, you're in school. Your mother *hates* me and she's right. I don't have shit going for me—"

"You have everything." He pressed a hand to my stomach. "And now you have this, too." Asher's eyes darted between mine. "Did you hear that heartbeat?"

I nodded slowly.

"It was *strong*. Loud. Real." He exhaled and smiled wider. "So real. It was amazing."

"So amazing," I echoed.

I released a shaky exhale and felt the weirdest urge to smile so big. I dropped my head into my hands a second later and laughed. "This is insane."

"Life is insane," he added. "But we do what we can to live it right."

"I know, but... this is a baby. A person." I stared at him. "And we're gonna have it? Like... together?"

Asher's smile grew so big I could count all his teeth. "Yeah."

"We hardly know each other like that, though."

I said the one thing that was true and that neither one of us had acknowledged before that moment. Asher and I had only known one another for a few months. Only three seasons. Barely. There were things he still didn't know about me and that I didn't know about him. I hadn't even met his father yet.

I loved him, and until that moment with him in my bed, I believed he loved me, too. But could that be enough?

"We know this iteration of each other well, Lauryn." He smiled. "We're never really the same people. Who I was last year isn't who I am today and isn't who I'm going to be years from now, nor should I be. I know who you are now, and I know I want to grow with you to learn who you will become years from now. And that's what matters, sweetheart. The commitment to grow and learn all the yous you will become. A chance to fall in love with all the versions of you all over again."

I bit my bottom lip and smiled even bigger. "But, how?"

He held his stare with me.

"How will we have a baby together when neither one of us knows anything about babies?"

"With faith." He winked. "And not the Faith at the clinic. Genuine faith."

I giggled.

"We'll move with faith because genuine faith isn't faith if we only believe in it when everything is certain and going well." He nodded, then blew air out of his mouth. "Genuine faith is when you trust everything will work out when it seems it won't."

I nodded.

"I didn't see this coming but, fuck it. Everything happens for a reason and this just feels right, so... let's do it." Asher reached his arm out to me, and I went to him, laying my head against his chest as he brought us back to our reclined position on my bed. "We'll figure it out."

"Yeah," I agreed, even though I was still unsure. But something about this, something about that moment, had me willing to do whatever I could to make it work, too.

"We got this," he affirmed.

Asher kissed the top of my head, then my forehead, changing positions and moving me beneath him. He lifted the sweatshirt I still wore and leaned forward to kiss my stomach, too.

I sucked in a breath to hold the tears back.

"What a blessing you are to us already," he said to my stomach before pressing another kiss there.

Tears welled in my eyes.

"You're too good for me," I said to him. Honestly, I said it to myself. Because it was true. He was too good for me.

Asher looked up at me.

"You could do better," I whispered through the tears falling down my face. "Be with a woman who has her shit together and who you could confidently build a life with. Not someone with all my shit, all my problems that now you must settle with—"

"What are you talking about?" He asked, crawling his way to me. "I'm the luckiest man in the world."

I rolled my eyes and was focusing elsewhere when he guided my attention back to him with his grip on my chin.

"I am the luckiest man in the world who has a woman who is so resilient," he told me, his eyes unwavering. "And she deserves the world in every facet I can present it to her, and that's what I'm going to do. You inspire me so much. You don't understand how *much* you inspire me. So, you should at least get every amazing thing the world has to offer and that I can give you."

I tried to fight my smile, but there was no use. It busted through, aching my cheeks and making him return one back.

"You're my world now, Lauryn," he told me, his smile slowly falling off his lips as he maintained a serious expression on his face. "And we're going to create a beautiful life together." He pressed his hand to my stomach. "Just like we did with this precious one. Right now, everything feels insane, but, sweetheart, this is a blessing to me. And so are you. I promise."

Thirty-One

LAURYN

I peeked up from the pages of the book I was reading to step off the elevator car. My eyes were back on the black words as I blindly fished through my pockets for my keys.

I had them only a few moments ago. Fished them out of my pocket when the elevator arrived at the fifth floor.

That wasn't my floor these days. Not after Asher asked me to move in with him shortly after we agreed to keep our baby.

It had been a month since then and today was my 30th birthday.

With the keys in hand, I approached the door, holding the book against my body to make sure I didn't turn the page by accident.

Living with Asher was different, but a good different. We didn't see each other as often as I liked. One reason he asked for me to move in was so we could make up for the times he'd be away in school. But when we were together, it was always nice. No arguments, no disagreements. Just... easy. And that was new to me.

The only thing that hadn't changed was my insomnia. Though it had gotten better, especially with Asher aware of it now. It was still there.

But I'd coped.

By reading.

"Hey," he said to me one night when he found me sitting up in bed with my back to his headboard.

The room was dim thanks to the light he kept on in his bathroom at night. He was turning over in his spot to face me when his eyes opened a little and caught me sitting there in the dark.

It was the first night I moved in. My stuff was still down in my apartment, but most of my essentials were now in Asher's apartment. But it wasn't the change in home that was keeping me up.

"I don't know a thing about being a mother," I said to the air. "Like... nothing."

He exhaled, then pushed himself up into a seat beside me, pushing his back against his headboard.

Since deciding to keep the baby, we held brief discussions about it.

It was still early. I was only eleven weeks, but the baby was growing and would eventually be here between us. We had our first doctor's appointment later that week, an appointment the receptionist at the doctor's office insisted we schedule before I reached twelve weeks. Everything was moving so fast to me, and I still knew nothing.

"I know nothing about being a father," Asher rasped, sleep still very much in his voice. "But I can learn. And you can too."

"I don't know Asher," I whispered.

Asher slid his arm behind my lower back and used his hold on me to pull me closer to him. I leaned my head against his shoulder, and he laid his head against mine.

"Studying psychology is hard," he admitted to me. "And I find it's really hard when I don't read whatever my professors give me to read."

I looked up at him and he moved in briefly to kiss my forehead.

"So, I read," he said with a smirk. "Everything. I read and I practice. You can do the same thing."

I furrowed my brows.

"You know there are a ton of books on parenting, right?"

"What?"

"There's a book for everything." He winked. "Anything you want to know is in a book, including parenting. There are literally a bunch of books on having babies, raising them, teaching them."

"For real?"

He chuckled. "For real."

So that's what I started doing. Reading everything I could get my hands on. Books on pregnancy. Books on childbirth. Books that explained the first year of a child's life. I'd been reading them all. Finishing them within a few days and starting on new ones.

The bookcase Asher built for me was now full of books and I was just getting started.

Reading also helped with my insomnia. Whenever I couldn't sleep or got up from sleep and couldn't go back, I'd turn on the book light Asher got for me and crack open a book and start reading until my eyes got heavy. I was learning all there was about this change that was happening in my life, and it made me sleepy. It was a win-win.

Finally.

The moment I pushed open the apartment door, my eyes fell on balloons on the island, along with flowers and a woman standing in the kitchen.

I stood at the door, my eyes bouncing from the balloons to the woman.

She wore a double-breasted black chef's coat and an apron at her waist. Busy moving around the kitchen, she didn't notice me standing at the door.

"Hey, sweetheart," Asher greeted straight ahead of me.

"What's going on?" I quizzed through my smile. "What are you doing here? I thought you had class?"

Asher spent most of his time either at school or resting because of it. He was nearing the end of his first year in his Ph.D. program, so his studies had picked up, taking up more of his time.

"It's your birthday," he explained, taking the book out of my hand, along with the bag of books I'd just gotten from the bookstore. He was removing the strap of my crossover from my shoulder when he added, "You know I couldn't miss your birthday."

"But—"

"But nothing," he interjected, moving in closer to me. "I'm not missing my girl's birthday. Come on. Her first birthday with me, too?" He shook his head. "It wasn't going to happen."

Asher's hand was on my belly soon after, rubbing it and placing another hand against it to rub too.

"How are you two?" He was already searching my eyes for the answer.

I was showing now at fourteen weeks. Nothing too obvious. Because I wore joggers, I hadn't really noticed the change in the fit of my clothing, but I did when I was getting out of the shower the week prior. My belly was comparable to my belly after I'd eaten too much. It was cute. Something I was getting used to.

"We're good." I licked my lips. "Hungry."

He smiled big and took my hand. "Perfect."

Asher walked me into his kitchen to where the woman, who I saw there wearing a chef coat, moved around the space, organizing everything.

"This is Molly," he said, gesturing at the dark-skinned woman who wore her hair in a neat bun and who was now facing us, smiling. Asher pulled out one of the island stools for me to take a seat. "Molly is going to be our chef for today."

My brows arched. "Our what?"

She giggled. "First, happy birthday."

I smiled. "Thank you."

"And yes, I'm here to make anything you want today. So please, don't hold back."

I turned to look at Asher.

"Molly is going to make us a little lunch and while we're out at the movies," he explained, "she's going to make us dinner and bake you a gourmet chocolate birthday cake."

My face lit up.

I could literally feel it warming at just the breakdown of our plans. "Are you serious?"

"He is." Molly nodded. "I'm all yours all day. Anything you want, I'll make it."

My focus was back on Asher.

"You love watching those cooking shows." He chuckled. "And I didn't want to just get you anything for your birthday, so..." He shrugged. "I hired a chef for you to recreate any of those dishes you saw being created on TV."

My heart could leap out of my chest. If it were physically possible for it to push through and leap out, it would have, and I would have let it because this man of mine was truly exceptional.

"I don't know what to say." I smiled so big my cheeks hurt.

"A food name would be nice," he joked.

I burst out laughing and so did the chef.

"Any food, sweetheart, come on," he encouraged, reaching his hand to my belly and running his palm down the small curve. "It's time for us to feed the baby and I'm hungry, too."

A giddy feeling rolled through me and made me squeal, then shake my head at myself.

They both laughed.

"Okay... *ummm*." I tapped a rhythm on the island's surface with my fingers. "Fried chicken, mac and cheese, and waffles with whipped cream and strawberries?" I clapped my hand together. "Can you put lobster in the mac and cheese? Is that possible?"

"Oh, it's possible." Molly smiled and nodded once. "And it's coming right up!"

I pressed my hands to my lips to cover my smile.

Best birthday ever.

———

Later that night, I rolled over off my side to face in Asher's direction in bed. Stretched my arm out to him but found his side of the bed empty. My eyes slowly peeled opened next.

It was dark around the room. The light in the bathroom was on, like always. I scanned the room to find it empty.

I immediately knew where he was.

I kicked my legs off the bed and stood to my feet. Took steps out of the bedroom to make my way to the kitchen.

The hour was after two in the morning. And even in the night's quiet, I could hear cars driving over the blacktop road outside through the closed windows.

I walked past Asher's second bedroom. That was one of the other reasons he wanted me to move in with him. Besides being able to see me after returning home late from the university, he wanted me in his apartment for the extra bedroom. We planned to decorate it and turn it into a nursery, starting the next month after Asher completed his first year of his Ph.D. program at LU. For now, it was still his study.

When he wasn't hanging out with me watching movies in bed or on the couch, he was in the second bedroom he'd turned into a home office.

I stepped into the kitchen and lifted the lid on the single serving coffee maker. Added the plastic cartridge filled with ground coffee and immediately closed the lid, pressing the brew button last.

He would need to be up in the next six hours to get ready to head to LU. On Tuesdays, he was the busiest, and he was preparing for finals.

When the coffee finished brewing, I took it off the drip tray. Only added honey to the black coffee, the way he liked it. I grabbed it by the handle and walked it to the office.

Asher's home office was simple. A desk that faced the window, bookshelves on either side of the door that displayed all of his textbooks.

When I walked in, he was leaning his head against his arm as he turned the page of his textbook.

He lifted his head when he realized I was there.

"Hey," I said, placing the coffee on the desk at a comfortable distance from the textbook.

Asher wrapped an arm around my waist and brought me close enough for him to kiss my belly.

He loved that I was showing. Ever since that curve beneath my navel became pronounce, he found it impossible to keep his lips off it.

I placed a hand at the top of his head to run my hand down his fade.

"You coming to bed soon?"

He nodded at me. "Was wrapping up right now."

He sounded so tired.

Asher told me I inspired him but he inspired me. He worked hard and was always present and available to me. It was admirable and made me love him even more.

He kissed my belly again, then moved his kisses up my torso, kissing me on the underside of my breast and making me giggle.

He kept kissing his way up until he was out of his seat and on his feet, kissing me on my neck.

I pressed my hands to either side of his face and smiled.

I leaned my head back to meet his gaze. "What are you doing?"

He folded his bottom lip into his mouth and smirked.

I tossed my head back and laughed. "You gotta go to bed, Asher."

He nodded and closed the space between us to kiss my lips. Against them, he said, "I do."

His hands, though, were at my waist, sliding his palms down to my ass to grab both cheeks in his hands to assist with lifting me to place me on top of his study desk.

Asher walked between my splayed legs, parting my lips, opened with his and guiding his tongue into my mouth.

And I didn't continue to put up a fight.

Soon I was in his arms, and he was walking us both to his bedroom, still kissing me along the way.

In the room, Asher didn't waste time placing me on the bed and climbing on, too. He was leaning his weight onto me in our kiss when I pressed my hands to his bare chest.

"Wait, wait."

He stopped immediately.

"You're gonna crush the baby," I expressed, peeking down at my tiny baby bump.

He chuckled, dropping his head between his arms that he kept me caged between. "I'm not gonna crush the baby."

"How do you know that?"

He licked his lips.

I used my elbows to push myself off the mattress. "I'll get on top."

Asher shook his head next. "I don't want you to do anything right now."

I smiled at the thought because I knew what he meant. He wanted control. He wanted me to relax. But there was no way I could do that with thoughts of our baby being squished by their father laying on top of me.

Asher moved to the side of me to take a seat beside me. "We could do it *another* way."

I turned to face him.

"Both of us lying down." His eyes moved to the mattress, then back to me. "Me behind you."

I bit the inside of my lower lip.

It was the one position we hadn't made love in. The last time Asher tried to embrace me from behind, he ended up with a black eye and a bruised knee after he fell off my bed because of it.

"I'll take my time," he promised low. "Like always. Your pace. Only if you say it's okay to, though."

His chest was rising and falling. A quick glance at his crotch in his boxers showed he was rock hard.

I licked my lips at its presence, really wanting it now that I saw he was more than ready to give me him.

Asher palmed it a second later, trying to relax it, and that brought a smirk to my lips.

"I don't think you doing *that* is going to work."

He hung his head forward in a laugh, which made me giggle.

Asher set his eyes on mine again when I noticed they were smoldering. He clenched his jaw and swallowed, visibly doing his best to remain calm and in control.

His discipline.

It was so sexy.

"You want me, huh?"

He nodded slowly, eyes closing briefly as he licked his lips too. "Badly."

I giggled.

"But I want your permission more than that."

My smile fell off my lips. I rubbed my lips together and glanced down at the mattress.

"But... if you're not for it," he said next, "then we can—"

"You're so patient with me," I interjected.

He smiled and his brilliant white smile lit up my heart in his dim room. "You deserve as much patience as I can give."

I glanced at the bed again and inhaled a deep breath. I was still unsure about it, but I figured Asher had done so much for me. He's always been patient, even patient when patience seemed hard for him to pull on.

And I trusted him.

I trusted him not to do me any harm.

The least I could do was to challenge the fear that was holding me back.

"Okay." I nodded. "Let's do it that way."

He lowered his chin to stare me right in the eyes. "Are you sure?"

"Yes." I nodded again.

I swallowed hard as I turned in my seat on the bed to lie down on the pillow.

Asher took a moment to join me there. But when he did, he gently draped his arm over my waist and moved in close.

The first thing I felt was his breath against my ear. That made my breathing hitch and my heart race. But then he kissed my neck. Then he kissed it again. And my body came alive, making it easy for a soft moan to escape through my lips.

Asher moved his hand off my waist and was sliding it down between my thighs when he asked me, "May I touch you here?"

I smiled and nodded, placing my hand on top of his and moving his fingers there myself.

And he didn't hesitate to spread my wet lips opened to guide the pad of his fingers down the soft folds in search of my tiny ball.

He massaged it slow. His breathing and kisses increasing. The sensation he stirred in me was growing hotter inside me, too.

I gyrated my hips and moaned in time with his finger movements, feeling his erection pressed against me from behind.

He slid his hand from between my thighs to behind me and breathed, "May I?" into my ear.

And I nodded, quickly adding, "Yes," not wanting him to take too long to get back at it.

Asher slid in slowly. My walls fluttered in rhythm with my heart as he buried himself inside me. His fingers returned to my clit, rubbing as he stroked.

He groaned in my ear. And it was the sweetest sound. Sounded so good. I pressed myself closer to him so I could turn my head a little to hear a little more.

Asher moved in too, using his free hand to turn my head a little so he could kiss me.

And I melted.

On that bed, joined with him beneath the sheets, I melted into a puddle of everything that felt good. In his arms, feeling all the things that were right.

He stopped circling my clit and stroking in and out of wetness to kiss me deeper. Moaning each time my walls contracted around him as he laid still behind me.

I couldn't take the wait for him to resume any longer, though, so I did the job for him. Kissing him back while moving him in and out of me with just my waist and hips.

His eyes flew open, and he released a guttural groan inside my mouth.

I moved slowly, shaking a little each time I pressed my ass against him before sliding him out again. The grip of his fingers against my pussy tightened and his fingers started massaging my clit faster, making me want to push myself even more on him.

I was close when everything picked up in pace.

"Yes," I exhaled into the air, closing my eyes to collide with the sweet sensation sweeping through me in no hurry.

Asher's fingers moved from between my thighs to my hip. He gripped my hip as he thrusted quicker. Slapping noises competed with our cries and it was like music to me.

He stroked one last time and pressed his lips into my hair to moan into my strands, sliding in deep and just staying there, inside me, holding me tight as he caught his breath against me.

"Fuck," he whispered against my hair. "Damn."

I bit my bottom lip and extended my arm behind me to hold his head in place against the back of mine.

I asked, "Are you okay?"

He laughed lazily before taking another breath. "I should ask you that."

I smiled. "I'm great."

Asher kissed my shoulder and said, "Then I'm great, too."

His hand was against my belly, rubbing it slowly.

There in his arms, covered in his warmth and his love, I felt safe. Something I believed I would know nothing about.

But it's like I said. I learned that with Asher everything was possible.

Unfortunately... that wouldn't be enough.

THIRTY-TWO

ASHER

"Good morning, you two," the ultrasound tech greeted the moment she pushed opened the door to the room.

Lauryn sat at the exam table while I relaxed by her side in the room's chair.

"Good morning," Lauryn returned with a smile.

"Good morning, Jillian," I echoed, smiling too.

Jillian was a petite dark skin woman with jet black short hair and big bright brown eyes. When Lauryn and I arrived for our first appointment after deciding to keep the baby and we met Jillian, she instantly became one of our favorites at the doctor's office.

Jillian was gentle with Lauryn. On the intake form, Lauryn and I were transparent about Lauryn's past, and both our doctor and the rest of the staff in the office have been accommodating in every way.

"Today is a special day," Jillian announced as she took her seat in front of her computer. She clicked a button, and the mounted flatscreen ahead of us turned on, displaying a black screen.

There was a private bet going between me and Lauryn's aunt Evelyn. Lauryn, carrying low, convinced Evelyn that Lauryn was pregnant with a boy. I wasn't knowledgeable about old wives' tales. But based on the type of foods Lauryn was eating, based on my scientific knowledge, she was having a girl. Lauryn was obsessed with sweets and fruits and, according to my classmates at school who had children of their own, Lauryn was carrying a girl.

Lauryn had mentioned none of her predictions. While she's done well with caring for herself and being extra cautious and thoughtful about the baby, she's never voiced what she wanted.

I figured she was like most moms. She wanted a healthy baby. Nothing more.

"Okay," Jillian announced, standing to her feet. "As always..." She giggled next. "This gel is going to be a little cold."

Lauryn smiled and nodded. "As always."

Jillian squirted the gel on Lauryn's stomach and placed the transducer's smooth edge against the tiny puddle of gel. Jillian's eyes remained on the mounted flatscreen as the picture brightened to a grainy black and white capture of our baby.

The moment I heard the baby's strong heartbeat, my smile grew big. It grew wider when I realized how big the baby had gotten. I could make out their forehead, their nose, and their mouth. When Jillian moved the wand to a distinct part of Lauryn's stomach, I noticed the baby's hands and feet.

"Growing so well," Jillian commented with a smile. "You've been eating good, huh, Lauryn?"

Lauryn chuckled. "Like all the time. I'm ready to eat right now."

She was showing a lot more now, too, especially since her birthday the month prior. It was like her belly experienced a sped up growth. Her waistline was rounder. Wide hips even wider now.

I loved everything about the changes happening with Lauryn's body.

Some mornings, I'd wake up just a little earlier so I could caress her stomach before having to get out of bed to go to class.

My life felt so right these days and it was honestly a shock sometimes.

"So, we want to know the gender, right?"

"Yes," I confirmed, straightening my back in my seat.

Evelyn made me promise to text her as soon as we found out. I was reaching in my back pocket for my phone to have it in hand so I could keep my promise.

"Well, get the pink ready because it's a girl!" Jillian confirmed.

My smile grew so wide. "I knew it."

I chuckled and was lowering my view to my phone when I heard Lauryn whisper, "Oh no."

My attention shot over to her to register what I'd just heard her say.

I could see the stunned gaze weighing her dainty facial features down even in the dimly lit room.

Lauryn's expression was wide-eyed. She wore an almost horrified stare as she gaped at the flatscreen.

"Are you sure?" Lauryn asked, eyes darting to the screen, then to Jillian before refocusing on the screen again.

"Yup!" Jillian confirmed, even cheerier. Jillian was too busy directing her attention between the mounted flatscreen and the knobs and dials on the ultrasound equipment she operated. She was so busy working to recognize Lauryn's growing discomfort with the news. "Over here." Jillian used the mouse to point the arrow on the monitor at the baby's legs. "Baby girl is making it clear she's all girl. Congrats you two."

Lauryn turned her head to face me. If there was any doubt that she wasn't happy about the news before, the wrinkles in her brows and the frown on her lips would certainly give that away.

We spent another few minutes in the ultrasound room before we stepped into our doctor's office.

Dr. Carmen Blair, who insisted we just call her Carmen, was a godsend. It was like the stars aligned when the receptionist placed us in her care.

She most of all was aware of Lauryn's past. We were transparent on our first doctor's visit, retelling the story of leaving the abortion clinic and deciding to have the baby.

Carmen's been honest. Letting us know that although the decision to have the baby is good, we would need to prepare. Lauryn was already ready to stick her nose in as many books as possible and Dr. Carmen was her guide, giving Lauryn recommendations Dr. Carmen believed would benefit us during the first years of our child's life.

When we stepped into Dr. Carmen's office, Lauryn was in a daze and remained that way for the first few minutes. Dr. Carmen fielded questions about Lauryn's pregnancy symptoms, her cravings, and if Lauryn had been experiencing any discomforts.

And Lauryn answered all of them. But she appeared visibly dejected as she responded.

"So, a girl," Dr. Carmen said, her deep brown eyes lighting up as they bounced between Lauryn and me. "I know you said you and Lauryn's aunt have been betting on the gender and I see you've won."

I laughed. "Yeah, I can't wait to share the news—"

"Is it too late?" Lauryn asked in a low tone.

Dr. Carmen's brows knitted as she leaned forward in her seat at her desk to give Lauryn her full attention.

"Too late for what?" Dr. Carmen queried.

"To end the pregnancy."

Dr. Carmen and I reared our heads back at that same time, but Dr. Carmen added some blinking, to her shock.

"Lauryn," I said, placing my hand on her forearm. "What are you—"

"You want to end... the pregnancy?" Dr. Carmen asked, dipping her chin a bit to stare Lauryn square in the eyes.

Lauryn inhaled an audible deep breath.

"Sweetheart?" I asked in a whisper.

Lauryn looked at me with the saddest eyes. They were watering and my heart sank. Her asking was a shock. I'll admit that. But seeing the weight in her mood that was so palpable I could touch it on her face as the tears slid from her eyes tore me up from the inside.

"Asher." Dr. Carmen rolled the office chair she sat in back quickly and stood to her feet. She pointed at the door. "Let's, *umm...*"

"Yeah." I moved my eyes off Lauryn and stood up slowly.

We were fine.

At least, I thought we were.

Dr. Carmen motioned for me to step away from the doorway of her office, out of earshot of Lauryn once we were outside of it.

"I..." I started, turning my head to her office door. "I don't know... I don't know what happened."

Dr. Carmen smiled warmly, pressing her palms together as if she were about to say a prayer. "New moms at different stages in their pregnancy can experience doubt about having their baby. It happens. Rarely. But it does."

I blinked in response.

"But with Lauryn, it can be a little concerning."

The inhale I did as I ran my hand down my mouth did little to calm the build of anxiety happening inside of me.

"Have you considered getting her some help?"

I turned my attention to Dr. Carmen.

"I know you two have shared her past and although I'm sure pregnancy hormones can affect a mother's mood; it can also bring up traumatic memories they keep in the recesses of their minds. Triggering situations can bring those memories to the surface and it's overwhelming to deal with."

"We've been good though, you know?" I tried. "She's been happy. Excited. Reading all the books you recommended to the point she's now searching for a new batch—"

"And although that is all great," Dr. Carmen interjected. "That may not be enough. She's asking about terminating in the second trimester of her pregnancy, Asher."

My eyes collapsed closed, and I held my lids together in a tight squeeze.

I nodded next, agreeing.

As a student of psychology, I've always wondered if Lauryn spoke to someone other than her aunt. I wondered if she would be okay with speaking to someone about any of what she's felt or was feeling.

"My goal has always been to make her comfortable enough to speak to me," I revealed, eyes pointing to the floor. "I'm in a Ph.D. program at

LU. Studied in a program at Brookville for five years before dropping out for reasons I really don't want to get into right now."

"Understood," Dr. Carmen acknowledged.

I lifted, then held my shoulders in the air before letting them drop. "I just... I figured I could be the person she talked to; you know?"

"And you still can be." She nodded. "What you've done together is amazing, but she may benefit from having just a little more."

I bobbed my head up and down. "Okay."

Dr. Carmen smiled, reaching forward to press a hand to my shoulder. "I have a doctor. Friend of mine. Her name is Liz Peters. Her daughter, Eryn, graduated from LU years ago, so you will be in splendid company. I'll write Dr. Peters's information down and will call ahead to let her know to expect you and Lauryn's call."

"Okay."

"Dr. Peters is excellent, Asher." She nodded. "One of the best, and she will be the perfect resource."

"I hope so."

When we returned to Dr. Carmen's office, Lauryn was motionless in her seat, her attention focused straight ahead, not really acknowledging Dr. Carmen and I had returned.

Dr. Carmen explained to Lauryn what she called me outside of her office to discuss. She told Lauryn that she was going to be giving Lauryn and me the psychotherapist's information and calling ahead to let the therapist know to expect our call.

And all Lauryn did was nod. No words, not even a sound. Just a nod.

She remained quiet after we left the OB-GYN office and after we climbed into the ride share, I ordered. Lauryn spent a lot of the ride staring out of the passenger window at the blur of activity happening in Brooklyn that afternoon as our driver drove.

"Sweetheart?" I asked ten minutes into the ride. The doctor's office was only a few miles away from our apartment building, so the ride would be short. "Are you okay?"

She twisted her lips to one side and simply shook her head.

I pressed my hand to her stomach and ran my hand along the surface, then leaned in close to press a kiss on Lauryn's cheek.

When we arrived at our building, we boarded the elevator and rode the car to the eighth floor. Lauryn stepped out first, pulling out her keys to open my door. I tailed behind her and entered after she opened the door to my apartment.

Inside, I watched as she removed her crossover bag and dropped it on the couch and then her denim jacket, leaving it in the same spot, and made her way into my kitchen.

I struggled to find the words. I was also very concerned.

And that concern didn't subside when I heard the sudden crash of glass in my kitchen.

My head whipped that way to see the tears in Lauryn's eyes and her reaching for another one of my glass cups to slam with all her might against my floor.

"Lauryn!"

A third glass was in her hand when I ran into the kitchen to grab her wrist. She tried to pull away.

"Let me go!" She screamed at the top of her lungs, freeing her wrist, and immediately turning to throw the glass cup at me. I ducked in time, hearing as the glass crashed violently against a nearby wall. Shards of glass flew everywhere. Lauryn yelled a blood chilling cry with that glass's crash.

I wrapped my arms around her to hold her and to keep her from reaching for any more of my drinkware.

There was glass everywhere, catching the glint of light overhead.

I was inhaling so hard and forgetting to exhale that my head was feeling light.

"Calm down, sweetheart," I could muster up. "You must calm down for the baby. We have to keep her safe."

"She's a girl," Lauryn uttered in a defeated tone, shaking her head slowly. "She's already not safe."

I blinked with realization. Gradually released my bear hug on Lauryn to turn her to face me. I took her face, that was wet with tears, into my hands to look into her eyes.

"I'm scared for her already," she admitted through trembling lips and with wild eyes.

I squeezed my lids closed and resisted, dropping my head in defeat.

Not at what she said, but at me not realizing the toll hearing she was pregnant with a girl would take on her.

How could I be so damn naïve?

I pulled her to me and wrapped my arms around her. Kissed her at the top of her head, then exhaled the breath I'd been holding.

Lauryn wasn't angry. Scared was more accurate of a description. And I missed that fact.

Dr. Carmen was right. We needed help.

And fast.

Thirty-Three

LAURYN

Her office was pleasant. Something about it was calming, too. I'm sure the tiny forest of plants situated around the room and the soothing rushing sound from both the desk water fountain and the slightly larger fountain on her bookshelf helped with the mood in the office.

But it was something else.

She sat behind her desk, writing something into a black book. The woman had a youthful radiance, skin lacking many wrinkles and eyes were so bright you could see the natural light in them. But her beautiful crown full of salt and pepper curls she kept in a high puff confused me.

Confused me because she looked so young but was still mature.

"Did you two find the office well?" She asked, lifting her eyes off the black book.

"We did," Asher answered beside me.

I refused to come here without him.

"You can try a session," Asher proposed. "One therapy session and if you don't like it, we can seek help somewhere else."

I shook my head. "Asher, I'm not going alone."

"Sweetheart, you have to," he tried.

We were in bed, him behind me with his arm draped over my waist and his hand laying on my belly. He stroked it with his palm and his touch was feeling more sensual than innocent.

I'd fallen in love with him, holding me in this position. We weren't having sex, although I hoped that would change in the next minute. Laying there in his arms with his breath against my neck was a kind of intimacy that was so satisfying.

"I'll only go if you go with me."

"Then done," he agreed. "I'll go."

"Your office is nice," Asher added. His thumb stroked the back of my hand as the rest of our fingers remained interlocked. "It isn't set up like your typical psychotherapist's office. At all."

She winked. "That was the goal."

Asher chuckled.

Her name was Dr. Elizabeth Peters, but she insisted I simply call her Liz.

"Doctor offices," she commented, "at least the ones I've been to are so stuffy and unwelcoming. All business."

"All business," Asher echoed. "I visited a few when I was studying at Brookville. It was one reason I believed psychology might not be for me. I wanted something more fluid. And I didn't think that existed because of the stuffiness I experienced."

"Well, I'm glad you could get a better view of the familiar, but from a different perspective," she added. "Sometimes a different perspective is all we need to confirm the direction we're headed is right. We're just traveling along the wrong road."

Her eyes switched over to me before they lowered to my belly, and she smiled adoringly.

I couldn't hide it if I wanted to. My growing belly had grown to a cute width, as my Aunt Evelyn put it. The width that made people's eyes soften at the sight of it. Aunt Evelyn couldn't keep her hands off it every time I visited. Asher was none better.

Dr. Liz asked, "Do you know what you're having, Lauryn?

I nodded. "A girl."

I twisted my mouth to one side, feeling the inside of my nose sting like it usually did right before I started crying. I knew the tears weren't far behind.

Every time I remembered what I was carrying, my heart ached.

I loved my baby girl already. But the world left me scared for her more.

"Girls are cool." Liz smiled as she reclined back in her office chair. "What makes them great is they all have distinct personalities."

I blinked in response.

"I have a daughter." Liz chuckled. "Eryn. She was five kids in one when she was a child."

That made me fight back a smile.

"Fireball energy from the womb, I tell you," Liz added through her laugh. "And not much has changed as she's reached her 30s."

"Were you scared for her?"

I saw when her smile wanted to get small. "Oh yes. Absolutely."

She had my attention.

"Although Eryn was my second born, her older brother, Everett, being four years older than her, I was still nervous after giving birth to her."

"Why?" I queried.

"I wasn't sure I'd know how to raise a girl." Liz folded her hands on her desk. "I grew up in a house full of boys. Heck, I was a tomboy for a good portion of my childhood and, until I was a teenager. I wasn't girly or feminine in the least. I'm still not."

"Same," I agreed. "The not being girly part."

"How about the having the girl part? She asked next.

I held my stare with her.

"Were you as scared as I was about having a girl?"

"Not *were*. I *am*," I admitted. "I'm petrified."

Liz nodded. "Because she's your first baby?"

"Because I don't want what happened to me to happen to her. And it could because she's a girl."

I felt the tension in Asher's hand around mine tighten, then quickly release.

When I glanced in his direction, I noticed the tension in his jaw, too. He released that too the moment he noticed my attention on him.

My attention returned to Liz, who relaxed her elbow on her desk, then balanced her arm on that elbow to lean her chin into her open hand. "Your assault is what you're referencing."

Not a question. A statement.

Asher filled out Liz's new patient form online and asked if it was okay for him to put on the form why we were seeking her help. I knew the topic of my assault would come up. Asher warned me it would. And oddly, I didn't have as much of a problem with it now that I was here, sitting across from her.

Liz gave off a maternal vibe. It surprised me a little she was nervous about having a daughter. I guess to me that humanized her some. Learning she was also a tomboy, something I've been told I am from the time I was younger, made me feel more understood by her, too. More comfortable. She didn't have to share anything about herself. Could have asked me a bunch of questions trying to get into my head. A part of me wanted to reciprocate, and it felt easy to, being that we had so much in common.

"Yes," I said in response. "I'm talking about my rape."

"Do you feel what happened to you happened to you because you were a girl?"

"And because it was my fault."

Her eyebrows reacted before she could say anything else. "What about what happened made you feel it was your fault?"

I twisted my lips to one side to bite the inside of my cheek. "Because I..." I cleared my throat. "Because I had a stupid crush on him before he raped me." I inhaled a deep breath and released it through my mouth. "I thought he was cute."

"How did you two meet?"

"He was my dad's friend." I clenched my jaw. "Him and my dad met when my dad was in prison. My dad got out before him and when he got out seven years after my dad, my dad allowed him to stay with us until he got back on his feet."

Liz nodded, lowering her eyes for a moment to write something into the black book she kept on her desk.

She focused on me and asked, "Was he much older than you?"

"Yeah. About ten years. He was in his mid-twenties." I shrugged. "But he had a younger appearance because he had a smoother face than most guys. He was a pretty boy, as the girls around the way used to say. Had a baby face, so he seemed younger than his age."

Liz nodded.

"He reminded me of the singer DeVante Swing from Jodeci." I gritted my teeth. "Same skin tone and light eyes. First thing I noticed when he walked into our house." I rolled my eyes and scoffed. "Used to imagine being his girlfriend." I squeezed my eyes closed while shaking my head. Only thinking about it had me bouncing my legs on the arch of my foot. "But after getting to know him, after seeing how he treated a girlfriend he had that he never mentioned... I didn't like him as much anymore."

"How did he treat her?"

"Terrible," I whispered.

"Terrible, how?"

"Like he didn't like her. Never answering her phone calls, talking bad about her to my dad and his friends whenever they were hanging out, and they thought no one was listening. But I was always listening. And I was always watching the way he moved too." I shook my head. "There was this one time he brought his girlfriend to the house for one of my dad's weekend card games. Him and his girl got into an argument in front of everyone and he hit her a few times in her face with his fist. One of my dad's friends had to pull him off the girl. If not, he probably would have kept hitting her until he got tired."

Liz's eyes were down on the book again, writing. "I want you to know I'm writing a few of the things you are telling me down because I'd like to return to them in the future. Are you okay with that?"

I nodded. "Yeah, it's fine."

She smiled as she lifted her eyes to focus on me again. "Great."

Asher leaned over in his seat to kiss me on the cheek and to whisper against me, "You're doing great, sweetheart."

I was feeling like I was, too. But I couldn't get myself to stop biting the inside of my lip or bouncing my knee up and down on my foot. It was both uncomfortable and relieving to get the thoughts out of my head. Finally.

"So, after you witnessed your father's friend hitting his girlfriend, was that when you stopped liking him?"

I nodded. "That was the start. Me liking him changed when he would bring random women to the house when my parents were out the house. He would have sex with the women on the couch right there out in the open. Always doing it when I got back from school, which was weird, but I figured he was a jerk and that's what jerks do, so..." I shrugged. "I just ignored it. Then he started getting weirder and scarier. I really knew I wanted nothing to do with him when I got up to him standing in my room over my bed one night."

Liz's brows rose. "I can see that being very scary for you."

I inhaled a stuttered breath. "It was weird, more than anything. And I couldn't understand why. I wanted to ask him what he was doing there, but he'd left my room as soon as he saw I was up. And I thought about asking him about it the next day, but he wouldn't pay me any mind that morning. He didn't say one thing to me that morning after I woke to him standing in my room. So, I excused it as one of his many other weird things he did, but I also decided I'd keep my distance from him. He stopped bringing random women around. Stopped talking to me. And I was happy he was out of whatever mood he was in, but I didn't realize the damage was already done."

"Why do you say that?"

"Because a week later, he ruined my life. He took everything from me. My childhood. My parents. *Everything.*" I tried to blink back the tears. "In a matter of hours, he raped me on my living room floor minutes after I walked into the house after returning from school. He shot my mother when she walked in the house minutes after and tried to fight him off me." I tucked my lips into my mouth and rubbed them together. I wanted to stop speaking, but I also wanted to get everything out, too.

Like vomiting. I wanted to stop, but my body wanted what I had to say purged out of me. Finally. "He forced me out of my house with the same gun he shot my mother with, promising he would kill me if I didn't follow him to the abandoned house down the block from our house."

Asher's grip around my hand tightened. The strokes on the back of my hand were soothing me and strengthening my resolve to continue in ways I wasn't sure he was aware of. It helped me keep going.

"He kept me in the basement of the abandoned house," I continued, squeezing my eyes closed, my knee bouncing a little harder. "It didn't have any windows, so I couldn't tell when it was night or day. I'd fight going to sleep until I couldn't help it, and that's when he would attack me. I'd wake up to him inside me." I released the breath, and a cry escaped. "And I'd fight him. Every time I'd fight him but he'd hit me so hard, just like he would hit his girlfriend, until I stopped fighting and gave in. And every time he'd tell me..." I exhaled a shaky breath. "He'd say it was my fault, and that I made him do everything he was doing to me. After a while, I believed him and felt guilty. I found no use in fighting him off me anymore. So, I gave up and gave in. I didn't think anyone would come for me. I started praying to die because I felt like I'd already died and it would be my only eventual escape."

I heard Asher release a stuttered long deep breath beside me. Followed by another before he could silence that, too.

There was silence in the office for a moment. Only the sound of water falling down the rocks in the tiny water fountains was evidence I wasn't alone.

Liz broke the silence, asking a question I wasn't expecting.

"At any point, before it happened, did you want him to do it?"

I darted my eyes to her. "What?"

"Did you want him to attack you? Did you want him to do any of what he did to you?"

I narrowed my eyes at her. "Of course not! What kind of fucking question is that?"

"A question I hope will be your first step, your foundation, for healing. I can see why you would think it was your fault. Your feelings are valid to blame yourself because it shows your part in it. Your feelings are valid because you feel them, and they are real. But your need to take accountability, though understandable, is not your job to do. Because of course you didn't want him to do it. Of course, you did not want to be attacked. So it could not have possibly been your fault, Lauryn," she explained lowly. "As many times as your attacker may have said those words to you and as many times as you convinced yourself to believe them, to take on a blame that wasn't yours, that doesn't change the absolute fact that none of what happened was your fault."

I shook my head quickly. "I'm the reason he raped me because I used to like him, and I thought of him like *that* at least once. I'm the reason my mother is dead. I'm the reason my father is in prison for killing him. All because I didn't—"

"No," she asserted. "*He* is the reason for all of that, because *he* caused all of that to transpire. Remove him from the scenario and none of what happened to you would have happened. Including your assault. You are not to blame. You did nothing to harm anyone for it to have been your fault. You liking someone, you even imagining them sexually, is no warrant for them attacking you. It's not a justification, and your feelings about him before the attack does not make the attack justified or right."

I released a breath of relief. Although my head didn't agree, my heart needed to hear those words Liz spoke to me.

"And you may not see that right now." She acknowledged while smiling. "But I promise you, Lauryn, you will. We will get there. But I need you to be as open and as transparent as you have been today. For someone who has never taken therapy, this, what you've done today, is amazing work. You've done really well."

"You really have, sweetheart," Asher acknowledged out loud. His eyes, when they locked with mine, were soft and a little red. "You did amazing."

"And you have, too, Asher," Liz added. "I'm truly proud of the both of you and I can already tell you two are off to a great start as parents."

Asher stroked the back of my hand with his thumb. When I peeked over at him, he winked, and that made me smile.

"And your fear, as a soon-to-be new mother, is a natural fear, Lauryn," Liz started. "Despite what you've experienced, fearing the things that happened to you, happening to your children, albeit big or small, is something that is natural. Making decisions based on that fear is not, and that's what we're going to work towards: reclaiming your power." Her eyes switched over to Asher. "How about you, Asher? Do you have any fears about having a girl?"

I moved my eyes to him.

"Few," he replied. "I have few. But I know Lauryn and I will figure them out. As far as protecting our little girl, I don't have any fears about that."

"And why is that?" Liz challenged.

I recognized when the side of his mouth lifted in a smirk. "Because her daddy can take down a club full of goons on his own and his mama has a *nasty* right hook, I know all too well about."

Liz looked at me the same time I did her, and we both burst into a loud laugh.

"Well, all right," she expressed through her laugh. "Those reasons sound assuring." Her eyes returned to me. "Lauryn, I'd like to continue to work with you. I have tools I want to share with you today that I want you to use and return here to let me know how they worked for you so I can share more, and you can share more of those fears you have with me. We can address them and work through them all."

For the first time in my life, the weight on my shoulders and my heart felt lighter. I could feel the sun, without seeing it, inside of me. And it felt good.

"How does that sound?" She asked. "You think we can continue doing stuff like this, having conversations similar to this, after today?"

My head was bobbing up and down before I could even think to. It was like my heart was answering for me and I followed it in a way I never have done before.

"Yes," I answered, a smile coming so naturally to my face. "I would like that."

Thirty-Four

ASHER

I followed at a safe distance behind the correctional officer as he walked me to the visitation room.

"Usually, you'd meet him in the in-person visiting room, but he's only allowed no contact visits right now."

I nodded my understanding, finding it difficult to speak.

The day was harder than I expected, and I'd already expected it to be hard.

"Oh, my God!" Lauryn's Aunt Evelyn shrieked the moment her eyes fell on the ring. "It's beautiful."

Her eyes filled with tears that she quickly wiped away before the tears could fall as she stared at the 3-carat diamond engagement ring.

It was a Tuesday evening. I told Lauryn I was meeting up with a friend from Brookville, but really, I was stopping by her aunt's apartment.

The one and only lie I'd ever tell Lauryn.

"It's definitely beautiful," William, Evelyn's boyfriend, expressed from the kitchen. "Got my woman crying and shit."

I chuckled.

"Don't be giving her no ideas over there."

"Aht!" Evelyn shouted. "You are not supposed to say that."

"You know I'mma always keep it real with you, love."

Evelyn rolled her eyes and gestured toward her kitchen with her thumb. "Now I'm gonna have to break up with him."

I hollered a laugh.

"I heard that," he said.

"I meant you to," she replied through her giggling.

Evelyn's gaze was down on the ring again when she sighed. "This is all so crazy good."

She lifted her attention to me as she placed the ring box on her coffee table, her eyes returning to it.

"Only a year ago, I just..." She inhaled a deep breath. "I was so unsure about where life would take her. Lauryn was so closed off. Scared but never saying so. But now, it's like..." She smiled. "When I look into her eyes, I see someone else. Someone so much better. Lighter. Still my Lauryn, but... better. Lighter." She snickered. "I don't know any other way to describe it."

I nodded. "Therapy has been great for her."

"It definitely has been." Evelyn inhaled another deep breath and laughed in her exhale. "Everything is moving so fast. First, she's bringing you here. Then she's pregnant and now you're telling me you want to ask her to marry you. I can't keep up." She snorted. "And I love that so damn much."

I smiled.

"This looks expensive, too."

"It was." I nodded. "I cleared out my savings, but it's worth it."

Her smile melted off her face when she said, "Since we're talking about money." Evelyn moved in closer. "Lauryn has some money I've put away for her."

I knitted my brows.

Evelyn exhaled deeply. "The abandoned property of her attack was supposed to be boarded up. There were a bunch of abandoned properties *around the neighborhood she grew up in that weren't boarded up, which was against the law. A lawyer who was more like an ambulance chaser talked me into filing a civil suit with the city. We ended up winning and they awarded her $2.2 million."*

I blinked hard. "What?!"

"After the lawyer took his cut, Lauryn kept over $1.4 million. But she wants nothing to do with the money."

"Understandably."

Evelyn laid her hand on my forearm. "But it's hers. I haven't touched a dime of it and honestly, with you in school and her out of work, you two can use it."

I shook my head. "Evelyn, if she wants nothing to do with it–"

"Talk to her about it."

"Evelyn—"

"Please." She pressed her hands together. "Just, please think about it, Asher. If the money can benefit the two of you, why not take it? You wouldn't have to worry about work or clearing out your savings again and she wouldn't have to worry about work either and can just enjoy being a mother. I don't have kids of my own, but I remember watching her mother struggle, and I don't want that for Lauryn. She's been through enough. Just please think about it and talk to her."

"I will talk to Lauryn and will see if she will agree, but I won't force the issue."

"Understood, and that's fine with me, and..." She gestured at the diamond ring in the box on her coffee table. "You have my blessing." She nodded enthusiastically. "One thousand percent."

"Thank you." My smile grew wider. "And while your blessing is more than enough, I want to do things the right way."

Evelyn tilted her head to one side.

"I'd like to get her father's blessing, too."

Her mouth formed an O as she sat up in her seat. "Oh, umm." She scratched the back of her head next. "Did Lauryn tell you he's in—"

"Prison." I nodded. "Yes, I know."

She blinked in response.

"I just don't know if he's in New York or what his name is, which is why I'm here to ask you for that information so I can visit him."

She blinked hard this time and slacked her jaw. "You wanna... really?"

I nodded and affirmed, "Yes."

The small smile Evelyn wore slowly pulled at her lips until all I could see were teeth. "Okay. I'll write everything down. But Asher, I gotta tell you."

I focused in on her.

"Where you're going." She shook her head. "It is not a place for the faint of heart, so please be ready."

"Step in here," the correctional officer instructed, pushing open a metal door and gesturing into the room. "He should be out in a few."

The room was small, with only enough room to walk to one chair. Tiny windows, resembling tiny bank teller windows, filled the room. These windows had metal chairs on either side of them.

Nothing about the experience was what I expected. My knowledge of prisons was purely from film, and they failed to capture the energy.

It had a sullied vibe. Low vibrational and cold. I took a cab from Brooklyn to Upstate New York and caught the visitors bus that brought visitors to the prison's island. The second I stepped onto the bus, the energy was off and that would continue when I arrived at the visitor building and had to go through screening of my persons. Thankfully, they had lockers. I was able to store my wallet, my phone, and my watch. I knew from a head of time what to wear. I opted for a simple tee, joggers, and sneakers because of all the restrictions they warned, if violated, would be a reason to cancel any visit I had scheduled. I wanted to bring the ring or at least show a picture, but the rules were the rules.

I sat in the room inhaling the smells of things I couldn't put names to. Collectively, they smelled horrible. Metallic, sour, and pungent were the best I could gather. Despite that, I remained in my seat, waiting.

A metal door on the other side of the tiny window creaked opened. The harsh grate of rusted metal sliding against more rusted metal sounded around me.

I saw his shadow before I saw him.

On the surface, Jayshawn James was intimidating. Big arms, with tattoos covering every inch and a walk that didn't seem hurried in the least. He was searching for my eyes before I could think of finding him.

And when I did, all I recognized was Lauryn. In his light skin tone, in his eyes. Though his brows gave off the impression of someone curious, inspired by intimidation, I could still see Lauryn in his eyes.

I straightened my back in my seat when he arrived on the other side of my window.

In the movies there were phones to converse, but that day in the prison there was simply a slot beneath the window that somehow carried our voices.

"I almost didn't come out here," he revealed to me, his first words.

"Well, that would have been a shame," I replied.

"For you," he countered.

I nodded. "I've waited three hours to see you."

"For what?" He leaned back in his seat, the metal creaking beneath his colossal body. "Nobody never comes out here to see me, but based on what they tell me, my daughter's boyfriend did? For what?"

Jayshawn had tattoos even on his face. Initials on one cheek, tatted black tears under his left eye.

"I would like to ask your daughter to marry me."

For the first time, his eyes moved off me to dart around me, likely analyzing what I said.

He lifted his handcuffed wrists high enough to point his finger at his chest. "You wanna ask me?"

I nodded slowly. "Yes, sir."

He scoffed a laugh. Gritted his teeth next. "What's your name?"

"Asher Truesdale."

"Asher Truesdale," he repeated. "Where you from, little nigga?"

"New York."

"Nah." He shook his head, eyes still fixed on me. "Where are you from? What planet do you call home? Because why the fuck you *here* on earth asking me for some shit like that? What kind of pull I got? What answer can I give that's gonna mean something? Are you serious right now?"

"Yes, I am."

"Nigga, why are you *here*?"

"Because Lauryn told me *why* you're *here*," I replied evenly.

The muscles in his face relaxed.

"And I respect that," I continued, looking him right in his eyes. "I respect you."

My fists slammed against my punching dummy, rattling my entire body. Teeth clenched, muscles tight, I kept hitting to relieve myself of the coursing of rage that seemed to be clotted in my veins. It was after 2am and I couldn't sleep. Crept out of the bed, leaving Lauryn asleep in it because the more I laid there and did nothing, the angrier I felt inside.

Earlier that day, we'd visited a psychotherapist's office. Lauryn's first therapy visit. She wanted me to go and although I didn't think I'd be ready to be present; I agreed. Lauryn needed to get the help, and I wanted to be there for her. And although I thought I had prepared myself to hear her, recall the most traumatic thing in her life, I was wrong.

I grunted and pushed air through my gritted teeth. Tightened my fists in my boxing gloves and hit harder, wanting to scream as I did it.

I circled the bag, throwing jabs, crosses, and hooks, feeling my body grow hotter as I executed each punch. I imagined it was him, the man who hurt her. Closed my eyes to picture for only a moment, causing splits in his lips and blacking his eyes. Hearing his skull crack and crumble from the blows. I'd created a picture in my mind based on Lauryn's description. So his face was vivid, crystal clear. And enraging me. My grunts irritated my throat, the tightness of my clenched teeth causing my jaw to ache. In that moment, I wished I could've killed him myself.

I'd circled the bag again, prepared to hit it with another jab when I glimpsed her shadow in my peripheral.

I whipped my head in the direction I thought I saw her to see Lauryn standing at my bedroom doorway with her hand resting on her belly.

I pulled in air through my nose and let it out as roughly the same way, forcing myself to calm down. To breathe.

"Did I wake you?" I exhaled once I had the breath to do it.

She shook her head. "Got up on my own. Like always."

I used my glove to clean the sweat off my face.

"Everything okay?"

My eyes met hers again. "Everything's fine."

"You're upset."

I considered denying that fact but decided against it, not wanting to lie to her.

So, all I did was nod my answer.

"Because of what I said in therapy today?" she quizzed. "Me talking about what happened to me?"

I nodded again.

"I'm okay now, though." She tucked her lips into her mouth for a moment. "Maybe not okay, okay. But I feel a lot better after talking about it."

"I know," I whispered.

Hearing her say that slowed my heart rate and allowed me to pull on the calm needed for me to relax.

"Plus, I'm safe now." Her eyes darted between mine. "Right?"

"Absolutely," I replied, not missing a beat. "Beyond measure, sweetheart."

"I know," she said, softly.

I cleaned the sweat off my brow with my glove again.

A smirk pulled at one corner of her lips. "Can you come back to bed and use the rest of that energy on me?"

I chuckled low and nodded. "I'm going to hop in the shower, and I'll be there soon."

Lauryn smiled, then turned to enter my room again. I turned to the bag and gave it one last hit before removing my gloves, sure I would be back in front of the bag tomorrow night. Because I was pissed, angry, and needing to get all of that out to be the best I could be for Lauryn. I knew I couldn't undo the stuff that happened to her, but I swore I'd protect her and my daughter the same way Lauryn's father did. Without a doubt.

"You respect me?" Jayshawn challenged.

"Absolutely," I answered.

He blinked away, then refocused on me.

"She's pregnant," I revealed.

His jaw slacked a little, eyes lit up.

"Lauryn's pregnant and the baby's due in September," I added. "In three months."

"My birthday is in September," he said low, nodding to himself. "Fuck. Pregnant." He scoffed in disbelief. "Wow."

We were quiet for a moment. We had plenty of time to be. They made me wait for three hours but assured me all visits could last up to one hour.

"You said no one comes to see you." I ran my hand down my beard. "But she said she came to see you years ago."

He shook his head. "I didn't want to see her. I couldn't."

I knitted my brows.

"In here..." He gestured with his eyes. "Ain't no place for someone like her. I didn't want her here. I wanted her out of here the moment I heard she was under this fucking roof. So, I denied the visit. I said I didn't want it."

He kissed his teeth. "I've put her through enough. Being the reason, all that shit happened to her." He grunted, then sniffed. "I didn't want her to have to be here, too."

"She blamed herself for what happened to her, too," I told him. "But her therapist put it best when she said that the only person to blame was the man who did it—"

"Nah!" Jayshawn's voice echoed around us.

"Aye," I heard out of sight.

Jayshawn raised a hand in the direction the voice came from. "My bad," he said, before swallowing hard.

His eyes were back on me. "That shit was all my fault."

Jayshawn lifted his cuffed wrists high enough to run his fingers down the sides of his mouth. "I'm a fuckup. Been a fuck up all my life. From the time I was a kid. My mama was a crack fiend, my father was her drug dealer who accepted payment from her with sex. I ain't never met him. I raised myself and only knew one way to live. So, you know." He shrugged. "I got in trouble for petty crimes. Disorderly conduct and shoplifting. That evolved to robbery and shit. Sometimes they'd get violent. I was in and out of jail or whatever. But then I met Lauryn's mother, and we had a good thing. But I fucked up, got her pregnant by accident." He shook his head. "Had no fucking plan, couldn't get no job with my record. But when I saw my baby girl the day she was born. Beautiful, soft, everything right with life. I said I'd figure it out. But then, figuring it out was easier said than done. She needed diapers. Her mama couldn't work after just having a baby, so I figured I'd do a little something, swipe a chain off some mark, to pawn and get enough until I figure out something permanent. But I picked the wrong one. My mark wouldn't give up his chain without a fight. The gun I robbed him with ended up going off, shooting him in the chest. He survived, but my involvement only got me locked up on robbery in the first degree. And my time behind bars was for a while. Six years. By the time I got released, Lauryn was six years old. She wasn't the three-week-old baby I left. She was now walking, talking, and sassy as fuck."

He laughed, and I did too.

Soon his smile was falling off his face again. "We were good for a few years. Me and my little family. I got me a construction job working under a nigga who didn't give a fuck about my record. I was making decent money. My household was happy, eatin'. My daughter growing more and more beautiful every day. And smart as hell. Then I get that fucking call." He gritted out. "During my last bid, I met a little nigga." Jayshawn scratched his head and grunted as he slid his hand down to his face. "Corey."

His whole mood shifted with the mention of that name and a feeling of cold washed over me.

"He was getting violated on his first day. He was what we all called soft. I felt bad for the kid. He was young. Only a teen when they threw his ass behind bars, so *them boys*... shit, *them boys* couldn't wait to get their hands on him."

I held my stare with him, picking up on what he was explaining.

"One day, I fought one of them off him and you know, told him I would have his back. And I *had* his back while I was doing my time. But after I got out, I was done. I promised myself I would leave all that shit behind for good. Somehow, that motherfucker got my info and called me up when it was time for him to get released seven years after I got out. And my dumb ass agreed for him to come and live with me and mine."

Jayshawn inhaled deeply and let his exhale go like a growl.

"I suspected nothing." He shook his head. "If I knew he was even looking at Lauryn in any way other than a little sister, I would've whopped his ass and kicked him out. But he was a snake. Waited for me and Lauryn's mother to be out the house before he..." He released a stutter exhale. "Shot my fucking wife. That woman stayed alive long enough to hear I rescued her daughter, according to her sister Evelyn. That's the only peace I get with that."

I bit the inside of my cheek.

"What happened to my baby girl was my fault and can't nobody tell me different. Not you, not her. Nobody."

He sniffed back his tears, quickly cleaning his face.

"I'm in here for life now," he gritted out. "I don't give a fuck 'bout nothing, my nigga. I ain't got shit to look forward to. The only reason I got a no contact visit is because I violated the rules last month and that means for six months, I can't have no in-person visits, but that shit doesn't matter because no one comes to see me. No one fucking with me no more. So, Lauryn's good. I was barely in her life, anyway. And when I was, I let that happen to her. She gon' be all right without me."

"She misses you," I told him. "Writes you every day."

"Write me?"

"In a notebook." I smiled. "Several of them. They fill one of her bookshelves now."

His brows wrinkled.

"She's been afraid to write to you directly since you wouldn't see her. She thinks you're mad at her."

"Never." His bottom lip trembled. "I could never be mad at her."

"I'll tell you what." I leaned close to the window. "I'll mail a few of the notebooks to you with her permission."

"Yeah?"

"Promise." I nodded. "And, with your permission, when the time is right, I'd like to bring her and your granddaughter here for you to see them."

He smiled and his facial features softened. "Granddaughter?"

I smiled. "But Mr. James, I can't do that if you don't find your reason. Because your reason will make you want to follow the rules. And following the rules will allow you to have access to your daughter, who would like to see you, but that wouldn't be a possibility if you don't find your reason, you know?"

He nodded, then dropped his head, lifting it soon after. "Yeah, I hear you."

I nodded too, inhaling deeply.

"Aye," he said across from me through the glass.

When I looked up at him, he scoffed a laugh. "You a real one."

I shrugged. "I think I know what that means, but I can't be too sure."

He hollered a laugh, and I did too.

Jayshawn pressed his fist up to the glass and gestured with his head. "It means you got my blessing, Asher."

I smiled and pressed my fist to the glass on the other side of his. "Now *that* I understand."

———

I'd waited long enough.

At least that was my thinking.

I'd visited her father in prison two days prior and had gotten his blessing, also making a promise I had every intention of keeping.

But before then, I'd been trying to think of ways, creative ways, to ask Lauryn to be my wife.

I walked out of the bedroom, dropping the box with the ring into my joggers' pocket.

We were only two days away from summer, but the weather was already providing the heat New York City summers were famous for. With my first semester complete with no plans to attend summer school, I had all the time in the world. That made me available to Lauryn, which I loved.

The moment I stepped into the space that provided a view out into the living room, I saw Lauryn following along to a pregnancy yoga video online.

She'd been doing yoga for almost a month now, ever since her therapist, Liz, recommended it.

Well, *our* therapist now.

"Can I be honest with you?" I asked, sitting in the chair across from Liz's desk.

I'd just walked in through her door after she called a week prior asking if she could meet with me, independent of Lauryn.

Lauryn, a week prior, had attended her session alone. Her request.

And I was beyond thrilled that she'd gotten comfortable enough to meet with Liz alone. But then Liz called me after Lauryn's first session asking for me to come in to see her.

Alone.

She smiled. "Of course."

"I don't need therapy."

Liz nodded this time, smile still in place. "We all need therapy, Asher." Liz closed her book and moved it to the side. "We all need to talk to people, right?"

"Well, yes."

"So, we should speak to people able enough to not only listen to our concerns, our worries, or simply our random thoughts, but who can also provide tools in the event there are any blocks. Why should we only rely on people who are still navigating their own lives to listen to our issues and provide guidance?"

I pushed my tongue into my cheek.

"That's nice here and there, of course, but we all need therapy in some form."

"I don't want to take any time that Lauryn could use."

"You just completed your first year at LU, correct?" she asked instead. "I recall you mentioning that in one session you came to with Lauryn."

"Yes." I nodded before seesawing my head from left to right. "Well, it's my first year at LU, but not my first year in a Ph.D. program."

She tilted her head to one side.

"I... I dropped out of my Ph.D. program at Brookville U my fifth year."

Her brows rose.

"I know." I shook my head and dropped it into my hand. "It... umm... I wasn't clear on my purpose when I went for my Ph.D. and life was unclear to me. "

"I didn't know what I wanted to do with psychology, either." She smiled. "While many psychologists start school and stay in it until they get their doctorates, I went as far as only getting my master's degree in psychology. I decided a year after I would return to school for my doctorate. After my master's, I believed I was done. I planned to get a job and live my life as a mother and a wife, but this neighborhood way back when helped with

changing my mind. I realized how many of the people who looked like me needed someone who looked like them to lend them their ears."

I nodded. "I similarly realized this while I was away in Bali for a year."

Liz sat up. "Bali."

I smiled big. "I've lived many lives."

"Your parents must have stories about you and your many lives."

I scoffed a laugh. "My mother is never happy about my decisions and my father..." I shrugged next. "My father is the most absentee but somehow still present father I've ever met in my life."

Liz blinked in response.

"My mother has been a single wife for over thirty-years, and she doesn't even realize it."

Liz reached for her black book and flipped it open.

"And you're good." I chuckled. "Very good."

She giggled, her attention down in her book as she wrote. "Do you mind if I take notes?"

"I don't mind," I replied. "Go for it."

"You see, Asher." Liz lifted her eyes to me. "We all need someone to talk to. To make sense of things. Even me. I go to therapy."

That made me sit up. "You go to therapy?"

"I do," she confirmed, resting her pen inside the spine of her book. "Most great therapists do. Because even the helpers need help too. It's the only way we can be our absolute best for others and ourselves."

I nodded, understanding the logic.

"I want to meet with you because I see what you are doing for Lauryn." She smiled. "And it is beautiful, and I want you to continue to be beautiful together. And... therapy will help support that. For you both."

"Okay," I agreed.

"It can be a lot to take on," she added. "Let's share the weight of it all." She folded her hands together. "So, I'll meet with Lauryn privately and then with you privately, and then the two of you together. How does that sound?"

"Like a solid plan."

And it has been.

Meeting with Liz on a weekly basis, days after her private sessions with Lauryn, has been very beneficial to me. I look forward to it, especially Liz's insights on how to navigate my Ph.D. program at LU. She knows a few of the psychology professors personally.

It was from one session Lauryn and I attended together that I knew I was ready to ask her to marry me.

I couldn't figure out how.

Lauryn sat on her gray yoga mat facing my mounted flatscreen. Shortly after learning she was pregnant, I convinced her to move in with me. And she obliged by spending most of her time in my apartment, only returning to hers to get something she needed.

I thought I would be nervous today. I'd spent so many weeks trying to decide how I would ask her. Thought about taking her to dinner but knew she wasn't the type to like all the attention put on her.

Thought about going away with her, to Atlantic City, for symbolic reasons, but the crowds there during the summer wasn't something I wanted to deal with.

So, that morning, I decided to just go for it.

Her yoga practice was winding down. Lauryn returned to this video often in her weekly workouts, so I knew the practice was coming to a close.

Seated in an upright position with her legs folded in front of her, I got down into a squat behind her and stretched out my legs on either side of her.

When I wrapped my arms around her, placing my hands on either side of her round belly, she dropped her head back against me. I couldn't help but to kiss her neck.

She giggled. "Don't distract me. I'm almost done."

"Couldn't help it." I pressed another kiss to the back of her neck.

Our baby girl pressed her tiny body against the warmth of my right hand, making me smile to myself.

The yoga video was seconds away from ending. One of the final sequences was inhaling and exhaling for four counts three separate times.

By the final inhale and exhalation, I revealed, "I went to see your father on Thursday."

I noticed when she inhaled a staggered breath and held it in.

I rubbed her belly and held her closer. "Breathe, sweetheart."

She tried to turn in my arms, but I held her in place. "What did you just say?"

"Breathe."

"Asher," she gritted out.

"Please." I kissed her neck and continued rubbing her belly. "Continue to breathe for us, sweetheart."

And she did, albeit with them being sharp.

"I needed to talk to him."

"The fuck?! About *what*?" she spat.

"*Shh*," I shushed in her ear, rubbing her belly slower. "Calm down."

"Why would you…" She took in a long breath, and I appreciated her pause. Her mindfulness. Her doing so showed me she was honestly trying and, given the news I shared, it showed a lot of restraint on her part. "Why would you visit my father, Asher?"

I gently pulled my hand off her belly to slide my fingers into my joggers' pocket, retrieving the ring box. Stretched my arm out in front of her with the ring box in hand and flipped it open.

She gasped softly.

"So I could ask him if I could marry his daughter."

Her inhales and exhales were sharper now, but in a good way.

I moved from behind her, changing position so that I was in front of her now.

She was both shocked and smiling. Lips trying to form words that her mind wouldn't meet her halfway on.

And I smiled. Even more sure that this is what I wanted with her.

In my new position in front of her, I stretched my legs out on either side of her, caging her in and sitting directly in front of her now.

"I love you," I decreed, running my thumb down her cheek. "And as crazy as it's going to sound… I knew this from the very first night I laid eyes on you outside of this building."

Lauryn's eyes watered with tears. I balanced her head in my hand so I could catch her tears when they fell.

"We've done things a little backward." I chuckled. "Life has been unfolding for us in ways that seem unplanned, but it feels like this is God's plan for us."

She dropped her head in front of her to gather her breath. I lifted her chin gently with my finger to lock eyes with her again.

"You are many things, Lauryn." I nodded. "Many amazing things. Including my heart, sweetheart."

She blinked, and the tears fell. And as planned, my hand was there to catch them and I planned to be there to catch her too. Every time.

"Will you make me the happiest man on this planet and be my wife, Lauryn? Will you marry me?"

She was fighting back tears and nodding before the words, "Yes, I will," came out of her mouth.

And it was the second sweetest thing I'd ever heard in my life.

I'd hear the sweetest thing in only a few months.

THIRTY-FIVE

LAURYN

Our silverware scraped against the porcelain plates as we ate in silence.

Every so often, I'd lift my eyes out of my plate and survey the surrounding faces.

If someone would have told me, I would sit in Asher's childhood home, eating across from his parents. I would've told them they were crazy.

"Will you have dinner with me at my parents' home on Long Island next week?" Asher asked me, randomly. We were walking through the park in silence. Allowing the summer afternoon activity to provide all the surrounding noise. With schools out, there were children all around us. Interestingly, after getting pregnant, I tolerated them a bit more.

That's why we were in the park that day walking. My doctor insisted I up my physical activity, so I'd be ready for labor.

I twisted my neck in his direction.

Asher glanced at me before facing forward. "My mother has been asking—"

"I remember what happened the last time you said that," I said to the blacktop road ahead of us.

Prospect Park was always busy with activity, regardless of the hour these days. I was thinking at the moment that's why he asked me here.

"I'll agree if..." I stopped walking and turned to him. "You answer more questions about what happened when you went to see my dad."

"Whatever you want to know," he obliged with no hesitation. "Ask away."

I had so many questions.

When he revealed to me he'd seen my father, I needed time to process that. Although Asher revealed his reasons for going to see my father without asking or telling me first, I still needed time to wrap my mind around a few things. To be honest, I was a little afraid to ask more questions about what happened when Asher visited my dad at the prison. Not afraid that Asher wouldn't tell me. Afraid of what I would learn.

"Did he seem happy?"

Asher inhaled a deep breath through his mouth. "Not really." He slid his hands into his pockets next. "It was a non-contact visit because he's gotten himself into trouble and the penalty has been non-contact visits for several months."

"How many months?"

"Six."

"Did he say what kind of trouble?"

Asher shook his head.

I rolled my eyes off his and ran my fingers through my hair, feeling the diamond on my new engagement ring comb through my strands.

I was still getting used to the feeling.

The ring and being engaged.

That prompted me to ask, "Was he okay with you asking me to marry you?"

He smiled. "Yes, he was."

I fought my smile at first, but gave in the next.

My next question weighed my smile down. Because I wanted to ask it, but was too afraid for the honest answer.

"Did he ask you to bring me next time, or did you suggest it?"

"It was my suggestion."

I collapsed, my eyes closed and turned away.

Asher wrapped his arms around me from behind, resting his hands on my round belly.

He ran his fingers around my stomach a few times, lowering his head enough to press his lips into my neck.

"'Cause he doesn't want to see me."

"He has his reasons, Lauryn," Asher insisted, "but I promise it's not what you think they are."

"Because it's my fault he's in there."

"He thinks it's his fault."

I turned in his arms.

"He blames himself, too."

"What?" I asked, feeling my heart pick up in rhythm. "Why... why does he..."

"That's something you two would discuss, sweetheart," Asher answered. "But he wants to see you. He just doesn't want you being uncomfortable being in the prison after everything. He wants nothing to make you feel uncomfortable anymore."

I closed the space between us and leaned my head against his chest.

Bicyclist whizzed by us and joggers pounded the pavements as they ran past.

"I still can't believe you went to a prison." I lifted my head to lock eyes with him. "If you could do that, I can at the least eat with your parents."

"How's the steak?" Asher's mother, Patricia, asked across from us.

I focused her way and forced a smile.

"I hope it's well seasoned," she joked. "I left the salt within reach for you."

"It's fine." I licked my lips. "No extra salt needed."

She giggled, and I had to fight to keep my brows from wrinkling.

"Do you two have a name picked out yet?" Asher's father, Jonathan, asked next.

I glanced at Asher at the same time he looked at me. We nodded.

"Yeah," I said, moving my eyes to Jonathan. "We're going with Eres."

"Oooh," Patricia expressed with more breath than tone. "That's beautiful. It's perfect."

I turned to Asher again, and he read my expression perfectly, chuckling.

"I'm kind of disappointed," Asher started, cleaning his mouth. "I've spent all week preparing Lauryn for a weird evening with you two."

Jonathan scoffed a laugh and Patricia giggled.

I bit back my smile because it was true.

Asher invested so much time in preparing me for an awkward evening that he failed to let me know he lived in a mansion.

The space was immense. The dining room we sat to eat in was larger than my apartment. The dishes we ate from were fine China, the glasses crystal. There were so many utensils on the table I thought I'd go crossed eye trying to figure out which one to use.

And the maids.

There were so many for only us four.

I knew Asher came from money, but I didn't realize it was *this* much.

"Why would we make things awkward?" Jonathan cleaned his mouth and sat up in his seat.

He was a larger man than Asher in weight, but just as handsome. They shared the same complexion and the same handsome smile. Demeanors weren't that far off, either. Asher was just as quiet, but observant. But even with the similarities, they were different.

"You two have a way of doing that, I guess," Asher answered.

"Oh, Asher," Patricia exclaimed.

"You've made your decision, Asher," Jonathan continued. "Lauryn is a lovely woman who is carrying your child and wearing your ring. What objections could we *possibly* have at this point?"

"So, is this tolerance?" Asher queried. "Sufferance?"

"It's acceptance," Patricia chimed in. "Repentance."

That made me shoot a glance her way.

"Repentance?" Asher challenged.

Patricia sighed, balancing her elbows on the dining room table to interlock her fingers together. "Last year, this time, things were so strange. Uncertain. At least to me."

Asher shut his eyes for a moment. I took his hand underneath the table, and he focused on me and gave me a small smile.

"You'd just returned from Bali after turning off your phone and going completely off the radar." Patricia inhaled deeply. "You're about to have a child of your own, so you'll understand how tumultuous that was for me."

"She barely slept," Jonathan chimed in.

Asher clenched his jaw in reaction, but quickly released it.

"You've never been an amiable person to guide, Asher," Patricia added.

"You mean control?" Asher asked.

Patricia tucked her pink painted lips into her mouth, then slowly released them. She pushed her chair back to stand.

"Lauryn," she said next.

I trained my eyes on her.

"Can we speak privately?"

Asher tightened his grip around my hand underneath the table.

"Are you kidding?" he asked.

She sagged her shoulders. "Asher, please. Do you really think I can do something heinous?"

"I didn't *think* you could talk my fiancée into having an abortion without my knowledge."

"She was your *girlfriend*, and there was a lot unknown." Patricia pinched the bridge of her nose. "Look, I would like to show her something and speak with her alone. Of course, with your permission and you have my absolute promise I will not harm her in my care, okay? She's carrying my grandchild for God's sake." She pointed her eyes at me. "I promise you're safe with me. Okay, Lauryn?"

I narrowed my eyes at her and saw no ill intent in her eyes.

I focused on Asher next and said, "I'll be fine."

"If you need anything," he reminded, glancing up at his mother before returning his attention to me. "You call me."

With that, I was on my feet and walking beside Patricia.

She gave me a brief tour of their estate, as she called it. Gave me a history of when architects built it and how it belonged to a French entrepreneur in the 70s before Jonathan bought it with his first biggest check.

"We were so thrilled when he did," she gushed, pressing her perfect hands to her chest. "With seven bedrooms and only the three of us, everyone thought we were insane but, we knew we'd always have plans for the rooms."

We stopped in front of double doors. The wood on the doors appeared thick, the doorframe thicker. I could smell the wood's rich smoky notes, only standing in front of the door.

Patricia turned on the brass doorknobs and pushed opened both doors.

My eyes grew at what she kept behind those doors.

The walls were powder pink and outlined in shiny foil gold.

A white crib with a silk curtain draped over it was straight ahead. Gathered at the top and held suspended over the crib by a large gold tiara.

Stuffed animals almost as big as me decorated the corners of the room. A giant giraffe on one end and the cutest gray elephant on the other.

My heart couldn't help but to melt at the sight of it all.

"I always wanted a girl," she said to my left. "After having Asher, of course. When I found out I was pregnant with Asher, I didn't care what I had. I wanted a baby after trying for years and getting nothing."

Patricia left my side to approach the crib, running her hand along the white railing of it.

"As soon as Asher told me you were having a girl, I got ahead of myself." She smiled. "Hired an interior designer to create a nursery, not once thinking my granddaughter's mother might hate me after everything that has happened."

I folded my arms.

"I do that sometimes." She nodded. "Act before thinking. Then regret sets in." Patricia pressed her hands together, then she brought her fingers to her lips. "I am so sorry, Lauryn, for everything. It just..." She inhaled a breath while shaking her head. "Everything was happening *so* fast. I finally had Asher back after he'd left the country for a year. I felt he'd made such poor decisions, and I was worried that you—"

"Were another one of those poor decisions?" I finished.

She blinked twice.

"Don't feel bad. I thought so too." I walked towards the crib, taking in the room along the way. Noticing the tiny details I missed from the door. I smiled as I fell more and more in love with it all. "Deep in my heart, I still feel he could do so much better than me, so I can't hold it too much against you that you felt the same way."

"How I felt was stupid and based on a fear which makes it wrong." Her hand was to her chest again when she added, "He loves you *so* much."

"He does," I concurred.

"And you love him."

"I do."

She inhaled a deep breath and let it out as an audible exhale. "Then that's all that matters to me. It's what should have mattered when you and I first met but, I can't undo that. All I can do is do better. Be better. And supportive."

My focus was on the room again, finding it impossible to fight back my smile.

"I would love for my granddaughter to spend time here whenever the time is right," she admitted. "Obviously, I know it'll take some time for you and I to get to know each other well enough for the trust to be there, but I want you to know I'll be patient and ready whenever you are."

"Geez," Asher said behind us. "Could it get any pinker in here?"

Patricia giggled.

"What is all this?"

"Ten minutes," Patricia said instead, turning away from the crib to face Asher. "You left us alone for ten minutes."

"Actually five," he clarified, entering the room, his eyes on everything around him. "I took my time making it up here behind you two, shortly after you left the table."

When he was close, Asher wrapped his arms around me from the back, like always, resting his hands on my belly.

"This," Patricia started, "Is my way of saying I'm excited for Eres. And obviously, Glam Ma is so in tuned with her granddaughter that she helped design a room fit for a princess."

"Glam Ma?" I asked.

"An alternative to grandma and nana." She cringed. "I couldn't."

I scoffed a laugh, and Asher chuckled.

Her eyes moved to Asher. "Your Aunt Priscilla gave me the idea. Said she would use it once Summer and Jayce gave her a grand baby. She's *so* jealous I beat her to it."

Asher snickered, and I smiled.

"Anyway." She pressed a hand to Asher's cheek, then peeked over at me to flash a warm smile. "I'm going downstairs to be with your father, Asher. He's hardly home, so I'm going to take up as much of his time as I can."

"*Hmph,*" Asher huffed.

"You two stay up here as long as you want," she said, exiting the room.

Asher walked opposite me to face me.

"It's like meeting two different people," I remarked. "I obviously like *this* Patricia way more."

"Same," he echoed, and I giggled.

"Liz told me to expect the best when I told her about this dinner." I moved my eyes off Asher to focus on the surrounding room. "I did, and it seems to have worked out."

Asher bobbed his head up and down.

I pressed my hand to his chest and moved in closer.

"I knew you were rich, but I didn't think *this* rich."

Asher broke eye contact and furrowed his brows. "Money doesn't make you rich."

"I know, I'm just saying..." I bit my bottom lip, then released it. "I didn't know your family had this much money."

"And I didn't know you did, too."

I reared my head back. "What?"

"Evelyn told me about the money she's keeping for you..."

Me waving my hand in the air and creating space between us kept him from finishing his sentence.

"And sweetheart, I get it."

"Then *why* are you bringing it up if you get *it?*"

"Because she made a valid point regarding it."

I kissed my teeth.

I've lost count of how many times my aunt has reminded me of that dirty ass money sitting in several bank accounts somewhere in New York.

"Do we need it? No," he continued. "I get money from my trust every month. A slow release of it until I'm 40, according to my father. I'll receive what's left of it on my 40th birthday, which will be at least 9-figures.

My parents handled tuition and will continue to do so for the length of my Ph.D. program. And that is the only other extra money I'll allow myself to accept from them, although I'm sure they'll insist otherwise. They always do."

I blinked in response.

"Would it be nice to know you will have money of your own to take care of yourself and our daughter in the event something happens to me? Yes. Would it be nice to be home as much as possible to take care of you and our daughter when I'm not in school, at least for her first year without a worry or care for how we will pay for things without having to ask anyone? I would *love* that."

I bit at my bottom lip.

"And as much as I love our living situation, I would love to change that, too."

Asher closed the space between us to hold me by my belly. On brand like always, our baby girl moved around the moment she felt her father's touch against me.

"I understand your reservations regarding the money, but they awarded it to you because it belongs to you. It was the *least* they could do in a situation that was far from ideal and completely out of your control. And I think, you should take the money and make a life you've always dreamed of having. Because…" Asher shrugged. "Money doesn't make you rich. But it can help to get the things you know that will help build a rich life. It can help make your life a little more doable."

Asher pressed his lips to my forehead, leaving a kiss.

"But that is only my two cents." He wrapped his arms around me and held me tight. "I'll support you in whatever decision you make."

I wrapped my arms around him too and held him close, knowing he meant every word.

Thirty-Six

LAURYN

"You look so beautiful," my aunt Evelyn mused, fighting back tears.

I rolled my eyes up to keep my tears from forming. "Please don't start."

Our voices echoed down the empty, wide corridor as we spoke.

I expected little from today. But Asher and Aunt Evelyn wanted it to be so special.

And it was.

I just wasn't used to all this fuss.

"They said we're next," Asher announced behind us.

I turned his way and couldn't help the smile pulling at my lips.

He looked good in all white. Insisted we both wear it today.

Because we were getting married.

"Do you think we can avoid making an enormous deal over the wedding thing?" I asked.

We were in his kitchen, an hour away from noon, working together to make something to eat.

"What do you mean?" He asked, his attention down on the cutting board where he was slicing carrots.

"I don't want a big wedding."

Asher peeked over his shoulder at me, then focused on the cutting board again. He shrugged. "Then we don't have to have a big wedding."

"I don't want a wedding, period."

That got his full attention.

He turned to face me immediately.

"You..." He tilted his head to one side. "You don't want to get married?"

"I want to get married. I just don't want a wedding." I licked my lips. "I was thinking City Hall?"

His brows shot up. "City Hall."

"Yeah." I tucked my lips into my mouth to rub together. "I wanna marry you and to me, that's the most important part. Going through all the getting a dress shit, picking bridesmaids which I don't have a variety of ladies to choose from."

"I don't have a variety of guys, either."

"Exactly."

"But is that what you really want?" He asked, lowering his chin to focus on me. "City Hall?"

I nodded and smiled. "That's exactly what I want."

The building we all stood in was very business. No one barely spoke and every conversation we'd had was through a plexiglass and only after our number was called.

Aunt Evelyn made a Gatsby style gold and ivory brooch bouquet for me. She made the bouquet with satin and chiffon ivory flowers, sparkling gems, draping pearls, and a beautiful gold handle. Took her a week to put it all together. She insisted she do my hair, which was styled in an immaculate top bun. Makeup was light, which I argued with her about wearing. But the result didn't cover up what I usually looked like.

It enhanced everything.

"Asher?" We heard up the hall.

I glanced that way to see a dark skin gentleman, tall, lanky. The camera he gripped tightly in his hand hinted it weighed more than him.

"Vic." Asher smiled. "You're right on time." Asher focused on me. "Sweetheart, this is Vic. He's going to photograph everything."

"Photograph?" I glanced at Vic before looking at Asher again. "I thought we agreed to keep it simple."

Asher laid his hands against my belly and gave me a warm smile. "It's still simple, but I want the memories too."

"*Aww,*" Aunt Evelyn cooed behind me, and I shot her a mean glare that made her giggle.

"Hey," Asher said, guiding my attention back to him. "Today is our wedding day and I know you wanted little, but you must give me a little, too. I want something that will help us remember today. Can I please have that?"

Couldn't stop the smile from pulling at my lips. "Yes."

Asher's cousin Summer and her fiancé, Jayce, arrived right before a clerk ushered all five of us into a room.

It resembled a small office. Complete with four pews and a wooden podium.

The clerk of courts was waiting for us when we stepped in. He was the warmest personality we encountered that day, and he didn't waste any time getting started.

Asher and I had applied for our marriage license a month prior, literally a few days after deciding we would get married at City Hall. The process was quick. In comparison, deciding on a wedding date took the longest time, but thankfully we had sixty days to pick our date.

Through it all, I didn't get hyped over the process. I was happy to be married to Asher, but I didn't allow myself the giddiness of it all.

It seemed it arrived the moment Asher, and I stood opposite one another.

The clerk began reciting the vows when Asher said to the clerk, "I wrote my own vows, if that's okay?"

"I'll allow it," the clerk replied.

"Oh my God," Summer gushed from the front pew.

I narrowed my eyes at Asher. "I didn't know you wrote vows."

He smirked. "Well, now you do."

I scoffed a laugh.

"Lauryn," he said, running the pad of his finger over the back of my hand. "From the moment I moved into the same building as you, our love story began in my eyes."

I took a breath, feeling his words.

"A tale of two hearts finding their way. Believe it or not, life had me feeling lost, sweetheart. Allowing life to just carry me because the life I thought I knew was mine wasn't, and I honestly didn't know what I wanted in my life that would feel purposeful. Until you."

He nodded.

"I discovered a warmth that drew me closer to you and away from a world I felt was cold. Today, in front of the people we love and trust, I vow to cherish the love that has grown between us."

Asher placed a hand against my belly and the tears gathered on my lower lids.

"As we step into this union, I look forward to more of the unexpected surprises that will only deepen my love for you. With joy in my heart and anticipation for the family we're creating, I promise to be your partner, your confidant, and your steadfast through every twist in our beautiful journey together."

Asher winked at me and looked at the clerk, offering a single nod.

"That was wonderful," the clerk commented with a grand smile. His deep brown eyes were on mine when he asked, "Do you have your own vows to speak?"

"No." I sniffed back my tears and giggled a little. "Because I didn't know we were writing vows." I playfully tapped Asher on his chest, and everyone laughed in the room. "But I have some things I would like to say in place of them, I guess."

The clerk smiled and gestured for me to continue.

I ran a finger under my eye to stop the tear that was falling, and Asher caught the lone tear that escaped from my other eye with his finger.

"Asher, I stand before you with a heart once uncertain, but it is now anchored in trust. You say there was a warmth that drew you to me, but there was a warmth in you I immediately wanted to seek refuge in. My life before you made me guarded, unsure if I'd find someone real to rely on. But in you I discovered a safe space, and a love that stood strong even in the face of my crippling fears." I took a breath to keep it together. "I never knew where life would lead me, and that uncertainty once terrified me. But with you beside me as first my friend, then my boyfriend, then my fiancé and now my husband, I'm confident my fear will continue to transform into bravery, and I am excited to finally live and to unravel life's mysteries with you. I didn't write my vows, but I think about you and what I want with you often. So today, as we say our vows, I promise to trust you with my deepest fears, to walk beside you through the unknown, and to cherish the courage you've ignited within me."

"Amen," Aunt Evelyn shouted from her seat.

I looked Asher deeply in his eyes and he did the same with me, and I finished it all with, "You are my anchor, my genuine solace, and my bravest and greatest adventure."

Asher folded his bottom lip into his mouth, shutting his eyes for only a moment. He said when he locked eyes with me again, "Damn, I love you."

"And I love you."

"And now I'm a mess," Summer cried out from her seat.

I dropped my head in a laugh, hearing as everyone voiced their humors around us.

"Wow," the clerk expressed, pressing his hand to his chest. "This has to be the best ceremony this year for me." He shook his head, then cleared his throat. "Okay. Let me get myself together."

Asher and I chuckled.

The clerk proceeded with asking if Asher and I would take each other in matrimony and, of course, we said we would.

After we exchanged our wedding rings, I honestly tuned everything out, staring ahead of me at the man who would be my husband.

Feeling, in that very moment, that if going through all that I went through was necessary to arrive at this moment, maybe, *just maybe*, God wasn't all the way bad if he was indeed orchestrating all of this.

"As the power vested in me in the state of New York," the clerk started, "I now pronounce you husband and wife. Young sir, you may kiss your bride."

Asher wasted no time, drawing me close to him to press his lips against mine and in that room in front of everyone, I melted in his arms like butter.

Aunt Evelyn, Summer, and Jayce applauded to the right of us, and Asher and I laughed on each other's lips.

My heart was doing leaps, and our baby girl was making her presence known between us.

Asher gave me another kiss on the cheek then pulled me in for an embrace and I closed my eyes against him, sincerely feeling every wonderful emotion a person could feel at once.

I said I wanted something simple today because this wasn't that big of a deal.

But it *was* a big deal and for the first time in any time I could remember... I was happy.

THIRTY-SEVEN

LAURYN

I laid in bed with my side table's light dimmed low. At two in the morning, I was awake.

I'd fallen asleep in the night. All I remember was Asher stroking my hair before I dozed off.

But our daughter's movements hours later made it difficult to sleep through. And instead of lying there in the dark, I did my next new favorite thing in the middle of the night besides reading.

Leafing through Asher and my wedding photos.

I giggled to myself. I did it every time I reached for the photos that I kept in the side table drawer. Because I was the same one not for it when the photographer showed up the day we got married at City Hall.

We had two of each photo made once we got the final prints on a disk drive. We put a bunch of photos in a wedding album we bought and had customized at a local gift shop in Brooklyn.

The other photos I kept in the drawer beside my bed and was leafing through them now.

There was the photo of Asher and me at the altar, the other of us sitting on the picturesque stairs of the courthouse that had this giant gold door that reminded me of the architecture from the Art déco era.

For a wedding at City Hall, the photographer sure made our wedding photos appear iconic and dreamy.

Every time I pulled the photos out and sifted through them, I became more and more happy that Asher didn't listen to me and booked the photographer. And that Asher insisted we both wear white. Because the results of him thinking ahead and living in the future created a memory, I loved revisiting.

It was like living in *my* romance novel sometimes.

I still couldn't believe this was my life now.

It had been two months since we got married, and I was finally in my ninth month. And life has been so amazing. I often feared I'd wake up from it all.

But now I was growing tired again.

I peeked at Asher to see him fast asleep as he rested on his back with one arm draped over his head.

When I was up like this during the night and I didn't feel like sifting through pictures, I'd wake him for his attention, and he'd give it every time.

I was feeling like doing that at the moment, but decided against it, switching off my lights and reclining back on my pillow.

But when I did that, as soon as my head touched the pillow, I heard and felt a pop.

I gasped and immediately grabbed my belly.

I suddenly felt the urge to pee and sat up in bed because of it.

Struggled a little to roll over to stand to my feet off the bed.

The moment both of my feet touched the floor, what felt like a ton of water rushed out of me, making an enormous splash around my feet.

"Oh, my God!" I shrieked.

Asher sat up immediately. "What?! What it is it?"

"I..." My eyes lifted to him, then fell to the floor again. My head got light next. "I think my water broke."

I watched Asher's face morph from shock to even more shock before he shook his head and was getting out of the bed almost mechanically.

"Okay, all right," he said to me as he made his way to my side of the bed. "Oh shit!" He shouted when he stepped right into the small puddle of water.

"Should we clean it up?" I asked, my throat growing dry.

He looked at me and chuckled. "Sweetheart, I don't think we have time for that."

Asher left my side to get his phone, and I felt like I was stuck in place.

I'd been reading the books and Asher and I had taken a virtual parenting class. I believed I was ready but, in that moment, I felt stuck.

"I'll call Dr. Carmen," Asher assured. "You want to sit down, sweetheart?"

I heard the question, but I couldn't get my attention off the floor or my belly.

"Lauryn."

His tone pulled me out of whatever head space I was drifting into.

"We got this," he pledged with conviction, eyes fixed on me. "We got this."

It took one call to our doctor for her to tell us to make our way to the hospital.

And I was overall fine. Through gathering my things that were already packed away in a bag and washing up quick and getting dressed, there were no contractions.

But the moment we sat in the four-seater Asher bought a month prior, and he drove over an unavoidable pothole, the impact triggered the first contraction, and then they kept rolling in.

Asher would reach over the center console to take my hand each time and coach me through.

"Just breathe, sweetheart," he told me, eyes on the road. "Just breathe through it."

Arriving at the hospital was nothing like how the women on TV arrived to give birth.

Asher and I needed to park the car in the hospital parking lot. Then we needed to check in and the check in was not only a couple of questions. It was a series of them. They asked us so many questions. Even after we completed the hospital's pre-registration for labor and delivery and had it sent in from last month.

The contractions were getting stronger by the minute. And each time one hit, my belly felt like it was hardening and shrinking against me, which was freaking me out like no other.

"You can follow me," one nurse instructed, as she walked us from the intake room to the delivery room.

Every move I made, breath I took, seemed to trigger another contraction.

And they were long.

I stopped walking toward the room when one of those long, strong contractions hit me harder than any other time before. I pressed my free hand against the nearest wall and dropped my head as I tried like hell to ride through the wave of the pain.

It was gripping. And I swore I felt it everywhere there was a nerve. Including on the inside of my toes.

Asher walked behind me and held me by my belly, taking the hand I pressed against the wall to hold it in his. I leaned my forehead against the wall instead, feeling another contraction fade in as the last one was fading out.

I rolled my forehead back and forth over the wall's cold surface, squeezed Asher's hand, and he held me firmer against my belly.

"I can't do it," I whispered, shaking my head.

"We need to get her to a room," I heard the nurse say to Asher.

"No worries," he replied gently and with so much calm, it filled me with a sense of security I have never felt. "I'll get her there. Give us a moment."

Her footsteps retreated up the hall when another contraction slammed right into me, making my knees buckle a little.

And Asher was there to catch me.

He pressed his face against my cheek. And then his lips, kissing me softly on a trail from my jaw to my ear.

"Do you understand how strong you are?"

I winced, feeling the tears well in my eyes. But not because of the pain. Because of his words.

"The strongest woman I know." Asher ran his hand around the circumference of my stomach. "Already, you are doing an incredible job of bringing new life into the world. You've got us this far."

I squeezed my eyes closed and squeezed his hand even tighter as a new contraction held me so stiff I thought I'd break in two.

"And you're about to create a miracle right now," He breathed, his exhale stuttered. "But you gotta keep going, okay?"

"I'm not ready."

"You're more ready than you think."

"Hey Lauryn," I heard softly on the other side of me. I instantly recognized the voice as being Dr. Carmen. Her hand pressed into my shoulder blade and that added to the calm Asher was evoking in me. "I hear they have your room ready."

"I was just telling her how resilient she is," Asher said beside me, still rubbing my belly slowly.

"Oh, extremely," Dr. Carmen concurred. "And that resilience is bringing you two closer to meeting your precious little one."

"That's right," Asher seconded.

"Lauryn, how about we get to that room so we can see how determined your baby girl is in making today her birthday?"

"Come on, sweetheart." Asher pecked my cheek with a kiss. "I got you."

I pushed myself off the wall. Face covered in tears.

Dr. Carmen ran her hand down my shoulder and gestured at Asher and me with her head toward the delivery room assigned to me.

Asher guided me the whole way, and the contractions didn't cease.

In the room and on the bed, Dr. Carmen asked for my permission to check how dilated I was.

I remembered her explaining to me my cervix needed to be one hundred percent effaced and ten centimeters dilated before I could begin pushing. With all the pain I'd been experiencing, I didn't believe I was anywhere near there.

The smile on her face when she zeroed in on Asher and me told me differently.

"You're fully dilated," she informed jumping to her feet.

My jaw dropped. "Wh-what?"

Dr. Carmen giggled. "Your little girl is excited to make her debut and is not trying to wait," she joked, as she removed the gloves she slid on to check me. "This explains why your contractions are feeling intense for you right now. You're ready to get this over with, too."

Asher kissed me on the cheek. "I knew you were ready." He winked next.

Dr. Carmen approached the front door of the delivery room and poked her head out, calling to two nurses. "Can we get everything set up? She's just about ready."

Another contraction ripped through, causing me to cry out.

"Is there time for an epidural?" I whined.

Dr. Carmen shook her head. "There might not be enough time for us to get you out of your clothes completely. Asher," she called, focusing on him. "Can you help her get her pants off?"

Asher didn't hesitate to help me to my feet and to assist with pulling my pants down over my hips.

"May I, sweetheart?" he asked before removing anything.

"Yes," I answered with a nod.

At that very moment, another contraction rolled through, but this time, instead of bracing for it to pass, I felt the urge to push.

I folded over and did just that, Dr. Carmen instantly noticing.

"Get her on the bed, get her on the bed!" She shouted, pushing up her sleeves.

Asher helped me up and onto the bed. One nurse was on the other side of me, adjusting the height of the bed, lifting the back of the bed on an incline.

Dr. Carmen took one look between my legs, then shot a glance up at me. "Lauryn, I can see her head, okay?"

"Oh, my God." My heart dropped. "What?"

"It's okay." Dr. Carmen smiled big. "She's ready to come on out. I need you to be too, right now. Can you do that for us?"

"She can do it," Asher asserted, his eyes locked with mine. "You can do it. I'm right here. You got this."

"With your next contraction, I want you to do *exactly* what you did when you were standing up." Dr. Carmen instructed. "I want you to push down like that for ten counts, okay?"

As the words left her lips, the beginning of a contraction built like a crescendo. It was growing when I held my breath.

"Breathe, sweetheart," Asher reminded, taking my right foot, and holding my leg back with it in his grip. "Breathe."

It was like my body took over. Because while I wanted to slam my legs closed, I widened them and bared down, pushing with everything in me.

"Good!" Dr. Carmen coached. "Keep pushing, Lauryn."

I growled and clenched my teeth the entire time, feeling every pain there was to feel.

The power of the contraction. The width of my daughter's head stretching her exit wide enough to accommodate her, the pressure my back molars were putting on each other as I bared down and pushed.

After the first ten counts, I fell back.

The whole thing took everything out of me and I sincerely believed I had nothing left. Barely could inhale my second breath.

Right when I was thinking I couldn't do all that again, Asher told me I could.

"You're so powerful right now," Asher said to me for everyone to hear. "Focus on that strength, Lauryn. I swear to God, you're stronger than you think."

I inhaled more air than I believed my lungs could take and took in even more air than that.

Another contraction was threatening to take stage. And instead of cowering from it, I met it head on.

I lifted off the pillow, brought my chin to my chest, and pushed against the contraction. I fought back against it. Used the rage slowly building in me. Pain always made me angry. So angry. Because it made me feel powerless and weak. But that day, and in that moment, I used my rage for pain for good this time. With the air I inhaled, I used it to scream out at the top of my lungs as I pushed.

"Good, Lauryn," Dr. Carmen shouted. "Here she comes!"

The sting of the baby's head pushing through me, followed by her limbs and then her feet, made me look to Asher to find his jaw slacked and his eyes widened as he watched our baby slide right on out.

"Oh, my God," he whispered, his head turning to me. "You did it."

I was prepared to drop to the bed, depleted, until I heard her cries.

And it was the sweetest sound.

Her voice shot through me and jolted my body with energy from a place in me unknown until that day. I sat up immediately to see her.

Red and white covered her, but through it all, she was so beautiful.

Asher pressed his hands to both sides of my face and leaned in, kissing me and holding his lips on my lips.

"I did it," I said against him.

"Yes, you did," he smiled, pulling me into the warmest hug he'd ever given me. "Just like I knew you could."

———

Four days later, on our second night home, I couldn't get any sleep.

Seems I lucked out and got one of those good babies, as Aunt Evelyn put it.

"She is so quiet," she noted as she sat in the armchair in my hospital room. "With her cute self just chillin' and relaxing."

I had the entire room to myself, Asher's doing, and Aunt Evelyn was in the room only hours after Eres was born.

"I still can't believe she came so fast," I said. My voice was still raspy from all the yelling I was doing when I arrived at the hospital. My throat was sore before I took the ibuprofen the nurses offered me soon after Eres was born. Now I couldn't feel a thing but pure bliss.

"'Cause your daughter's a blessing," Aunt Evelyn said to Eres as she rocked her great-niece in her arms. "And you're one of them good babies, huh?"

I smiled, watching them.

"Girl, I'm gon' spoil you." Aunt Evelyn smiled so big at Eres it made me smile wider, too. *"Yes, I am." She nodded. "Yes, I am."*

My daughter.

I was still getting used to the idea of being someone's mother.

I sat on the edge of my side of the bed where Eres's bassinet aligned with Asher's bed.

Though the night table's light was on, I had it turned away from her so that it wouldn't shine in her face.

She laid in the pure white bassinet, her head covered with a cute pink hat I got as a gift from Aunt Evelyn. I swaddled Eres in a monogram print swaddle blanket. The pattern of black girl ballerinas on the swaddle cloth made my heart melt when I saw a picture of it online. In person and with Eres swaddled in it, I wanted to burst into tears.

She was perfect.

Eres had her father's eyes and his full lips. The only thing she seemed to have gotten from me was my light brown skin tone. And according to Aunt Evelyn, Eres's ear color hinted she wouldn't get much darker than she was. So, at least Eres got that from me.

"Hey," I heard Asher rasp behind me.

He'd fallen asleep shortly after returning home from classes. Asher had taken off a few days after I gave birth to spend time with Eres and me in the hospital and then her first day at home.

Between classes and adjusting to having a new baby at home, he was tired. So when he returned home, ate the takeout he picked up on his way back from school, Asher showered and fell asleep the moment his head touched his pillow.

"What are you doing up?" he asked, peeling himself up and off his pillow. Asher balanced himself on his hands to move closer, wrapping an arm around my waist, to lean his chin on my shoulder.

I leaned my head against his. "Just watching her."

He snickered lowly. "Watching her?"

"She's better than TV."

Eres moved a little, her tiny mouth opening to let out the cutest yawn.

"Oh, my goodness," I gushed quietly, blinking back tears. "She is so beautiful."

"Like her mama."

I kissed my teeth. "She looks just like you."

He chuckled.

"I carried her for nine months, only for her to come out looking *exactly* like you."

"As she should," he mumbled.

I elbowed him playfully, and he chuckled while wrapping his arms tighter around me.

"You being up before the baby arrived I said little about," he started low. "But now that she's here, sweetheart, you need to be getting your rest when she's resting."

"I know," I agreed. "I just…" I smiled next. "I feel so good I can't sleep."

Asher lifted his head off me, using his arm to turn me a little.

I winced a little as I adjusted myself in my seat. Though I was healing well, only needing one stitch according to Dr. Carmen, I was still sore down there. Ibuprofen did most of the work. But I was wide awake. Up at a sleeping hour, as Asher suggested.

But like I said, so much joy and giddiness filled me to see Eres's face just one more time before I went to sleep.

"I still can't believe that she grew inside of me, you know?"

Asher ran a hand down my cheek.

"After everything I've been through, all the doubt about if I even wanted or could even be a mother because of my past." I shook my head. "To still produce someone so beautiful, so precious." I focused on Eres in her bassinet, still resting so peacefully. "I thought some really shitty things about God and feeling like I wasn't being watched over like everyone always says God does but, now…" I smiled so easily. "Now I see God really is amazing. How he could help me grow this life inside of me? Me?"

Asher pressed his forehead to mine, then pecked at my lips with his.

"Because of you, life has become something I could love, Asher."

"No—"

"Yes," I whispered, leaning away to look him in his eyes. "And you can't tell me any different. I am so thankful to have you. Seriously."

Asher smiled.

"I love my life." I inhaled a breath to keep the tears in, but decided against holding them back.

Because I've cried because of the pain. Cried because of disappointment. Cried because I was angry. So, for once, I was shedding tears because of something good.

Something great.

Genuinely great.

"Come here, sweetheart." Asher guided me down onto the bed and into his arms. He used his free hand to stroke my hair and my eyes grew heavy. "Get some rest for her and me."

I smiled while nodding and closing my eyes. Grateful to be loved so deeply and, for the first time, excited to see what magic tomorrow would bring.

THIRTY-EIGHT

ASHER

I smelled the scent of cooked food, salting the hallway's air the moment I stepped off the elevator.

Smiled when I realized it wafted through the gaps of my apartment's door.

As many times as I told Lauryn not to worry about cooking anything and to only concentrate on adjusting to having a new baby around, she didn't listen.

And I wasn't too mad about it.

I moved the bouquet to my other hand so that I could slip my key into the door. I'd been making it a habit to return home from LU at a reasonable hour after I made the mistake of staying late last month.

The door to the classroom opened, attracting our attention to the sound of it opening.

I was sitting across from Sharon, a young lady in my doctorate program group at LU. She'd been complaining about not remembering the material in time for an exam, so I promised I'd go over it with her.

I jumped the gun, telling her that. Especially when I hadn't told Lauryn I'd be staying late after school.

The hour was after 9pm, when I turned my head to glance at the opening door.

Never did I expect my wife with our newborn daughter strapped to her via the carrier to be standing at the entryway.

"What the...?" I was up on my feet the moment our eyes locked. "Sweetheart, what are you doing here?"

Lauryn's eyes looked past me for a moment, focusing on Sharon before Lauryn's beautiful eyes returned to me.

Since having our daughter, Eres, Lauryn didn't wear her red lipstick like always. Said she didn't want to leave lip prints on the baby. Though I loved her lips painted, seeing the natural pink hue of her lips always did it for me.

Lauryn lifted her hand to show me the plastic bag in her hand. "I brought you your dinner since you were late coming home."

I approached her and my daughter. "Sweetheart, you didn't have to do that." I pressed my hand to the baby's back in the carrier. "I don't want you two out here in this cold." I leaned closer to peck Lauryn on the lips and then left a kiss on Eres's warm, tiny forehead, making her stir a little in her sleep as she rested against her mother's chest in the carrier.

Lauryn's eyes focused past me again and at Sharon, her attention staying on Sharon a little longer.

"What's going on in here?" Lauryn asked, focus still on Sharon. "Why are y'all in here, all alone?"

I smirked, sensing her vibe. Thought it was cute more than anything else because this woman really did not know how much I loved her.

I guided Lauryn's eyes back on me by twisting her head to face me until she looked up at me.

"Down girl." I dipped my chin to lock eyes with her. Lauryn fighting back her smile made me chuckle.

"This is Sharon and I'm only sharing my notes with her so she can pass this mid-term. She's been worried about failing it."

Sharon raised a hand. "Hey."

"Hi," Lauryn replied softly, still grilling Sharon with a little suspicion.

"And Sharon is well aware of how much I love my wife," I said out loud.

"Oh my God," Sharon shrieked, holding her hands up. "Of course! I promise I just want to pass this course so I can get sleep again."

I gathered my things soon after and me, Lauryn, and the baby exited the university soon after.

I told her never to do that again. I didn't want her taking the train to bring me food, and she understood. Lauryn promised she wouldn't do that again if I didn't stay out too late without letting her know first.

Tonight, when I opened my apartment door, the scent of cooked food traveled up my nose, making me moan a little. Hearing Lauryn singing lowly to our daughter as she rocked the little girl in her arms made me smile so big. She sat in the middle of the couch, Eres swaddled in the cutest blanket, and asleep in Lauryn's arms.

Lauryn looked up from Eres and twisted her head to focus on me and I swear I skipped a breath.

Lauryn exuded softness. She appeared delicate, only sitting there cradling our daughter. Long black hair pulled up to the top of her head and secured in a bun. Strands of her straight hair, stuck out here and there, resembling an artist's sketching of a doll.

She smiled, then stopped singing to whisper, "Hey."

"Hey," I whispered back, removing my satchel to leave on the island's stool.

I rounded the couch, and Lauryn's brows rose at the sight of the bouquet in my hands.

"Flowers?" She asked softly. "I wasn't expecting that."

"And I wasn't expecting that voice." I took a seat beside her, and she met me halfway for a kiss. "How did I not know you knew how to sing?"

She rolled her eyes playfully and shook her head. "I'm not Whitney Houston or anything..."

"Yeah, because you're Lauryn James-Truesdale." I grinned. "With a voice of an angel."

She pursed her lips to keep herself from smiling.

It was like she was undergoing yet another transformation right before my eyes. The woman who I met when I first moved into the building, on the elevator, clutching a book in her grip on how to be soft in a world that was hard, differed totally from the woman who sat beside me holding our greatest creation.

She was her own story now. One that was beautiful and rich with so much to discover.

And I could not wait to uncover all her mysteries.

"I wonder what other things I'll discover about my wife." I bit my bottom lip and winked at her. "I'm eager to get to know this era's Lauryn."

She giggled, her attention lowering to Eres again.

Our daughter was perfect. Many people say that about their children, but my baby girl was perfection in human form.

And as much as I loved seeing Eres, I needed Lauryn tonight.

"I got these for you," I told her as I placed the bouquet of roses on the coffee table in front of us.

"Me?" she questioned. "What's the occasion?"

I licked my lips. "Today is the one-year anniversary of when we first... you know."

A grand smile took residence on her face now. "You remembered that?"

"Oh." I pressed my hand to my chest. "Of course. It was a commemorated moment. One of the best nights of my life. Only second to the birth of our daughter."

She giggled again.

I leaned in close, pressing my mouth to her neck. Trailed my kisses from her neck up to the lobe of her ear. "Lay the baby down in her bassinet so I can take care of you for the rest of the night."

She turned her face to look at me and I pressed my lips to hers, opening her mouth with mine and guiding my tongue inside in search of hers.

Lauryn moaned, making me instantly hard.

It was officially past the six week wait Dr. Carmen made Lauryn and I promise to respect. And though we'd found other ways to please each other, her giving me head for the very first time by week four, I've missed her.

Truthfully, I would wait as long as Lauryn needed me to. But the way she was kissing me back and moaning the whole time, she was as ready as I was.

I broke our kiss gently, pecking her on the lips at the end. She opened her eyes to mine, and they were smoldering. I grinned at the heat she was giving me in only her gaze.

"Go ahead," I told her, licking my lips slow. "I'll be patiently waiting for you to get back to me."

Epilogue

February 2022 - Three Months Later...

ASHER

"This is the last box," the moving guy announced as I approached.

"Cool," I told him, extending my arm to take it from him. "Then I can walk this one in."

It was moving day for us. We were moving into our new house. A literal dream come true.

"And this is the bedroom," the real estate agent, Moriah, presented as she pushed opened the double doors. "This room is, of course, the largest room in the house and has a skylight with the perfect view of the stars at night."

I heard Lauryn's gasp in awe up ahead of me.

She'd been gasping since we stepped onto this property. This had been

*the third house our real estate agent had shown us. Seems the third one
really was the charm.*

*Moriah continued to detail the features and benefits of the room. A
walk-in closet, generously sized en-suite with his and her sinks complete
with shower stall and whirlpool bathtub. I could see the glow on Lauryn's
cheeks.*

*She was in her own world, smiling, eyes moving around the room in
wonderment.*

*I allowed for Moriah to continue to do her job. But the look on
Lauryn's face from downstairs in the kitchen was all I needed to see to
know that this was our forever home.*

After a few lengthy discussions and sessions with our therapist, Liz,
Lauryn, accepted the money from her aunt. And two of the ways she
wanted to spend it was to buy us a house and give her aunt enough to
put a down payment on a house, too. We planned to put the rest away,
some of which we invested. I had my friend Tyler give us sound advice
about what places were lucrative and how to best manage the money
that was left. When he wasn't visiting strip clubs trying to rendezvous as
a rapper, he was an intelligent financier who knew his stuff, putting his
degree from Brookville to good use.

I stepped inside of the house and made my way to the kitchen. My
eyes traveled up the curving staircase, excited to spend the night in our
new home later.

It was only Lauryn and me for now. Eres was with Evelyn in her new
home, so that Lauryn and I could move into the house and setup before
bringing Eres home.

When I wrapped around the wall that led into the kitchen, I saw
Lauryn opening one box to pull out dishes and glasses.

"This is the last box," I announced, placing the box on the
counter.

She glanced up at me. "What's in that box?"

"Your sneakers," I answered. "I didn't know we were unpacking."

"We're not." She turned to place the stack of bowls into the large
overhead cabinet. My eyes fell to the curve of her jeans.

She wore jeans now. High-waist and killing me softly since she
started wearing denim.

Like everything else, she wore them beautifully. The jeans were one of the obvious changes she'd undergone since therapy.

For as long as I've known her, she's only worn hoodies, big tees, joggers during the colder months and biker shorts in the summer.

But jeans?

These were her first pair. And they looked amazing on her.

"I wanted to put a couple of these away so if we order takeout..." She turned to face me again. "Then we'll have something to eat the food out of."

Lauryn took one look at me before a sly smile pulled at her lips.

I smiled back, pushing my tongue inside of my cheek.

She folded her arms over her chest. "Distracted?"

I kissed my teeth. "Don't tease me."

She tossed her head back in a laugh.

Happy looked so damn good on her. It's like every day she gets better and better right before my eyes.

And she was *my* wife. My riches in human form.

"You know what those jeans do to me," I told her.

"What do they do again?" She asked, taking slow steps towards me.

I pressed my backside to the lip of the island behind me to keep my eyes on her.

Lauryn closed the space between us, only stopping when our lips collided.

"Where are the movers?" she asked against my lips.

"Gone."

She smiled. "Good."

Lauryn wasted no time parting my lips with hers and sliding her tongue into my mouth.

Her initiating making love was also new, and another welcomed change. Because she was skillful in how she moved. And comfortable too.

I lifted her into my arms and walked her out of the kitchen and into the sitting room that was steps away from the kitchen.

It was the closest place in the house with furniture, the other being our bedroom. But I didn't feel like placing an obstacle like stairs between us and interrupting the christen of our home.

I fell back onto the couch cushion, placing her on my lap. She returned her lips to mine, kissing me softly. She broke our kiss only to slide down off me, moving to her knees between my legs.

I didn't stop her as she dipped her hand into the waistband of my joggers, palming my erection, then pulling it out.

Lauryn lifted her eyes to find mine peering down at hers as she slid her hand up and down the length of me.

I moaned at the sight because the sight was a turn on.

Her mouth covered the tip soon after before guiding me deep into her mouth and I tossed my head back, biting my bottom lip to calm the hell down.

The first time she'd done this, please me orally, I asked her about it.

I didn't want her to do anything she didn't want to do, so it was important that I understood how she felt.

"It was good," she confirmed, laying in my arms.

Eres was asleep, like always, in her bassinet. As our daughter got older in weeks, she slept less during the day. But mostly, we'd gotten her on a good sleeping schedule at night thanks to her Aunt Evelyn and my mother giving us suggestions.

"What was good about it?" I asked next.

Lauryn tilted her head back to look up at me. "Watching you."

A smile pulled at my lips. "Watching me?"

"Mm-hmm." She nodded, wrapping her arm tighter around me to move in closer. "I loved watching you come because of me."

And as she bobbed her head up and down on me, I could see that was the goal at the moment.

But as much as I loved how she looked and felt with me in her mouth, I wanted her sweet pussy more.

I ran my fingers through her hair, and she tightened her jaw, causing me to groan.

"Come here, baby," I instructed, while reaching for her.

Watching her slowly slide me out of her mouth was one of the sexiest things I'd ever seen her do.

And sexy was new for the both of us.

Lauryn didn't delay lifting onto her feet, leaning forward over me to kick her legs on either side of my legs.

Since giving birth and making love again, and consistent weekly therapy appointments with Liz, Lauryn has been a little more explorative. From the first night, over six weeks after she birthed our daughter, which was appropriately the anniversary of when we first made love, she's been interested in trying new things.

At her insistence, we've tried several positions so she could discover what she liked the most and this, her on top, has been an undefeated favorite of hers.

Lauryn held me in her hand and slowly sat back, sliding me inside of her with only her stationary hips.

She locked her eyes on mine, watching me, her new favorite thing to do, wanting to capture every expression I made.

So, I never held back.

Biting my bottom lip, moaning when she circled her waist and gyrated her hips while sliding back and forth on my lap, moving me in and out of her wet pussy.

When I moaned, she moaned, her hands moving up the sides of my face to hold it stable so she could lean forward and press her lips to mine as she rode.

Sex had become fun between her and I. We were still in the newlywed phase, that's true. But since she's been doing the work to heal and sort through her past, she's been open. More present. And I've been able to enjoy the fruits of that.

Sex between us was more than the physical. It was beautiful. Sacred. Our way of retreating into our own world of bonded bliss, I allowed myself to get lost in every time... with her permission.

I felt her walls firming around my shaft and her ride becoming a little staggered. She angled her hips so that the tiny ball between her thighs could brush against my coarse hairs and I angled my hips to have her make an even better contact with it.

"Here you go," I whispered. "Do you like that better?"

Her eyes flew open to mine as I matched her pace with well-timed upstrokes.

"Yes," she cried out, dropping her head back between her shoulders. "*Mmm-hmm.*"

Lauryn moved her hands to the couch's shoulder to grip. I took her by her waist and changed positions, lifting just enough to lay her on her back.

I drove into her on top, the way she told me she liked it. Long deep strokes I breathed in rhythm to inhaling when I retreated, deep breaths when I slid back in.

Her hands held me by my backside as we made love, the tension of her lids increasing as she squeezed her eyes closed.

"Are you coming, Lauryn?" I whispered. "Are you coming with me, baby?"

She nodded quickly, her face gradually relaxing, walls fluttering, body growing rigid beneath me.

And I pressed my lips to hers gently, slowly peeling her mouth opened with mine and slowing my pace to rock us through ecstasy. Slowed everything down and lost myself in her sweet whimpering, her consuming warmth, feeling my release crescendo with hers, sincerely grateful I'd get to do this for the rest of my life.

———

LAURYN

I stood over Eres's crib, stroking her tiny forehead and the soft black hairs on her head, humming "When You Wish Upon A Star," low, like she loved it.

Didn't know why that song came to mind the first time I hummed it to her weeks after her birth... until my aunt revealed why.

"Are you singing?" She asked, folding clothes to put away.

As always, her boyfriend William was in her new kitchen, cooking up something. This was her first Sunday in her new home. It was a no brainer for me to help her get this house. Didn't even tell her I was going to do it because I knew she would refuse my help. But I loved Aunt Evelyn with everything in me. She's always been good to me and took me in without question. She was like my mother, and I wanted her to have this house. So, I helped her buy it around the same time Asher and I bought ours and I presented it to her as a surprise.

"Yeah," I answered, nodding my head, eyes focused on Eres as she laid

in my arms, out-staring me with the cutest dark eyes I swore I'd ever seen before. "She likes it. I don't know why I thought about singing that song."

"Because your mother used to sing it to you when you were a baby."

I shot a look over at my aunt.

Aunt Evelyn giggled. "You remember how your mother was obsessed with Disney. Mickey Mouse this Mickey Mouse that. Insisted you have a room decked out in Minnie Mouse decal and stuffed dolls from the ceiling to the floor." She nodded next. "She used to hum 'When You Wish Upon A Star,' all the time. You probably remembered it and didn't realize it."

I blinked to myself.

"She's always with you, Lauryn," Aunt Evelyn said next. "Even though she's not here in the physical, your mother will always be with you. This is her way of connecting with you, I'm sure."

Learning that made me hum and sing the song to Eres more often than before.

This was technically our first night in the new house.

It was magical to me.

I knew I wanted to call this house my home the second I laid eyes on it from the outside.

But the kitchen sold me when I saw it.

"Do you like it?" Asher asked. The agent had shown us the last room of the house and told us we could take a moment to peruse on our own. We'd already toured the kitchen, but I had to return to it.

"I love it," I expressed. "It's too big, though, right?"

He shook his head. "It's the perfect size."

"Yeah, well." I sputtered a laugh. "You grew up in a mansion, so I don't expect for you to get what I mean."

He chuckled. "That's not fair."

I smiled. "It's only you, me, and Eres."

"I mean." He slid his hands into his pockets. "Eventually, there would be more, right?"

I lowered my chin to look at him from the top of my eyes. "More... what?"

He grinned. "I would love to give Eres siblings, is what I mean, and there is plenty of room to do that here."

"You..." I couldn't fight my smile if I wanted to. "You wanna have more kids with me?"

He scoffed a laugh, then reached for me to pull me close. "I want to have all of my children with you and only you."

The warmest feeling rushed through me, and it felt so damn good. I wished I could bottle it.

"I want to have all my children with you, and only you, too." I coiled my forearms around the back of his neck. "But how many are we talking about? 'Cause making them is a lot of fun, but getting them here hurts like hell."

Asher tossed his head back in a laugh and I snickered in response.

He leveled his head and pressed his forehead against mine. "We have plenty of time to discuss that, but only a small amount of time to agree that this house is our house."

"It's perfect." I nodded enthusiastically, because it was our house. "Let's tell her we wanna take it."

We'd given everyone we knew a tour of the house, including Asher's parents, his father giving the final approval. According to what Asher told me, the real estate world considered his dad Jonathan an expert. He knew his stuff, so his approval meant something.

The relationship between Asher's mother, Patricia, and I have improved and getting better every day. She wasn't too happy we didn't invite her to our wedding at City Hall or the dinner after. She eventually got over it. Patricia reasoned she and I weren't close, and it probably would have been uncomfortable for her to be there, which it would've been for me.

So, to make up for it, I gave Patricia her wish when we were in Long Island a few weeks ago.

She stood over the white crib, watching as Eres laid on the mattress sound asleep. Patricia turned on the sound machine. She couldn't keep quiet about turning it on to see if Eres would like it.

While we visited Asher's childhood home, Eres fell asleep against her father as he was holding her. Patricia hopped up out of her seat and reminded us Eres could sleep in the room Patricia had renovated into a nursery.

"Only if Lauryn is okay with it," Asher said, checking with me for confirmation.

So, I gave it, walking Eres up to the room and laying her down gently inside of the crib.

Patricia stood over the crib almost in tears.

"She is so beautiful," she commented to me, but focused on Eres. Patricia finally glanced over at me, her eyes welling with tears. "You two have made me the happiest woman on earth."

It would take a little more time for us to really be good. If ever. But for now, I was happy with where Patricia and my relationship were.

Most of the house was still in the dark. Asher and I agreed to keep the hallway light outside of our bedroom on at night, or at least for the first night, so we could see our way around. Eres's nursery was the only room arranged. Asher and I bought the crib the day we closed on the house and had it set up for our baby girl soon after. Because of how they built our house, her room was accessible through ours via a connecting door, which made it easy to move between our rooms to get her if she got up through the night.

I'd walked through the connecting door and stopped at the threshold when I saw Asher in bed. He was shirtless, with our bedding covering his lower half. In his hand was an opened book, his attention so focused on the words on the pages he didn't realize I was standing there watching him.

I loved doing that these days. My new favorite sport. He was fascinating. Asher has always been fascinating to me. But after several sessions with Liz and using the tools she provided, she has helped me to get the most out of my therapy sessions. I've been able to really be in awe of the things that surrounded me. Especially my new life.

Asher lifted his eyes out of the book long enough to glance over at me and smiled.

He extended his arm in front of him and in his hand was the book I'd started earlier that week.

It was a fantasy novel he recommended. And it was good. I was a few chapters away from finishing it and was eager to start the next book in the series.

"Thank you," I said, making my way over to him. "I'm happy you got them out of the box."

"You're more than welcome."

I lifted the down comforters on my side of the king-size bed and climbed on. Our room only had our bed and dresser set up. My mind raced with all the things I wanted to do with our space, and I would have all the time to do it.

For now, I got cozy beside Asher, who raised his arm so I could rest beneath his bicep and against his shoulder.

His natural scent drifted up my nose because of the covers' billowing. And I leaned in because of it. I just couldn't resist.

I placed a kiss against his shoulder, then his cheek.

"*Mmm*, uh-uh," he moaned, shaking his head. "I have been trying to finish this chapter for a week now and I always let you stop me."

I dropped my jaw dramatically.

He closed the space between our lips to press his against mine and whispered, "I'll take real good care of you after. Just be patient."

I pressed my hand to his face and pecked his lips softly, leaning my head away a little to tell him, "Okay."

He pecked me again. "I love you."

I caressed the side of his face. "I love you too."

He gave me a third kiss, then returned to his book, and I nuzzled myself up under his arm to read mine.

My life was beautiful. Four words I never believed I'd ever say in this lifetime.

And I wasn't mad about that at all.

Finally.

The End.

FINAL WORD

Dear reader,

Thank you for reading *Wrath*. And when I say thank you, I sincerely mean that from my heart. I hope you enjoyed it as much as I did creating it.

I dreaded writing this story when I first mapped out the story summaries for the *Love is Cure, Vol. 1 – Vices & Virtues series*. Before I wrote a single line for any of the books, I created brief summaries that included basic background information about the characters and what I wanted to happen in their stories. *Wrath* differs from the other stories in this series. Mainly because it's capturing triumph from trauma.

I created a series of blog posts on my website BrookelynMosley.com leading up to the release of *Wrath*. I wanted to give readers an idea of how *Wrath* came to be and what to expect before *Wrath's* release. One of those blog posts explained how I named Lauryn. And the real news story about a girl from Humble, Texas, gave me the push I needed to write a happily ever after every woman who has experienced trauma deserves.

Asher.

Oh my goodness. When I developed his character and before I wrote a single line of dialogue for him, I adored him. He was everything Lauryn needed, and then some. Patient, understanding, selfless. His need for consent and sharing control in their relationship was both refreshing and attractive. He's in my top five of book baes who appear in my stories and he's not the five or the four or the three!

I really loved watching their love bloom on the page. We literally watched them go from strangers to married with a baby.

Before Asher, Lauryn did not expect much from life. Her outlook was grim as she viewed life as something only to exist in. She was taking it day by day and doing it scared. On the surface she was a 29-year-old woman just existing, but inside, she was stuck at the age of her trauma. Her past and refusing to discuss it left her fearful and angry, but angry as a protective measure. I loved seeing her armor come down with the natural progression of this story and I hope you did too.

As I promoted this story, I felt it was important to note that this story was a slow burn. It took its time and unfolded organically, because in life, which I like my stories to mirror, slow and steady is a must in many situations. And it was necessary for Lauryn.

She needed someone who was patient. She needed an Asher. And when they say the right person for you is going to want to do the work with you and not see it as a burden, Lauryn and Asher are the perfect example of that.

I couldn't have picked a better couple to serve as characters for book six in this series.

There is just one book left in the LIC series. I can't believe we are here. And book seven is going to be everything! Eryn and Simeon will not disappoint at all! Have you met them? Be sure to meet them in Gluttony

(Eryn) and in So This is Love (Simeon). You can find those stories online on Amazon as of the time of *Wrath's* publishing. You can also find them listed on Also by Brookelyn Mosley.

If this is your first book by me, and you enjoyed it, I would like to say you are a Brookelynite. Welcome! To my readers who have been with me from a book or many books ago, y'all, this book is in the 40+ club. We are one book away from having another completed series! And you have been rocking with me through it all, and I am so grateful to have your love and support. I write for me and you. We are living and loving these stories together lol. I am so thrilled to do it all again and I can't wait to deliver another one to you soon.

Thank you for reading and thank you for trusting my pen yet again.

I'll see you at the end of the next book!

Love,
BK.

Book Club Questions

1. What was your first impression of Lauryn James?
2. What was your first impression of Asher Truesdale?
3. What did you think about Lauryn and Asher's first sighting of each other on Asher's move-in night?
4. What did you think about Lauryn and Asher's dynamic?
5. What are your thoughts on the way Asher gave Lauryn the space to let her guard down?
6. Did you root for this couple? When did you start rooting for them?
7. What did you like most about Asher?
8. What did you like most about Lauryn?
9. How do you feel about the ending?
10. What did you think about Lauryn's growth throughout *Wrath*?

Character Cameos

In the order they appeared or were mentioned in Wrath...

Desmond Ellis II
Envy

Ayanna
Forbidden: An Anthology
So This is Love

Dallas
Forbidden: An Anthology
So This is Love

Summer
Pride
So This is Love
Glimpses

Jayce

Pride
So This is Love
Glimpses

Priscilla
Pride

STORY EXTRAS

(Type this link into your browser to view story extras from *Wrath* on BrookelynMosley.com - https://brookelynmosley.com/wrath-extras/)

About Brookelyn Mosley

Brookelyn Mosley is a captivating voice in the world of black romance literature. With a gift for weaving heartfelt narratives and steamy encounters, she invites readers on journeys of love, passion, and self-discovery. Through her compelling storytelling, Brookelyn celebrates the beauty of black love and explores the complexities of relationships with authenticity and depth. With over 40+ titles, her stories resonate with true-blue readers, touching hearts and inspiring conversations about love, identity, and resilience.

Connect With Me Online!

Twitter: @brookelynmosley
Facebook: http://facebook.com/brookelynmosley
Facebook Reading Group: Brookelynites Book Lounge
Instagram: @Brookelynmosley
My Website: BrookelynMosley.com
My Readers Website: BKBookLounge.com
My Mailing List: BK Insiders (*Sign up at BrookelynMosley.com and receive 4 complimentary shorts in your email when you sign up as a new subscriber!*)